QUARRY

QUARRY

C. Terry Cline, Jr.

NAL BOOKS

NEW AMERICAN LIBRARY

NEW YORK AND SCARBOROUGH, ONTARIO

PUBLISHER'S NOTE

This book is a work of fiction. Names, characters, places, and incidents either are the product of the author's imagination or are used fictitiously, and any resemblance to actual persons, living or dead, events, or locales is entirely coincidental.

NAL BOOKS TRADEMARK REG. U.S. PAT. OFF. AND FOREIGN COUNTRIES
REGISTERED TRADEMARK—MARCA REGISTRADA
HECHO EN CHICAGO, U.S.A.

SIGNET, SIGNET CLASSIC, MENTOR, ONYX, PLUME, MERIDIAN and NAL BOOKS are published
in the United States by NAL PENGUIN INC.,
1633 Broadway, New York, New York 10019, in Canada
by The New American Library of Canada Limited,
81 Mack Avenue, Scarborough, Ontario M1L 1M8

Designed by Sherry Brown

Library of Congress Cataloging-in-Publication Data

Cline, C. Terry.
  Quarry.

  I. Title.
PS3553.L53Q3   1987   813'.54   87-15218
ISBN 0-453-00514-8

First Printing, November, 1987

1 2 3 4 5 6 7 8 9

PRINTED IN THE UNITED STATES OF AMERICA

To Hennie and Bozie Dietze
For all the good times

CHAPTER ONE

The scene was as ancient as the Rocky Mountains themselves, unchanged since primordial man. Shafts of sunlight stabbed through a coniferous canopy, melting the last patches of snow which seeped into loam that had been undisturbed for centuries. The aroma of damp humus was a heady, musky scent that wafted between thick stands of hardwoods.

Borden Wilson moved like a shadow, his rifle blackened to avoid reflection, no clasp loose to tinkle and give warning. His step, first to toe, then heel, was as deliberate as a cat's. He slipped slowly from tree to tree, dissolving into the gloom. Below, scarcely fifty yards away, walked his quarry . . .

The boy was four, maybe five; he was shrieking happily as he darted up the trail. He ran ahead of his parents who followed, unhurried, but never out of sight. They were not yet acclimated to being ten thousand feet above sea level. Their hearts hammering, limbs heavier, they might not even recognize altitude sickness. They were tourists from New England. Borden knew this by the license plate on their car parked a mile and a half away in a designated area. He knew, too, by the clipped inflections and nasal twang that gave an edge to their voices when they called their son.

"Stay on the trail, Tony. Tony, do you hear me?"

"Look, Daddy—ugh—what is that?"

The child was squatting, knees out, peering at the earlike lobes of *Auricularia auricula*—the only one of the jelly fungi that are commonly eaten in North America.

1

Borden was surprised to hear the father say as much.

"When it dries," the man told his son, "it looks like liver."

"Ugh, I don't like liver."

"It becomes tough and hard," the father said. "In China, they call it *Yung Nge* or *Muk Nge*."

The lesson was wasted. The child bounded ahead, his shrill voice stilling the call of native fowl. But creatures were there: chipmunks peered over stones gray with lichen, perching birds in boughs overhead watched the intruders.

The trail meandered upward, marked by color-coded signs advising the hikers as to distance traveled, how far yet to go. Borden kept pace with the family, putting himself in strategic places to intercept at will. But he wasn't ready. Sometimes he stood no more than a dozen yards from them and they suspected nothing. On the other side of the trail, invisible except to Borden's trained eye, Wang tracked the same threesome, the same way, letting them draw nearer the crest, nearer their destiny.

"What's this one, Daddy?"

"That's *Phlogiotis helvelloides*."

The boy touched smooth gelatinous folds, the mushroom a deep rose in color. "Can you eat it?" the child inquired.

"You could eat that one."

"I don't want it, though."

The man said to his wife, "That's the same kind we used to make candied red jelly fungus, remember?"

She nodded, absently. Borden detected a subtle shift in mood, in her stance, a barely perceptible change in demeanor. Like a fawn which has not yet smelled or heard—but senses—danger.

"Don't you think we ought to be going back, Harold?"

"The trail circles back."

"The way we came, I mean."

"Are you tired?"

"No . . ."

He pulled her under his arm, protectively. "Tony is enjoying himself, Donna."

She yielded, but again she scanned the hillsides. She had seen Borden without realizing it.

"Here's another one, Daddy!"

The husband stepped off the trail to join his son. "That's a different kind, Tony. I don't know about that one. When you aren't positive, you should never taste it—right?"

"Right."

Watching the woman, Borden saw her exhale short, thin, misty vapors, her breath warmed by the exertion of the climb.

Perfect. Late twenties, body firm, almost athletic—a good figure under those blue jeans, well-rounded buttocks. Her eyes were large, expressive, complexion fair.

Wang was thirty meters beyond, also watching. He was a dappled shadow in a patchwork of sunlight, his camouflage suit and greasepaint breaking the contours of his face and body.

"Harold," the woman said in a low voice, "let's go back."

"It's only a two-mile trail, Donna. We're more than half-way already."

"Let's go," she urged.

He came back to her. "Is something wrong?"

"A little queasy."

"It's the altitude." He looked about, a subconscious response to her distress, civilized man reacting to primitive stimuli. "It's probably closer to go on ahead," he said.

"Then let's go."

Harold called to his boy as the child labored toward the summit. "Tony, stay on the trail."

The crest was a hundred meters more, the boy almost there. Wang flowed like water, putting himself in the lead. Borden remained with the parents, listening to the woman's apology for cutting short their hike. The husband's response was generous, but he was disappointed.

The child topped the trail, paused to look back, beckoned his father and mother, then turned to race downhill.

In that instant, Wang had him.

Beautiful! Not a sound. Like a whisper of wind in the

forest, a soft sigh *en masse*—out of the thicket came a hand to muffle cries, and the child was gone in the blink of an eye.

A magpie called, *wink-wink-wink!* A squirrel quarreled afar. The parents continued to climb, slowly, toward the summit. Borden turned away, moving quickly to a vantage point on the far side of the precipice. He heard the mother call, "Tony—wait for us!"

Her husband laughed. "It's all downhill from here."

"You told him to stay on the trail," she said.

They paused where the boy last stood, gazing across the crowns of trees, up a canyon that bordered the National Park area.

"Tony!"

The reply was her own voice, rebounding in ever-diminishing echoes.

"Ho, Tony!" the father shouted. The name rode the canyon walls in dying ripples. *Silence.* Distantly, the murmur of a mountain stream came as a muted drone. A hawk rode air currents along red and yellow cliffs, turning his head this way and that in search of sustenance.

"Yo, Tony!" The father, again. Before the wife could speak, Harold said, "He's gone on to the car, Donna. Playing with us."

She knew better. Borden could see she knew better. Women had a sixth sense about these things.

She began to run, scrambling, slipping, an awkward grace in the way she flung her legs out at the knees, grabbing passing vegetation for support, stones skittering. "Tony!"

Borden watched their panic ascend, voices drawn with mounting fear, the mother coming down the trail with no care for her own footing, impelled by a mindless dread.

He stepped into the open and she screamed, falling backward.

"Easy, lady, easy—what's the trouble?"

He saw himself in their eyes: armed, booted, face painted, weapon blackened, clip in place. It was a clash of cultures. They were from the cocoons of civilized man, hot tubs, and

thermostatically controlled environments; he was an atavistic apparition, as alien as a grizzly, part-man, part—
"My son," she gasped. "Tony. We've lost him."
"How long ago?"
The husband was here now. "A few minutes. Seconds."
"Then he can't be far. Give another shout."
"Tony!" called the mother.
"Tony!" called the father.
Borden slung the rifle over a shoulder, joining them. "Tony!"
"Does this trail return to the parking area?" the father asked.
"Which one?" Borden mused. "There are dozens."
"Oh, my God." The woman shouted again, "Tony!"
"The park isn't open," Borden said. "It won't open for another few weeks."
It was a subtle accusation of irresponsibility and the husband rose to it. "We're experienced hikers," he said. "We hadn't planned to go far."
"No," Borden said, ruefully. "They never do. This can be dangerous country."
"Danger?" the woman said. "What danger?"
"Cougars. Bears. Mountain streams so swift a man can't stand in them, can't get up again if he's knocked down."
"Oh, my Lord, Harold."
"City folks have died of dehydration a few yards from good water," Borden expounded. "They become disoriented, careless. Fall in a crevasse, break a leg. Sound is funny in the mountains. Up canyon, if the wind is right, you hear a whisper. Another time, another day, you can't hear screaming."
The woman was trembling. Borden put an arm around her, squeezing. *Firm. Supple.*
"Hey, hey," he said, "this happens every year. We'll find the boy. But it *is* this kind of thing that keeps the park closed until the rangers check it out."
"Check out what?" the husband snapped.

"Landslide," Borden said. "Trail markers vandalized. Things like that."

She drew away, stepping back. He had been stroking her shoulder as if distracted, but comforting.

"We can go to my place and call the rangers," Borden offered. "Thirty minutes later, men, megaphones, maybe a helicopter—they don't take this kind of thing lightly."

"I . . . this . . . surely this doesn't call for that kind of response," the man asked his wife.

"Thing is—" Borden massaged his jaw— "up here tiny mishaps can become needless tragedies. We look an hour or two. Maybe we find the boy, maybe we don't. It gets dark—well—"

"Harold," the wife said, "you go to a telephone. I'll stay here."

"Oh, no, you don't," Borden said, gruffly taking her arm. "By the time we get back, there will be two lost tenderfeet."

"I won't be lost. I'll stay on the trail."

"First rule of hiking," Borden said, "stay together."

"Tony may find the trail; he'll come down. Harold, you make the call."

"Amateurs get fearful and do fearful things," Borden sighed. "I can't leave you wandering around out here."

He caught a wary glint in her eye and turned aside to put her at ease.

"Perhaps you could make the call for us," the father reasoned. "We'd both stay here, on the trail."

"Could, I suppose. Trouble is, I can't describe your boy, what he's wearing—or your car, or where you parked it."

"It's back up this trail."

"Which trail? There are several converging into this one." Borden consulted his watch, squinted at pure blue sky. "About four hours of day," he said.

"Donna? What do you think?"

"You go. Tony may show up."

"What we've got here is a deadlock." Borden smiled. "I'm of a mind to leave you both and go alone. But the last time I did that, the rescue party came and the folks had found one another and left, too embarrassed to stay and admit how stupid they had been."

Borden watched a solitary hawk swerve, dive at the cliff. *Missed.*

"I've lived in these mountains all my life," he said. "If I leave you and things don't work out, I take a lot of lip from folks. 'Borden, you knew better,' they say. And I do. City people are found frozen to death. This minute, it's comfortable, but it's midday and still. If we were wet, if a brisk wind came off those snowcaps—"

"Donna, he may be right."

The husband extended a hand, "My name is Harold Morris. This is my wife, Donna."

Borden shook their hands. "Borden Wilson," he said.

"How long will it take us to reach a telephone, Mr. Wilson?"

Borden hunched his shoulders to ease the bite of the gunsling. "Be there in a few minutes," he advised. "It's a rough ride, but my rig can make it."

"Let's go, Donna."

"No, Harold. I'm not leaving."

"Donna, damn it—what he says makes sense. We'll be back—half an hour at most. Right, Wilson?"

"Right it is."

"Donna?"

Borden was moving away downhill. The mother screamed her boy's name, listened to it fade away mockingly.

"Donna, please!"

"If you want to stay alive in these mountains," Borden noted, "stay together. That's S.O.P. Know what that means?"

"Standard operating procedure." The husband's voice dropped to an insistent command. "Donna!"

"S.O.P.," Borden continued, moving away. "That's how to stay alive."

In double-low gear, with all four wheels pulling, Borden drove across streams swollen by melting snow, water rushing up the hood and over the windshield in roaring gulps,

the mud tires clawing at slippery banks, lurching over turning stones. Their passage was parallel to two electric lines
snaking up the canyon. Donna sat beside Borden, answering
his questions with leaden dread.

"So how many kids you got?" Borden shouted over the
deafening voice of the river.

"Just Tony."

"Nice little family. Where you from?"

"Boston."

"Boston—Massachusetts? I hear they have good lobster
in Boston."

"Yes. Good lobster."

The husband leaned around his wife. "How much farther?"

"Two miles total from where we were. It seems slow, but
we're making way."

The vehicle jolted, lurched, throwing the passengers back
and forth. Borden deliberately paused, midstream, gunning
the motor as if for added power. The vehicle broached,
swept downstream a few yards. The woman gasped, clutch-
ing the dashboard with both hands. It was a bit of drama
Borden had performed many times.

"So, what kind of work do you do?" Borden yelled.

The husband responded, "I'm a teacher."

"Teaching what?"

"Botany."

They struck a hole, water, blinding, ferocious, pummeling
the windows, sweeping over the windshield. Borden backed
away. His passengers were white, their lips bloodless.

"Too fast for good fishing," Borden said. "You fish for
trout, Harold?"

"No."

"Pan-fried," Borden reminisced, "splash of lemon—you
like trout, Mrs. Morris?"

She made no attempt to answer, her knuckles jutting,
fingers glued to the dashboard.

"So where are you folks staying?"

"Gatlin Pass."

"Gatlin Pass—where?"

"Rocky Mountain Lodge," the husband said.

"Used to," Borden volunteered, "I lived down in Longmont. Got too crowded. I moved to Gatlin Pass, but that gets crowded too, come summer. So I built a cabin back up in here. Hunt, fish, it's a good life. Nobody comes this way."

He changed the subject unexpectedly, with another question. "You have people hereabouts?"

"No. Goddamn, Wilson, this is a rough ride."

"Said it would be. Just tourists?"

"Tourists," Harold said irritably.

They reached higher ground, the stream more shallow, its flow slowing, the floor of the valley a narrow corridor between towering peaks strewn with boulders larger than houses. In the lee of one of these, Borden's cabin was built hard against the side of the incline. There were two outbuildings. A cord of cut wood was stacked in a lean-to shed.

"There's a telephone out here?" Donna questioned.

"And electricity and good water from the stream," Borden said. He snatched up the emergency brake, retrieved his rifle from behind the seat, getting out.

The husband dismounted, helping his wife. The moment her feet touched the ground, Borden leveled his weapon at them. "Do exactly as I say," he said, "and nobody gets hurt."

"What is this?" Harold demanded.

"You want to see your boy?" Borden asked. "Do as I say."

"You have Tony? You sonofabitch!"

"Come this way," Wang called. For the first time they saw him. Wang held them in his sights every second. He stood in shadows that made his eyes dark slits, his white teeth stark flashes when he spoke.

"Hey, you guys, what's going on?"

Wang lifted a door that was almost at ground level, the type covering a root cellar—which is what it was meant to seem.

"Get below," Wang said sharply. "Move!"

"Is this a robbery, Wilson?"

Wang jabbed Harold with his rifle.

"We're going nowhere." Harold stiffened.

"Do it or die," Borden said casually.

"Where is our son?"

"In the cellar. Go and see."

Donna ran down the steps. The husband was facing them now, as if to block their passage below.

"Oh, my God, Harold," the woman wailed. "They have Tony chained."

"We will kill you," Borden said, softly, "if that's your wish. But if you do what we say, this will soon be done and you'll be on your way home to Boston with an interesting tale to tell."

It was a lie. Harold knew it—Borden could see it in his eyes. But his choice was nothing. One step at a time, the trembling man backed into the cellar.

"What are you going to do?" Donna cried. "Why are you doing this?"

Wang searched the husband, backed him to a wall. The cellar was deep—twelve feet from hard-packed soil floor to the thick beams overhead, with a foot of dirt atop that. The walls were built of similar timbers. It was cold year round, but fairly constant winter and summer.

Wang shackled the man's wrists to pitons embedded in grommets slightly higher than Harold's shoulders. He shoved Harold's legs back, cuffing the ankles. The bottom restraints were so close to the wall, with the top ones built out a bit, that the captive was thrown forward, off center, hanging by the wrists, helplessly.

"Please," Donna wept, "please—what are you going to do to us?"

"Make you a star," Wang said laconically.

Borden watched the young Oriental close the top outer door, then bolt the lower, heavier bottom door. Borden lit a cigarette, his weapon still slung on one shoulder, and took a seat on the corner of a heavy worktable.

Wang stepped back, studying the weeping woman. "What do you think, Borden?"

"Looks damn good to me."

"Little thin."

"Those eyes, Wang—she's the best one yet."

Wang dabbed his fingers in cold cream and wiped greasepaint from his face with slow methodical strokes. "Man then boy?" he contemplated aloud. "Or, boy then man?"

"You're the director."

Wang peeled away his shirt. He had a tattoo of the U.S. Marine Corps emblem on one forearm. Borden set up two cameras, one on a tripod, the other hand held.

"Oh, merciful God," Donna shrilled. "Harold, do you see what they're going to do?"

The man bucked against his shackles, blood tracing one arm from the wrist. "Bastards!" he screamed. "You bastards!"

Wang transferred the boy to another place, the child dumb with shock.

"Please," Donna begged. "Please don't do this."

Wang looked back at a TV monitor, moving this way and that in the picture. He adjusted a light to reduce a hot spot, another to eliminate a shadow. He looked at the woman, then the monitor. "Yeah," he said. "You're right about the eyes."

The camera on the tripod focused automatically. Borden picked up the other, facing the husband to catch his response.

"Ready, Borden?"

"Ready."

Wang reached for her blouse. "Action," he said.

CHAPTER TWO

O nly in the Rockies were the nights so clear. A million stars sparkled in a moonless sky, each pinpoint as hard and crisp as a diamond. Insects burred in the dark, the whir of crickets undulating as they fiddled for their mates. Richmond Bell sat on the front steps of his cabin, lit a cigarette, inhaled deeply, debating what to do next. Years of experience had taught him, when he didn't know what to do, do nothing.

Stupid.

No other word for Borden—*stupid.*

Richmond pinched the head of the spent match and a smell of phosphorus brought back a memory in vivid detail: Borden sitting in a corner of a Saigon bar, his fingernails filthy with accumulated grime from his work as a mechanic in the motor pool, his eyes reflecting the boisterous scene of servicemen, of women selling themselves. The noise was incessant, the air rank with the smell of stale beer.

"It takes a particular personality to kill, Borden," Richmond had said.

"I could do it."

"You have a man in your sights, he's two hundred yards away, you squeeze the trigger and he falls. You could do that?"

"I could."

"But that's not the same as standing next to him, his breath in your face, your hand behind his neck, driving a blade into his solar plexus."

"I could do it, though."

"That kind of killing is personal, Borden. That contact, that touching, the feel of the hilt as he quivers, paralyzed. That kind of killing requires a certain type of man."

He remembered Borden as mesmerized, taking a long draft of beer, foam making a mustache on his upper lip. "I know I could do it," Borden had said, huskily.

"Okay," Richmond had taunted, "suppose it were a woman?"

Borden had blinked. Richmond had laughed at him. "You hesitated, Borden. That's what I mean—"

"I could do it!"

"Suppose she's young, she's delicate." Richmond had lowered his voice to enhance the image. "She's beautiful. Big brown eyes, skin smooth, her waist tiny, her hips firm and round. You've got her. She sees you mean it, begging for mercy. Could you cut that lovely throat?"

Borden had swallowed more beer, foam mustache renewed. "I could," he had insisted.

A mechanic from headquarters motor pool. A Colorado mountain boy who had seen war in movies, joined the army. The nearest he'd been to battle was there in Saigon, keeping the officers in rolling stock.

Remembering it, Richmond cursed himself. He should've seen Borden for what he was. His only excuse was his own state of mind at the time. He'd come in from missions so emotionally exhausted he wasn't thinking. Drank himself senseless to sleep at last, numbed his mind with drugs until it was all a dream, a horrible dream.

"What if it were a child?" he'd mocked. "Wide-eyed and innocent, caught in a cruel quirk of fate—have you ever thought about fate, Borden? What brings two beings to a precise instant in an exact place—one to die, the other to live another day?"

Like a cobra rising from a basket, Borden had swayed, hypnotized by the vision of it.

"Could you cut the child's throat?"

"I would," Borden croaked, "if I had to."

"But you don't have to! You can stay here in Saigon, get through your tour, go home, and forget about it. There's no blood on your hands. For most men, that's the way this war will be. There are very few who actually kill; fewer still will kill as I do. Kill without a qualm. That's the difference between them and me, Borden. I kill and walk away. Never a second thought. No nightmares. No recriminations, no regrets."

Fodder for another letter home. It was Richmond's payment to Borden for uncut snow, for black market delicacies, for girls.

Thinking about it now, he must have seen Borden for what he was, even then. He must have. A grease monkey yearning for the glamour of infiltration and assassination, a warrior with no scars, living a fantasy.

He'd thought he was using Borden. Returning from every job, his confidence slightly thinner, his bravado more forced, Borden bought the drinks and offered the solace of illicit relief. *No charge,* Borden would say.

Not money, but there was a price.

A falling star, spraying celestial grains across the firmament, brought him back to the present. Richmond ground his cigarette under a heel, field-stripped the butt, put the remnants in his top pocket.

He'd grown close to Borden. No apology for that. Battle did it. Scum became companions, your life depended on them. You didn't question morals or political inclinations. Could he kill, that's what you wanted to know.

There is in every intimate relationship an instant that welds. It may be as subtle as sex appeal and a sympathetic response, or as remarkable as the trauma of combat. In battle, when a new man proves his mettle, he's accepted. If he stays in the face of death, endures to help his buddies, then you know he can and will do what he must to survive and keep you alive. After that, he's your friend.

With Borden it came one sober night in a new bar where they'd never been before. Officers were there, Borden had said, but it was open to anyone with the money. No ear-shattering electronic guitars and amplifiers here—the music was violins, Mantovani, and symphonic orchestras. The cuisine was superb, the wines vintage French.

"Saying I can do it doesn't make it so," Borden had proclaimed, his voice guttural. "I tell you I can, and I can. But how will you ever know?"

"I'll never know."

"So I'm going to do it."

"Kill somebody?"

"Pick one." Borden indicated the room of people.

Richmond remembered thinking, *He's crazy.* He'd lit a cigarette, leaned back in his chair, surveying the patrons. American officers, mostly. A few counterparts from the South Vietnamese IV Corps. Two European journalists sat at a nearby table talking to three women in French.

The women—expensive. Their perfume was a hint of florescence, their hair coiffed, their jewelry real. They comported themselves with dignity, spoke in cultured tones. It was a class act. Richmond had been impressed with that.

"Pick one," Borden had urged.

He meant it. The entire evening had been aimed at that precise moment, in that exact place. There was no way out. Richmond had started the goddamned game, enticing, taunting—and he dared not flinch. He'd forced utter nonchalance, blowing smoke toward the ceiling. He'd selected the most beautiful woman there, the one least likely to respond to a mechanic with dirty fingernails. Even then, he had stalled as long as he could, his words the same, but his motive altered, trying to joke Borden out of it. He'd spoken the truth when he said only a particular kind of man could kill as he killed. Unfortunately, Borden was that particular kind of man.

It had taken two penetrations of the blade. Analyzing it later, Borden told Richmond the first faulty stab was due to inexperience, not hesitation.

Standing over the body, calmly wiping his hands and weapon, Borden had proved himself that night. In so doing, he'd welded them one to the other.

The insanity of warfare has a certain sane balance. The most wanton killing serves a perverse purpose as a thread in the fabric of war as a whole. But this—what purpose this?

Even in war, there's such a thing as murder.

When his tour ended, Richmond had gone home to West Virginia, to the rolling smoky haze of verdant mountains where he'd grown up. He tried to farm again, but failed. He'd taken a job in the city, making cigarettes. The din of machinery was disturbing. People irritated him, the voices, their words, a meaningless prattle that gave him hives. He didn't want to be touched, not even intimately, by anybody.

The dreams he'd never had, now came: sudden flashes of dying faces, of mutilated bodies, their anguish inflicted on him in sleepless, fitful onslaughts. He could smell the sweat, feel the shiver in the hilt of his blade, hear the whispery sigh of air from a punctured lung.

Then Borden had called. In Colorado. Describing impassable mountains and the flash of striking trout in pure rushing waters. He'd built a cabin, remote and quiet, he said. He hunted deer in the fall and salted it for winter. The world was far away, the nearest town several miles. *Alone. Tranquil.*

It was seduction, and like in Saigon, nothing was free from Borden. Richmond knew that. But he came anyway.

For a year they had lived together. Hunting, fishing, trapping, the old horrors more bearable and less fearsome somehow in the retelling of them. Winter snow cloistered them, a roaring fire was a lulling magnet. The two men were bound by the murder of a lovely woman in a far land as a ritual act of passage into manhood.

Instinctively, he must have known Borden was doomed. Richmond never accompanied the man to town. Inventing excuses, he had avoided contact with people Borden knew. *Thank God.*

During that time, he'd taught Borden military tactics and strategy—tutored him in camouflage, tracking, quick kill techniques as opposed to stun blows that rendered the target helpless and mute. Augmenting the fantasy of Vietnam, still playing the game, he'd paid the price for living with Borden Wilson.

They had parted company, finally, friendly adversaries. The rapport had run its course. Borden's territory was his own. They'd seldom met thereafter. Two years, then three, finally four had passed.

He should have killed Borden in Saigon, the night of the murder. He'd unleashed a psychopath with a deadly fantasy. Why hadn't he?

Richmond lit another cigarette, pondering the question. *Should have and didn't.*

He held the cigarette between his lips, eyes squinted against smoke, flesh crawling with a restlessness he hadn't experienced in years. His body was demanding action, his brain declined—*think—think—plan.*

He was nauseated from lack of food, his system unbalanced by nicotine. He sighed repeatedly, listening to the diminishing cricket chorus, his head throbbing with the prospect of a brain-buster. The night air was going cool, insects falling silent as their metabolisms slowed.

He stood up, walked away, turned, walked back and sat again. He twisted his shoulders to ease taut muscles. He massaged his hands, rotating his head with the cigarette in his mouth, eyes closed. *Relax.*

He'd done good work these past three weeks. Sensing freedom, Wynona and Joyce had cooperated with every directive, producing the penultimate scene of the video.

They were whores, of course. He had hired both of them in Las Vegas, promising a thousand dollars each for a skin flick he was making. They sold their bodies anyway, so why not? It would only take a few days, he'd said. There would be a bonus when the job was done.

They had accompanied him willingly for a hundred-dollar deposit.

There was no need to do as Borden did, taking people here in home territory. Richmond had hired his actors in Reno, Los Angeles, San Francisco, Chicago, and New York— the temptation of an "easy" thousand was, to a hooker, something of a vacation. Besides, they fancied themselves stars even if only in a porno flick.

They had helped him apply the shackles. It was expected in something of this sort. They did not resist when he took away their clothing to clear the scene.

Then—he had them.

There was never any hurry. Who would be looking for them? Their line of work did not engender reports of missing people. The pimps would find others to replace them.

From the viewpoint of a casting director, which Richmond was, in a manner of speaking, prostitutes were perfect. The choice was a matter of personal discretion. They came in all sizes and shapes: blondes, brunettes, and redheads, from children to syphilitic old women. They were unabashedly immodest, completely willing to do anything he suggested.

So dumb, Borden. Using tourists when prostitutes were so plentiful.

Richmond had had Wynona and Joyce for twenty days. He fed them, bathed them, tended to their sanitary needs. He gave them magazines to read. Except for being chained to the walls, they had it as well as could be expected under these circumstances.

They were fairly good at acting, too.

It should have been ended today. Then, there would be the arduous task of final editing. Much of the editing had already been accomplished after each night of recording. All he lacked was the last scene, the crucial one, carefully planned.

He did what he must because it was the only way to accomplish the job. The job happened to involve death. Unlike Borden, the act of killing held no morbid fascination for Richmond. He would be willing to work tirelessly to give the illusion without committing the act. But the viewers knew. They always knew. The producer who did not make it absolutely, positively real defeated his own purpose. The viewer paid for the guarantee that what he bought and saw was true.

In the beginning, when he and Borden made only porno films, it was good sport. They went to a city, found girls, used the opportunity to have fun, and made the films. But with the easing of laws against pornography, ten thousand people were in the business. You could make a few hundred dollars, a couple of thousand, maybe—but nothing like *these* videos!

It took a particular kind of man to do it.

Do it—without qualms of conscience.

Richmond ground out his cigarette, permitting himself a moment of regret. He would miss their company, such as it was. At age fourteen, Wynona wasn't exactly a fountain of culture; Joyce was older by four years, larger of stature, more streetwise, faster with insults, and quick with a comeback. He would miss Joyce most of all.

Women in this situation were not like sweethearts or wives, demanding more, using him for all he had or would ever hope to acquire. Chained to a wall for three weeks, they were more like dogs—eager to hear his footstep, anxious about meals. If they grew fractious, he could understand.

Like pets. Yes, like pets.

Richmond went inside, placed a pot of stew on the stove to reheat. He stoked the fire, adding fuel.

He wished he could bring the girls inside to sit at the table, but he didn't dare.

He warmed plates, placed them in a picnic basket with the food in covered dishes.

He tried to be a benevolent captor, giving what they needed as much as he could. Even as he held them he teased about the money they were going to get, promising a bonus that would more than compensate for their incarceration. It never occurred to them they wouldn't go free, financially rewarded for their discomfort and inconvenience.

He strolled around behind the cabin to the fuel tank and used a dipstick to check the contents. Gasoline was the most precious commodity here—every drop had to be carried in, up a torturous incline, to this tank. It took strength and endurance he didn't always possess, so he used the gasoline sparingly. When he was not actually in need of electricity for video recording, he resorted to kerosene lanterns. As for the girls in the darkened cellar, kerosene and Coleman lanterns were not allowed—there was the threat of fire, or more likely, asphyxiation. For them he provided Durabeam battery-operated lights with brilliant halogen bulbs—very nice for reading, long-lasting six-volt alkaline cells—very nice.

In a year or two, he planned to take his money and leave. Go back to the Orient, maybe. A potentate could ask no more than he would have.

Nothing was forever.

He had a good life here. Isolated and self-sufficient, the world was at bay except when he wished otherwise. The nightmares had subsided, slowly, then vanished altogether. Richmond had discovered the formula for peace of mind and it had surprised him. When he was committed to violent acts, the horrors past were swept away. Probably a chemical thing relating to the glandular flow produced when under the stress of violence.

As long as he continued, the dreams did not haunt him. But when he stopped, the specters were only in remission. His mental defenses eroded. Out of the dark came the moaning ghosts of dead men past—bloody maws, voiceless mouths wide as if screaming with their throats slit.

Last night, the viscid sucking pool of his subconscious was bubbling, fermenting, threatening to erupt in his sleep. The visages of agony lurked in that pit, clawing for attention, lunging at him in the deepest levels of slumber.

He carried the basket of food across the ledge upon which he'd constructed his cabin. This place was ideal for his purposes. Inaccessible, with a commanding view of the valley below. He'd dug a cellar much like Borden's—it would seem to be a root cellar beneath a massive granite boulder.

Tonight he would stay with them, talk awhile. Listen to their appeals, endure their entreaties. He would treat them to his best liquor. Give them all they wanted. It helped ease Wynona's pain. He, too, would drink. Drink himself drunk!

He'd been so close yet he had failed. The thought angered him, but he banished the emotion as fruitless.

Of the two captives, Wynona had seemed the most vulnerable. Her youth had lulled Richmond.

When she attacked, day before yesterday, she threw a loop of chain around his neck, dragging him toward Joyce. In the clutches of both, he would've been finished.

Frantically, he'd fought for his life.

He was fairly sure he'd broken Wynona's arm.

If so—well, he couldn't wait for mending.

And that was his quandary.

If he must begin the video again, he had to have another performer. It might take days, weeks. Imprisoned as she was, Joyce required daily attention.

He would examine Wynona's injury, resist the urge to berate her for the assault. They would drink and eat and maybe—miraculously—Wynona's arm was only sprained and not broken.

He hoped so.

Otherwise, dumb or not, he'd have to do what Borden did.

As he lifted the cellar door, Joyce screamed from below, "About time, you cripple sonofabitch!"

CHAPTER THREE

C olleen watched her husband stuff clothing into a duffel bag. His shoulder-length hair was styled, streaked. He wore a new Nehru jacket over designer jeans and clashing red Reebok running shoes. *Punk rock à la 1960.*

"Ginger got us this gig in old Mexico," he said. "All the standards—Presley, Fats Domino, Little Richard. But with a Tijuana Brass feel, only no brass, see—I can sense it, Colleen—we're making new waves here."

Going to split, he said. *Wanted out.*

His out was in the living room. She sat on the divan, shapely legs crossed under a miniskirt, bleached blond hair teased and striped with purple—a ludicrous blend of flower child 60s and latter-day punk. She chewed gum, popping it, reading a month-old copy of *Billboard* magazine.

"I always told you to hold me with open arms," Timothy said. "If you let a thing go and it returns, it's yours; if it never returns, it was never yours."

"Are you planning to return?" Colleen asked.

He spoke of "true love" with a whispery monotone, pausing to take massive inhalations through flared nostrils. He composed his reply along some pseudo-philosophic theme. "Even the gods are capricious," he said.

"What will I do, Tim?"

"Your own thing, babe. No other way. Listen, have you seen my bikini silks?"

"In your drawer. Tim? Please. Can we talk this through?"

"What's to say?"

The telephone rang and the girl in the living room answered without permission.

"Look, Colleen." Tim held her shoulders, his eyes darting across her face earnestly. "We gave this marital gig a turn, right? It's too goddamned confining—admit that."

"Tim!" the girl called. "Somebody about the rent."

He extended a hand toward Colleen as if putting her in a spotlight center stage. When she didn't react, Tim hollered, "Tell them, 'Up yours,' Ginger."

Dutifully, Ginger relayed the message and hung up. The gum popped, pages turned.

"Tim," Colleen reasoned, "we got married. You lost your job with the band a month later. You've been unemployed for two years. All this time I supported us—"

"Until you lost your job. *You've* been unemployed for six months. See what I mean? Restricting."

"Marriage demands responsibility, Tim. True, that carries some restrictions."

"Too many for me, babe. Hey, look, let's stay friends."

"We're married."

"In spite of that." He swept things from a vanity into his bag. "If you want a divorce, go for it," he said. "I won't contest it."

"Nor pay for it, I imagine."

"Money," he said, placidly. "That's the sum of it with you. Okay, for what it's worth—money is part of why I'm going. I can't take the bitching anymore."

"When did I bitch?"

"You eye-bitch, babe. Better than anybody I ever knew, you eye-bitch. That sad, hurt, green-eyed veil of condemnation. Without a word, sigh-bitch-sigh-bitch. Mostly with the eyes. That's your act and you're good at it."

"I didn't realize—"

"Gin's got a car and enough money to get us to Mexico City. The rock stuff is going to be big there. When I make some dough I'll try to send a little."

"The value of their currency is nothing," Colleen protested. "If you make a thousand pesos a day, it's worthless!

What can you do in Mexico City that you can't do here in Los Angeles making more money?"

"A prophet is not without honor, save in his own country," Tim said. "I got to go just to return, babe. Don't you see that?"

"For a few pennies."

"Who gives a damn? Tequila for a buck a bottle; eat like a king for a few dollars more."

He pulled a cord, closing his bag.

"My advice," he said, "is go home to Gatlin Pass. Go before they find the car and repossess it."

"Gatlin Pass? How would I make a living in Gatlin Pass?"

"Feed off your famous daddy, babe. Necessity is a mother."

The phone again. As the girl reached for it, Colleen screamed, "Don't answer the goddamned phone, you bitch!"

"Now that," Tim said, "is bitch without the eyes."

They contemplated one another and Colleen said, "We should not have married."

"I hear you."

"But since we did, we should work at it."

"When it's work, it's over."

The telephone rang, rang, rang.

"Go home to Daddy," he said, gently. "You weren't meant to live among wolves."

She followed him into the living room. The phone seemed to intensify with each pulse.

"Take this with me?" The girl held up the *Billboard* magazine.

"Why not?" Colleen said. "You're taking my husband."

They shut the door behind them. The lock clicked. Colleen stood in the empty room, listening to the phone.
Go home.

She had no money. The car needed servicing, nearly empty on gas. The rent was three months overdue. No food in the kitchen.

She answered the telephone.

"Colleen, this is Mrs. Pfeiffer."

"I don't have it, Mrs. Pfeiffer."

A pained sigh. Colleen felt ill.

"It takes six months to evict," Mrs. Pfeiffer said. "Must we go through that?"

"No. I'll leave tonight."

Another sigh.

"Mrs. Pfeiffer, would you take a check for cash and let me send the money when I get home to Colorado? I promise to send it as soon as I get there."

"Why don't you have them wire money to you?"

"My folks don't know I'm in trouble, Mrs. Pfeiffer. I'd rather be there to explain it."

"I'd like to help," Mrs. Pfeiffer said. "But I can't bail out the world."

Colleen hung up. *Home to Daddy.*

He'd never met Timothy. She'd given no hint of difficulty. *I'm married,* Colleen had reported, after the fact. Working at the *Free Press.* A "reporter" in the entertainment section, she'd met Timothy Lichtenfelter and wow!

Yeah, wow.

The phone again.

Colleen wandered into the bedroom. She saw Tim's blue silk bikini underwear on the back of a chair.

The phone quit. Maybe they cut it off—electricity would go next.

She went through her closet, found a battered autumn-orange Samsonite pullman and opened it on the bed. Take what she could, forget the rest.

How could she have screwed up her life in twenty-three years? Unemployed, abandoned, destitute.

"Home is the place where, when you have to go there, they have to take you in," Daddy often quoted Robert Frost.

Gatlin Pass was home.

They would take her in.

But, oh, how she hated to admit the mess she'd made. She thought about calling for money, but Mom's real estate was all that kept Daddy's weekly newspaper afloat.

"Everything all right down there in L.A.?" Dad always asked on the telephone.

"Everything's fine, Daddy."

"That's my girl. Got your mama's good looks and my backbone."

"Good genes," Colleen would reply.

She wanted them to be proud of her and they were. Colleen wiped a tear with the back of a hand. So proud, and so deluded. She'd worked at building the illusion—always a cheerful tone, always "too busy" to run home.

"Why aren't you sending me your latest columns, Colleen?"

"I will, Daddy. When I'm proud of something I write."

"Nonsense."

"Hey, I have a lot to live up to," she would insist. "Nothing I do can match your Pulitzer stuff."

"Um. Well, darling, I don't match up to that Pulitzer stuff, either. Don't judge yourself by a rare and lucky happenstance."

Now, like a splash of ice-cold water, she was going to face them. "Hiya, folks! Remember your daughter, Colleen Colter? Lost a vestal virgin and gained a new name: Colleen Lichtenfelter."

If she got a divorce, she was going to dump that name. The jokes she'd endured—*Lichtenfelter*.

Somebody knocked on the door and Colleen froze, her stomach knotted. When she opened it, Mrs. Pfeiffer stood there in stout resignation, charcoal-colored bags under her weary eyes. She extended a paper.

"This is a release for the furniture so we can sell it," she said. "I can spare fifty dollars as a loan."

Colleen signed the document. "Thank you, Mrs. Pfeiffer."

"I saw your husband leaving."

"Going to Mexico, he said."

Mrs. Pfeiffer's upper lip was a hairy critter in motion, driven by a nervous tic. She walked through the living room, looked into the kitchen and bedroom. "K-Mart," she observed.

"I'm afraid so."

"I don't know how you young people make it these days," Mrs. Pfeiffer said. "Use to be I could live a month on what it takes for a week these days. We can thank the politicians for that. All right, Colleen—" She delivered fifty dollars in folded currency. "Pay me back when you can. Be careful going home."

Alone again, Colleen saw the rooms as the landlady had: spindle-leg coffee table, plastic veneer. Soiled paper shades on cheap lamps. Nothing of quality. Little value.

It had not been a happy two and a half years.

Go home.

She left the door keys on the Formica kitchen counter. Leaving the place dirty—that was not like her. But nothing about her life had been like her, lately.

She took her luggage downstairs. Passing the resident manager, Colleen said, "Thank you, Mrs. Pfeiffer."

Outside in the night, smog burned her eyes. The Volvo threatened not to start. In the next car, a drunk slept with his head back on the seat, mouth wide.

Whatever lay ahead, it couldn't be worse than this.

Richmond closed the heavy lower door to the cellar and bolted it out of habit. He placed his picnic basket on a worktable beside the video cameras and monitor.

"Why don't you turn on some lights, you stingy bastard?" Joyce demanded. *She knew why.* To save fuel.

Both women were tethered by their ankles, with room to move about on individual pallets, but too far apart to touch one another. "When I get my hands on your gimpy ass," Joyce threatened, "I'll rip you apart."

"Is it day or night?" Wynona asked softly.

"Night," Richmond said. He served her plate first. "How's your arm?"

"It hurts real bad."

"What you call this shit?" Joyce stared at her plate. "You expect us to eat this crap?"

"I like stew," Wynona said. "My mama served stew all the time." She tugged her chain nearer to ease the strain on the swollen left arm. "If you came from a big family like I did," Wynona said, "you'd know good stew when you tasted it."

There wasn't much doubt her arm was fractured. The flesh was discolored, distended.

"In Juarez," Wynona said, "we used a lot of jalapeño peppers in stew to give it flavor. The one thing we had was peppers."

Joyce swore at length, food untouched. "A honky cook and a Chicano whore—never heard of soul."

Richmond sat beside the worktable, watching Wynona struggle to eat with her good hand, the other arm useless. No, there was no doubt. *Pity.*

"Girls," he said, "this is our last evening as a threesome."

Wynona lifted chocolate-brown eyes, hopefully.

"It is obvious we cannot continue with a wounded performer," Richmond said. "This means I must throw away everything we've done and begin again. It represents a loss of time and money."

He lit a cigarette, trickled smoke through his mustache. "The good news is: Wynona goes home in the morning. The bad news is: Joyce, for having encouraged Wynona to attack me, you will not receive extra pay for the time it takes to repeat our work. You are going to be here longer than expected and it's your own fault."

"This ain't no big-time movie and you ain't no Metro-Goldwyn-Mayer, asshole," Joyce snapped. "Keeping us down here like some kind of animals! You better kill us while you can."

"No!" Wynona cried. "I won't tell anybody, I swear it."

"Of course you won't," Richmond soothed. "It isn't your fault we had this unfortunate accident. Until you assaulted me, you'd done a good job, Wynona. Therefore, I am going to give you full pay plus a bonus. That's four thousand dollars."

"You believe that," Joyce said to Wynona, "and you believe your mother is a virgin."

"I won't tell the police," Wynona promised.

"I know that." Richmond stroked her hair, soft ebony strands between his fingers. "You'll have more money than you anticipated and I'll pay the doctor for tending your arm. In a few weeks you'll be as good as new and no worse for wear. In fact, I was wondering if you'd consider coming back next year to do another feature."

He saw disbelief in their eyes.

"You're probably thinking, Why has he done this to us?" Richmond brushed hair from Wynona's face. "The answer is simple: to help you gain proper intensity, the right mood. Professional actresses have to do things to themselves to achieve a level of performance that's real. Neither of you is a professional—you needed the realism of this uncomfortable situation."

"Bullshit," Joyce said evenly.

"Tomorrow," he spoke to Wynona, "I'll take you to a doctor. After he takes care of your arm, you and I will go to a fine restaurant for a sumptuous meal. We'll sip wine and the candlelight will play in your eyes. You have beautiful eyes."

Joyce swished water in her mouth, cheeks puffed. She swallowed, watching Richmond skeptically.

"This hasn't been so bad," Wynona said.

"Hell it ain't."

"I've had tricks do me worse for a whole lot less," Wynona said.

"How long we been locked in here?" Joyce demanded.

"Three weeks."

"Three weeks and I work four johns a night minimum," Joyce said. "That comes to more than four thousand dollars, I promise you."

"Push me your plate, Joyce," Richmond said.

She flung it at him.

Unprotesting, Richmond retrieved the metal utensil, put it in the picnic basket. "Anybody want anything else?"

"You're really going to let me go?" Wynona questioned.

"We'll leave in the morning."

"And pay me my money?"

"Every cent."

Wynona began to cry quietly.

"I'll bring some whiskey and pills to ease your pain," Richmond said. "Later on, I want to give you a bath, clean your fingernails, shave your underarms and legs. By this time tomorrow night, you'll be laughing and happy."

"What about me?" Joyce asked, brusquely. "I'm supposed to sit in this hole for how long?"

"Until I get another girl and train her. You brought this upon yourself, Joyce. No one to blame but yourself."

"I don't want to be left down here by myself, man."

"It can't be helped. You should not have fostered an attack. Because of you, Wynona was hurt. Just imagine that you'd succeeded—how would you get out of here? Nobody to look after you, bring the food? It was an idiotic thing to do, Joyce. Really stupid."

As he started up the steep steps to the outer door, Joyce hollered, "I don't want you leaving me here alone, jerk-off! Hear me?"

He pushed open the sharply slanted doors and cool night air felt good on his face.

By the light of a lantern, he rinsed the utensils and dried them. From a cupboard he took a bottle of bourbon and four Percodans. Enough to assure Wynona a restful night. He placed two buckets of water on the cast-iron stove, fed the fire, stoking it.

When he returned to the cellar door, he heard Joyce urging, "Call my pimp, understand? Tell that sucker, come get me!"

They heard Richmond and fell silent.

"Take these, Wynona," Richmond directed. He steadied her with a hand behind her head as she gulped the painkillers. She leaned against him, responding.

"The water will be hot in a little while," he said, pouring whiskey for each of them. "After the pills take effect, I'll bathe you. Tomorrow is our last day together. I can't send you home looking a mess, can I?"

"You promise to let me go?"

He touched her face reassuringly.

"You promise?" she persisted.

"I wish I hadn't hurt you, Wynona."

"Promise!" she cried.

"Very well," he said. "If it makes you feel better. I promise."

High on adrenaline, incited by anger, Colleen had been driving like an automaton. When she thought of Tim and that blonde moron, she swung from weeping to fury, subsiding at last into self-pity.

What possessed her to marry him in the first place? She'd known her parents wouldn't approve. She hadn't been home for a holiday since college. She'd fibbed about so many things—the bliss of marriage, the prospects of working for the L.A. newspapers. Lies they would recognize in retrospect.

She hadn't wanted to worry them. Didn't want Daddy pressuring her to come home and work with him.

She dozed. A truck hurtled past, horn blaring. Shaking, Colleen clamped her hands to the steering wheel with arms straight, pushing herself back into the seat. *Stay awake!*

Of Mrs. Pfeiffer's fifty-dollar loan, she had four dollars remaining. Her stomach growled with hunger. She was thirsty.

Again she nodded off only to jolt awake as the bump of the median threw her this way and that. *Idiot!*

To stay alert, she sang as loud as she could. She jiggled in place. She stuck her head out the window, the cool wind bracing, blowing her hair wildly. *So sleepy.* She closed one eye in a futile attempt to rest it, using her other eye to navigate.

Still, she fell asleep. She shook her head, slapped herself, cursing. Had to stop. No choice. The motor hesitated, caught up again. The needle of the gas gauge was firmly on empty.

The eastern horizon was serrated by the tips of the Rockies, the sky glowing pink. The Colorado state line loomed and passed.

She left the four-lane highway at the next intersection.

One service station and it was closed. She coasted to a halt beside the gas pumps, rolled up the windows, locked the doors, and immediately fell asleep.

Colleen awoke to an urgent tapping on the window. She squinted up through a dusty windshield at a man's face.

"Blocking my pumps, little lady!"

"I'm sorry."

"Want gas or what?"

"Gas . . . no, wait a minute . . . sir?" She blinked away slumber. "Sir, would you take my spare tire for a tank of gas?"

"What'd I do with a Volvo tire out here?" He examined her vehicle with watery gray eyes. He was elderly, unshaven.

"I'm broke," she said. "I'm trying to get to Gatlin Pass. One more tankful and I can make it."

"Some folks call these Volvos," he said. "Some call them valvos. I don't recollect anybody hereabouts owns a valvo."

"Suppose I give you a check?" Colleen bartered. "The check is no good. But when I get home to Gatlin Pass this evening, I'll send the money. You'll have my tire and my check for leverage."

He kneaded his jaw. She heard whiskers bristle. "Let me look at the tire."

She opened the trunk. The tire was new.

"That's a cheater tire," he said.

"A what?"

"It ain't a tire," he said. "You have a flat and that tire is good for maybe forty miles. Meant to get you to the next station, that's all."

He slammed the trunk lid, slammed it again, slammed a third time and it latched.

"By looks of the rubber on the ground," he advised, "you best keep the cheater anyway."

"That tire came with the car!"

"Yep and you paid full price for a spare. That's why they're called cheaters."

A headache spawned at the base of her skull and swam upward. "Can you help me?" she asked.

"Last time a sweet missy come in here, she swung her hips first one way and then the other, holding her own hands, smiling like innocence itself. Stung me for thirty bucks, she did."

"Please," Colleen implored. "My father owns a newspaper in Gatlin Pass. My mother owns real estate. As soon as I arrive, I'll send a check to replace the one I give you."

"If I don't get it," he said, "I swear out a warrant."

"That's fine. I will send the money."

He pumped gasoline into her tank, directing, "Write down your pappy's name and address on the check. I'm telling you fair, if I don't get my money inside a week, I'm going to the law. Colorado has mean laws about bad checks."

"I know. Thank you."

He took her check, held it at his best focal length. "Lichtenfelter?"

"Yes."

"Lichtenfelter," he said, making note of her tag number. "Knew a fellow back east name of Greisedieck once. Down south, there's a family name of Badcock. But I never heard of Licked-and-felt-her."

He gave Colleen his address and a final warning. She started the motor. "Thanks for your help."

"No money—into jail you go."

"You'll get the money."

As she pulled away, he said, "Lichtenfelter . . ."

Colleen followed the Interstate to a familiar turn north. The days of free road maps were gone and she was driving by memory alone. It had been several years since she'd come this way. The mountains rose on her right. She drove in their shadows along clear streams gurgling over smooth stones. The air was fresh, cold, invigorating.

As bad as it was to be going home in trouble, it was good to be going there. She'd decided to be blunt, admit her errors, remain unemotional. She had allowed false pride to rule and that had to go.

The sky was utterly blue here, but higher up she saw heavy clouds darkening the peaks. Pockets of snow formed patchwork quilts on the sides of mountains.

Timothy had never been here. He'd never know what he had missed.

The road wound ever upward and she dropped to a lower gear. For want of a tune-up, the car was sputtering as the atmosphere rarefied.

"Come on you—valvo! Get me home and you can die forever. Come on—"

It coughed. She smelled steam. One more spastic jerk and it quit. *Overheated.*

Colleen set the brake. Dense fog shrouded the highway. She got out, walked to the next hairpin curve. Giant flakes of snow wafted down. She saw a sign and strolled toward it. TRAIL RIDGE CLOSED.

She'd forgotten to consider the opening date of the high-winding, scenic drive traversing the Rocky Mountain National Park. Her only thought had been the shortest route to Gatlin Pass. Should've gone to Denver, then north.

As she returned to her car, snow dappled her blouse. She attempted to start the motor and it turned once—then, nothing.

The last town was at least fifteen miles back. Where had she seen a house? On both sides, mountains rose into the clouds. The altitude made her giddy, cold air burned her throat.

Who knew when anyone would happen this way?

She blew her horn long and hard, three times. It echoed briefly, the sound absorbed by falling snow.

If she went east toward Gatlin Pass, she faced forty or fifty miles of steep climbs and precipitous grades on a closed road. She'd hiked the Trail Ridge as a high school student, but never the full length and never from the western limits.

Her watch had stopped, but the quartz clock in the Volvo ticked steadily. Nearly two o'clock Mountain Time. A walk back to the last town would take, say, four hours.

Despite the snow, it wasn't unbearably cold. She could sit

here at least one hour in the hope that somebody would come along.

In the meantime, she would change into jeans and better shoes.

Might as well relax. If she had to be stranded, she couldn't ask for a more beautiful location. It was good to be back in familiar territory.

CHAPTER FOUR

Gatlin Pass was—*bucolic.*
Gary Colter searched his brain for synonyms: *pastoral, rustic, unsophisticated—simple.*
And he was—*stagnating, vegetating.*

With his ankles crossed, heels on a corner of his desk, he leaned back in his swivel chair. Through the gilded letters on the plate-glass window of his office he watched a lone car drive slowly by. The sun had not yet burned away the morning fog and the town was gray, humid, unoccupied.

"Coffee, Gary." Barbara placed a mug on his desk, sat across from him, her short blond hair still moist from the high humidity of outdoors.

This is what they had come for, wasn't it? At *his* urging. He had wanted to own a small-town newspaper. A weekly, he had insisted. No pressure. No underworld, no dock disputes, no aching abdomen as he checked under the hood of his car each morning. Peace and quiet. A good place to raise his last child, Marcus, where they didn't have to lock the door every time they stepped out.

"Worrying about this week's story?" Barbara guessed.

"No news," he said, "is *not* good news when you have a front page to compose."

"Marc has some good shots of deer. You could do another wildlife article."

"We did that twice last season."

"Tourists like it."

"Yeah. Well . . ."

Somewhere in the files he had a document. *Pulitzer.* Investigative reporting.

Every major newspaper in the nation had been his plum. He could have gone to any of them. Offers from the *San Francisco Chronicle, The New York Times* for God's sake!

"They're opening the Trail Ridge Drive next month," Barbara suggested.

He nodded glumly.

The telephone rang, drawing his wife away. "Rocky Mountain Rentals!" she said pleasantly.

Making more money in her real estate business than he was with this rag called a publication. His biggest story last season had involved a man who threw his wife off the third-floor balcony of a motel. She had landed in the swimming pool—no harm done. But sobered by the fall and the dunking, she had gone back upstairs and thrown her husband off the same balcony, breaking both his legs.

"How many in your party?" Barbara said into the phone.

Okay, so he wasn't going to do an exposé on teamsters' union executives. He wouldn't be facing death threats and the chance of acid hurled into his eyes. He was safe, secure, his wife happy back in this, her hometown. His son Marc was now sixteen, tall and gangling, healthy and athletic, a pretty fair amateur photographer—what more could a husband and father ask?

"The chalet has a fireplace, nice modern kitchen . . ."

The summer season was upon them. Soon the population here would swell, almost overnight, from twenty-eight hundred to forty thousand. During June, July, and August, for three bright months, the shops would prosper, nature trails would be crawling with humanity, and the biggest story would probably be another drunken brawl.

"Minimum is seven nights," Barbara said to a potential customer. "The price is one-fifty per day."

Of which she received twenty-five percent. She managed over one hundred units, plus the property she had bought—a four-plex, two duplexes, three cottages.

The good life. Barbara said that often. "We're leading the good life, aren't we?"

As if to convince him. To reassure him.

Only a fool would deny it. Coming here was probably the best thing they had ever done, would ever *do*. Marc was popular, a fine skier—and happy. They'd seen their daughter, Colleen, graduate with honors, go to Los Angeles and college. If the proof was in the pudding, Colleen was the proof.

How could he be so selfish as to want to change any of that?

Truth was, he didn't want to. He just didn't want to feel this hopeless, *dull* throb that pulsed in his body. Like—"Is this it? Forever—*is this it*?"

"August fifth," Barbara concluded, "through August nineteenth. Yes, I have your credit card number. Thank you."

She returned to her coffee, pursed angel's-bow lips, and sipped. "It's going to be a good season," she said.

A moment later, "Gary, are you all right, darling?"

"Oh, yeah. Just—you know—I have to put this paper to bed tomorrow afternoon, or we'll be off schedule again."

"So?"

She meant, *So what? Who cares?*

"So," he labored, "I need a feature."

Barbara rounded the desk, pushed his feet off, and sat on his lap. She had a nice bottom, round, firm. "You miss the midnight calls from obscene men of sinister intent—is that it?"

He constructed a smile.

"I'm sorry you aren't revealing corruption and degradation this morning," Barbara chided. "But as for me, I get a tingle when I see you sitting here going through the editorial process."

"What editorial process?"

"The one that inevitably ends with, 'Gatlin Pass, Great Place.' "

"That's the way it ends, all right." He moved to unseat her, but she didn't budge. Her eyes—he could do the Australian crawl in those viridian pools—were blue-green and now teasing.

"Is this condition temporary or permanent?" Barbara asked.

"Temporary. I get the itch now and then."

Barbara stood up. "How about a headline that reads: CRIME WAVE IN GATLIN PASS?"

"There is none."

"Aha! That could be your subheading, in parentheses: THERE IS NONE."

"Therefore," Gary said, "Gatlin Pass, Great Place."

"Exactly—and why not?"

The telephone rang again and Barbara turned professional. A second phone rang even as she answered the first call.

For the next ninety days, tourists would roar through this canyon like a flash flood. They would leave fattened bank accounts and tons of debris in their wake. Gary's sales pitch notwithstanding, leather handbags, silver and turquoise jewelry, trout amandine, and beer would sell whether they were advertised or not.

July fourth was his "Christmas." The usual eight-page paper would grow to twenty-four pages. It was make-or-break time, fiscally, but the merchants didn't truly need the *Gatlin Pass Sentinel*.

Hell, this wasn't a newspaper, it was a swap shop, a trader's forum. "Wanted, good four-wheeler, low mileage." Next column, "For Sale: good four-wheeler, low mileage."

Whatever it had once been, Gatlin Pass was now a western mountain amusement park. The leather goods came from Mexico, the trout from commercial ponds. In stables where they rented horses, the steeds had names like Melody and Bronco to fit the psyche of the novice horseman. In any case, they were all more like melodies than broncos.

Across the street, Barbara's brother, Clint, dressed in the uniform of deputy sheriff, had paused to chat with a couple of flatlanders. Tall, broad-shouldered, amiable, Clint Ferguson was a peace officer in the truest sense of the word. He was as far removed from a streetwise Chicago cop as one planet is from another. Clint was a man who liked to hunt, loved to eat, cherished his homelife and sweet wife.

But still—that had appeal, didn't it? The gentle giant and his tender persuasions. A modern mountain man. These canyons were full of them—rugged individualists as solid as boulders, as clear as the rushing brooks. No better friend had any man than one of these people—and no worse enemy, if it came to that.

Watching Clint, he could imagine the man's great-grandfather as he must have been a hundred years ago. Battling bitter winters and trapping for a grubstake, living on hardtack and what he shot, dreaming of finally finding it— whatever *it* was.

Clint walked through the office door, its bell tinkling. "Morning," he said. His face went to leathery folds, as close to a grin as he would ever get. "What's the story this week?"

"Crime," Gary replied. "In Gatlin Pass."

"My most memorable case," Clint pondered aloud.

Gary sharpened a pencil, distracted by Barbara as she issued orders for the day to their son, Marc.

"Go up to Deerfield Chalet and clean units thirty and thirty-four," Barbara instructed.

Marc kept step beside her, standing close, head and shoulders above his mother. "Mom, I have a chance to work this summer."

"You have a chance to go to work this minute."

"I mean a real job."

"This is a real job. Be sure to make all the beds, including the sofa sleepers."

Marc shifted from one size twelve-D foot to the other. Patience was not his strongest attribute. Charm was. He grinned to lower her defenses, lifted a strand of Barbara's hair with one lean finger, almost flirtingly. "See Mom"— he arched pale blond eyebrows— "you and I have a problem."

"I don't have a problem." Barbara gave him an armload of towels.

"The problem is," Marc persisted, "we disagree over my hours worked, salary earned—"

"I pay for every hour you work, Marcus."

"You say you do, Mom, but then you always cut the number of hours you say I work."

"I don't pay for time spent arguing, Marc. I don't pay for you to stop at the drugstore and flirt with girls."

"Hey, Dad, you hear this?"

Gary raised both hands in surrender. "Not me. Leave me out of it."

"I don't pay for you to run a cute little tourist up the Trail Ridge Drive." Barbara pressed her point.

"You say be nice to the tourists," Marc responded. "You say they're our stock in trade. You say—"

"I say go clean up the Deerfield units, Marc."

"The girl's moped was out of gas. I couldn't leave her to walk two miles with a can of gas, Mom!"

"Deerfield Chalet. Units thirty and thirty-four."

"You know," Marc growled, "someday you're going to be old and need somebody to push your wheelchair or something."

"And someday you'll have a surly son who wants to be paid for making kissy-kissy instead of performing janitorial duties. When you asked to borrow five hundred dollars to buy ski equipment, you agreed to work it off."

"We read about this in school." Marc turned to Gary. "It's called indentured service. That means slavery."

"I know what it means."

"I've sold my birthright, for what?" Marc tramped toward the office door. "For what?"

"For five hundred dollars, no interest, pay as you can, half of what you earn—that's what."

The door slammed, glass rattled, the bell rang furiously.

"I had to arrest old man Murtry a few years back. He was accused of rustling."

"Cattle?"

"Chicken."

"Clint, how do you rustle a chicken?"

"In a burlap bag."

Barbara was talking on the phone again. "We have adjoining rooms which make a suite."

Outside, Marc reached his jeep, shot a glance at the office. A girl ran to jump in beside him. They pulled away, west toward Deerfield Chalet.

"I told the rancher," Clint reminisced, "stealing cattle is rustling; stealing a chicken is petty theft. Truth is, Gary, there is no crime around here. Even when the tourists are in bloom, we're a peaceable town."

"Yes," Gary sighed, "I know. That's the crux of the article. It has to be."

"We had an armed robbery once," Clint offered. "But nobody got shot. There was no high-speed chase."

"What I'm after," Gary explained, "is more of a profile on you and your men."

Clint pinched his cleft chin between thumb and forefinger. "Well, we're part of the Sheriff's Patrol, like you know. The sheriff's office is in Fort Collins and this is the sixth-largest county in Colorado—so we have deputies in various towns, each patrolling a certain area."

"I meant a personal profile, Clint."

"Personal? Like what?"

"How you came here, what your dreams and aspirations are."

"I was born here, you know that."

"What do you hope to accomplish?"

"Keep the peace."

"You've done a good job."

"I think so."

"That's sarcasm, Clint," Barbara advised, dialing the phone. "The last thing Gary wants this morning is peace. Hello? Just so you'll know, Marcus, I saw that girl get into the jeep with you. May I assume she is going to assist in your work?"

The doorbell sounded and they all looked up.

"Clint, I want to speak to you. Morning, Barbara, Gary."

Tom Albright was a small man, almost delicate. He lived

up Thompson's Canyon near Estes Park. He declined an offer of coffee, but sat down to discuss his problem.

"You know Borden Wilson?" Tom asked Clint.

"Lives down at Meeker Park."

"Used to. Built him a cabin back up the canyon about six miles, near Rush Falls. Know the place?"

"I think so, Tom. What's the trouble?"

"He took up with that Chinaman, or Korean, or whatever he is. Man named Wang."

"Yeah, I've seen him."

"Not from around here."

"Don't think he is, Tom."

"I know he ain't. I know everybody who is."

"Okay."

"I think he stole a shotgun from me. I know he has it."

"How do you know?"

"I saw my gun in Borden Wilson's four-wheeler. Laying in the back. He'd covered it with a blanket, but I saw the butt and it's mine, all right. Remington special."

"Could be similar."

"No. It's mine. I know the etching. No other like it. The Wang guy was driving the four-wheeler at the time. In the hardware store buying ten-gauge shells and that's what my gun is, ten gauge."

"Tell you what," Clint suggested. "Next time I see Borden, I'll ask him about it."

"I want you to go get my gun."

"Borden comes to town every week or two, Tom."

"You get it, or I'll get it."

"Suppose they have it and say it's theirs, Tom?" Clint said. "Suppose they claim they bought it from somebody else?"

"I won that gun in a contest," Tom said softly. "Remington made just that one. Silver plates on the butt, marked as a one-issue gun. I want it back."

"What's it worth?"

"Six hundred, maybe more."

"Well." Clint slapped his knees, sitting back. "Would

you like to run up the canyon with me, Gary? This is about as much crime as we're liable to see."

"I'm going with you," Tom said.

Clint hesitated, nodded. "Let's be going, then."

They drove along a timber trail, crossing creeks roiling with water. Conversation was difficult. Clint drove in double-low gear, all four wheels churning.

"I've known Borden Wilson all my life," Clint spoke as they hit high ground. "You remember him, Gary?"

"I think so. Wears fatigues when he comes to town?"

"Rough sonofabitch. His parents raised him down near Meeker Park. I don't know what ever happened to them—you know, Tom?"

"Never had much to do with them."

Clint drove into another, deeper creek and for one breathtaking instant, it felt as if the vehicle would be swept away. Lurching, motor growling, the truck lunged free and gained the other bank.

"Next day or so that will be impassable," Clint noted. "That heavy snow last winter is beginning to come down."

They approached a log cabin built hard against an over-hanging cliff. As Clint turned off the motor, the cabin door opened and the man they sought appeared with a rifle cradled in his arms.

"What say there, Borden?"

"Clint."

"You know my brother-in-law, Gary Colter, and Tom Albright?"

"To see 'em."

"Mind if we talk a bit?"

The man nodded, but he still held the rifle, his stocky legs slightly spread. He made no effort to seem friendly.

"I'd like you to put away the rifle," Clint suggested.

Wilson did so, leaning it inside the door. Something in his stance made Gary stand fast, awaiting an invitation to advance.

"Where's your friend, Borden?" Clint inquired.

"Which friend is that?"
"The foreign fellow—what's his name?"
"Wang."
"First name or last?"
"Never asked."
Clint strolled across the ground, looking up at the cliff, across the far creek, his comportment unthreatening.
"Been catching any trout, Borden?"
"Enough to get by."
Clint kicked at a stone, squinted into the afternoon sky.
"Where's your truck?"
"Wang has it."
"Gone where?"
"You looking for him, me, or my truck?"
"Looking for a shotgun."
"What kind of shotgun?"
"Remington special," Tom Albright said. "Ten gauge."
"Shotgun." Borden seemed almost relieved.
"Tom says he saw the gun in the back of your truck."
"I never saw it," Borden said.
"Wang was driving at the time."
"Sonofabitch."
"What?"
"If that sonofabitch—listen, Clint," Borden said, stepping out of the doorway, smiling, "when Wang comes back, I'll find out about the gun. If he's got it, I'll skin him alive and bring him into town."
"We need to talk to him," Clint said. "If he stole it—it's an expensive gun, Tom says."
"Six hundred. More maybe."
"Ain't that some shit." Borden laughed, shortly. "I can't imagine him doing that—"
"You known him long?"
"Three, four years."
"I've been seeing him around." Clint was between Borden and the door now, leaning through to peer inside. "He calls this home, doesn't he?"
"Been staying here awhile."

"Where's he from?"

"San Francisco, I think."

Clint picked up Borden's rifle, turned it appreciatively. "How'd you meet him, Borden?"

"I went to one of those survival camps. He's a former marine, like me."

"Mind if I look around for my gun?" Tom Albright asked.

"I wouldn't like you to do that, no."

"I just want my gun back, Wilson."

"It isn't here. If it's in my truck, Wang has it. I'm not saying it is—I never saw it."

"I'm sure we can straighten this out," Clint said.

"If he stole it—" Borden's voice faded a moment. "That'd be a dumb thing to do."

"How old is he?"

"Twenty-four."

"Kids do dumb things. We all did."

"Not this dumb." Borden glowered.

Clint looked at his wristwatch. "Why don't you come on back to town with us and we'll get a description of your vehicle—"

"I said I'd bring him in."

"I know you did. And you would, too. But this is grand larceny, Borden. Suppose the kid stole other things?"

"Not likely."

"But just suppose. We'd have to get a search warrant and look the place over, to be sure."

"I'd know if strange stuff showed up here."

"But you say you didn't see the shotgun."

Gary saw the man's hand tremble. He was fingering the lapel of his fatigue jacket, tracing the stitching.

Clint checked Wilson's rifle, saw it was loaded. Methodically, he emptied the chamber. When he looked up, he wasn't smiling.

"I think we'd better drive to town, Borden. The worst you'll have is some good food and hot coffee."

"Mind if I get some fresh clothes?"

Clint stood in the doorway, blocking passage. "We won't be gone long."

Gary and Tom Albright got into the rear seat. Clint and Borden Wilson sat up front.

"Say you've been getting some trout?" Clint inquired.

"Enough." Borden's voice was strained.

Clint started the motor. "I love it while the fish is still quivering, don't you? Catch him, clean him, throw him in the pan!"

Borden stared out the window, silent.

"Quivering in the pan and basted with lemon," Clint said. "That's the best way to eat trout."

CHAPTER FIVE

W ynona's eyes were dilated from too many Percodans.
Richmond helped her dress, hooking her brassiere.
Joyce had screamed herself hoarse, pleading, "Don't leave
me alone!"

She flung her bedding at Richmond.

"After we leave," he said, mildly, "you'll be wishing you
had something to sleep on besides hard ground."

Joyce scratched dirt from the floor and hurled dust at his
face. She had lunged against her chain until her ankle bled.
Now, with bitter resignation, she stroked Wynona's face,
crying.

"Find my pimp and tell him, Wynona."

"I'm not going there."

"Please," Joyce begged. "Call him, tell him."

Richmond held Wynona's good arm, ascending the steep
narrow steps. On the ledge in the light of midafternoon, she
closed her eyes a moment. She carried her arm in a bandana
cradle that Richmond had fashioned.

"Do you want another pill for pain, Wynona?"

"No."

He steadied her, crossing the ledge, past the cabin, down
a rocky incline toward his Jeep Wagoneer parked far below.

"Does your arm hurt?" he asked.

Obviously. But she said, "I'm all right."

He eased her into the front seat. "How long will it take to
get there?" she questioned.

"We have to take timber trails for several miles. It's a rough ride and slow driving."

He tucked a lap blanket around her legs, strapped her in with a seat belt. He adjusted the shoulder harness and tightened it gently. "There we go. Are you comfortable?"

"Yes." She gazed up the embankment down which they'd come. His cabin was hidden from view at this angle.

His destination was thirty miles away, but the route was through isolated canyons along seldom-used passages. He reached Highway 34 and followed it briefly before turning off.

"Why don't we take the paved road?" Wynona asked.

"It goes east to Gatlin Pass," he said, truthfully. "We're going west."

"It goes west!"

"Yes, for a little while. But higher up, it's closed. Every winter they have rock slides and trees fall. Remember the way we came in? That's the way we have to go out."

Tree branches squealed against the sides of his Wagoneer, the wheels churning slowly, lurching over stones.

"Beautiful day down here," he said. "Snow up there."

He had wandered through these mountains for the last few years. He knew every rill and cliff. Wynona moaned as the vehicle jolted.

He patted her leg. "It won't be long now."

A buck in full rack, followed by three does, ambled across their path. Richmond pointed and Wynona attempted a tearful smile.

Forty minutes later, if a straight line were drawn from their starting point to where they were, they had traveled less than five miles, skirting a mountain through wilderness areas. Streams became freshets, fed by melting snow from surrounding peaks.

Wynona grimaced, reached for the clasp of her seat belt.

"Don't take that off, Wynona."

"It's hurting me."

"You'll hurt a lot more if you get thrown forward suddenly. Leave it on. I'll try to be more careful."

To distract her, he asked, "What are you going to do with your money?"

"Buy my mama something nice. Go home to Juarez."

Another two miles. Ascending now, wheels clawing shale loosened by winter freeze and subsequent thaw. So steep was the rise, the front wheels vaulted from the ground and for an instant they seemed poised to topple backward. Wynona was racked with pain, groaning.

"What will you buy your mother?"

"TV."

Then, abruptly, they struck pavement and Richmond stopped to shift into two-wheel drive. This was the western edge of the range and for as far as they could see, the macadam wound down through towering trees and disappeared into the foggy depths of mountains below. Huge flecks of snow fell like wintry leaves.

"Beautiful, isn't it?" he said.

She blinked away tears.

"Hold on a little longer," he soothed.

"Can we hurry now?"

"Wish we could. But a wise driver takes a descent in the same gear he'd use coming up. We wouldn't want to go off down there."

Down there was a plummet of a thousand feet, the road bound by cliffs on one side, a sheer plunge on the other. The passage was a series of steep hairpin curves. Here and there, piles of fallen stones scattered across the right of way. This stretch was closed to the public for another week or so. Other than Richmond and a few mountain families, nobody came this way until summer.

"Glad to be going home?" he asked.

"Yes. Please, hurry."

"A TV set," he said. "That's nice."

Her lips thin, face taut, she nodded.

"One more stop and we're on our way," Richmond said.

"Stop—where?"

"To get your money."

They rounded a curve and Richmond touched the brake. Far below, through a veil of snow—a car.

"It won't be long now," he said, distractedly.

A tourist, maybe. Took a wrong turn at Granby. *Lost.* No—stranded. He saw a woman get out. She had tied a handkerchief to the radio aerial, a signal of disability. The reflection on her windshield hid the interior. *A Volvo.* Warily, Richmond picked up speed. The woman began waving as he neared.

When it became apparent he wouldn't stop, she stepped toward the center of the road. Richmond shifted gears, gaining momentum.

Pretty. Young. And alone.

She wore a long-sleeve sweater and blue jeans. Petite, slender, sexy figure. Her windblown curly hair was reddish blond. Richmond drove past and her expression changed from apprehension to anger.

In his rearview mirror he saw California license plates.

"We can't stop," he commented to Wynona. "You need a doctor. I'm worried about that arm."

He stroked her knee to reassure her, but Wynona pulled away.

"It won't be long now," he said once more.

"Damn you!" Colleen shook a fist at the departing Wagoneer. Her first thought was, *Flatland tourists!* Such people had been conditioned by urban crime to ignore anyone in trouble. But then she saw the Colorado tag and recognized Larimer County.

It was unthinkable that any local person would ignore someone in distress. People here survived in an inhospitable and unforgiving area by being self-sufficient. But they were also generous with consideration for their fellowman. Daddy used to quote Housman, "Luck's a chance, but trouble's sure."

The Wagoneer became a pinpoint of blue, made a final turn, and disappeared in slowly falling snow.

Coming this way had been a mistake. *Tired. Not thinking.*

She rubbed her hands briskly. Gray scudding clouds obliter-
ated the sunshine but they could pass as quickly as they
came.

Thinking of the blue Wagoneer, she swore softly.

She thought of Timothy and that gum-popping wench
he'd found to finance him. Probably eating guavas and
mangoes in the warm Mexican sunshine by now.

Incongruously, she had a memory, doubly painful because
it was happy—the time she and Tim drove to Cuernavaca to
stay for a week. The future of Tim's rock group had seemed
so promising then. The villa was owned by the leader of the
band. There'd been a high wall around the compound,
beautiful gardens, the heady scent of tropical flowers. They'd
gone swimming in a huge pool of warm blue waters, then
joined other musicians for a breakfast of chilled mangoes,
fresh bananas, thick slices of bacon, and eggs-to-order. Tim
had been euphoric, she contented.

Maybe she'd done something wrong.

Eye-bitching.

The recollection turned sour and she put it out of mind.
But it crept back, tiny fragments like specks floating in a
pond, first a jumble, then a recognizable mental picture:

"When we've got a couple of hits," Tim had said, "I'll
start my own band. I've got a feeling the public is ready for
a return to the solid beat of the fifties rock. But with a punk
flair. What do you think, Colleen?"

She tried to remember what she'd thought. She had encouraged him, of course. That was the duty of a spouse. But
what did she think, down deep?

"You're a writer," he'd said. "I'll compose the music,
give you the gist of my thoughts, and you do the lyrics.
What say, Colleen?"

But she had never been a poet. Not even a writer, actually. Oh, yes, being Daddy's daughter, newspaper editors
might grant an interview. But she wasn't creative.

"Solid reporting," Daddy called her style, inadvertently
damning her. *Without flourish,* an absence of adjectives.
Who-what-when-where-why and nothing more.

Nevertheless she'd tried to help Timothy. Searching the dictionary, poring over *Roget's Thesaurus*, trying to bring life to rhyme and help Tim achieve his goals.

Did he ever have a goal? Maybe the whole punk-rock thing was a device to avoid a job and the strictures of marriage.

"A baby?" he once objected. "Jeeze, Colleen. We can't have a baby. Can you imagine a snotty-nosed kid on concert tours?"

By then the band had dissolved. The leader had wisely "upgraded" his retinue and his songs were hitting the charts. He'd moved from acid to heavy metal to mainstream to full orchestra. Synthesizers had replaced the twang of Tim's electronic guitar.

The realization that Timothy was second rate had taken time. Colleen's earliest doubts were dismissed as "unfaithful thoughts." But he *was* second rate. As a musician, a husband, and as a person. *The bastard.* He'd used her money, depleted her emotions, wrung her dry, then left for a chicle-chewing moron with an IQ calculated in Celsius.

Okay. She wrenched herself back to this moment. Here she sat. The Volvo had gasped its last and she'd decided a radiator hose must have burst. Whatever the problem, it wouldn't start. Back to Granby was maybe fifteen miles. East through the Rocky Mountain National Park was out of the question.

Going down would be easier than up. It meant easier breathing, less exertion, and she would walk out of the snow eventually. It also meant calling Mom and Dad to come get her. They might send Marc.

A fine homecoming. The troubled daughter estranged from a worthless husband, costly to raise and now, dear to maintain. The car would have to be hauled in and that would be expensive. If she repaired it—they were about to repossess the thing.

God—thinking about Tim again—*damn!*

She quelled an impulse to cry. This was awful, but somehow it would be for the better. Marriage hadn't done a thing for her. Poorly dressed, ill-fed, she'd suffered a lapse of confidence. Except for the painful confession of failure to her parents, this *was* for the best.

O-damn-kay, then. Sitting here was a prelude to something better. She got out, stretched the muscles of her legs. Forcing exuberance, she yelped and her voice caromed, rippled, died.

"Timothy!" she hollered. His name rode away in audible bounds. "I hope Montezuma gets you!"

You . . . you . . . you . . .

Yes, this was a beginning. For the better. It *had* to be.

She threw back her head, shut her eyes, stuck out her tongue and let snow drift down on her face. She breathed deeply of mountain air so rare and clean it seared her nostrils.

Should never have left here.

This was home.

They would be glad to see her, pleased to have her here.

This was the first day of the rest of her life! The least she could do was enjoy it. Smiling, she began to walk—down toward Granby.

The jostling had increased Wynona's pain. Traveling was arduous, creeping along rocky terrain. Here and there, the braceworks of abandoned mines stood against slag heaps. Richmond drove under one warped sluice and around another.

"Lot of lost hopes here," he said. "People came to dig for silver or gold. Some died trying."

"Is it much farther?" Wynona asked.

"Another mile or two."

"To town?"

"To your money."

A slurry had choked the creek. Gray scars formed mounds—detritus from abandoned claims that pocked the mountainside.

He stopped the Wagoneer, turned off the motor. The snow had ceased, the clouds breaking.

"Come along and we'll get your cash, Wynona."

Eyes glazed, she peered at the colorless scene.

"I keep the money hidden in that mine." He pointed at a shaft two hundred feet up.

"I'll wait for you."

"Can't do that," he said, jovially. "I need your help to get it down."

"I can't help," she protested. "I hurt too much."

He pursed his lips. "Well. Let's see. I can't get the money without assistance. My bad back. I guess I could mail it to you."

"You said you'd pay me."

"And will. Would now, if you help me get it. But I have to climb a ladder to reach the strongbox. I see you're hurting, Wynona. I'll do whatever you wish."

She was rocking to and fro, crying. Richmond waited.

"How long will it take?" she asked.

"Few minutes."

"How far is it?"

"You see the opening—that far plus that far again inside the mine."

"Why don't you put the money in a bank?"

"Now, Wynona," he chuckled. "In my line of work, that's not possible. How would I explain so much money? The tax people would be all over me and—"

She cursed in Spanish, trembling with frustration and anger. "It had better be there—you hear me? It better be."

He circled the van and opened her door. He helped her out and she staggered. "We'll get your money," he promised, "then we'll beat it back to the highway and go to a doctor."

Her feet slipped on loose gravel and Richmond held her. "I tell you what," he said. "Since you've gone above and beyond the call of duty, I'll give you another five hundred dollars."

He kept a flashlight hidden in a recess a few feet from the small entrance. The beam was yellow, but strong enough. They could hear the drip of water somewhere within. Wynona balked.

"I don't want to go in there."

"It isn't far."

"I don't want to go. You can send the money."

"Now, now, Wynona—after all you've been through? We can almost spit on that strongbox from here. Come along." He took her elbow and she moaned. She looked toward the opening, a rectangle of dull light. "A few more feet," he reasoned. "There's nothing here to hurt you." He kept the light toward the floor, off her face.

"I'm scared of bats and rats," she said.

"No bats. No rats. Come on, now, let's get this done and find a doctor."

"Let me hold the light," she said.

"That's what I need you for."

She took it, flashed the beam along earthen walls, the low ceiling, the floor.

"You'll have to lead the way," Richmond said. "You have the light."

Cautiously, her breathing making short, sharp gasps, Wynona inched forward.

"Take a left at the next tunnel," Richmond directed.

"You said it wasn't far."

"And it isn't. Turn left here."

The shaft descended; crude steps had been fashioned and were now rounded and powdery with dust. It was noticeably cooler.

He'd discovered this mine by accident. The unlucky soul who dug here had carved his way through granite only to find himself in a natural cavern.

"It's a cave," Wynona said. Stalactites hung like the flutes of a gigantic organ. Eons of seepage had built corresponding stalagmites on the floor. To Richmond they appeared to be the serpentine teeth of a prehistoric monster with mouth agape.

"Let me have the light," he said. "The money is over here."

She gave it to him and he flashed it in her face. Blinded,

she could not see him draw the pistol. But she heard it click as he cocked the hammer.

"You're going to kill me," she said.

"I'm sorry, Wynona."

She crossed herself, praying in her native tongue. He would do this the humane way. He held the barrel inches from her head.

The sound was deafening. She stumbled backward and fell.

He held the light on her. The remains of others lay nearby. He watched for movement, his ears ringing from the percussion.

Then, with a sigh, he turned and began the climb out. The cold aggravated his limp. The footing was slippery until he cleared the cavern and reached the shaft again.

Fate.

He was thinking of the California girl stranded up the highway.

He replaced the flashlight. Must remember to bring new batteries next time.

If he hurried, he could catch the girl. And, if not, then that too was fate.

CHAPTER SIX

C lint's office was the largest of seven rooms in the municipal building. His cluttered desk was surrounded by three walls covered with the bureaucratic tools of his trade: bookcases, file cabinets, and a large map of Larimer County. The fourth wall was an eight-foot window—chicken-wire mesh pressed between shatterproof glass, overlooking the admissions desk, radio room, and a hallway leading to four cells in the rear.

Borden Wilson sat in a worn mahogany chair, elbows on his knees, hands clasped, glaring at the floor. To Gary, he smelled of sweaty leather, like an old saddle pulled from a lathering steed. The hair on the nape of Borden's neck curled in thick sandy ringlets; his flesh was deeply creased.

He wasn't a large man in terms of height, but his muscular biceps and corded forearms suggested strength beneath the military-style fatigue jacket. He was unshaven, but not bearded, and oddly, his eyebrows were so perfectly shaped they appeared to have been plucked. He wore a heavy ring, the type awarded to graduates, on which an opened parachute was embossed. The backs of his hands were freckled and now his fingers were laced together as if to still the tremble which came when they were free.

"You finished school in Gatlin Pass, did you?" Clint inquired amiably.

"Longmont."

"I thought we were in school together."

"Couple years."

Clint examined the items on his desk, setting them aside or dropping them into a wastebasket.

"Are you arresting me?" Borden asked.

Clint seemed surprised. "No."

Borden glared at the floor.

"Tom wants his shotgun, that's all."

"That's all I want," Tom affirmed.

"Get his shotgun and this will be over."

"I don't have the gun."

"Wang has it," Clint confirmed. "What we need to do is find Wang. He's in your truck you said?"

"He'll be back in a few days."

"You must be close, him taking your truck. But you don't know his full name?"

"I let him use my truck because he's running an errand for me."

"Now we're getting somewhere," Clint said. "Where did he go?"

Borden massaged his hands with such pressure the fingers turned white.

"If he would steal a shotgun," Borden said, "chances are he wouldn't tell me where he was going."

"How can he run your errand and not go where you sent him?"

Clint looked at Gary a long moment, his gaze distant. "You know how, sometimes, you're out in the mountains and something doesn't feel right? Could be a she-bear watching you, or a cougar. Not sure why, but something is wrong. You know that feeling, Borden?"

"I sent him to Denver."

"And he'll be gone several days?"

"I said, No hurry."

In his years of investigative reporting, Gary had learned the subtle indicators of subterfuge—a certain posture, the way the pupils of the eyes changed during a lie. Clint saw it, too.

"Wang has been with you—three or four years you say?"

"About that."

"Long enough to need a Colorado driver's license. Does he have a license?"

"I wouldn't know."

"You let him drive your truck and you wouldn't know," Clint said softly. He looked at Gary, then at Tom, back at Borden. "You have insurance?"

"No."

"Driving your truck with your permission makes you liable, Borden."

"He's careful."

"Suppose he wrecks it. You're liable."

"I don't see the point of this," Borden said huskily. "Wang will be back in a few days. I said I'd bring him in and the shotgun too, if he has it. If Tom wants his shotgun back, I'll get the goddamned gun back."

"He wants it back."

"Making a lot out of nothing," Borden said.

"To Tom Albright, it isn't nothing."

"I don't believe Wang stole a gun," Borden said. "That would be so damned stupid it would be incredible. No disrespect, Tom, but you made a mistake."

"Borden, I want you to stay here tonight," Clint said.

After a pause, Borden lifted his chin. "I wouldn't want to do that."

Clint sighed. "Tom, you willing to sign a complaint?"

"I am."

"It's too late to see this through today," Clint advised. "With a complaint we can ask for a search warrant."

"You accusing *me* of stealing your gun?" Borden confronted Tom.

"It was in your truck."

"I am not a thief."

"All I know is I saw my gun in your truck."

"When we find Wang it'll straighten out," Clint predicted. "Hell, we're having roast beef and potatoes tonight, Borden. How can you turn that down?"

"And I say," Borden said to Tom, "you made a mistake."

"You mean lying."

"I mean you made a goddamned mistake. If that boy stole something—he wouldn't have to steal nothing!—but if he had, it would be the dumbest—he did *not* do it."

"It was in your truck," Tom said flatly.

"Jesus," Borden swore, "I can't believe this. If I'm being arrested, I'll stay. If not, I'm going home."

"That's the hard way, Borden."

"That's the only way I'll stay. Fair warning, Tom—if you're wrong, your ass is mine."

"It was my gun. In your truck."

They sat in silence, Clint watching Borden, waiting.

"Arrest me or let me go," Borden said.

"Tom?" Clint questioned.

"No gun like it," Tom said. "It was mine."

"I can't hold Borden without a complaint."

"If a man steals one thing he'll steal another," Tom said.

"Shit." Borden sneered.

"I know my gun," Tom insisted. "I seen it. I ain't saying Wilson took it. But it was in his truck."

Borden's face was contorted, dark.

"If it's at his cabin," Tom argued with himself, "come tomorrow he'd be rid of it. Maybe other stuff, too."

A few decades ago, this dispute would have been resolved in a flash of temper, a moment of violence. The fathers of these two mountain men would never have turned to a third person to settle a disagreement. But this was today, not half a century ago.

"With a complaint I can act," Clint said.

"If I have to, I'll sign it."

Borden sat back in his chair, taking a deep breath. His expression changed from fury to sadness.

"Ain't this some shit?" Borden said softly.

Alone with Borden, Gary watched the man twist a long thread in his jacket, pulling loose the stitches. In the outer office, Clint and a secretary were taking Tom Albright's statement, typing a formal complaint.

"What's your interest in this, Colter?"

"I happened to be there when Tom came looking for Clint," Gary said. "I was preparing an article."

"Article? About what?"

"Crime in Gatlin Pass. There is none."

Borden lifted his perfect eyebrows and looked at Gary sidewise, bemused. "Crime in Gatlin Pass," he said. "That's funny."

He tugged the loose thread, unraveling the hem of his garment, chin to his chest, watching it. He laughed softly, "Crime in Gatlin Pass—there is none." Without looking up, Borden said, "I heard you won a Pulitzer Prize."

"Yes."

"Big underworld story, somebody said."

"Yes."

Borden laughed again. "I swear before God. I think Fate is a proctologist."

The comment was unexpectedly learned. Gary grinned.

"A big Pulitzer prizewinner and a suspected petty thief sitting in a halfass deputy's office in a town so quiet you can hear a dog cough. Jesus, ain't this some shit. You ever wonder how you came to this exact moment?"

"As a matter of fact—"

"I'm hung," Borden marveled. "Hung for a crime I did not commit. Hung nonetheless."

"This man, Wang—what does he mean to you?"

"Not a damn thing. Dust on my boot. If I knew where to find him and could get my hands on him, I'd—"

He laughed again, grimly, fingering the hem of his jacket.

"When they catch up with Wang," Gary said, "this will all blow over. Give Tom his shotgun and I suspect he'll drop the whole thing."

Borden put something in his mouth, rolled it over his tongue. "I've often thought about Fate," he said. "I was in Vietnam—"

"I assumed so."

"Once I had a sniper in my scope—I could see a little scar right here." He touched his chin. "I sat there, my finger on the trigger, asking myself what brought us to that place at

*

that instant? Me from the mountains of Colorado, him from some village in North Vietnam."

Borden pushed his tongue into one cheek, gazing past Gary at the outer office.

"He was dead and didn't know it," Borden recounted. "One squeeze and he was gone."

"That must be an awesome moment."

"That's the word, awesome. What brought us to that meeting, two strangers in a foreign field? God, or the stars, or whatever? One to die, the other to live another day. Makes you wonder."

Borden sighed wearily. "I didn't shoot him. I don't know why I didn't, but I didn't. He never knew I was there. Like I was God, with the power to—and didn't."

"Did you know Wang in Vietnam?"

"He's twenty-four. He was a child then."

"Damn," Gary said. "Has it been that long?"

"Yesterday. Eternity."

"What drew you to one another?"

Borden picked at the thread, breathing heavily. "Hell, I don't know," he said. "Why does a man keep a worthless dog?"

"Is Wang worthless?"

"I've known men I could trust less, and my life depended on them."

Through the window they could see Tom Albright leaving. "I hate being shut up inside," Borden said.

Clint returned to his office. "I have to search you, Borden. Put your hands on my desk and lean into it."

"Tom signed the warrant?"

"Yes."

"That's it," Borden said. "That's the end of me."

He yelled suddenly, stiffened, then fell to the floor.

"What the hell?" Clint put his hand under Borden's head as the man writhed, snorting, teeth bared.

"Convulsion." Clint looked up at Gary. "Could he be epileptic?"

Gary opened the office door, "Call Doc Johnson—get an ambulance."

A bloody froth rose in Borden's mouth. Gary felt for a pulse—rapid, feeble, irregular.

"Clint, I saw him put something in his mouth. I think he poisoned himself."

Clint shouted toward his outer office, "Get Doc Johnson!"

"He isn't breathing, Clint."

"Jesus!"

Stunned, they watched the man go limp. Doc Johnson ran in, sank to his knees, felt for a pulse.

"Dead," he said.

"Dead," Clint stated. "For what? Over a shotgun?"

Doc Johnson sniffed the man's face. "Almonds," he said. "Looks like cyanide."

"Sweet Jesus!" Clint met Gary's gaze. "He killed himself—for what?"

Doc was calling the coroner.

"Nobody commits suicide over a stolen gun," Clint said gruffly. "Why would he do that?"

"I don't know," Gary said.

"This was nothing. Nothing! I saw you talking to him, Gary. What did he talk about?"

"Fate. He was talking about fate."

Lowland clouds were mountain fog at this altitude, thick and penetrating, a shroud that cloaked Gary as he walked the five blocks home, morose. As he entered the front door, Barbara called from the kitchen.

"That you, Gary? You're early. Wash up for dinner."

He removed his muddy shoes, went to the kitchen in stocking feet.

"Barbara, do you know Borden Wilson?"

She turned. "Wash up, Gary. I can have this ready in a few minutes."

"He killed himself."

"Borden Wilson?"

"Yes. He had an ampule of cyanide sewn into his jacket.

Clint brought him down to the station to question him about a stolen gun and he killed himself."

"Why would he do that?"

"I don't know." Gary lathered his hands at the kitchen sink. "Damned if I know."

"You were there?"

"Right there."

"Don't drip on my pasta," Barbara warned.

"Where's Marc?"

"Where do you think? Chasing girls."

"One minute Borden was talking, calm, next minute he was dying. He said he didn't like confinement, but nobody dies to avoid it."

"Not that towel," Barbara cried, then smiled sweetly. "That one is for dishes. Why don't you men wash in the bathroom?"

"Was he friendly, unfriendly?" Gary asked.

"I didn't know him all that well, Gary. We went to the same school. I knew his sisters slightly. They kept to themselves. Hurry up, the sauce is just right."

"Did he date? Play sports?"

"I don't remember." Barbara delivered spaghetti, meatballs, and sauce, steaming. It was one of her specialties.

Gary blessed the food with a murmur, sat with head hung thinking about Borden Wilson. *God rest his soul.*

After a moment Barbara asked, "Is this going to ruin dinner? I worked hard on this meal."

"It looks great."

Unsmiling, she watched him help himself to salad. "I'm glad we live here," she said.

"What prompts that?"

"That expression. The way you're acting. Like Chicago."

"Sorry, Barbara."

"This morning you had no story, and now you have one."

"A stolen shotgun?"

"And suicide."

"I can't publish that. The family has to be notified."

"Would that stop the *Chicago Tribune*?"

"As you keep reminding me, this is not Chicago."

The telephone rang and she swore shortly. "Rocky Mountain Rentals!"

He pushed the food with his fork, thinking of the dead man, reliving images that, at the time, had seemed unimportant. He felt Barbara's eyes on him as she spoke to the caller. "One double, two people—I've got it."

When she hung up, she sat there gazing at him, her food untouched.

"What is it, Barbara?" *He knew what.*

"Is it good?" she asked pleasantly.

"Very good."

"You haven't tasted it. How would you know?"

He tasted the pasta. "Very good."

"Are you planning to publish the paper tomorrow?"

"I think so."

"Big story, hold the presses," she mocked.

His belly turned, knotting.

"You'd have a hard time readjusting to the real world again, Gary. You've become spoiled."

"What does that mean?"

"Deadlines are now artificial. Appointments will keep. Schedules can be altered."

"This morning you said it didn't matter if we published on a strict schedule."

She stood up. "Do you need anything from the kitchen?"

"No."

Oh yes, he knew this knot in his belly. The digestive juices soured even as he swallowed. And goddamn, he resented it!

The telephone rang, rang again, a third time. He glanced toward the kitchen, then answered. "Hello?"

"Got the time to go with me tomorrow?" Clint's baritone was unmistakable.

"To Borden's cabin?"

"Right."

"Yes."

Clint disconnected.

"Big story, hold the presses," Barbara intoned.

"Clint wants a second opinion," Gary said testily. "I am not inexperienced, after all."

"Not at all inexperienced."

This emotional flagellation was something Barbara did well. Her tone of voice changed and her lips tightened as if he had a history of drunkenness and was about to go out and drink with the boys.

He pushed his plate away, stood up. "I think I'll go to the office and set up tomorrow's story, Barbara."

If she had said, Don't, if she had yielded even slightly, he would have remained. But she didn't. She returned to the table, sat with both hands in her lap, peering at her plate.

They had moved here to Gatlin Pass at his urging, yes. But hundreds of domestic scenes just like this had prompted him to make the decision.

"So," she said, "what's the story tomorrow?"

"Wildlife—as usual."

Walking through the fog toward town, he remembered countless evenings he had left the house in bitterness. She had married him knowing he was a reporter, a writer. She had accepted the long hours and the sordid subjects briefly, then without ever actually saying so, she had begun to try and reshape him and his career. The Pulitzer had been frightening to Barbara. She got no joy from his accolades. To her, public recognition was mortar to cement them in place.

He unlocked his office door. What the hell was he doing here after hours? What was he doing in Gatlin Pass, for God's sake?"

He composed the front page with Marc's photographs of elk and deer and wrote some tourist-oriented captions.

What he had been through a moment ago was one of those marital performances men and women learn to master eventually. The same accusations, the same thorn of discontent festering in their relationship. They had spoken the lines so often it took only a word of disapproval and, in an instant, they catapulted to furious conclusions that had once required hours to reach.

To hell with it.

Something had to change. He couldn't stand this lifestyle. It might be good for Marc and wonderful for Barbara. But here he was, at fifty years of age, printing pictures of an elk!

Colleen was wise to have gotten out of here. As much as he missed her, she had done the smart thing—in L.A. where things happened, where news had meat on its bones.

If there was a story behind Borden Wilson's death, he was going for it. Little-town sensibilities be damned.

Nobody dies for a stolen shotgun.

CHAPTER SEVEN

A n easterly breeze swept the canyon overnight, pushing clouds up the mountains to snowy peaks, turning thick fog to torrential rain. Gary spent the night putting the paper to bed, and nursed the antiquated press through fourteen hundred issues of the *Gatlin Pass Sentinel*.

Marc's photograph of deer and elk covered the top half of page one. He would like that. The photo credits were his.

Waiting for the ink to set, Gary sat at his desk watching sheets of rain pour from the roof, gathering in the street, hurtling toward the valley below. He saw Clint drive up to the Sheriff's Patrol office. Here and there down the slopes, house lights winked on.

The phone rang. Gary knew before answering that it was Clint.

"Still want to go?" Clint asked.

"I sure do."

"We'll have to cross that river on foot."

"That's all right."

Gary hung up. The rain beat a steady drum overhead. Thunder boomed, rumbled away to infinity, rolled anew.

The phone again. "Hello?"

"Gary? I love you."

"I love you, Barbara."

"Only a puppy loves a bitch."

"Arf."

She laughed softly. He could tell by her voice she had only now awakened.

69

"Raining," she yawned.

"Heavily."

"I'll bring coffee and cinnamon rolls, 'kay?"

"That'd be good."

"Love you," she said, and hung up.

They had a policy, he and Barbara. Don't go to bed angry. In this case he had not gone to bed at all. The second policy was the one that had probably saved their marriage: don't get up with a grudge. For nearly twenty-four years, the no-grudge vow had kept them together.

Clint crossed the street in a long sou'wester, his face hidden under the wide brim of his hat. He stamped through the door, shook off his wet coat, and hung his hat on a rack.

"Search warrant is on the way," Clint said.

"Do you have to wait for it?"

"Not really. The judge signed it. We ought to wait for the rain to let up."

"Suits me."

Clint studied a proof copy of the front page. "Isn't that the same story you did twice last season?"

"Same subject. Different story."

"Same elk, though."

"Different elk."

Clint put a finger on the photo. "Looks like the same elk."

"Why would I lie about the elk, Clint? It's a different elk."

Clint bit the tip off a cigar, rolled it between his lips. "What happened to the crime story?"

"Working on it."

Barbara drove up, windshield wipers thrashing, horn honking.

"Pretend you don't hear her," Clint suggested.

The horn blared again.

"I think she's delivering coffee and hot rolls."

"Take my slicker," Clint said. He turned the page, muttering, "An elk's an elk."

Barbara shoved a sack through the car window. It was

instantly soaked, and Gary rushed back inside. From the doorway he waved at her and Barbara backed away from the curb.

"Did you locate Borden's family?" Gary asked.

"Not yet."

"Where's the body?"

"Fort Collins. Autopsy." Clint bit into a steaming hot roll. "Barb knows about cinnamon," he said.

"I didn't mention it in the paper," Gary said. "Out of deference to the family."

"I noticed. Pour the coffee."

The two men sat at Gary's desk, eating their rolls, watching the rain fall.

"Been thinking," Clint said. "A man who carries a capsule to commit suicide must be into something."

"I'd say so."

"I put out a statewide APB on the truck. We got the vehicle information during the night."

"Good."

Clint swallowed coffee, shut his eyes tightly. "Jesus, that's hot."

"Borden said Wang was going to Denver."

"I figured if Borden would die over it, Wang must be someplace else and up to something."

"Maybe Wang had something incriminating with him."

"Are you going to eat that last roll?"

"I'll share it."

Clint unfolded a knife, cut the bun cleanly. He took his half in a single bite. "Remember that rifle he was holding when we got there yesterday? I think that was a Russian gun."

"You do?"

"There wasn't an English word on it. You know how they write in wiggly lines."

"Cyrillic," Gary said.

"It looked Russian. Would you know?"

"No, I wouldn't."

Clint rose to his six-foot-four height and looked out at the rain. "Every important day of my life it rained. Day I got married. Day I die, I guess."

Marc arrived in his jeep, jumped out in the rain and dashed for the door. He slammed it behind himself, grinning. "The bridge down the way is flooded."

"Sign says flash floods," Clint reminded.

Marc peeked into the sack Barbara had brought and came up disappointed. "Mom said she sent a dozen buns."

"Sorry, son."

"Hey!" Marc noticed the newspaper. "That's a good reproduction, Dad."

"That elk," Clint said. "Good shot."

"That's the same one we ran last January."

Clint looked away, feeling his gums with his tongue in search of a final morsel.

"Dad, I want to go with you this morning to Mr. Wilson's cabin."

"I need you to start labeling the papers for mailing, Marc."

"I can do that when we get back. That only takes a couple of hours."

"We don't know how long we'll be up there."

"If I have to work late tonight, I'll get it done. You might find a roomful of hot goods up there. We'll need photos."

"Clint?"

"Strong back, weak mind, always welcome." Clint put on his rain gear. "Be ready in half an hour?"

"We'll be ready."

Their eyes met and the men grinned. "Kind of exciting," Clint admitted.

Yes. It was.

As they worked their way up the canyon toward Borden Wilson's cabin, Gary compared the stark landscape to the swamps and bayous of South Florida where he had spent his childhood. His father had taken him on extended camping trips in the vast Everglades, boating over the sluggish black waters of hyacinth-choked canals. He had gigged frogs, stalked deer, angled not for sport, but for food. He knew the flora and loved it—frangipani, mimosa, banana trees growing wild.

Colorado, by contrast, was barren. Devoid of lush tropical vegetation, the mountains were massive boulders and stiff evergreens. An experienced woodsman could judge the altitude by the growth around him. From the frost line down, firs and spruce gave way to pine, ponderosa, limber, and lodgepole. Along the banks of streams and moist canyon floors, mountain alder mixed with maples and broadleaf hardwoods.

In an academic way, he could appreciate the majesty of the jagged peaks, the grandeur of bottomless chasms, but never would the landscape be a part of him like it was to Clint and Barbara, and now, Marcus.

It was almost as if his son were learning an alien religion not his father's. For no reason that Gary could call logical, he was uneasy about it. But whether better or not, Marc had developed an appreciation for flora that was not tropical, for creatures no swamp would ever see. He had failed to teach Marc those things he had learned to appreciate from his own father. Absurd though it may be, he felt as if he had broken a familial link in the chain of generations.

In the back seat of the jostling car, Marc leaned forward to listen to Clint.

"Navajo made red dye from the bark of the alder," Clint was saying. "It grows from sea level to about nine thousand feet. In lowlands they call it river alder."

Gary remembered his father walking marshy soil, counseling, *Take the gum of staghorn sumac and put it in a cavity to ease toothache.*

Clint was not a talkative man. But with Marc he sometimes poured forth. *No children of his own.*

He spoke of Arapaho, Cheyenne, and Ute, always with respect and a tinge of sadness. With little more than a high school education, Clint was steeped in Colorado history. He liked to say his family had been here when the territory became a state, in 1876, and he planned to be here for its 150th birthday.

"You'll be how old?" Marc asked.

"Old enough to know better."

"But not too old to care," Marc concluded.

They followed the river that had been a mere stream a day ago. Rainbows rode columns of mist as the sun moved higher. The needles of evergreens were jeweled with shimmering beads of moisture, a billion tiny mirrors reflecting a sky now astonishingly blue.

"We'll have to hike from here." Clint halted, set the brake. He called in on his shortwave radio, "Going on foot."

"Have to go well upstream," Clint said to his passengers. "Watch your camera, Marc!"

He didn't need to be told.

They surprised a doe and her fawn. Men and deer froze for a moment before the doe led her baby into a thicket. Marc turned to Gary, grinning. "Wow," his lips said.

Leaping from ledge to boulder, crossing over water so vicious it seemed to snatch at them, they reached the other bank and scaled a steep incline toward drier ground. Over the precipice, two hundred yards inland, the roar of the river was muffled; their ears rang in newfound silence.

Unerringly, Clint broke out on the flat shale canyon floor a quarter mile from Borden's place and they walked toward the cabin.

"Anybody home?" Clint yelled. His voice caromed, mocked, died.

The lawman was casual, long legs taking him toward the secluded cabin, but under the broad brim of his hat his gray eyes moved here, there, alert. "Ho, there," he called. "Anybody here?"

The overhang against which it was built made the cabin a citadel with a single approach, from the front. Behind them, the meandering headwaters of the stream were a murmur again, the call of a bird crisp and sharp.

Clint reached the door, rapped, calling once more, "Anybody home?"

He shoved the door open. Leaning against the inside wall was the rifle Borden had carried—was it only yesterday? Clint handed it to Gary. "See the writing?"

It was Russian.

In so rustic a setting, electric lights seemed out of place, but they were there, along with kerosene lamps for times when the lines were down. A rough-hewn table sat centerpoint in the room. Two benches, two chairs, two beds, a woodbox beside a heavy iron stove used for heat and baking. There was a hot plate for skillet cooking, utensils hanging on a wall. Clint pushed open a door into a second, smaller room. The walls were hung with rifles, shotguns, pistols, a commercial crossbow with telescopic sight.

"Damned arsenal," Clint grunted.

Gary lifted a weapon from a wall hook. "Looks like a submachine gun."

"The bore is too big." Clint took it, breached the weapon, and looked at a dozen twelve-gauge shotgun shells loaded in a cylinder. He read the manufacturer's logo. "South Africa," he said. "There's no way this is legal here."

"Looks like more than one stolen gun is involved," Gary said.

"Maybe. There are ways to buy this stuff, but not legally. Still, nothing to die for."

In drawers they found boxes of ammunition, shotgun shells loaded for bird, others for big game. Clint discovered a tubular contraption wrapped in oilcloth—a grenade launcher, or bazooka, the ominous missiles neatly boxed in a corner.

Stacks of magazines reflected the mentality of the residents—*Soldier of Fortune*, periodicals dwelling on weaponry, advertisements for "men of action with combat experience."

Marc photographed one wall after another, the flash vivid for a split second, capturing the armaments on film.

In cabinets, on shelves were survival kits, military rations, dehydrated foods, stocked as if for a siege.

Amid it all was a console with a large color TV set and video player, a box of tapes. Marc inserted one in the tape deck, turned it on.

"Better leave things alone until we know what we're dealing with," Clint advised.

"Looks like homemade movies," Marc said.

Clint picked up razor-sharp projectiles, some shiny silver, some coal black. "Throwing stars," he said. "They use them in the Orient—hand-to-hand combat."

Gary glanced at Marc, the TV—a naked girl.

"Marc, turn the damned thing off."

"Dad—"

They were all looking at it now—a young girl, eyes wild, weeping, apparently pleading.

"I said, turn it off, Marc."

"Dad—wait—"

Gary reached for the button and Marc seized his wrist, hand trembling.

"Wait, Dad—I know that girl."

The men stared at the images, the girl looking here, there, crawling backward to a wall.

"I met her last winter," Marc said. "I'm sure I did. She was here on vacation."

A lithe young man moved toward her.

"That looks like Wang," Clint said.

The girl's terror was mesmerizing, the menace of the assailant unmistakable. He shifted slightly, showing the camera the blade of a knife, light refracting on the serrated edge.

"You remember, Dad?" Marc said. "She came by the office a couple of times. I took her skiing."

Wang had her by the hair, drawing her head back, the blade crossing the trachea as if to cut.

"I know it's her," Marc insisted. "I'm positive of it!"

Suddenly, the blade slashed, blood flew and Marc gasped, recoiled.

"Jesus Christ!" Clint said.

The camera held as the girl's hands clawed the air, grappling to staunch the lifeflow, her head held back by Wang.

"Was that real?" Marc gasped. "Did he do that?"

"It had to be trick photography," Gary reasoned.

But her face—*sheer terror*. She wasn't acting, couldn't be.

"Jesus," Clint whispered.

Marc staggered for the door, gagging. He didn't make it, vomiting, turning away from Gary. "I'm sorry, Dad—I'm sorry—"

Gary grabbed him, held him tightly.

"I'm sorry, Dad—I'll clean it up—"

He pushed Marc out into blinding sunshine, the boy heaving, weeping.

"He did it, didn't he, Dad?"

Clint emerged, flesh the color of algae, gulping air, mouth agape.

"He killed her, didn't he, Uncle Clint?"

Clint blinked, hard.

"I knew her," Marc said. "I took her skiing."

Clint walked to one of two outbuildings, kicked in the door, hand on his pistol. *Woodshed*. He reached the second building, hurled the door inward.

"Sonofabitch!" Clint yelled. He rounded the building, tore aside a slanting door to the root cellar.

Gary left Marc on his knees crying.

The descent was narrow, to a heavy door at the bottom, at least ten feet underground. The chamber reeked of a stench like that of beef left thawed and wrapped too long.

There were manacles embedded in the walls, chains with cuffs, a table display of garrotes, knives, razors, video cameras on tripods, lighting equipment to serve the grisly studio, a recording device, an editing machine.

"Sweet Jesus," Clint murmured. "Sweet Jesus."

They stumbled and fell, senses numbed, crawling over rocks and through the river back to Clint's truck. Gary, who had never suffered from altitude sickness, was breathless and ill. Marc had wept himself to dry heaves, shock making him gaze fixedly, slow to respond, face pallid.

"I need backup," Clint radioed, hoarsely. "Forensics. Call Fort Collins—we need copters. Do it now."

The shortwave radio crackled, the dispatcher's voice responding, "You need medics, Clint?"

"No."

"What did you find?" the voice inquired.

"Awful," Clint said, but not into his microphone. "Something awful."

They sat on the hard ground, the indelible horror of the video images crisscrossing their minds. Clint lit a cigar, sat with forearms on his knees, his back to a tree, the smoke going to waste.

"I didn't take pictures," Marc said dully.

"There'll be time for that."

"Dad?" Marc came beside him. "I'm glad I came—okay? I know you wish I hadn't, but I'm glad I came."

Gary pulled the boy to him, a child now larger than his sire, and held Marc closely.

"I knew that girl," Marc said. "I knew her."

CHAPTER EIGHT

C lint's office had always been a haven for Marc, and Gary knew it. When the pressures of peers or the stress of adolescence became too great, Marc turned to his uncle. As Clint once said, "He could do worse." From Clint there was no parental displeasure for juvenile transgressions and no recriminations. He was philosophical about "the things boys do." When it isn't your son it's easy.

Sitting here now, Gary wondered if Marc would ever find this office a sanctum again. When he was distressed, or ill, his childish bravado dissipated, Marc most resembled his mother. At the moment, his green eyes had gone gray, his lips were drawn; he was emotionally exhausted by the events of the day. Nevertheless, Marc insisted he would meet a special agent of the FBI, Roger Beecham. Clint and Gary observed.

"The girl you recognized," Beecham asked, "what was her name?"

"Charlotte. I'm not sure she told me her last name."

"Where was she from?"

"Illinois, I think. Or, Indiana. Some state starting with *I*."

"Iowa? Idaho?"

"I think it was Indiana or Illinois."

A portable tape recorder captured their voices, the reels slowly turning. The agent spoke to Marc in a low, almost conversational tone. "How did you meet her?"

"I was driving around. I saw her walking with skis."

"She came to ski?"

"I told her I knew the best slopes. Places where tourists didn't go." Marc looked at Gary, sickly. "I snowed her a little."

"She was about your age, then?" Beecham inquired.

"She said twenty-two."

"Was she with her parents?"

"She was in college, she said. She came with other students who pooled their money for the ride."

Beecham straightened the cuffs of his already-smooth shirt-sleeves. He was all neatness with his buttoned-down collar and his tie the hue of his eyes, dark blue. "Did you take her skiing?"

"Yes. Up trail into the park. Near Hidden Valley."

"Did her friends go with you?"

"They weren't her friends. They barely knew one another, she said. Somebody had put a notice on a bulletin board at her college asking for anyone with fifty dollars to join the motor pool. She didn't really know how to ski. The skis she had were too long and narrow. She rented them."

"The two of you went alone?"

"Yes."

"Often?"

"Every day—just about."

"When was this?"

Marc squirmed, eyes averted. "End of December, right after Christmas. She was here a week."

"Where was she staying?"

"See, she—" Marc chewed his lower lip, tears in his eyes. "Dad, I let her use Mom's cabins."

"Don't worry about it, Marc."

"They were in a motel room, five of them, two guys and three girls. She was odd one out, she said. I kept moving her around when a cabin was vacant."

"It isn't important," Gary reassured him.

"Tell me as much about her as you can, Marc," Roger Beecham urged. "Describe her as completely as possible."

"She had brown hair with some red in it."

"Auburn."

"Brown eyes."

"How tall?"

Marc stood up. "Her head came to my chin."

The agent made verbal note. "Five-four."

Sitting, Marc said softly, "She had a scar from where she had run into a barbed-wire fence when she was a little girl."

"Where was the scar?"

"She said it had once been on her hip, but it climbed as she grew."

Clint coughed, peered out the office window at the dispatcher's desk.

"She'd had her appendix out," Marc said weakly.

"That's a good description," Beecham said approvingly. "About how much did she weigh?"

"Hundred ten, maybe."

"Anything else?"

"She liked pistachio ice cream and Madonna."

The agent's expression made Marc explain, " 'Like a Virgin.' "

"Religious symbol?"

"No, the song, 'Like a Virgin.' Madonna is a singer."

Beecham patted Marc's shoulder. "You're doing fine. Did she say anything about her family? Where she grew up? What her father does for a living?"

Marc pondered, bouncing one long leg, his weight on the ball of his foot. "We didn't talk much."

Clint coughed again, excused himself. He sat behind his desk, winked at Gary, but received no response.

"I remember now," Marc said. "They didn't see much of her. They sent money for school, but didn't check up on her."

The agent furrowed his brow, pushing back short curly hair. "Not so good for us, is it?"

"She didn't drink, but—"

Beecham supplied the ending. "A little pot now and then?"

"Yes."

"Did she say what she was studying in college?"

"Oh, yeah! Film. She was taking courses in that. We took pictures of deer and elk at Hidden Valley—we did more of that than skiing. She knew about depth of field and different film qualities. She liked Ilford HP-5, 400 ASA, because it has such a broad range of tones. We would have to special-order it here and I'd never used it before. She gave me two rolls."

Marc addressed his uncle. "We used that film to shoot the elk."

"Good shot," Clint said.

"When you first met her," Beecham persisted, "where was she staying—with her companions?"

"Rush Falls Lodge."

"Did you meet the others?"

"Not by name."

Clint interrupted. "Where did she rent the skis?"

"Rush Falls Lodge."

"Now a tough one, Marc." The FBI agent lowered his voice. "Did she leave on schedule? Or did she disappear?"

Marc sobbed. "I thought she left because—I didn't know—"

"She didn't say good-bye," the agent surmised.

"I went to the cabin and she was gone."

"What about her clothes, her baggage?"

"She wore a backpack."

Beecham turned off the tape recorder. "You've been helpful, son. You're very perceptive."

"Dad, when Mom finds out about the cabins—"

"Circumstances don't justify mentioning it, Marc."

After the agent departed, they sat in silence, letting Marc regain his composure. "If they want to know what she looks like," Marc said, "they can look at the video."

After a moment, Marc stood. "I'm going home, Dad. I don't feel good."

In the office alone with Clint, Gary sighed, "This could take days or weeks. They have to match faces to names, verify they're missing."

"We had a missing family not long ago," Clint said.

"Man, woman, a boy about four years old. They found the car down around Denver and we dropped it."

A detective leaned through Clint's door. "We made duplicates of the tapes. We're taking the originals for evidence, one copy for analysis."

"Sign a receipt." Clint lit a cigar, watched thick smoke trickle upward. "Wang or Borden could've moved the car to Denver. Could've done that—who knows how many times?"

He turned in his chair and stood up, reaching for his hat. "Want to run over to Rush Falls Lodge?"

"What for?"

"The girl rented skis. If she did that, she had to leave a hundred-dollar deposit, a credit card, or—"

Gary snapped his fingers. "Driver's license!"

"If we're lucky," Clint said.

On his back, under the labeling machine, Gary spoke to Clint, who leaned down from above. "See that cog? Not that one, the smaller one next to it. The cotter pin has slipped."

Clint tried to adjust it—a surgeon in boxing gloves. He swore under his breath.

The office doorbell tinkled and Clint spoke. "Hi, Barb."

"Gary, it's ten o'clock and you've had no rest. Can't this wait?"

"No. Clint, use the needle-nose pliers."

"The last time you tried to repair that," Barbara said, "it took hours. Let's label the papers by hand and be done with it."

Clint's grasp slipped and the pliers fell into the gears.

Gary inched out. He was unshaven, greasy, and so tired his vision was blurred. Barbara had a stack of newspapers that she was labeling by hand.

"Did you see Marcus?" Gary asked.

"Yes. Came home, fell on the bed, and died. I tried to get him up to shower. Next time I went in, he was sleeping on the floor."

She pointed at a chair. "Sit there, Clint. Grab a handful of labels and don't mix the zip codes."

"There's not but one."

"We have out-of-town subscribers, too."

"Marc told you what happened?" Gary questioned.

"Everybody in town knows. Gary, wash up and let's get this done, honey. You must be exhausted."

The telephone rang and Barbara answered. "The Trail Ridge Drive opens in June," she said.

Returning from the toilet, sleeves rolled, Gary took a stack of papers and joined them.

"Her name was Charlotte Minoretti," Clint was saying. "Student, Carbondale, Illinois. Mother in Europe. Father in New York City."

"Clint thought of the ski deposit," Gary said. "She posted her driver's license and didn't return to get it."

"Terrible." Barbara's hands flew, expertly.

Clint lifted each label from waxy paper as if removing a Band-Aid from flesh. He took care to place it squarely on the newspaper.

"Mr. Minoretti thought she was in school," Clint reported. "Everything fine. I told him what we knew. He called the college. Called her friends."

"He's flying out here," Gary said.

A long pause, working by reflex, each immersed in thought.

"Marc told me he put her in the cabins," Barbara said.

Clint chuckled. "What'd you say, Barbara?"

"I told him not to do it again." She set finished papers aside.

"Remember the time you and I made love in the front porch swing at your father's house?" Gary grinned.

Barbara shushed him with a quick flap of a hand.

"Didn't get away with it," Clint mused.

Barbara paused.

"I watched." Clint bit his lip, shoulders pulsing with contained laughter.

Barbara said to Gary, "Remember the night down at the

rock pit? Clint's little bare butt and that squealing Annie what's-her-name?"

Clint's shoulders jiggled again. "Good old Annie," he said.

They worked several minutes in silence.

"Seeing that horrible videotape was bad enough," Barbara commented. "But how unfortunate that Marc had known her."

Hands flicking, long moments passed, each working the stacks lower.

"Every boy's dream," Clint said soberly. "Sixteen with a willing older woman. Too bad he got caught."

Gary sorted papers for bundling. His head ached and his eyes were burning as if dry.

Barbara laughed unexpectedly. "I can imagine Marc shuttling that girl from cabin to cabin. I remember thinking how diligent he was back in December. I had assumed it was gratitude for a good Christmas."

Clint passed his stack of papers to Gary. "Any more?"

"That's it. Thanks."

"Better head home." Clint stood, stretched, putting the flats of his palms against the ceiling.

"What about Wang?" Gary asked.

"Oh, we'll get him. He's out there somewhere."

"Out there—*where*?" Barbara cried.

"If he's got any sense, not around here," Clint replied.

"If he had any sense," Barbara said, "he wouldn't have done such things!"

Letting Clint out, Barbara locked the door. She turned to Gary, distressed. "I can't remember locking a door because I felt insecure in Gatlin Pass. In Chicago and New York, yes, but not here."

"I know."

"I resent it," Barbara said. "It's as if Borden has assaulted us all."

She came up behind Gary, her arms around his waist as he worked. "I guess he did," she said, softly. "Assaulted all of us. And there's the other man—out there."

* * *

When a dream went sour, Marc had learned to rewrite it, slipping back into slumber, returning to create a different ending. In that twilight of semiconsciousness, he had undone automobile accidents, returned stolen goods, beat the hell out of a bully, regained his balance on a lofty precipice. It was a matter of editing, mentally revising the unpleasantry until it suited him. Then, and only then, would he allow himself to awaken, satisfied.

Charlotte was on top, facing his feet, the curve of her back flowing into muscled buttocks. She pushed against his ankles for leverage, the movement all hers, meeting his climax with a quiver and a moan, as if it had been her own. Then, she would massage his feet—

He sat up abruptly—damn! He had soiled the bedding, himself—but wait, he was clothed. His trousers rumpled, still wearing socks.

No dream.

He drew his lips taut across clenched teeth. He sucked his lungs full of air, fighting images intruding on his mind. *Her eyes. The terror!*

Through the sheer curtains on his bedroom window he could see the first pale of dawn. Somewhere in the valley a single dog barked, his cry returning in echoes. The dog barked again to reply.

Marc wanted a shower but feared he would wake the folks. He changed clothes, tiptoed down the hallway, pausing at their bedroom door, listening. *Nothing.*

When he reached the kitchen he took time to write a note, considering the tone and content before each word.

"Good morning!" he fashioned block letters. "Gone to label papers. Then for breakfast. Love, Marc."

No date, no time. If they awoke in a minute or slept another three hours, they wouldn't be certain when he had left the house. The wall clock said six.

He put the jeep in neutral, rolled from the driveway. Downhill half a block, he started the motor. The town was still, the air cool, clear.

When he reached the *Sentinel* he discovered the papers already labeled, neatly bundled, reach for dispatch.

Once more he had failed to keep a promise. Dad had picked up the slack, as he always did.

Across the street and down the block, one car was parked at the Sheriff's Patrol office. It was not Uncle Clint's.

Marc took the Trail Ridge road, driving slowly, without conscious thought as to where he was going. But he knew where—drawn as if by gravity, afraid, ill with the prospect of it, and unable to turn aside.

He had never known a girl—a woman—like Charlotte. If she had not encouraged him he would never have made a move. But everything was so relaxed with her. Want to do it? *Why not?*

Some guys had pimples on their faces. Some had them on their chest. He had them on his bottom.

"You need some baby powder, that's all," she had said. She smoothed it on, bending to kiss his butt, and it seemed so natural.

She had shown him that tiny piece of flesh that would give her pleasure, then taught him how. Afterward, she held him to her breasts, breathing heavily, thanking him. *Thanking him!*

They made love in the cabins, in the shower, in the jeep, on a blanket in the snow.

They smoked pot. Sitting nude, legs folded Indian style, passing the joint back and forth through bleary-eyed giggles.

She stared at his toes, tickling with her tongue, moving up his leg.

Marc stopped the jeep, cut the motor, sat gripping the steering wheel with tight fists, sick—sick at heart, sick with guilt and shame.

"Little-boy stuff," Charlotte had once teased. "When you grow up you find out everybody's done it, everybody has felt the same, thought the same—people are all alike. Just enjoy it, and as long as you aren't hurting someone, it's all right."

Not hurting someone.

When he went to the cabin New Year's Day, she was gone. No call, no note—gone.

At first he was sure she would be back. He'd sat there half a day, waiting. Finally, it became obvious she was truly gone.

He was angry. Disappointed. But mostly, he was furious! He had imagined her doing with other males what she had done with him. Why *not*?

She'd taken her camera, her skis. Maybe she'd walked up toward Hidden Valley where they had shot photos of elk a few days before. He had tramped through the snow, looking for footsteps—she must have taken the trail. But he didn't find her up there, either.

Her companions had probably called and on the spur of the moment she had left, that was all. Not a thought of him, not a moment left to telephone—he'd been nothing!

And yet . . .

And yet . . .

He started his jeep, turned up a steep incline going toward the cabins Mom rented. Each was placed on a different facet of the slopes so each had a view. One cabin could not see another. The dwellings were very popular, and it was here he had moved Charlotte from one vacant lodging to another the whole week.

His mouth was gall, tongue so dry it stuck to the palate. There were no visitors here now. The crest of the small mountain allowed him to see all three cabins at once. Here, centrally located, was a combination storage room, workshop, and laundry. There was a washing machine, clothes dryer, both coin operated but not yet connected for this season's use.

With quivering hands, he unlocked the storage door, stepped in onto a concrete floor. On one wall, there were shelves filled with towels and linens, two folded portable beds in a corner—accoutrements of the rental trade.

He walked through, opened a second inner door, and felt for a light switch.

There.

Marc closed the door behind himself, bolted it from the inside. His ribs hurt as if he had been running too long, too far.

For security, a padlocked cabinet had been built to the wall and lined with metal to seal against insects and rodents. In here were spare dishes, Mason jars with sugar, salt, the staples so often forgotten by transient clients.

There, on the bottom and deepest shelf—Charlotte's backpack.

Should have known something was wrong. Leave that? Stupid.

But he had been so hurt, disappointed.

He pulled it out into the light. He had been through it a day or two after she disappeared. Toilet articles, cough drops, a medicine for "premenstrual pains," and a small jar with marijuana; another small box held cigarette papers used to fashion the smokes.

How could he have been so dumb? Would she leave her razor, her postage stamps, her marijuana?

He had found two rolls of Ilford film that New Year's Day, taken it to the *Sentinel* darkroom, and developed the exposures.

From a contact sheet he had selected several shots, blown them up.

The shot of the elk that everyone liked—it was one of those. Marc had been so upset with her he'd presented the magnificent photographs as his own. Every hair was crisp, distinct. The animal was stately, the very essence of the Rocky Mountains.

It was her picture, not his.

He had said it was his to—to punish her.

He spread everything on the floor, no two items touching. What was her last name, her college, her address?

The sweater was wool, thick and worn. She must have been wearing the only other sweater she had. He held it to his nose, smelled. The perfume was gone.

The panties were bikini style, very sexy. He pressed one

to his mouth, choking, tears rolling from his cheeks to the fabric.

If he had told anyone, would they have searched?

What could he have said? What could he have done? He drew the garments around himself, piling them on his lap, caressing them, weeping without a sound.

While he had fumed selfishly, fretted egotistically, she was being tortured and slain.

Her eyes.

He wished he had told Dad the elk was her shot.

He wished he had told somebody about the pack—but then they would all know he let her die without reporting her absence.

Her eyes—God, God—he would never forget the way she had looked—pleading, the knife at her throat—begging— and then the gaping of flesh, the horror, the terror—

Her eyes.

CHAPTER NINE

The Staghorn Café was a focal point in Gatlin Pass. Businessmen gathered there for coffee that curled the tongue like a dead leaf. The waitresses called everybody by first name, serving the house specialty, flapjacks. "Three parts sand, one part batter," Clint had once described them. Maple syrup poured over the porous flapjacks simply disappeared, adding to the specific gravity but seldom spilling onto the heavy porcelain plates.

The Mexican-American cook was a burly cigar smoker, a former wrestler from Tijuana. He emerged from the kitchen periodically, apron rolled around his waist, to go into the toilet. "Kidney trouble," Doc Johnson confided.

Joining the locals for morning coffee was not Gary's favorite activity. They seemed to accept him with a certain uneasiness, making a place for him to sit at the large round table. But clearly, Gary felt, he had never become one of them.

He had delivered bundles of newspapers to the post office for mailing, serviced the three vending machines owned by the *Sentinel*. His last stop was the Staghorn where he left twelve copies for sale across the counter.

"Cyanide," somebody mouthed the word. "That a painless way, Doc?"

Gary took an empty seat. "Kinda like rotgut," Doc said. "After a minute or two it doesn't matter."

"Cyanide," the first speaker said. "Ain't nothing like it used to be. Used to, a man shot himself. Used to, a man

91

who took a pill left folks thinking he was kinda sissy like.
No self-respecting man would take a pill."

"Ain't nothing like it *used to*," George Nolan, proprietor
of the hardware store, said. "Used to, Memorial Day was
the thirtieth, and today's the thirtieth and the government
says it was last Monday."

"Cyanide." The word went around the table. "We killed
rats in the grainery with that once. Not the best way, though.
They died in the burrow."

Pete McHenry, the druggist, paid a quarter for the *Sentinel*
and shook it like a stiff cloth, holding it at arm's length.
"Colter, how many times you going to tell us about the
birds and the bees?"

"We're playing to the tourists," Gary said. His smile felt
as if it trembled.

"That's the same elk as last time," somebody said. "Is
that the same elk?"

"How come there's no story on Borden Wilson?" McHenry
questioned.

"Waiting on notification of next of kin," Gary said.

"What about that Wang guy?"

"What about him?"

"*Denver Post* said he's a former marine, born in Hong
Kong, lived here with Wilson."

"The *Post*?"

Doc took a newspaper from a chair, gave it to Gary.

Front page. God *damn* it.

"What did you win that Pulitzer for?" McHenry looked
over the tops of spectacles. "Wildlife?"

The men sipped coffee, enjoying it.

Dishonorably discharged. For stealing! A photo of Wang
covered three columns upper right.

"Word is," George Nolan said, "Borden and Wang were
torturing and killing people. That true, Colter?"

"Nothing has been positively—"

"On videotape, they say."

"It seems that way."

"You saw it. You and Clint and your boy. That right?"

"Yes."

"Wang was in the film?" somebody marveled.

"Yes."

"How come that's not in your paper?" Doc asked.

"We can't print what isn't positive, Doc."

"Did you see it or didn't you?"

"I saw a tape, a girl and Wang—"

"Cut her throat, I heard."

Pete McHenry refolded the *Sentinel*, put it back on the pile for sale. "Borden was always nice to me and the wife. Never out of line."

"Odd, though."

"Who ain't?"

"Odder than most."

"Thought I saw him stealing some stainless-steel bolts once," Nolan said. "Can't stop a man for suspicion. Most times he was a good customer."

"Seemed to leave folks alone so long as he was let be."

The waitress poured refills. The men sat for a few moments without speaking. "Known Borden all his life," Doc said.

"His family still down at Meeker Park?" somebody queried.

"Borden's pappy, Ned Wilson, pulled stakes and moved deeper in the mountains, I heard. He didn't like a crowd."

"Borden never got in trouble that I knew about": another opinion.

"Park marshals got him once for hunting out of season."

"Man has to eat," somebody said.

Several men nodded. They didn't hold to regulations aimed at tourists.

"He went to school here, didn't he?"

"Borden? Here and Longmont. He was a few years behind me."

"What was his sister's name?"

Nobody could remember.

"Friendly enough."

"Borden? Hell, yes. Nothing wrong with Borden."

The hardware store owner stood up, chair rasping the

floor. "You being on top of it," he said to Gary, "looks like you would know the story better than people in Denver."

"Yeah."

"Not a bad picture of the elk, though."

"That is the same elk, ain't it?"

Gary put change on the table, nickels from the vending machines. He left a dollar at the cash register, face burning, walking as casually as he could when he felt like running.

He crossed the muddy street, entered the Sheriff's Patrol building and Clint's office, unannounced. "The *Denver Post* had a story, a photo of Wang."

"Saw that."

"Where did they get it?"

Clint was sorting papers—original, two copies, three piles.

"Who the hell is handling information on this?" Gary demanded.

"FBI."

Gary stabbed Clint's desk with a forefinger. "I'm sitting here with a goddamned newspaper doing Disney stories, Clint. First man on the scene and Denver scooped me! Who's heading up the investigation?"

Clint licked a thumb, peeled one paper from another. "Minoretti will be here today."

"Interviewing a victim's father wasn't what I had in mind. I can't believe I let hard news get by me like this. I've been in this burg so long I've lost my touch. I could've called the wire services, called the networks."

"How's Marc?"

"Out and about."

"Seem okay?"

"He was gone when I got up," Gary said.

Clint stuck an unlighted cigar in his mouth, speaking around it. "Cora took it hard."

Cora was Clint's wife. Half his height, nearly the same weight, she was a butterball who adored Clint. "Mutt and Jeff," they referred to themselves.

"Cora put a gun in every room. Locked the doors. Borden is dead, I told her. Wang isn't going to come to *my* house. Most likely shoot me."

"Can she handle a gun?"

"Enough to shoot me."

Gary massaged his forehead. "I've got to get a grip on this thing. Scooped by Denver—I'll be laughed out of business. You're sitting on the inside, the least you could do is keep me advised, Clint. What about Wang?"

"I'm a deputy," Clint said. "FBI. State Police. Sheriff. Not likely to tell me much."

And, of course, he was right. Information wasn't here. It was in Fort Collins, in Denver, and in half a dozen other places. Laboratories to process suspected blood spots, computer centers to trace legal records, fingerprints to be checked, missing-person reports to verify. The crime was here, but the investigaton had a ripple effect.

"Do what you can, Clint," Gary insisted. "Give me any news you get."

"Minoretti is coming. I said that."

Gary left, feeling absurd, as if the entire town were laughing as he passed. In a vending machine outside McHenry's Pharmacy, that lousy elk was front and center.

When people spoke to him, it was not to be sociable. It was an interrogation: Was it true? Murder? Torture? Borden Wilson?

Inside the *Sentinel* office, the telephone was ringing. Gary grabbed it. Barbara's voice was up, in her saleswoman tone.

"I'm taking a prospective buyer to Rush Falls to see a chalet," she said. "I wanted you to know."

She never had before.

"Male?"

"Yes."

"Who is he?"

"I couldn't say." *With her. Listening.*

"Want me to go with you?"

"No, no." She laughed as if he had made a joke. "We'll be back around four. I have to bring him to his car. You see it in front of the office—Plymouth, powder blue."

"Got it."

After he hung up, Gary read the salient points: male, Rush Falls, Plymouth, powder blue.

What good was this? If Barbara were missing, what would the authorities have in these bits of information?

Cora Ferguson worked outside her home only during the summer, and only from noon to five. Her job, she said, was looking after Clint. "Marriage goes sour if a woman isn't there when her husband needs her. The Muslims say, 'A wife should answer the call for sex, even if upon her camel.' "

"One hump or two?" Clint had inquired.

But she was dependable when she worked, and she knew Barbara's business. She had a pleasant voice, the patience to endure petty complaints, and she cared for Barbara and Gary.

Her working months began tomorrow.

"Cora," Gary had pleaded, "Barbara is at Rush Falls with a prospective buyer. Clint says the father of one of Borden Wilson's victims is on his way here from Denver airport. I need to be there for the interview. The phones— you hear them. They're driving me crazy."

There had been a long pause.

The streets that had been devoid of traffic yesterday were now bumper to bumper. The motels were booking steadily— already there were "no vacancy" signs. By nightfall, lodging would be scarce. It was the opening of the scenic Trail Ridge Drive next month that brought them.

"Until five?" Cora had asked.

"If you can."

The fifty-mile drive at rarefied heights lured visitors from around the world. Seen from the air after June eighth, the mountain lanes would be like a jointed snake, vehicles wending from Visitors' Center to Scenic Overlook.

"It's two o'clock now," Cora had debated.

The other phones were a cacophony. Gary let them ring for her benefit.

"I suppose I could," Cora yielded.

It was after three when she entered the *Sentinel* office carrying a huge woven straw bag and a shotgun.

"What's that for?" Gary protested.

"Need you ask?" She grabbed a phone even as she placed her bag beside a desk. "Rocky Mountain Rentals!" As she spoke, she leaned the double-barrel shotgun against a filing cabinet. "A busload of how many?"

A few minutes later, as her presence bestowed order, the calls lulled and Cora spread the contents of her bag on the desk—one pistol with a long barrel, a container of tuna salad, a jar of mayonnaise, plastic utensils, home-baked bread neatly sliced.

"Clint said to stay as long as I'm needed." Cora's eyes fluttered rapidly, two black buttons in a pale round face. "He said not to believe you would be back by five."

"Thank you, Cora."

"Lock that door," she said. "If I don't know them, they can't come in. If I don't know them and they *try*—" She patted the pistol, then covered it with a paper napkin.

"Aren't you overreacting, Cora?"

She lifted a dimpled chin, tiny mouth a shocked *Oh*. "Clint watched every one of those horrible picture shows," she said. "Borden and that Chinese boy raping and torturing."

"He did that at home? When?"

"Last night. They brought them to our house and sat there looking at them. Clint, two deputies, state trooper, that FBI man. Horrible, filthy, decadent. Not just women. Did you see the one with a man, woman, and child?"

"No."

She halted long enough to catch a call, then another. Business concluded, she picked up her thoughts, "Sod-oh-me, hurting for the fun of hurting. Well, I never saw such things. I've known Borden Wilson, knew his *mother* and sisters. The war must have done something terrible to him. Made him insane."

"Was Borden on film, too?"

"Yes, God-in-heaven-rest-their-souls. Yes! That FBI man called them 'snuff' films. 'Splatter films,' he said. What kind of men do such things? What kind of men watch them? I've been sick and shivering ever since."

"You watched?"

"God forgive me."

She dabbed her eyes with a paper napkin. "Then they wanted sandwiches and beer. Clint said it was their job. Men get used to violence, he said. A damnable thing to say. He got used to it quickly. I was furious. Scared. How could they think of food? They watched them over and over."

"For a purpose, Cora, surely."

"Counting the victims, they said."

"That had to be done. Why did you stay?"

"Because I . . . when they told me what they were . . . when they told me to leave the room . . . I didn't want Clint to know such things without me. Like going to war. I wanted to share the terrible part so he wouldn't suffer alone."

She twisted bodily. "He didn't suffer, though, Gary. None of them did. I could see in their eyes. They watched and it was horrible and they *watched*."

"Cora, they had to watch."

"You can watch without seeing something. You can do your job even in disgust," she sobbed.

He put an arm around her shoulder, standing beside her chair. A tear hit waxed paper with a brittle spatter.

"I know Clint looks at other women," she said.

"Cora—now, Cora, that's ridiculous."

"I'm not blind," she said. "I look in the mirror and see myself and I don't blame him. He's handsome—"

Gary shook her gently. "Cora—"

She held up a pudgy hand. "I can forgive Clint for that. I do the best I can with what I do best and I can forgive him for seeing slim women."

"Cora, really, now—"

"But I hated him for looking at those pictures like he did. It was frightening. The *way* he looked."

The telephone rang and Gary took it.

"Minoretti is here, Gary," Clint advised.

"Be there in a minute."

He hung up, looking at Cora. "Will you be all right?"

She wiped her nose, reaching for a ringing telephone. "I'll be all right. Hello? Rocky Mountain Rentals."

Through the office window, Gary saw a car pull up at the Sheriff's Patrol office. A gentle breeze pushed vapor toward the valley below. Clint and Minoretti were waiting, but he felt compelled to stay.

Cora covered the telephone with a hand. "Go on," she urged. "I'll be all right."

Vincent Minoretti wore a tailored suit, imported Italian shoes, a ruby ring where a wedding band would be. He listened to Clint with an expression that seemed almost hostile, his deep brown eyes steady.

"This is the driver's license." Clint pushed Charlotte Minoretti's identification across his desk. The girl's photo was on the license. Minoretti looked without touching it.

"Is that your daughter?" Clint asked.

"Yes."

Clint nodded, grimly. "I'm sorry, Mr. Minoretti."

"May I see the body?"

"We haven't found a body."

"Then how can you be certain?"

Clint gazed at Gary, then away. "They made videotapes, Mr. Minoretti. There is no doubt."

"Who did this?"

"One is dead. Suicide. The other is being sought."

Minoretti took a deep breath, nostrils flaring, staring at the girl's driver's license. "What the hell was she doing here in the first place?"

"She came to ski. She left the license as assurance she'd return the skis."

"Going off without telling anyone," Minoretti said, caustically. "This is the sort of thing her mother would have done. I assumed Charlotte was in college where she belonged."

His countenance portrayed anger, his voice anguish. "Free spirits, they call themselves."

"I'm sorry," Clint said.

"I telephoned the college. They said she dropped out last semester. I called her friends. Friends! They didn't know where she was. Was she missing? They didn't know!"

"Would you like a cup of coffee, sir?"

"You give the most you can, you try to do what is right. Education, support without intruding. Young people today pride themselves on being 'free spirits.' "

"Yes, sir."

"Don't ask where they've been or with whom. Don't demand information or the names of their companions."

"Yes, sir."

"How did she die?"

"Mr. Minoretti—"

"Gunshot? Stabbing?"

"Knife, yes, sir."

"Did she suffer?"

Clint turned to Gary, as if helpless.

"Mr. Minoretti," Gary said, "do you want us to notify your daughter's mother?"

"I'll do that."

"Is there anything we can do? Anything at all?"

"Did she suffer?" he insisted.

There was no way to lie. There would be a trial. The tapes were evidence.

"It wasn't easy, sir."

Tears swam in the man's eyes. "Is that all you need from me?" he asked.

"We could have wired the picture of the license, as I told you."

"I wanted to come."

Gary took his arm. "Let's go have a drink, Mr. Minoretti. My name is Gary Colter. My son knew Charlotte."

"Your son and the legions of Rome."

"Come on," Gary said.

They went to the Rocky Mountain Lodge bar, half a

block away, with secluded booths and picture windows looking out at ski slopes, now idle.

"Wouldn't go to NYU," Minoretti related. "It had to be Carbondale, Illinois. What would a girl see in Carbondale, Illinois?"

"Youngsters feel a need to pull away," Gary said.

"To be a filmmaker." Minoretti downed his third martini, waved a hand for another. "I tried everything when she was growing up—spankings, taking privileges away, reason—"

"Mr. Minoretti, your daughter didn't do anything wrong. The men who attacked her were wrong, but not your daughter."

"Her mother will say I caused it," he continued. "She will remember this incident and that, this fight or that, this time or that when we might have changed the course of our lives by doing something we did or didn't."

He took the next martini in a gulp, then ordered again brusquely. "Make it a double and put gin in it."

A boisterous party came in and, before they were seated, Gary asked the bartender to put them in the solarium. Still alone with the grieving father, Gary offered to arrange for a room and Minoretti nodded, despondently.

"This will kill Charlotte's grandmother," he said. "She lost her husband last year. Eighty-four. She won't live when she hears this."

Minoretti lit a cigarette and extended the pack, which Gary declined.

"I'm in textiles," Minoretti said. "Three hundred thousand jobs lost in our industry these past four years. Cheap imports. Dollar high. Federal deficit. The unions keep screaming for protection. They destroyed the American textile industry—steel industry, too. Labor has actually come to believe they're worth those outrageous salaries."

He inhaled deeply, trauma making furrows in his olive face. "Unions, crime—the world is going to hell."

"People have a way of coping," Gary said.

"When I was a child," Minoretti murmured, "we would

walk through the Village, to Washington Square. Thought nothing of it. Wouldn't do it now."

"No."

"Movies glorify violence. TV pours it out nightly. Sometimes they make the bad guy the hero. Nothing to admire, but admirable, know what I mean?"

"Yes."

"Vulgar language on the radio. Free expression, they call it."

Another round of martinis. Two strangers linked by tragedy in suffering no words could alleviate. Gary sat through long minutes of silence, Minoretti's breathing labored as his stupor deepened.

"She was a nice girl," he said.

"I'm sure of it."

"Free spirit or not—nice girl."

The bartender came to the table, voice low as if he sensed the moment. "The gentleman's room is ready, Mr. Colter."

"Thank you."

"She loved pistachio ice cream," Minoretti said weakly. "For her eleventh birthday we had a cake with pistachio icing, pistachio ice cream, bowls of pistachio nuts."

He made a peculiar sound, like a tiny green frog, the kind with sticky feet that can climb walls and cling to glass. *Breep-breep*.

"I think her mother is in Milan," he said. "Hotel Cavour, I think. She *was*, last week. Knowing her—who knows?"

"We could try to call from your room," Gary suggested.

"Not yet. Charlotte isn't dead so long as she doesn't know. I'll call from New York. No body. No funeral."

He looked at Gary directly, the first time he had done so. "As long as she doesn't know, then Charlotte is still alive. You see?"

"I think I do."

"It's true," Minoretti said. "Charlotte is alive in Milan until I say otherwise. Then she's dead there, too. When I tell her mother, it'll be like I killed her. That's what her mother will say. If I never called, for months, Charlotte would be okay."

A few minutes later, bitterness curdled the man's face. "Pornography stores, sleazy X-rated theaters. Good is losing out to evil."

"No, it isn't," Gary said gently. "Society is a centrifuge that rejects evil, otherwise mankind would be destroyed. Evil men, isolated and left to themselves, must become good if they are to exist."

Minoretti fought a quivering lip. "The men who killed Charlotte should be shot like rabid dogs."

He finished his drink, regaining control over himself. "Shot," he said. "Like rabid dogs."

CHAPTER TEN

C olleen had been walking about an hour. Dusk filled the valleys with shadows, the sun settling behind the westernmost mountains.

He came up behind her, his blue Jeep Wagoneer coasting at walking speed to keep pace. "Sorry I passed you by earlier," he said. "I had an injured girl. Going to a doctor."

She was exhausted from nineteen hours of driving, two days with no sleep except for a few minutes at the last service station. The rumble of the Wagoneer sounded comforting. Yet she was properly wary, still walking.

"Were you lost?" he inquired.

"Car trouble."

"I saw that. Were you lost?"

"I was going to Gatlin Pass by the Trail Ridge Drive."

"Isn't open."

"I know that, now."

"The name's Bell," he said. "My mother christened me Richmond Cathedral Bell. She did it, she said, because our name was Bell and I was born in Richmond, Virginia, on a Sunday morning with the cathedral chimes in full voice."

"I'm Colleen Lichtenfelter."

"Colleen. Well, Colleen, of course you can walk to Granby but nothing will be open when you get there. Or, you can forgive me for snubbing you earlier and let's start over. I'll take you to Gatlin Pass."

"This is the wrong way."

"That's true." He watched her with sky-blue eyes behind

round metal-rimmed spectacles. Beneath a handlebar mustache, his teeth were white, even. "I could've gone on home, you know. I came looking for you."

Looking for her. *Yes.*

"How do you get to Gatlin Pass with the Trail Ridge Drive closed," she questioned.

"Timber trails, rough and winding—but I can."

After a moment he said, "Okay. My advice is this: go back to your car and wait. I'll call somebody when I get to Gatlin Pass. Will you be warm enough until morning?"

She halted, assessing him.

"I guess I'm still angry because you drove by and left me earlier."

"Couldn't be helped. The girl was in pain."

"If it's no bother, I'd appreciate a lift."

They returned to her car, got her suitcase. Farther up the mountain, in the last glimmer of twilight, he turned off down a slope so steep Colleen gasped. Through trees, around boulders, wheels skidding, brakes locked—only the seat belt held her in place.

Between them lay a wide-brim leather hat. He wore western-style clothing, scuffed boots, a bandana around his neck, the raiment of a working mountain man. He spoke with the inflections of someone native to the region, except for the slightest hint of a southern drawl. But his speech was educated, diction precise. He mentioned a buck and three does he'd seen earlier, commented on fishing as they crossed a stream that flashed in the headlights.

Not once did he make a gesture that was intimidating; nothing untoward.

"What takes you to Gatlin Pass?" he asked.

She didn't want to say why; she didn't want to mention Daddy for fear he knew him. When people knew Daddy, all talk turned to writing and the inevitable question, What are you going to do for a living?

"Visiting friends," she said.

"What time did they expect you?"

"They don't know I'm coming."

"Coming—from California?"

"Los Angeles."

"Is that your home?"

"Yes." *For two and a half years.*

"I get over there now and then," he said. "I like it here better."

The vehicle jolted and jarred, making her muscles sore from tension. Her headache had ascended to full force now and he seemed to sense it, falling silent. Typical mountain man. In the light from the instrument panel she saw him whistling, but the motor drowned the sound.

"Mind if I detour by my cabin for a minute?"

What could she say?

"I might as well take a couple of jerry cans and fill up with gas while I'm in Gatlin Pass."

"How much farther?"

"Ten miles, give or take."

They hit pavement and a moment later he took another rutted lane.

"Man with a bad back has to be calculating," he said. "Anytime there's help, take it."

He needed the gas for his generator, he said. Would she help him?

He was doing her a favor, wasn't he? What else could she do?

They climbed a slope under a sprinkling of early stars. The cabin was nestled in the lee of a promontory, built on a ledge with an incredible vista of valley and distant peaks.

"Why would you build up here?" she asked.

"Privacy."

He lit a kerosene lantern. Colleen saw a television set and two video players. Following her eyes, he said, "That and reading is all there is up here. May I give you a tour?"

In a cul-de-sac behind his cabin, he'd constructed a cold-storage room in the side of the mountain. A trough collected seeping water. Across the ledge, under a huge boulder, he had a cellar—would she like to see it?

Before she could decline, he yanked the starter rope on

his generator and the engine buzzed. "Come on." He grinned. "You're in for a surprise."

When he lifted the slanted doors, down below Colleen could see a second door with a sliver of light from within. "Go on in," he urged. His tone was a promise of the unexpected; like Daddy at Christmas presenting a box within a box within a box.

Just as she entered, a naked woman came into view. "Who-ee!" the woman cried. "There's a sucker born every minute. You ain't never earned a dollar harder than the one you going to earn now!"

Colleen wheeled and froze. He pointed a gun at her, the lights reflecting off his glasses. "Easy," he said. "Easy now."

"What day is it?" the black woman demanded of Colleen.

"Wednesday."

"What month?"

"May. May twenty-eighth."

The woman scrutinized Richmond. "Least you ain't lied about that."

"I wouldn't lie to you, Joyce."

"Hell you wouldn't. Wynona gone?"

"Yes. Gone."

"Some lucky bitch, you ask me. Break my arm one time and let me go. You take her out to dinner like you said?"

"Yes, indeed." He held the gun at arm's length, pointing at Colleen's face. "Joyce, this is Colleen. She'll be working with us." Then, to Colleen, "Take off your clothes, please."

"Like hell."

He cocked the hammer of the gun. "Do as I say. Do it or suffer."

"What are you going to do?"

"Kissy-licky," Joyce said. "This gimpy sonofabitch thinks he's Metro-Goldwyn-Mayer. Hire him a whore and makes kissy-licky movies. See how he treats his stars, don't you? Sitting up here in the Rocky Mountain Hilton."

"Take off everything," Richmond commanded. "Put that clasp around your ankle. Then lock it."

"I'm not going to do that, damn you!"

"You do it or I do," he growled. "Easier if you do."

"How much he promise to pay you?" Joyce challenged.

"Pay?"

"How much you promise her?" Joyce taunted Richmond. "I ain't working for a penny less, I can tell you."

"Lie down," Richmond said. "Extend your leg so I can check the clasp."

Her first fear was rape. There was no rape. He gathered her clothing, enduring Joyce's insults stoically, then shut the heavy door and bolted it. A few minutes later the lights went out and Colleen panicked, snatching at her chain.

"Hey, hey, hey," Joyce soothed. "Take it easy. Was it day or night when you come in?"

"Night."

"Probably be messing with supper. Jeeze I hope it ain't stew again. I am O-double-Deed on stew."

"What is he going to do with us?"

"Making smut films, honey."

"Pornography? But why me?"

"Because he broke Wynona's arm, that's why. We jumped his ass. Scared him, too. Wynona had that chain around his neck, dragging his gimpy butt over here—he got a bad leg, you saw that. We nearly had the sonofabitch, too." She cackled gleefully.

"You came here willingly?"

"Aw, hell, it ain't as bad as I make him think. Wynona said she's had tricks treat her worse for a whole lot less and that's the truth. We get done, we get our money and be gone home."

Frightened, quaking, Colleen asked questions to keep Joyce talking. "Where did you meet him?"

"Las Vegas. Me and Wynona both."

"Does he hurt you?"

"Naw, hell, naw. I mean, yeah, he hurt Wynona, but that was because we jumped on him." She laughed again.

"Where'd he get you?" Joyce asked.

"I was walking. I had car trouble."

"Car trouble!"

Colleen felt the floor, the pallet, the wall, following her chain to a bolt that held it.

"You ain't a whore?" Joyce asked.

"No."

"He just snatched you off the road?"

"Yes."

An instant later, Joyce turned on a battery-powered lamp and shined it on Colleen. "No shit now," she said huskily, "you ain't a hooker?"

"No, I'm not!"

The light went out and Colleen heard a ripple of chain as her companion moved in the dark. The absence of light was absolute, as if the air were ink and yet, somehow, they could breathe.

"Can't keep up with time down here," Joyce murmured. "Feeds us two meals and takes out the chamber pot and I figure that's about a day. Got no way to know day from dark except by what he does. I figured he'd been gone a long time. Where was you when he came along?"

Colleen told her.

"You see a girl with him? Chicano girl? Broken arm?"

Colleen explained, voice tremulous, how Richmond passed her by, came back about an hour later.

"Without Wynona," Joyce confirmed.

"He couldn't have gone far," Colleen said. "Town was ahead of me and he came up behind me down off the mountain."

"Sonofabitch," Joyce whispered.

"What is it?"

"You ain't a whore and Wynona is gone," Joyce said. "That ain't nothing but bad news, honey. Real bad news."

Nobody expecting her. Nobody to report her missing. Timothy in Mexico.

"Real bad news," Joyce muttered.

A nightmare.

And nobody would miss her.

Colleen wrapped herself in a blanket that smelled of

perspiration. Wool in the fabric gave welcome warmth but made her itch.

Richmond lit a cigarette, held it between his lips, examining items from her pocketbook.

"Tell me about yourself," he said.

She tried to remember what was in her purse. Driver's license, stubs from unemployment checks before the benefits expired.

"What's there to tell?" she asked.

Smoke curled around his nose, rising past his glasses.

"I'm married," she said.

"This your husband?" He displayed a photograph from her wallet.

"Yes."

"Timothy Lichtenfelter," he said. "What does he do for a living?"

"Musician."

He breathed around the cigarette, an intensity to his manner that overrode softly spoken words. "Where is Timothy?"

"Mexico."

He sucked smoke, inhaled, shuffling pictures.

"He left me," Colleen said.

"Pretty girl like you?" He examined her checkbook. "Little on the light side," he remarked. "How long have you been out of work?"

"Several months."

He knew that. He dropped unemployment vouchers back into her purse.

"Don't lie to me, Colleen."

"Why would I lie?"

"I don't know why—but don't."

Joyce sat against a wall, immodestly exposed, listening.

"Why would Timothy leave a pretty girl like you?"

"You'd have to ask him that."

"I'm asking you."

"Because I could no longer support the bastard. He found another woman who would."

Joyce snickered.

"What kind of work do you do?"

"I was a reporter."

"Reporter," he said. He held up an ID card from the *Free Press*, then dropped it in the pocketbook.

"Were you a good reporter?"

"Obviously not. They fired me."

He lifted a tampon, tossed it in the bag. "When was your last menstruation?"

"None of your damned business, you sonofabitch."

He glanced at her, eyes hidden behind reflected light on the round spectacles. "Who do you know in Gatlin Pass?"

"What are you going to do with me?" Colleen demanded.

"Answer the questions. Who do you know?"

The edge in his voice made her chest constrict. "I have no friends there."

He raised a small address book and shook it gently. "Have I explained the consequences of lying? They can be severe."

"What difference does it make?" Colleen shouted.

He took a final puff on his cigarette, mashed it under a booted foot. "Perhaps we need an understanding," he said. "I am asking questions for a purpose. This is not idle curiosity. I expect truth and nothing but. Is that clear? When I first found you, you said you were going to Gatlin Pass to see friends. Who are they?"

"It . . . it was a loose use of the term 'friend.' "

"Names?"

It was in the address book. Colleen answered carefully, "Barbara and Gary Colter."

"Colter. He owns a newspaper."

"I met him once in Chicago. I was hoping he'd give me a job."

"Reporting," Richmond said.

"Yes."

"It's a small paper. How much would you hope he'd pay?"

"When you're stone broke, three meals looks good."

"Yes, I suppose." He thumbed through the address book.
"Do you mind telling me what you're going to do?"
Colleen asked.

"Didn't Joyce tell you? We're making a movie."

"Pornography," Colleen said.

"To some, the *Kamasutra* is art, to others it is not. Who
else do you know in Gatlin Pass?"

"Nobody."

"You were very sure of employment, going there with no
money, your checking account overdrawn, your automobile
failing."

"If I didn't get a job at the paper—it's a tourist town—I
hoped to find work as a waitress, maybe."

He reached for her blanket and Colleen shrank back,
holding it. He yanked it away, standing over her.

"Not as photogenic as Wynona," he mused. "What do
you think, Joyce?"

"I think you a suck-egg-yellow-mane dog."

"You deserve an explanation," he said to Colleen. He
reached for her hair and she knocked the hand away.

"If you cooperate, in a few weeks you will be out of here.
The degree of discomfort is up to you. This can be a reward-
ing, even pleasant adventure."

"Bullshit," Joyce said.

"Suppose I'd told you I wanted you for a porno film?"
Richmond suggested to Colleen. "You would have refused.
You don't know me. You have inhibitions. No amount of
money could have induced you into this. Am I right?"

"Yes."

"Ah, yes, you see! But now, you have no choice whatso-
ever. You are here, a captive, and you are going to make
the film. For the rest of your life you can declare that you
would never have done this willingly."

He reached for her hair again and when Colleen tried to
push him away, he slapped her head, gently, then stroked it.

"You have no money, Colleen. Now you are about to
make some. I pay a thousand a week for three weeks. If you
do a good job, if you put your heart into this production,

there's a bonus when the film is completed. Most directors can finish films of this genre in a few days. They ignore story lines, go for sex alone, and the end result is generally terrible. I take pride in what I do. I worry about lighting, about nuances of body movement. Emotion is the name of the game. Would you like to know the story line?"

His hand was cold, fingers slipping through her hair. Colleen was rigid, trembling, eyes shut tightly.

"Two women prisoners share a common dungeon," he said. "As you see, one is black, the other white. At first, there is animosity and distrust. But gradually, they come to admire one another. Ultimately, love . . ."

He lifted her chin, wiped a tear from her cheek. "One never knows who will see these things. A producer, a director—who can predict what this will open for you? A new career, maybe."

He held her chin, shook it. She opened her eyes. She could smell his leather jacket.

"Where do your parents live, Colleen?"

"They're dead."

He stared down at her, holding her head back. "Where were you born?"

"Chicago."

"School?"

"Chicago. Then UCLA."

"Brothers, sisters?"

"No."

"I'll find out if you lie. It is best to begin without lies."

"I'm not lying."

"For the moment I'll take you at your word. Is there anything you'd like to alter or add?"

"No."

"Very well, then." He pushed back a strand of hair, smoothed it. "I think you'll do fine."

When he reached the door, Colleen asked, "What if I refuse?"

"It would merely take longer. You would do it eventually. As I said, the degree of discomfort is up to you."

"What does that mean?"

"Food is a motivational factor. Nutritionally adequate, but unpalatable. It can be the difference between dog biscuits and prime steak, for example. Also, I provide lamps and reading materials. Those can be withheld. The potty needs to be emptied daily. Imagine it overflowing and left here for a week. As I say, the degree of discomfort is your decision."

"You sonofabitch," Colleen said.

"I can be," he agreed. "Don't want to be but I can be. On the other hand, if you get into the mood of this, you come out a winner and we all make some money."

He shut the door and Colleen heard a bolt slide into place. She shook violently.

The lights went out and she fought sudden claustrophobia. The air felt thicker.

She remembered Daddy's comments about the making of a good investigative reporter: collecting tiny facts until they meshed. Intuition and data.

Richmond Bell hadn't taken that girl to a doctor. He'd gone into the Arapaho National Forest. Thousands of acres of wilderness; nobody lived there. No towns. Certainly no doctors.

He'd told Joyce they'd gone out to eat—another lie. Time and place did not allow.

Colleen had sensed danger in his quiet inquiry. *Intuition and data.*

"Joyce, I think he killed Wynona."

Such a lapse passed that Colleen said, "Joyce, do you hear me?"

"I heard you."

"We've got to get out of here."

"Get the key and we're gone."

Colleen grappled with the chain, following it to the bolt that anchored her. She fingered the stanchion, the texture of the beam in which it was embedded. *A sharp tool would—*

The lights came on again. Richmond descended one careful step at a time. He brought a picnic basket and placed it on the worktable.

"If it's stew I puke," Joyce said evenly.

"Biscuits," Richmond replied, pleasantly. "Scrambled eggs and thick-sliced bacon. Oh, and rich creamery butter. Coffee—"

He served their plates and passed the food. It was hot, steaming. Colleen ate because her body demanded fuel. She wanted to hate it, but it was good.

All the while, he sat on a high stool, smoking, watching them.

"You're serious about producing a quality film?" Colleen asked.

"Do a thing, do it right," Richmond said.

She swallowed the last of her coffee, tossed the cup to him. With her other hand, she pushed her spoon under the blanket.

"Okay. I'll cooperate."

"Wise decision."

"If it's truly quality," Colleen insisted.

He smiled enigmatically and said, "Fair enough."

He took their plates, putting them in the basket. He stood with his back to them a long moment.

"Who kept the spoon?" he asked.

He turned, stared first at one, then the other. "Who has the spoon?"

Joyce looked at her and Colleen said, "I have it, Richmond."

He snatched it from her hand and then slapped her so forcefully she fell on her side, ears ringing.

"Must we do this the hard way? Have you ever heard of Pavlov? I can train you to sit up and beg if need be. Must we do that?"

"No, Richmond."

"Don't test me again. There's a limit to my patience."

"All right, Richmond."

He shoved her away and turned on Joyce. "No more nonsense, Joyce."

"I ain't done a damn thing!"

"There's a limit to my patience," he said.

CHAPTER ELEVEN

B y Saturday afternoon, Gatlin Pass approached its satura-
tion point. Pedestrians clogged sidewalks under brilliant blue skies. The shops were bustling. Motels were booked
to capacity. The restaurants had waiting lines. Traffic crept
through town.

To clean the streets and maintain public facilities, students from the University of Colorado were trained in school
and hired for the summer. Fourteen of these came as peace
officers, tripling Clint's staff.

To welcome them, Clint and Cora held an annual barbe-
cue, invited their neighbors, and enlisted the help of the
family. Sides of beef simmered over pits of glowing embers,
the spatter of grease sizzling, the aroma maddening. Beer
flowed from kegs on a table near a patio wall. Tubs of soft
drinks gathered beads of condensation. In deference to the
youthful newcomers, music was loud and contemporary.
The party was a celebration of the beginning of summer, an
inauguration for the novice officers, and it lasted from noon
until midnight to accommodate the changing of shifts at the
Sheriff's Patrol office.

"They're burying Borden tomorrow," Clint advised Gary.
"Glade Memorial Gardens."

"Who arranged it?"

"A sister."

"I've been trying to find his family. I think I'll go down
there. What time?"

"Two o'clock. Turn those ribs, will you, Marc?"

"Mind if I go, Dad?"

Barbara responded, "Absolutely not."

Gary used a paintbrush to swab sauce over ribs.

"Dad? May I?" Marc asked, softly.

"Did you hear me?" Barbara snapped. "No!"

A female rookie spoke to Marc. "Is it true what they're saying? Thirteen people murdered?"

"Yes."

"You saw it?"

"One film."

The young woman wore new, freshly pressed trousers, a shining badge. She took a space beside Marc, helping turn ribs with tongs. "I went to a bullfight once," she said. "It was awful. But it was fascinating. I guess that's how it was, seeing the murder."

"Young lady, get me a Coors," Clint said.

She called to a fellow student, "Mr. Ferguson wants a brew, Netta."

Gary watched Marc unobtrusively. The boy's forehead was gleaming with perspiration, his face red from the heat of the pit.

"That's the way it was," Marc said. "Like a bullfight."

"Will we get to see the videos, Sheriff?" she asked Clint.

"No."

"My interest is purely academic," she said. "I did a thesis on the pervasiveness of porn in the home market. The porn theaters are closing down, you know."

"They are?" Marc questioned.

"Oh, sure. Losing money. People can order porn in the mail and watch it at home without going to a sleazy theater. Cheaper, too."

The conversation was drawing others.

"My name is Rachel Winthrop." The girl grinned at Marc. "You're Marc, right?"

"Right."

"Rachel," Clint said, pointedly, "we need more sauce."

She spoke to her friend. "Netta, more sauce."

Back to Marc. "There were 800 porn theaters in America

at the pinnacle of their popularity. Vincent Miranda owned fourteen of them—he was the first exhibitor of *Deep Throat*. You saw that—"

Marc darted a look at his mother, basted the ribs.

"That was probably the best porn ever made," Rachel stated. "Most of them have bad acting, inferior processing. *Deep Throat* had some quality."

Cora, too, was listening. Her chubby hands flitted here and there over a table of covered dishes, but she wasn't changing anything.

"The big item these days is child porn," Rachel reported.

"My dear," Barbara said, "may we talk of other things?"

"Oh, sure. Sorry. I spent nine months on the subject, so I tend to view it dispassionately. Academically."

"How did you get your material?" Somebody laughed.

"Rented it. Bought some. It's for sale—are you interested?"

"I'd have to see it."

"Anytime," Rachel said. "I finished my thesis last quarter. Like I say, most of it is prurient with little attention to aesthetic value."

Barbara was at the far end of the patio now, animated in conversation, as if to cover this one with her own words.

"If I had to bet," Rachel said, "your two murderers were making snuffs, Sheriff."

"Let's find another topic for dining," Clint said.

"Oh. Sure. Sorry."

The listeners broke into smaller groups, but their comments were hushed and the topic the same.

"You saw such things?" Cora questioned Rachel.

"Researched it."

"Why?" Cora asked.

"To judge something, one must know it, Mrs. Ferguson. You see, the word 'pornographic' once included the works of Michelangelo and books by Mark Twain. Our definition has altered considerably, wouldn't you agree?"

"Cora," Clint commanded, "more sauce."

Cora walked toward the kitchen with Rachel, unhurried, the two women murmuring to one another.

"Screwing up my goddamn party," Clint growled.

Several couples had been dancing. No longer. They had joined one clique or another, voices low. Only Barbara could be clearly heard, her listeners politely attentive.

"Sonofabitch," Clint snarled. He sucked his thumb. "Burned myself."

Marc stood so near Gary they were touching. "Dad, I want to go to the funeral."

"Marc, I'm going as part of my job."

"You said you wanted me to learn reporting."

"There are better circumstances for learning."

"Dad, please. Mom says no, automatically. Please."

"Marc, I won't defy your mother. Whether she's right or wrong, I won't do that."

Marc stared across the patio, tormented. "Mom can't protect me from what I already know," he said. "There's no way she can take back what I've seen."

Clint reached over and drew Marc into a hug, gruffly. "Are you going to turn ribs, or not?"

They worked in silence, heads down, the guests withdrawn.

"I'll talk to Barbara," Gary offered.

"She'll say no."

"If she does," Gary said, "that settles that. But I'll talk to her."

Barbara dropped her blouse on the bed, kicked off her shoes. "The ribs weren't as good this year," she said. "But they ate like pigs. Blood and gore the subject of the evening and they suffered no loss of appetite."

"Young people are resilient," Gary said.

"Not to mention callous. I don't think Marc should associate with them anymore."

"Telling Marc who he can and can't see is a mistake, Barbara. He's not far from legal age, you know. He's already asserting himself, developing quite normally, actually. That's how he met Charlotte Minoretti. It's natural."

"You see what it got him, too."

"When some doors open," Gary reasoned, "they can

never be shut again. You wanted to come to Gatlin Pass to buffer the children from the world and that works for a while. But eventually the world intrudes. Colleen went to Los Angeles. Marc is too old to shield from reality."

"Reality is what you call it, Gary. As if, having been immersed in muck, there's no cleansing yourself. We don't have to wallow in it. Marc spent an evening listening to that horrible, chunky girl, Rachel, *dispassionately* discussing sodomy, cunnilingus, and fellatio."

He laughed. "Clinical terms are better than generic. It beats learning from lewd magazines and public rest room graffiti."

He stood in the bathroom doorway as she ran water in the lavatory, washing her face.

"Marc said something I thought was astute," Gary related. "He said you can't protect him from what he already knows. You can't take back what he's already seen. That's true."

"Cora insisted on telling me the horrid details of those videotapes," Barbara spoke between splashes. "She watched every one of them. I couldn't shut her up."

"I know."

"She watched so Clint wouldn't suffer alone, she said. Then she described the look in Clint's eyes, the way he smelled. Cora said her living room stunk of saliva and sweat and semen, like making love in a closed car. Then damned if she didn't have the gall to suggest his reaction had hurt her feelings for him. She told you, didn't she?"

"Yes, she did."

"She told everybody. But I didn't hear Clint describing the mutilation of that poor woman and her child—the murder of her husband and child, Gary—before her eyes!"

Barbara was staring into the lavatory, holding the sink with both hands. "Cora could talk of nothing else. She and that girl, Rachel. I couldn't keep Marc away from them."

She closed her eyes. "I don't want Marc associating with them."

"Does that include his Aunt Cora?"

"Until she regains her senses."

"She works with you. She comes to the office. How can you mandate such a thing without alienating her? I'm not sure it wouldn't make matters worse. We can't hide from reality—"

"You mean, if horror exists, we must face it—is that right?"

"Ignoring it won't eliminate it."

"I know terrible things occur," she said. "Evil men commit atrocities and always have. The cruelty is beyond comprehension and there's nothing I can do about it. But I don't have to hear about it. I don't want to see it. I don't want to think about it."

"Barbara, maybe people should know about men so uncaring that they kill for the thrill of it. To be horrified is to be repulsed and out of that repulsion can come fury. If we are furious enough, maybe we'll do something about it."

"Like what?"

"Like going after the people who buy the videotapes as well as the people who sell them. As for Cora talking about it, she's like the patient who has survived life-threatening surgery. She is compelled to talk it out, come to grips with it. This whole town is going through that to one degree or another."

She met his gaze, her eyes going to blue-green ice. "Gary, there's a part of you that is enamored with violent men and criminality. I would say it's abnormal, but after an evening of 'dispassionate' discussions about unspeakable things, I'm not sure what is abnormal. But it *is* atavistic. Before the brain developed in man, before bonding between humans, the ability to shrug off death had value—it was an anesthetic for survivors in a violent world. But I am the culmination of thousands of years of civilization, hundreds of generations of people who clawed their way out of violence. I realize a person can dwell on sick men doing sick things and finally that person becomes dispassionate. The girl Rachel is a good example—her clinical observations are frightening. You really must forgive me for refusing to participate."

"Barbara, this isn't going away. The story is only now beginning to unfold. Men are at Borden's cabin right now, digging up the place. There will be forensic scientists studying dental charts and bone shards and—"

She clapped her hands over her ears, eyes shut.

He took her in his arms.

"Children are starving in Ethiopia," she whispered. "I must ignore it or sell all that we own to feed them. Since there's nothing I can do, I must ignore it."

He caressed her back.

"Marc is destined to be hurt," she said. "He may go to war, become warped in ways I can't prevent—but not yet, not now. I can protect him a little longer, and I will."

She was rigid in his arms.

"I want a scalding hot bath," she said, brusquely. "I want to be by myself for a while."

"I'll run the tub."

"No. I'll do it."

She pulled away, closed the bathroom door. The tumbler clicked. *Locked.*

Marc attached a zoom telephoto lens to his Nikon and set up a tripod. Eddy Anderson sprawled on a rock, his incredibly long and skinny legs thrown wide. His posture suggested a spilled sack of angles. He had a disconcerting way of crossing his eyes to stare at the mound of his own nose, a feature that now cast a shadow across thin lips as Eddy chewed a twig and squinted against the morning sun.

"Your dad looked odd in a suit," Eddy observed. "I don't suppose he could wear jeans and boots to a funeral, though. Especially being Sunday."

Dad had told Marc to get exterior shots of Borden's cabin for the paper. It was dubious compensation for Mom's refusal—Dad went to the funeral alone. Down below, crews were digging up the grounds.

"So what's he going to ask them?" Eddy mused. He lowered his voice to a manly grumble, "Hi there! I'm Gary

Colter of the *Gatlin Pass Sentinel*. How does it feel to bury a mass murderer?"

Marc focused on the cabin.

"Tell me, Mrs. Wilson," Eddy persisted, "what was the first thing your son ever killed?"

The camera clicked. Marc advanced the film.

"And do you blame this on heredity, or environment?"

"Eddy, will you shut up?"

Eddy slapped his own face, muttering, "Mosquitoes." A moment later, "How long did you know Charlotte?"

"About a week."

Eddy spit between the space in his front teeth. "Did you make it with her?"

"Eddy, I'm trying to work."

Click. Click.

"Well—did you?"

"Grab my camera bag. I want to find another angle."

"Oh say, hey, you don't have to share with me," Eddy said as he followed. "Keep it, sure, just keep it. I'm your best friend. I tell you every teensy detail, but you keep this for yourself."

"Yes, we made it."

At a higher elevation, Marc set up the tripod again, focused through the telephoto lens.

"Well?" Eddy squealed. "Well, well?"

"Well, what?"

"Was she pretty?"

"Yes."

"Sexy?"

"Yes, Eddy."

Three more exposures and Marc disassembled his equipment. The mosquitoes were a steady drone. Pity the men working below.

"You never told me about her." Eddy kept pace, returning to Marc's jeep.

"I never tell you about any of them."

Eddy halted, drew back. "A multiplicity?"

"You're the one always talking about conquests. It's immature and a cheap shot."

"It is normal." Eddy slipped, regained his footing. "It is normal for two young men to discuss their amorous encounters. It's a learning experience. It fills that void between parent and progeny, that lack of communication."

"It stinks."

Eddy grinned, the gap between his incisors showing. "Odiferous, perhaps, but titillating. Well, okay—did I ever see her?"

"I don't think so."

"The week after Christmas, you said. Where was I the week after Christmas?"

They rode the steep winding road toward Gatlin Pass, trailing tourists who gawked at the scenery.

"Twenty-two," Eddy pondered. "Experienced?"

"More than me."

"Oh, God." Eddy squirmed down in his seat. "I can't stand it. So, okay, she's sexy and experienced and willing. I mean, she seduced *you*, right?"

"It was mutual."

"Mutual," Eddy rhapsodized. "Star-struck lovers destined for tragedy—God, that's wonderful."

"It's awful."

Eddy sobered. "It is, really. So, okay, did you take her picture?"

"I don't remember."

"Oh, come on, Colter. You take pictures of flowers and elk and football games—come *on*—"

"I took a few."

"I want to see them, okay?"

Marc parked in front of the *Sentinel*. The sidewalk was crowded, people sounds bubbling around them as he unlocked the door. The phone rang once, stopped. Mom must have answered at home.

"Are you going to the Rooftop Rodeo next month?" Eddy asked.

"To take pictures."

"Get a pass for me, too." Eddy couldn't walk through a room without fondling things. He seldom returned an item to the exact place he found it. "I'll get the girls."

"Dad will be back in a couple of hours," Marc said. "I've got to develop these shots for the next paper."

"That a hint?"

"Yes, it's a hint. I have to work."

"So, hey, okay, why can't I stay and keep you company?"

"I can't talk and work, too."

"Won't say a word."

"Once I start, you can't leave the darkroom."

"I know, hey, I know. I'll sit here on this stool and watch."

"Don't bug me. I mean it."

Marc mixed chemicals, prepared the trays, mentally checking himself as he went through the familiar procedure.

"Little later, maybe," Eddy said, "you can show me pictures of the girl."

Marc turned to face him, accusingly. Eddy made an "OK" sign with thumb and forefinger of each hand, winking. "Until then," he said, "I will sit by, silent and unnoticed."

Sometimes he did things he couldn't explain, even to himself. Marc hadn't wanted to talk about Charlotte. He certainly didn't want to flaunt her photographs before Eddy's leering eyes. But here he was, the newspaper work spread to dry, enlarging photos that he and Charlotte had made on their last day together.

Eddy whistled softly. "Oh, man, she is pretty."

Beautiful.

They had gone to Hidden Valley to ski. Instead, they shot pictures of elk. Then they made love on a blanket in the snow. That moment came back as vividly as if it had been a second ago.

He had grabbed his camera, teasingly threatening to take her picture in the nude. The anticipated objection didn't come. Charlotte had thrown back her head, breasts thrust forward, posing.

"God, what a body," Eddy murmured.

Marc had moved around her, shutter clicking, this angle, then another, farther back, from a point looking down, another, shooting uphill with snow-laden evergreen boughs as a backdrop.

He hadn't enlarged the photographs because—what could he do with a print of a naked girl? Having the contact sheets filed, it was unlikely anyone would ever discover thirty-six tiny prints on a single page. But an enlargement!

"May I have this?" Eddy asked.

"No."

"Hey, why not? It's no worse than a calendar pose. Better, really. You can make another one."

"No."

Eddy held the print under a light, using a magnifying glass. "Curly little hairs," he said.

"You're disgusting."

"If you were my mother," Eddy said, "my reaction would be more circumspect. I would speak of this remarkable art form, the symmetry of lines, the poetic flow of artistic perception. But you are my best friend. I feel free to express my fervent emotional response to this lovely, lovely girl."

Marc sorted pictures of Borden's cabin—exterior shots made today, other shots, from that first trip with Dad and Uncle Clint, of weapons, survival kits.

"Hey," Eddy said, "come here."

"I'm busy."

"Hey, man, come look at this."

Eddy brought the picture, magnifying glass trembling. "Look at the tree."

"Spruce."

"Take this glass and look—right there—"

A shiver streaked up Marc's back, goose bumps rippling flesh.

Through the boughs, barely perceptible—a man's face.

"And there," Eddy's finger moved slightly.

Another man. *Watching.*

CHAPTER TWELVE

There were no flowers, no mourners except Borden's father and two sisters. The sun was a blister in a cloudless sky; it was an unusually warm day. The Lutheran minister admitted he was a stranger to them all, and pleaded unconvincingly for the dead man's soul.

Mr. Wilson stood over Borden's fabric-covered plywood casket, his head bare, shoulders rounded, hat in hand, turning the brim between thick fingers. Borden's sisters each wore dark cotton dresses, old-fashioned shoes, and gloves. One held a paper tissue, but she did not weep.

In the shade of a nearby tree, two Mexican-Americans leaned on shovels, waiting. Headstones formed geometric patterns in a pea-green field.

The ceremony ended. Mr. Wilson gave the minister ten dollars as Gary approached.

"I will be writing about Borden," Gary explained gently. "I would like to say things only a family member would know. Good things to balance the not so good."

After an awkward silence, Mr. Wilson put on his hat. "Come to the house if you're of a mind to."

As the family got into their pickup truck, the laborers moved toward the grave to finish their task.

Gary had seen scandalized families many times in the course of writing about criminals. Humiliated, sometimes convinced that all accusations were lies, some took their loved one to the grave with bitterness. Others seemed almost relieved.

The one thing all criminals had in common was their lack of regard for others, Gary thought. He was convinced that the quality of unselfishness was stronger than law. Any potential criminal who loved someone more than himself would never chance disgrace.

Wilson's pickup truck reached the highway, the heads of the sisters and their father moving in unison as they bumped over a final hump.

Criminals were stupid. There were exceptions, of course. Con men who embezzled by artifice were not the dullards who brutalized with weapons. But overall, whatever the transgression, criminals were selfish and unloving.

He had known writers who claimed certain star lawbreakers as friends. Not *friends*. Criminals had an insurmountable problem: they couldn't trust one another. No, they didn't have real friends.

The pickup turned up a rutted road, Gary following. Monkeyflower, Mexican hats, and golden asters wove a yellow carpet along the roadside. Trembling aspens shivered in a breeze, the silvery leaves like a million minnows swimming in an invisible bowl.

Beyond another turn, the gully was darkened by trees, cooled by a mountain brook. He heard the truck gears grate as they went into low, ascending a rocky incline, briars rasping against the sides of the vehicles.

The stigma of criminal behavior stained the family as well as the felon. If he loved any of them, how could he blemish their name? Suicide had released Borden in a final selfish act, leaving his relatives to shoulder the burden.

Mr. Wilson pulled into a yard. When he got out, he placed stones under the rear wheels of his pickup. The two women climbed toward an unpainted cabin with a cedar-shingle roof and an open front porch.

"You knew Borden?" Mr. Wilson asked.

"Everybody in Gatlin Pass knew him."

"A man ain't nothing but what he is last," Mr. Wilson said. "That's what I blame him for mostly, killing himself. Can't change anything now. It's over."

They went up plank steps to the porch and Mr. Wilson removed his hat.

"This is Mr. Colter from the newspaper," Mr. Wilson said to his wife. "Wants to know about Borden."

She was of Indian blood, with dark eyes and cinnamon skin. The resemblance to Borden was obvious in her high cheekbones and perfectly formed eyebrows.

"Borden was a good boy."

"That's what I want to know," Gary said.

She seemed older than her husband, but her hair was still black while his had gone gray and thin.

They sat in rocking chairs with bottoms woven from cowhide thongs. The sisters, Frances and Emily, brought a fruit drink Gary couldn't identify by name. In the house, as if ready for guests, there were sandwiches, thick slices of deep-fried potatoes, paper napkins, and a bowl of punch. They asked if he was hungry.

These were the kind of people Gary had known growing up in the Everglades of Florida. Simple, honest, laboring people. They prayed for good and planned for bad times, their possessions so meager and their existence so hard they developed a personal ethic that demanded physical toil. They had intense pride, such people. If a man lost the respect of his fellowman, what had he?

"Did his chores good," Mr. Wilson said.

"Kept his word when he gave it," the mother added.

"Did he ever marry?" Gary asked.

"Long time ago." Mrs. Wilson rocked slowly. "Girl he met in a city somewhere. Painted her fingernails and ate garlic." She turned to her husband. "You remember."

He nodded.

"Any children?" Gary inquired.

"Not to know about."

Frances and Emily brought a plate of sandwiches, offered them. "Directly," the father said, refusing for now.

"Borden, he liked to hunt and fish," Mrs. Wilson said. "Give that boy a dry fly and rod and he'd be gone a week up in them mountains. Knew what to eat and what not, berries and all."

They rocked, rocked, the porch creaking time with each movement.

"Birds and animals—"

"Good trapper," Mr. Wilson said. "Sometimes he'd catch a thing and let it go just to say he'd held it."

"Raised rabbits—"

"Thought he could sell them down on Longmont, but a skinned rabbit looks like a tiny human baby and nobody bought."

"That's what Borden said," Mrs. Wilson remembered, ". . . look like tiny babies . . ."

"The war did it to him," Frances said, angrily. "The war made Borden different."

"That wasn't Borden they buried today," Mrs. Wilson said. "That was not my boy. My boy went away to war and never come home whole."

They rocked to and fro.

"That's why I didn't go to the funeral," she said. "That was not my boy."

"You say the war changed him," Gary prompted.

Emily responded, "Quit coming home. Was a time he'd be here Christmas if he had to crawl."

"Claimed there was no God," Frances added.

"Took to killing for sport," Mr. Wilson said. "He never did that before. If we didn't need food, we didn't kill things."

They brought scrapbooks to the porch. The sisters sat in ladderback chairs, eating sandwiches prepared for visitors who never came. They spoke of Borden the infant, Borden the first-grader, Borden the adolescent.

"The war did it." Mrs. Wilson wept over a faded photo of Borden as a child, his chin tucked, one eye closed against the glare, knees touching, bare feet turned inward, hair unruly.

"Mrs. Wilson, will you loan me these pictures? I'll take care and return them."

"Got no other," she said. "Pa?"

Mr. Wilson rocked, peering into the gathering shadows of late afternoon.

"Might as well," he said. "It's over, anyhow."

Streetlights glowed, tourists strolling the sidewalks past the *Sentinel*. Gary composed the front page in two parts. The headline: BORDEN WAS A GOOD BOY. His interview with the family followed. Below that, midway down the page, a second headline and a haunting question: SO . . . WHAT HAPPENED . . . ?

"Not a single vacancy," Barbara announced from her desk. "We're booked through the end of July."

"This is good writing," Gary said. "It may be the best I've ever done."

In the darkroom, Marc and his friend, Eddy, were making copies of all photographs from the Wilson scrapbook. Page two was filled with them: Borden on a sled, another as a student in high school, finally as a raw recruit in an army boot camp.

Mrs. Wilson had related things Borden wrote about while in Vietnam—the horror of battle, the wrench of his first kill, the emotional furnace that warped the personality and returned a son "changed."

The clincher to Gary's story was, "The war did it," quoting the tearful mother.

She had brought out letters, grammatically flawed, spelling terrible, but vibrant with the anguish of a combat veteran enduring the unendurable. Excerpts from the letters formed a box on page two with the childhood photos.

Good stuff. Under-the-skin stuff. Gary checked the press, aligned newsprint, pushed the start button.

"How many copies this week?" Barbara called.

"Two thousand—what do you think?"

"They will sell," she said.

No matter how many times he had done this, the sight of his words in print was still a thrill. He halted the press to check the proof.

"Typo, second paragraph, column one," Eddy said.

"Change it, will you?" Gary subdued irritation. Eddy Anderson was a state champion speller, runner-up in national competition. His vocabulary was exemplary, his command of English outstanding. And the little bastard could see a flaw at a glance, reveling in the discovery.

"Typo, column four, lower right," Eddy called. "Want me to change it?"

"Yes."

He heard the boy humming as he reset type, adjusted the paragraph. "Whoops—another one!"

"Good work!" *Insufferable creep.*

The doorbell tinkled. Barbara stood up to meet the man entering. "Stand clear," Gary warned. "Presses running."

The drums picked up cadence, paper moving through, belts drawn taut. The next edition was on its way.

"Gary!" Barbara brought over a young man, her voice raised to be heard. "This is Daniel Talbert!"

They shook hands. Something in Barbara's eyes—a spark— "Have we met?" Gary asked.

Barbara interceded. "You know—Daniel Talbert!"

He didn't know. But all right. Gary grinned, added strength to his handshake. He indicated the running presses with a helpless shrug and Talbert winked, a hand lifted to show he understood. Barbara took him to the front of the office and they sat at her desk. Eddy and Marc joined them.

Never heard of him.

Gary adjusted belts on the conveyor to insure a smooth run. He squirted oil on a cog that was warming. From the corner of his eye he saw his wife and son and Eddy in animated conversation. Much laughter. The stranger was known to *them*, obviously. He took out his pen and signed a piece of paper, giving it to Eddy.

Eddy was delivering an adolescent performance of some kind, long arms extended, hips wiggling as he acted out the story he told. Talbert was now sitting on a corner of Barbara's desk, listening, nodding, smiling.

Daniel Talbert—he tried to remember if he had heard the name. It had a ring to it, but so did *Porky Pig* and *Bugs Bunny*.

One thousand . . . the press developed a tiny clinking and Gary swore under his breath. *Run, damn you.*

Eleven hundred . . .

Barbara laughed so loudly he turned to see. Now Talbert was talking, acting out his own story.

Twelve hundred . . . the clinking escalated into a rattle.

Clint entered, his attention drawn away by Barbara, introducing Talbert.

Thirteen hundred fifty . . . a clank played counterpoint to the rattle, a tinkle coming from another part of the equipment.

Whang!

A breaker flipped, power failed, the press whining down to silence.

Everybody up front looked this way. Gary pursed his lips in a soft whistle, casually circling the *goddamned thing.*

"Need some help, Dad?"

"Nothing important."

"Sounded like a fan belt," Marc offered.

"Could be."

"Gary, Mr. Talbert has invited us to dinner."

"The Trout House," Talbert said. "Trout Eisenhower is their specialty, I'm told."

"How many copies did you get, Dad?"

"Fourteen hundred."

"Great! We'll fix the belt tomorrow."

"I planned to run two thousand."

"Last time we did that we took back four hundred."

"This time we have a hot item," Gary said, brusquely.

"Dad." Marc's voice lowered. "That's Daniel Talbert."

"So I'm told."

"You know—The Hillside Strangler, Ted Bundy, the society murders in Dallas—"

"Darling." Barbara's eyes were like a teenager's in the presence of an idol. "Let's go have dinner with Daniel. We'll finish the press run in the morning."

Daniel.

Gary washed his hands, Clint's voice rising above the others, " . . . an armed robbery once . . . no high-speed chase . . . nobody hurt . . ."

Now he remembered. The novelist. Daniel Talbert. The Gatlin Pass Library ran notices on new books once a month. He had seen Talbert's name in that feature. Something of a success, Gary recalled.

When he emerged, Talbert shook his hand again. "Your boy says you won a Pulitzer!"

"Yes . . . I . . ."

"What was your subject?"

"The underworld connection between the docks in major ports and the city of Chicago."

"A Pulitzer." Talbert's teeth gleamed white, eyes hazel, jaw square—a kid. Couldn't be more than thirty-five! "I'm impressed," he said.

Big deal—impressed. Barbara was turning out lights, Marc checking the back doors, locking up.

"Did you do the script on *Dallas Dead Man*?" Eddy asked.

"Scripts aren't my métier."

"The movie followed the book pretty well," Eddy said. "I loved that scene where the cops caught the villain in the express elevator of his unfinished high rise."

Talbert had Barbara's arm, escorting her. Clint fell back with Gary.

"You know him?" Gary asked softly.

"Read his books."

"A goddamned kid."

"When you're eighty, sixty seems young," Clint said.

"What's he doing here?"

Clint peered into windows in passing. "Writing a book, he said."

"About what?"

"What do you think?" Clint asked.

* * *

They sat at a round table in the Trout House. The restaurant was crowded, dim lights augmented by candles.

"You're my guests," Talbert said. "Have anything that appeals to you."

"Oh, there are too many of us," Barbara protested.

"Nonsense. I'm here to conduct research."

Twice before their order arrived, patrons approached Talbert for his autograph. They had seen him on talk shows, they said. Read his books.

"Bless your heart."

"My favorite was the one about Ted Bundy," Barbara effused. Gary put a crick in his neck snatching around to stare at her.

"Did you meet Bundy?" Barbara inquired.

"No, but I talked to hundreds of people who knew him. Everybody but his mother. I didn't want to get sued."

For Clint, Barbara, and Gary, he ordered an excellent dry white wine, urging Marc and Eddy to have all the soft drinks they wanted.

"How do you decide on a subject?" Eddy asked.

"First, it has to be a crime." Talbert sat back as platters of trout arrived. "Second, it must be a subject that lends itself to suspense. Finally, the villain must be an interesting personality. The reader doesn't want to spend an evening with a moron."

"Interesting—like Ted Bundy," Barbara persisted.

"Precisely so. An educated man, intelligent, witty, charming, and completely without remorse for the sadistic sexual attacks that culminated in brutal murders."

Handsome. Thick sideburns curled at Talbert's ears, hair wavy, professionally trimmed. His dress was casual, expensive—open-neck shirt, tailored jacket.

Barbara, who loathed discussions of crime, continued to ply him with questions. "For all his insane acts, Bundy was sane—that's your point?"

"Exactly." Talbert gazed at her as if they were alone. "We hear about gruesome crimes and we naturally presume such a criminal is insane. How else could he do such things? But we must remember, the most cruel acts are often sane ones—premeditated, logical, calculating the agony of the victim—"

"Isn't that insane?"

"Were the Nazis insane? They killed millions systematically. Evil, yes. Insane, no."

"Frightening," Barbara said. She didn't look frightened.

"On a broader scale," Talbert said as he filleted his fish, "we have the crimes of dictators like Stalin who engineered the deaths of twenty million of his own people, the massacre of thousands of Poles who were anticommunist officers during World War II. Christians have slaughtered in the name of Christ and the Moslem sects have declared *jihad*, 'holy war,' by perpetrating random acts of terrorism."

He munched trout, closed his eyes for a moment. "Delicious. But," he said, returning to the subject, "we are numbed by such staggering statistics. To feel it, we must reduce the gross to one-on-one. We *feel* the pain when it is intimate. We are anesthetized by dozens or hundreds or thousands."

Eddy held forth on the social aspects of crime, Daniel Talbert giving the boy full—and, it seemed, genuine—attention.

"A society can be judged by its acceptable extremes," Eddy concluded. "If we shrug about pornography, for example. If we accept abortion, we may be one step away from euthanasia."

"Point well made," Talbert said. "Having done this, our prurient needs escalate from shocking sex to more shocking acts—using people becomes abusing people and finally the murder of them. That was probably what Wilson and Wang were doing."

He omitted nobody. Asking Clint about certain aspects of his job, he responded intelligently and sympathetically to Clint's problems as the local peacekeeper.

"And now we are on the scene of a crime that seems

ghastly enough for literary consideration." Talbert lifted his drink in a toast. "The elements for suspense are here—the crime is inconceivable, recording death for sale on video-tapes, the locale is exotic, in the beautiful Rocky Mountains, and the criminals are not dullards."

Gary spoke for the first time since sitting. "You seem sure of that."

"I am. Or else I wouldn't be here. As I said, the reader doesn't wish to spend an evening with morons."

"I've always considered criminals stupid," Gary said.

"Then your book will be nonfiction this time," Barbara remarked.

"Always fiction."

"Aren't you wasting the research?"

"Not at all." Talbert sat with an arm over the back of Barbara's chair. "When I know these men, when my heart beats as one with theirs, then I am ready to write about them. Fiction allows the reader to live their reality, to understand the matrix that created such animals."

"Dad's feature in this week's paper is about Borden Wilson," Marc noted. "Super job, I thought."

"I have no doubt of it." Talbert turned to Gary now. "I'm trying to locate the family. Perhaps you could help me?"

"One small problem," Gary said, attempting to smile. "I intend to do a book myself." Barbara laughed.

"Oops!" Talbert laughed with her. "Fiction?"

"Nonfiction is my forte."

"Ah! No conflict, then. Thank goodness. I'll be more than happy to share my notes. Incidentally, I secured a copy of Borden Wilson's military records if you'd like to see them."

"What about Wang?" Clint asked.

"I released that last week. You may have read it in the *Denver Post*."

He spoke to Gary again. "The *Chicago Trib* and *The New York Times* asked me to feed them the story, which they syndicate or release through the wire services. It helps open doors and—why not?"

"Yes. Why not."

"You'll be here how long?" Barbara inquired.

"Who knows?" He placed a gold credit card on the bill. "As I say, my heart must beat as one with the principals in every story. Only then am I ready to write."

The waitress took the bill and credit card. Eddy kicked Gary under the table, uncrossing his long legs, sprawling with arms extended to adjacent chairs. He sucked his teeth for orts, nodding sagely. "Anything we can do to help, Mr. Talbert, we'll do it."

"I will need a guide," Talbert acknowledged. "To the cabin, to various points of interest."

"No problem," Eddy said. "By the way, Marc has some great shots of the cabin—weapons, survival kits, a bazooka—"

Talbert barely shifted his vision, but he took in Gary before answering. "I'd like to see them, but I can't use them. Mine is fiction, remember. No photos in that."

"Too bad," Gary said. He heard a tremor in his own voice. "Marc's a good photographer."

They stood to leave and Talbert put a hand on Marc's shoulder. "There's always a chance the wire service would buy a shot or two. We'll look them over and submit a few. What do you say?"

"Great!"

Face flaming, Gary followed as they sauntered toward the *Sentinel* office.

"*Dallas Dead Man* was better," Clint said.

"What?"

"*Dallas Dead Man*," Clint said. "It was better than the book on Ted Bundy."

"The pay isn't phenomenal," Talbert was telling Marc. "But national exposure and photo credits—right?"

"You bet!"

"Not better writing," Clint spoke in a murmur. "Better story. You read it, didn't you?"

"No."

"Watch the traffic," Clint warned at large. He looked into windows, walking by, paused to rattle a door to be certain it was locked.

"Guess we'll be famous," he said. He bit the tip from a cigar, rolled it in his mouth. "I'd want Robert Redford to play me. Do away with Cora."

Gary's expression made Clint shuffle slightly. "Hell, Gary, it's only fiction."

CHAPTER THIRTEEN

G ary arrived at the *Sentinel* office before dawn. The presses repaired, he impulsively ran off three thousand copies to complete the run he started last night. Before eight o'clock he had delivered bundles to the motels on consignment, watching them disappear as he stood there. He filled the sidewalk vending machines, sold some out of hand to passersby, people clustering to read his story. God, it was wonderful!

This morning, he looked forward to the Staghorn Café.

He entered unnoticed. Daniel Talbert was the center of attention, holding his audience with stories about nefarious men he had known.

"The theory was," Talbert said, "the killer had a split personality. According to the psychiatrist, one did not know the other existed. He was really two separate people living in a single body. The question was, how do you punish one without unjustly persecuting the other?"

"Shoot the bad one, let the other go," somebody suggested.

"You interviewed this weirdo?" McHenry the druggist inquired.

"Both of them, many times, for many hours. Good morning, Gary."

Gary sat down as McHenry nudged George Nolan, the hardware proprietor. "What's our nature story this week, Colter?" McHenry asked.

At the counter, tourists were buying the *Sentinel*, returning to their tables.

Back to Talbert: "What'd they do with the man?" somebody questioned.

"The judge ruled wisely, I thought. They put him in a mental institution. When one personality becomes dominant, the other will be eliminated. Which is capital punishment, if you think about it. The guilty personality would no longer exist. And if it did, he would be tried for murder."

McHenry went to the counter, put down a quarter. He snapped the paper between his hands, unfolding it. He examined the front page, then peered over his glasses at Gary.

"When they make a movie out of your book," somebody asked Talbert, "do you have a say in that?"

"Hollywood believes an author should take his money and go away."

Ten years. Ten years Gary had lived here and never felt accepted. But here was Talbert, a flatland foreigner, sowing tales and reaping some.

" . . . he'd breathed so much dust he had mud balls in his brain . . ."

Talbert pulled out a notebook, which didn't go unnoticed.

" . . . fair-skinned feller. Couldn't read in bright light 'cause it burnt the top of his head . . ."

Duly noted, Talbert smiling.

" . . . got flash burns when he opened the refrigerator door . . ."

McHenry the druggist returned to the table and put down the *Sentinel.* He slapped it with the flat of a hand. "Now that," he said, "is what I call a newspaper."

He announced the headline to all: "Borden was a good boy . . ."

Heartbeat ascending, keeping his expression nonchalant, Gary sipped coffee as conversation ceased. A clatter of dishes in the kitchen broke the silence.

Sold out. Within minutes! He wished he'd printed another thousand.

"Colter," George Nolan said, "I begin to see how you won that big writing prize."

Heads nodded, readers engrossed. Gary's eyes met Talbert's a moment, then looked away.

He was afraid his glow was showing. The waitress brought more coffee and he stirred it excessively.

"So . . . what happened," McHenry read the second headline aloud. "The war did it . . ."

Talbert gazed toward the street, watching people pass the windows.

"There's something any man can understand." McHenry thumped the newspaper. "Borden Wilson went through hell we can only imagine and it broke him."

"You knew Wilson?" Talbert inquired.

"We all did, more or less."

"These changes were noticeable?"

"Well, see, Borden was a fellow stayed to himself. These mountains are full of men like that."

"But they aren't murdering tourists, I trust."

A young couple at another table frowned at one another.

"If combat caused Wilson," Talbert suggested, "how do we explain his partner, Wang?"

"He was in the war, too."

"No." Talbert winced with the disclosure as if pained by his rebuttal. "Wang was in the Marines a short time. They mustered him out for stealing. He's also a pathological liar."

"He ain't from here," somebody said, as if that explained or excused it.

"Did any of you know Wilson well?" Talbert persisted.

"Nobody knows a man like that," McHenry countered.

"That is a point well taken," Talbert said. "Such a man doesn't encourage close relationships. But then you have to wonder—why did he come back here to commit these terrible crimes?"

"Knew the territory."

"Trapped and fished these mountains all his life. It says so right here in the *Sentinel*."

"But if he's going to do something as heinous as he is supposed to have done," Talbert mused, "he wouldn't do it among friends. I don't think Wilson considered any of you friends. Close relationships invite inspection."

"Folks hereabouts don't poke in another man's business," McHenry said.

Talbert stroked his nose with a thumb and forefinger, tugging toward the septum. "I guess what I'm trying to say is, Wilson was born and raised here, but he wasn't one of you. He never came to chat with you guys over morning coffee. He never confided in a single man here. You saw him now and then, but he remained a stranger."

"I allow that," somebody agreed.

"Which means, the community isn't guilty of anything, except tolerating a stranger."

McHenry bristled. "Who said we were?"

Daniel Talbert beckoned for more coffee, holding them with a pregnant pause, letting the waitress pour.

"You seemed relieved that Wilson had been explained." Talbert spoke to McHenry. "You said it was something any man could understand—the war did it."

"Anybody has a breaking point."

Talbert lifted his eyebrows. "What say, Gary?"

"About what?"

"Your story is really about the parents and sisters. Their observations and recollections. The letters they gave you were written by Borden, they said. I see no editorial content in your article, except, perhaps, in the headlines themselves. Would you agree with these gentlemen—the war did it?"

"I have to agree. If only a tenth of what Borden wrote about is true—his combat experiences could distort reason."

Talbert wore another pained expression of dissent. "Yes, that would be true, I suppose." He turned to Gary's article, reading aloud, " '. . . blood . . . flowing, coagulating , . . dried on the face and hands . . . the smell of it . . . the sticky feel of it . . .' "

"He was going crazy right there," McHenry suggested.

"I blame the government for what happened," George Nolan said, acidly. "They sent our boys where they shouldn't have been and put them through hell on earth."

"Combat will do it to you."

Talbert's wince deepened. "Only trouble is," he said, "Borden Wilson never saw combat a day in his life."

Stunned, Gary's ears were ringing.

"He went to Vietnam on three different tours," Talbert said. "Each time he was assigned to the headquarters motor pool in Saigon. He wasn't even there for the Tet offensive."

"Motor pool?"

"He never received a decoration for anything, except marksmanship in boot camp," Talbert said.

"He wore a ring," Gary said. "Parachute."

"Probably bought it. He owned various insignia which the FBI found sewn to shirts and field jackets. But it was a fantasy. His military records don't indicate a single jump from an airplane. He never qualified on anything but standard-issue rifle and a bit of hand-to-hand stuff."

Fantasy?

"I hope I'm not ruining the thrust of a subsequent article, Colter," Talbert apologized. "Maybe you were setting up your readers with this first article?"

Gary lifted fingertips, let them fall to the table.

"It's this kind of dichotomy that makes a man like Borden Wilson interesting to me." Talbert smiled. "All that you thought was wrong—surprise! Great cliff-hangers and plot twists—but real and true. He wasn't what his parents thought. Nor what any of you thought. He wove a tale of jungle horror while he was safe in Saigon with the prostitutes and gaudy nightlife."

Gary felt people looking at him.

"Stay tuned," Talbert said, dramatically. "More next week."

The telephones were ringing, the office empty. *Goddamned one-mule farmer!* Gary grabbed a receiver. "Hello?"

"Mr. Colter, this is Eddy. Is Marc there?"

"No."

"Ask him to call me when he comes in, will you?"

"Right." Gary hung up, then answered one of Barbara's lines. *No vacancies.*

He shoved things around in his desk drawer, moved to a bookcase, searching for an old address book. *Ah!*

The phone again. "Dad, is Mom there?"

"No, Marc. Eddy is looking for you."

"I finished cleaning cabins. Listen, do you mind if I go with Dan up to Borden Wilson's cabin?"

Dan. Dan?

"Dad, are you there?"

"I see no reason why not, Marcus."

Another phone rang, but he ignored it, dialing long distance. He listened as connections were made electronically.

"*Chicago Tribune.*"

"Good morning. No, well, it's afternoon now, isn't it?"

"May I help you?"

"This is Gary Colter. May I speak with Morgan in syndication?"

"Morgan, sir? First or last name?"

"Morton Rheinhold Morgan," Gary said, tersely.

Long pause. Daytime rates.

"Sir, we have no such person in syndication."

"Who took his place?"

"I wouldn't know, sir. One moment and I'll connect you."

"No, wait, I'll speak to—"

The phone was ringing. A woman's clipped midwestern accent. "Syndication."

"This is Gary Colter. I worked there for several years . . ."

"May I help you?"

"I was asking for Morton Rheinhold Morgan."

"I don't believe he's with us any longer, Mr. Colter."

"Who took his place?"

"What place was that?"

"Editor-in-chief, head honcho, big man on campus."

She didn't laugh. After a moment, she said, "Would you like to speak with a particular department, Mr. Colter?"

"Head of syndication."

The phone blipped, began to ring. Another secretary. No

nonsense this time. "My name is Gary Colter. I worked for Morgan Rheinhold Morton several years ago."

"You mean Morton Rheinhold *Morgan*."

"Yes, I mean him. I presume he left the *Trib*?"

"Are you a personal friend?"

"We worked together five years."

"I see. I'm sorry, Mr. Colter. Mr. Morgan died of a heart attack some time ago."

"Oh. I . . . well . . ."

"Seven or eight years ago."

"May I speak to his successor?"

"Mr. Feldstein is chief of syndicate services now."

"May I speak to him?"

"Is he expecting your call?"

"Of course not. I never heard of him! Tell him a man who won a Pulitzer Prize writing for that rag is on the phone *right now*."

He waited. Waited. *Sonofabitch*. Waited.

"Feldstein here."

Gary heard a tremor in his own voice. "Mr. Feldstein, I was working there some ten years ago under Morton-Rheinhold-Morgan."

"Yes?"

"I have a story I wanted Morton to see."

"What is the nature of the material?"

"Multiple murder. I'm living in Gatlin Pass, Colorado, where this happened. A man named Daniel Talbert is here—"

"Oh, yes."

"He says he's feeding the story to you."

"He is."

"Well, hell, man, I'm living here. Why didn't you call me?"

"Are you working with one of the Denver papers?"

"I publish a paper."

"Which paper is that?"

He heard his own swallow. "The *Gatlin Pass Sentinel*. I know everyone in this area. These are funny people, Mr. Feldstein. They're clannish."

"What did you want, specifically, Mr. Colter?"

"I'd like to submit my articles for syndication. For possible syndication. I would want to hold book rights, but other than that, the rights are yours."

"As you said, Mr. Talbert is there already."

"Going for fiction. I'm talking newspaper here. Feature. I think it could be another Pulitzer piece."

It wasn't. He knew it wasn't! He shut his eyes, sickly, waiting for a response.

"Of course, we'd be happy to consider anything you send us, Mr. Colter."

"To your attention?"

"That would be fine."

"I'll shoot off a package air express."

"Yes." Pause. "Thank you for thinking of us."

"Hell," Gary croaked, "that's home for me. I was sorry to hear Morton died. Where's Andy Riley these days?"

"Andy went with United Press International."

He mentioned other names. Two were unknown to Feldstein, the third he had lost track of.

"I'll get this off to you right away, Feldstein."

"Very good. Oh! Mr. Colter, be sure to include a stamped, self-addressed envelope."

He hung up.

Who was he kidding? The world had turned and he had stood still. Who in hell was he kidding?

His feet were swollen and felt weighted. His ears rang as they had when he'd first come to this altitude ten years ago. When he entered the bedroom, Barbara was propped up with pillows, knees raised, her round glasses giving her the appearance of a stylized owl. "Hi, darling. How was your day?"

"I've had better."

"We received some nice comments on your story. Dan said it was first-class writing."

Yeah. Well, screw Dan.

He noticed a stack of books on the bedside table. *Daniel Talbert. Seven of them.*

"I bought them today," Barbara said. "Dan offered to autograph them."

"I thought you had his books."

"Some. Book club editions. I couldn't ask him to autograph those."

He opened one. "Sixteen dollars? Sixteen dollars for a novel?"

"That's the price these days."

He pulled off his tie, hung it in the closet.

"Dan said your story captured the flavor and grief of the family. He said it was masterful poignancy."

Novels. Movies. People asked for his autograph. The bastard had hair and straight teeth.

"Did Marc tell you Dan is going to send his photographs to the wire services? He's so excited he can barely stand it."

"Good for Marc."

His tone brought up her guard. "Yes," she said. "Good for Marc."

Naked, he stepped from the closet to find her staring at him. "Yes?" he snapped.

"What's wrong, Gary?"

"Nothing is wrong."

"Something is. What is it?"

He laughed mirthlessly. "Sixteen dollars for fiction. What do you suppose his royalty is on that?"

"Ten percent of the first five thousand copies, twelve and a half percent of the next five thousand copies, fifteen percent thereafter."

"Told you that, did he?"

"I'm married to a writer and he's a writer. It's a natural topic of conversation. Besides, as he said, these things are common knowledge. They're in the trade magazines."

"You know, I just don't understand something." Gary paced two steps, turned. "I've been in this town for ten years and I'm still an outsider. Here comes Daniel Talbert wearing Gucci shoes and capped teeth and the guys at the Staghorn Café treat him like a celebrity."

"He is."

"They chuckle at his thinly veiled insults. They bring out their homilies and old war stories and revel in his notes about them."

Her eyes never left him.

"Ten years I've been going in there and you'd think I was after state secrets. They either take digs at me or ignore me outright."

"Come sit down, Gary."

He wheeled, pacing. "They don't understand half what Talbert says. He speaks of Rorschach tests and they think he means electrical response."

Barbara patted the mattress beside her. "Come here."

But he didn't. Stalking across the bedroom nude, he raised his voice. "You," he said. "You stick your head in the ground and your fingers in your ears—no, no, you do not want to hear about terrible crimes! But while we're eating at the Trout House last night, you couldn't get enough of the gory details."

"Now, Gary—"

"We're talking about my life here," Gary said. "My occupation, my career—and you refer to it as 'obsession'! But you hung on every utterance from Daniel Talbert. I'd like for you to explain that, Barbara."

"Stop running around this room like a baby elephant swinging his little trunk. Come sit down."

"Goddamn it, I'm serious! Tell me why you sit there starry-eyed over Talbert, asking about things you couldn't bear to hear from me a few nights before."

"All right." She closed her book, put aside her glasses. "For one thing, he doesn't sit at the breakfast table so depressed that he has to be jolted to get his attention. He doesn't come up in the middle of the night screaming his way out of a bad dream. Oh, he may do those things, but I don't have to sleep with him. I'm not required to hold his rigid sweat-soaked body, trying to wake him. I don't have to watch him lose weight as he destroys himself. And yes, *obsession* is the word!"

"You knew I was a crime reporter when you married me."

"You were *not* a crime reporter when we married. You worked for a twice-weekly paper in Champagne-Urbana. You did everything from obituaries to sports news and you were bitterly unhappy. You wanted to rise above the herd, you said, to climb over the pack of ten thousand reporters in America."

"You have never understood my work."

"Gary, your memory is short and convenient. When we married you came home nights complaining because you hadn't the time to write a 'serious' book. You dreamed of doing a series of articles with 'social relevance.' "

He put on a robe.

"Night after night we sat at that cheap chrome dinette table poring over every word in your articles. We wore out one thesaurus and two dictionaries, but it was worth it. The *Tribune* finally gave you a job."

"At which point you changed your tune. You hated my job."

"I hated what your job did to you. Prowling the streets, hounding the police—"

"That was my job."

"Twenty-four hours a day," Barbara enunciated. "You brought it home. You ate with it and slept with it. The doctor said your nervous stomach would turn to ulcers eventually. A knock on the door and you jumped as if they were after *you*."

He sank to the bed, hands in his lap. "I'm shorter than the shortest member of your family."

"Cora is shorter."

"She isn't blood."

Barbara took his hand and held it.

"Marc goes to Clint when he needs adult support. Now Talbert is sending those photos to the wire services."

"You could have done that, Gary."

"But I didn't. It didn't cross my mind. Besides, I'm not so sure anymore. I called the *Tribune* today."

He heaved a sigh, peering at his bare feet.

"Well?"

"Morton Rheinhold Morgan is dead."

"Oh, that's too bad."

"Andy Riley went with UPI."

"I didn't know him, honey."

"Fellow named Feldstein is in charge of syndication and he treated me like a cub reporter—"

"When he finds out who you are, he'll cringe."

"Hell, I told him! Pulitzer—know what he said? 'Send a stamped, self-addressed envelope.' "

"Oh, baby." Barbara pulled his head to her breasts and rocked him gently.

"I'm such a failure."

"That's absurd, Gary."

"What must I seem to Marc? His uncle is macho, his mother is successful in real estate, this bastard Talbert can open doors with the wire services—"

"However he sees you," Barbara said, "it is distorted by youth and kinship. But that's the way he views every adult. That's adolescence."

"I told Talbert I was writing a book." Gary squirmed. "He caught me off guard, asking for help. I opened my mouth and the words fell out."

"I understood that. It was a knee-jerk response."

He pulled away, sitting up. "But I am going to write a book," he vowed. "I'm going to peel Borden Wilson like an onion, find the seed that made him. No poetic license, no convenient fictional trickery. It'll be truth."

"All right, Gary."

"How could such a creature evolve among civilized men?" Gary said. "What created a man capable of torture and murder—"

Barbara touched his face with her fingertips. "There," she whispered. "That expression on your face—that's what I meant. *Obsession.*"

CHAPTER FOURTEEN

E ddy leaned on Clint's desk, chin in his hand, elbow supporting his upper torso. Marc waited nervously for Uncle Clint's reaction to the photo of Charlotte Minoretti, nude on a blanket in the snow.

"Better man than I thought," Clint said, looking at the picture. "Get a girl undressed in the snow."

"Probably suffering from hypothermia," Eddy said. "Her mental faculties were impaired."

"Snow-blind, too."

Marc sat back, face flushed.

"You see the two men," Eddy said.

"I see."

"Marc and Charlotte were probably in mortal danger and never knew it."

"Not likely," Clint said.

"They were there," Eddy insisted. "Watching."

"Wouldn't you?"

"Yeah, I would, but I wouldn't be dressed like that."

"You would," Clint said, "if you were hunting."

"Is that Borden Wilson, Uncle Clint?" Marc asked.

"No."

"You think it was just two hunters who found us?"

"Looks that way."

Marc reached across the desk, took the photo and put it into a manila envelope.

"Don't let your mother see that."

"Don't worry."

"I don't understand it." Eddy sat down. "Have you ever seen Marc undressed?"

"Missed that, somehow."

Eddy held up a little finger. "Like that. How can he get a woman undressed in the snow with something like that?"

"Makes me think of the most pitiful man I ever knew," Clint said. He put a finger in the crook of an arm, fist clenched. "Like that," he said.

"Really?" Eddy sat upright.

"Trouble was, when he got aroused, he fainted. Lack of blood to the brain."

"You guys are gross." Marc stood up. "I'm going."

Clint pointed at the manila envelope. "Take that with you."

Walking down the street, Eddy thumped the envelope with one knuckle. "Suspense, intrigue, sex in a snowbank—there ought to be a way to capitalize on this."

As they passed the *Sentinel* office, Marc saw Dad with the FBI man and Daniel Talbert. Mom was on the telephone.

"Smart as we are," Eddy said softly, "we ought to figure out how. What do you think, Marc?"

"About what?"

"Forget it," Eddy said. "I'll think of something."

Gary sat at his desk, facing Daniel Talbert and Roger Beecham, the FBI agent from Denver. Barbara was on a telephone talking to a plumber.

"We're distributing these to state newspapers," Beecham said. He placed a stack of photographs on Gary's desk. "These are people reported missing in Colorado."

"How many in Gatlin Pass?"

"That's what we want to know. We're hoping they will be recognized and somebody will come forward, placing them in this vicinity."

"There were thirteen victims on videotape," Gary said. "You know there are at least thirteen."

The agent tugged at his button-down collar, easing the pressure. "So far, we've uncovered nearly fifty pounds of bones around the Wilson cabin. With dental charts and medical records of known injuries, we may match some of the bones to the people in the videotapes. But until we get Wang, there will be a lot of unanswered questions."

"Any results on that?" Gary thumbed through the photos. Talbert and Barbara traded smiles.

"They found Wilson's truck," Beecham said. "In Cheyenne. We have reason to believe Wang went to Canada."

"Was the stolen shotgun in the truck?"

"No. Armed and dangerous."

Beecham frowned at Barbara as her voice rose, angrily. "Flushed a what?"

"On the back of each photo," Beecham said, "there's a name, age, date reported missing. That informaton might jog somebody's memory."

"Disposable diaper?" Barbara hung up, speaking to nobody but herself. "Can you imagine? And they're surprised the commode is stopped up."

"I'd like to know more about Borden Wilson," Gary said. "Who were his friends in school, in the military? Where is his former wife—is her last name still Wilson? Did they have any children, she and Borden?"

"I couldn't say."

"But she's been located?" Gary persisted.

"I couldn't say."

"Could *you* say?" Gary questioned Talbert.

"She's in Los Angeles. One daughter, age twelve."

"Where did you get that information?"

"Telephone book and the L.A. city directory. There's a copy in the Denver library."

"I see," Gary said. "You sat down and went through every city directory and telephone book until you found the uncommon name 'Wilson.' "

Beecham cleared his throat softly.

"I'm not too happy with you, Beecham," Gary said.

"I'm sorry to hear that."

"It only seems fair to share with me the information you give to Talbert."

"Colter, I don't *give* Talbert anything. He digs for it. He catches a plane and flies to Connecticut or Florida, interviewing families of people reported missing. Talbert supplied several of those photographs."

"And you swap information *quid pro quo*, is that it?"

"Do you have information to trade?" Beecham smiled dryly.

"I offered to share my notes, and I will," Talbert said. "You asked about Wilson's former wife and I told you. I'll get her address and phone number for you when I return to Denver."

Barbara lifted a photo and looked up, distraught. "Terrible," she whispered. "So many. Seeing their faces makes it personal."

"What I want from you," Gary said, jabbing a finger at Beecham, "is parity. Talbert wrote an article saying Wang may not be an American citizen. Is that true?"

"I'd have to check into it."

"Born in Hong Kong, according to Talbert."

"Colter." Talbert stood up. "I got that from Immigration, not the FBI."

"Who the hell are you snowing, Talbert? Nobody goes to Immigration without a tip. Or maybe you're more thorough than I imagined—have you called his parents in Hong Kong, too?"

"The advantage of wire service is manpower," Talbert said. "We do have a man in Hong Kong and he is talking to relatives. What they find will come to me. I will compose it for the wire services."

"Beecham, when Wang is captured will you be the agent to interrogate him?"

"Possibly."

"Fine. When he's caught, will you call me?"

Beecham's eyes darted once, returned cold. "I'm not in a position to give press releases, Mr. Colter. As far as Dan is concerned, he may know about Wang before I do. The press has reporters in every American city and Canadian hamlet. It's far more likely the press will tell the world before I'm told."

"I don't see the problem," Talbert soothed. "Like you said, we're after different facets of the same diamond. If you want me to keep you informed, I'll do it."

"After it runs nationally."

"Well, Gary, yes. This is a weekly paper, isn't it?"

The FBI agent stood up, brushed off the front of his trousers. He put a hand in his jacket pocket, the thumb hanging out. "If you can help us, Colter, we'd appreciate it. Thanks for your time."

"You're looking for Wilson's friends." Talbert lowered his voice, speaking to Gary. "Hell, I'm having trouble finding his friends myself. The man was a loner."

As the FBI agent and Talbert departed, McHenry entered, announcing, "Big Rexall one-cent sale. Two for the price of one, plus a penny." He placed his advertising copy on Gary's desk. He looked at the stack of photos.

"Isn't that unbelievable?" Barbara said. "So many."

McHenry held his glasses by the stem, leaning to examine the pictures.

"How many are there, Gary?"

"Forty."

McHenry stopped looking at photographs, contemplating Beecham and Talbert getting into the agent's car, across the street. "Folks are funny about tragedy," McHenry said. "This has been the talk of the town. Like when the dam broke down at Estes Park and washed the place away. But soon enough, everybody has had his say and they'll have had enough of it."

He pulled a roll of mints from his shirt pocket, offered one to Barbara and Gary, took one for himself. He peered toward the street, his eyes magnified by his spectacles. "This morning, tourists came into my place," he said. "Used to be, I knew by the way they walked and the expression on their faces what it was they needed. Hemorrhoids don't walk like indigestion. The arms are held different for poison

ivy and insect bites. Constipation or razor blades—I pretty
well knew. But these folks didn't come to buy."
  He shifted the mint on his tongue. "Where's Borden's
cabin, they ask. Did I know him or any of them he murdered? Not a word about unguents, ointments, or salves."
  "Any change in your advertising this week, McHenry?"
  "Not mine to change, Colter. Rexall co-op."
  The pharmacist walked to the door and stood with his
back to them. "Been a good season so far. Promises to stay
that way. Be a shame to mess it up with bad publicity."

  Friday was Richmond's day to relax. He always drove
into Gatlin Pass early, treated himself to breakfast, picked
up the local newspaper and read it over coffee. It was his
day to replenish supplies, top off the Wagoneer with gasoline, and fill the jerry cans to fuel the generator.
  Because of the new girl, Colleen, last week he didn't go.
So he'd been anticipating the ritual more than usual.
  He'd sat in the Staghorn Café at a rear booth waiting for
the publisher to deliver the *Sentinel*. In the meantime, he'd
salvaged an abandoned copy of the *Denver Post* as he
received his first sip of coffee.
  Borden Wilson dead—a suicide.
  Startled, Richmond had scanned the other patrons to see
if his reaction had been noted. Only then did he catch a
piece of conversation—a tourist writer talking about criminals he'd known.
  Stupid! Trapped not by investigation, but by a twenty-
four-year-old Chinaman. Never tested by war, a braggart
and a thief. Borden had taken a thief for a partner!
  Somewhere in the area of Borden's cabin, or in bank
accounts under assumed names, thousands of dollars waited
in cash. They could afford a dozen guns, except for the
notice of heavy spending. Yet the kid stole a shotgun.
  No other word for Borden—*stupid*.
  Reading the story in the Denver newspaper, Richmond
began to feel naked, as if everyone could see his thoughts.

But when he glanced up, all ears were tuned to the tourist writer and his tales of crime.

In the midst of it all, the local newspaper was delivered. Lest he be noticed, Richmond sat there as every copy sold.

Shocked, he heard his words from the past, reported as Borden's thoughts.

. . . flowing, coagulating . . . dried on the face and hands . . . the smell of it . . . the sticky feel of it . . .

Borden had taken Richmond's battlefield descriptions, sending them home as his own. Extending his fantasy.

Well. Borden wouldn't talk now. Buried last Sunday, the *Sentinel* said. The publisher had interviewed the parents.

At any moment, Richmond expected to hear his own name, all eyes turning on him.

But, no, Borden and his companion Wang were the subjects.

Wang was a worrisome prospect. What did he know of Richmond? Or think he knew? Had Borden ever revealed the truth?

Trying to think logically, he decided it wasn't likely. Not Borden who wove tales from the experience of others. The last thing Borden would want was two associates comparing notes. A slip of the tongue and Borden would be revealed for the vicious liar he was.

But still, somehow, Wang might know. He would be desperate when they caught him. He would barter frantically to save himself, grasping for every shred of leniency he could salvage.

Before it was over, the Chinaman would dredge his memory for anything that might, somehow, turn the wrath of his captors, alleviate the revulsion of his fellowman.

After the businessmen broke away for a day of work, Richmond dared to leave. He bought a copy of the *Sentinel* from a news rack and read it cover to cover. Then, taking a back trail, he went to Borden's cabin, the sun behind him, spying on the work below through powerful binoculars. Heavy equipment had been lifted in by industrial helicopters. Men were scooping dirt, sifting it through wire mesh screens, separating natural debris in search of bone fragments.

They would examine every article in Borden's cabin. The slightest detail would be questioned as they struggled to explain the unexplainable.

Would they find evidence he'd lived there? His name on a note tucked in a book and forgotten? Some *stupid* thing Borden might have done?

Even if they knew he'd lived with Borden, there was no crime in that.

But then they would trace the identities of the bodies, calculate the time of death. If they suspected he'd ever lived with Borden, they would descend on *his* cabin.

The video cameras, TV monitors, editing equipment, the cellar with chains and pallets.

He returned to his cabin bent on destruction, certain of his jeopardy. But now, sitting on the steps in the afternoon sun, he forced himself to pause, be analytical, be wise. He pulled his shoulders forward, easing taut muscles.

This morning, the writer, Daniel Talbert, asked at large, "Did any of you gentlemen know Borden well?"

Of course not. Not even his *mother* knew Borden. *A stranger tolerated.* Nothing more.

The crime was uncovered, the culprit named, the felon dead. Why would anyone approach Richmond?

Even if they did! Everybody knew Borden.

Law by its very nature was a sluggish entity. Crime-suspect-trial. Justice done. It would be over. When they caught Wang, that should be the end of it.

Richmond stood up, walked the lip of the ledge in ebbing sunshine, then back to the steps again.

He couldn't run. That would beg for suspicion. Anybody who came here would then have the truth. No, he could not run.

He must do what he'd always done here. The same routines, seeing the same faces. No more curious nor less so, then anyone else. His best protection was anonymity, the safest course was stay. No deviations; breakfast at the

Staghorn Café once a week, buying a newspaper every Friday, chatting with the townfolk if so inclined, but no more cordial than usual.

If they asked, he'd say, "Oh, yes, Borden. I knew him about as well as everybody."

No more. No less.

He consoled himself with the truth. He was not as dumb as Borden and certainly not as careless. Until he took the new girl, he'd never violated his own territory. She'd been here ten days and not a word about her. California woman. Husband ran away.

He had to be calm, deliberate. His reaction to people would be critical. Don't get caught in a lie. Don't say too much, or too little.

He stood up, shaking out his arms, trying to cast off the tentacles of tension and dread.

In the past, he had remained alive by staying calm in moments of panic. *Remember that.* It was a matter of conditioning, a trained process whereby reality was ignored, the mental faculties producing cold logic in the face of utter madness.

Supper.

He went inside, lit a kerosene lamp and adjusted the wick to a comfortable glow. He stoked the fire and waited for the stove to heat. Cornbread. He still had a pot of beans from last week. He sliced potatoes into a skillet oiled with lard, added onions. He checked the fire, suddenly salivating with hunger.

Joyce hated the potatoes and onions. Hadn't liked beans. But if she stayed irritated, maybe she would put pressure on Colleen to cooperate.

Things had not been going smoothly. Colleen was frigid, self-conscious.

He stirred the beans, then potatoes, steam fogging his glasses. He'd reconciled himself to a long-haul project. Colleen had to be reduced to a primitive animal drive before she would be natural. The final act demanded primordial savagery. The way Colleen was now, if Richmond chose to shoot the last scene tonight, the outcome would be predictable—Joyce would triumph easily.

The lantern light cast his shadow against the cabin wall. His nerves crawled like red wigglers in a bait bucket.

He shivered. "Get off of me," he growled aloud.

Dumb, Borden. *Dumb!*

Took a thief for a partner and paid with his life.

But as he ladled food, Richmond forced himself to a realistic appraisal of the moment. He too had been dumb. Forced to take a woman from a nearby highway. Even as he did it, he'd decided it was a risk requiring instant action if it turned out she was local.

Local girl missing? They would comb these mountains with thousands of men, search every cabin.

The only way he could survive would be to seem blameless. That meant no evidence, no video equipment, no tapes—and no bodies.

If the girl had been local, he would have executed her immediately; Joyce too. Better to begin again with girls from afar—or abandon the project altogether.

He placed containers in his picnic basket, banked the fire to preserve the embers.

Actually, having to begin again had served an unexpected purpose. Colleen on videotape had an innocence about her. Demure, shy. It was awfully hard to fool the camera.

She *was* trying, give her that much. If he could break through her reticence, banish the rigidity of self-consciousness, this could become the best one yet. More real.

He raised the cellar doors and a creak of the hinge brought Joyce's screaming vulgarities.

Joyce. She had spirit.

He descended the steps taking care not to twist his back while carrying the food.

It was a wise combatant who had a contingency plan. Rationally, he should be above suspicion. There was no reason anyone should tie him to Borden's activities.

But, just in case, he'd better call his distributor and be prepared to bail out of this.

If he had to run, he'd be running forever. Better to see this through and depart in an orderly manner after all evidence was destroyed.

But if he had to . . .

He would do what he had to.

CHAPTER FIFTEEN

M onday morning, Gary supervised repairs from above the
press. Beneath the mechanical monstrosity, Eddy
and Marc struggled to lift a roller for adjustment.

"Don't drop it," Gary warned. "There'll be no paper if
you do."

"Got it, Mr. C.," Eddy called. Then to Marc, "You do
have it, don't you?"

Clint came through the front door, dropped his hat on
Gary's desk, and stood waiting.

Eddy's voice rose to a high-pitched wail. "Watch it, Marc!
That's my finger."

"Little early with the paper," Clint observed.

"Special edition," Gary said. "It's a four-fold showing
pictures of the missing people and a recap of the news."

"Win another Pulitzer," Clint suggested, "buy a press."

"It's a thousand dollars."

"Thousand? Pulitzer?"

"Nobel is the big one."

"Go for that."

As the drums began to roll, Gary listened for oddities in
rhythm.

"How many copies, Dad?"

"Twelve hundred."

The front page carried three photographs across the top
with a one-word headline: IDENTIFIED.

Below, ten photos, and inside thirty more, unidentified.

Eddy examined the finished product. "Typo, column one, page one."

"Too late, Eddy."

"Another one," Eddy advised.

"Too late!" Gary shouted.

With a shrug, Eddy joined Marc tending the press.

Gary sat at his desk and Clint pulled a chair next to him. "Little family problem," Clint said. He placed a warrant before Gary. "Bad check—Colleen."

"Colleen?" Embarrassed, Gary opened the warrant. *Fifteen-dollar check*. Court and legal fees. Amount due: $108.50.

"Clint, I'm sorry. I'll get the money."

"Not the point," Clint said. "I took care of it."

Gary looked at the endorsement, "Gypsum, Colorado? Where's that?"

"Halfway between Denver and Grand Junction. Service station."

Gary looked at the date and his heart skipped a beat. "This was the day before Borden killed himself."

"No connection to Borden," Clint said. "Couldn't be. Not enough time. He used people, then killed."

"Well, I apologize, Clint. I'll get the money from Barbara and repay you."

"Don't worry Barbara," Clint said. "When Colleen calls, mention it."

"All right, I will. Thank you."

Clint stood up, put on his hat. He gazed out at the crowded street. "Been this way several days," he noted. "Good season in the making."

Gary placed the check in his center desk drawer, locked it.

Colleen in Colorado. Why hadn't she called, come by?

"Uncle Clint," Marc asked, "could Eddy and I borrow your International Harvester Travel-All?"

"Got some things to haul," Eddy explained.

"Gas guzzler," Clint warned.

"We know. We need the space," Eddy said.

"Eats gas so fast you can't fill it if the motor's running."

"We know. That's okay."

"Hauling what?" Gary questioned.

When they hesitated, Clint guessed, "Girls. Nine of them?"

The boys grinned and Clint gave them his keys.

"The press is going, Dad," Marc said. "May we leave?"

"Yes. Thanks for your help."

As the boys departed, Clint said to Gary, "Nine girls—or one mattress."

Gary ordered coffee, watching the businessmen engrossed in his special edition.

"Helluva thing this," George Nolan said. He wore a baseball cap with TRUE VALUE HARDWARE on it. He turned to page two, scanning pictures of missing people.

"It's all anybody talks about as it is," he grumbled. "Bad for business, Colter."

"Not *my* business," the manager of the Rocky Mountain Lodge said. "I've had three reporters this week and more coming."

"You have?" Gary was surprised.

"*Newsweek, Time,* and a crime magazine."

They hadn't come by the *Sentinel.* Gary covered his dismay, putting cream in his coffee.

McHenry shook the newspaper briskly, folding it, reading with chin lifted, peering through bifocals. "Full price for half a paper," he said. "Not a subject we like, but this had to be done, I suppose. Get these folks identified and be through with it."

"Business has never been better," the proprietor of the Trout House stated. "Tourists eat, but these newspeople buy on expense accounts. They drink and they tip good."

"I'm sorry to say it," Nolan said, "but I think this bad news is going to end up hurting us. Like that movie about sharks. People quit going to ocean resorts for a time."

"Listen, Nolan," Gary reasoned, "we can't hide from this."

"The Denver papers printed these photographs yesterday,

Colter. Everybody saw that. No need to have them in our home paper."

"I disagree."

"This can be good or bad," McHenry stated. "As bad as it is, it puts Gatlin Pass on the network news. Did anybody see it last night?"

"Two networks," somebody said.

"So long as we balance the bad with the good, we're all right," McHenry suggested. "That interview with Clint was probably edited severely."

Clint? Gary choked on a swallow of coffee.

"Now if Clint had said we are a law-abiding, God-fearing community in shock, that would've been good," McHenry expounded. "But when he said he never thought Borden Wilson was unusual—that is not the image we need."

"But hell, it's true!"

"Truth has nothing to do with it." McHenry put aside the paper. "I'm talking public relations. You think Miami says it's pouring rain every day? Hell no! They say it's partly sunny. They talk about palm trees and the temperature of the ocean. They *don't* say it's the cocaine capital of America with more murders per capita than any other city."

"There's no public relations in this." Nolan slapped the paper. "Forty pictures of people who might be buried just up the canyon."

"I agree," McHenry moderated. "But I say again, this issue probably had to be printed. If anybody recognizes these unfortunate people, let's hope they come forward."

He turned to Gary, rheumy eyes magnified. "After this, I'd like to see some more about deer and elk."

"A newspaper has a responsibility to news," Gary said.

"That's what they'd say in Chicago, Colter," Nolan responded. "Your best advertisers are sitting at this table. Maybe we should vote on what we consider your responsibilities."

"I don't think I can publish a paper based on a weekly vote, Nolan."

The waitress poured coffee as she rounded the table.

"They put me on TV," she announced. "First time I ever saw myself on TV."

"How'd you look?"

"Like I weigh a ton."

The men laughed, then fell silent. "When the national press comes in here," Gary said, "they're looking for different angles to the same story. They have to compete with one another. The more sensation, the better they like it."

"They asked me if Borden ever came in for coffee," the waitress said. "I told them, 'Sure! Everybody comes here for coffee.' I told them to say the name of the place, too, but they didn't."

McHenry studied Gary soberly. "You're saying we should stop talking to outside reporters?"

"It isn't possible to bottle up the town," Gary yielded. "But you ought to know, they're going to edit anything you say and get it down to a few seconds. It may come out with a different meaning than you intended."

"Might help if you stopped contributing to it," Nolan said. "Might help if you countered with a picture of that elk you seem to like."

Gary stood up, face flushed. "It would help," he said, "if we stuck to hard news. That's what this special edition is about. Forty missing people—how many were here and when? This is journalism, Nolan, not public relations."

"You could give us more elk," Nolan said, "and leave the bad news to the Denver papers."

"I'm not going to sit around writing about elk when the town is crawling with reporters."

"That's it!" Nolan yelled. "You're playing a game, Colter. You're not thinking about this town at all. Damned newspaper people will suck tears from a weeping woman's eyes if it sells papers."

McHenry rose between them, patting the air with his hands. "Now, now, boys—"

"You can cancel my advertising, Colter."

"Nolan, now, now—"

"Cancel my subscription, too." Nolan flung a dollar on the table and walked out.

"Sit down, Colter, sit down," McHenry soothed.

"I have work to do." Gary went to the cash register, legs trembling.

"Colter," McHenry said, "I ask in a friendly way. Do you think more of this would be in the best interest of the town?"

"McHenry, truth is what I'm all about. I learned the newspaper business with that credo pounded into my skull. *Truth.* If it hurts, and sometimes it does, it's still truth."

"The *Sentinel* isn't a Chicago newspaper."

"Oh, I know that. Oh, yes, by God, do I know that!"

He threw open the door, leaving. He met Clint crossing the street. "Did you give interviews to the networks, Clint?"

"Couple."

"Mind telling me why you didn't mention it?"

"What's to tell?"

"That they're here. That you did it."

Clint fell in step with him, walking toward the *Sentinel*. "I gave you an interview," Clint said. "How can I not give them one?"

"Forget it."

"You pissed with me, Gary?"

"I'm pissed with the world."

As they entered the *Sentinel*, Cora met them with a broad smile. "We got some calls," she said. "Three people think they recognized somebody."

"Did you get their names and where to reach them?"

"I told them to call the FBI."

"Call the—" Gary turned full circle. "Cora, this is a newspaper. When you answer *that* phone"—he slammed it with the flat of a hand—"it is not real estate, it is *news*paper."

"Okay, Gary."

"From now on," he quavered, "get the name, address, telephone number—so they can be interviewed."

"All right, Gary."

Clint fell back as Gary moved toward the front door. "It's

about time everybody realized that," Gary raged. "We do more than rent cottages around here."

He slammed the door.

Screw Nolan. Screw the hardware account.

Eddy and Marc drove by in Clint's nine-passenger Travel-All. It was filled with people, and the boys didn't see Gary. He turned down a side street to get out of Cora's view.

Screw everybody!

Gary went home, found Colleen's telephone number in Los Angeles and called.

Temporarily out of order.

He rummaged through Barbara's desk until he found the name of the apartment complex. He dialed the resident manager.

"Mrs. Pfeiffer, my name is Gary Colter. Colleen Lichtenfelter is my daughter. She's one of your tenants."

"I know Colleen, Mr. Colter."

"I've been trying to call her. Apparently the phone is out of order."

"It's been disconnected."

"I see. Well. Would it be an imposition for you to contact her? Ask her to call home?"

"Mr. Colter, Colleen moved out. She said she was going home to her folks."

"She did? When was that?"

"She left here May twenty-seventh. I loaned her fifty dollars to make the trip. She said she'd send it to me when she got there."

"I'll mail you a check."

"She didn't get there, you say?"

"No ma'am. We haven't heard from her."

"Car trouble, most likely."

"Was she alone, Mrs. Pfeiffer?"

He heard a long-distance sigh. "You know her husband left her, don't you?"

"No. I didn't know that."

"Colleen deserved better, I'll say that for her. She's a

good girl off on the wrong foot, that's all. Colleen supported that boy until she lost her job and then she was out looking for work every day. No offense, Mr. Colter, but he was a worthless young man."

"No offense taken," Gary said, heavily.

"Him and some floozy going to Mexico."

He verified the dates—a week ago last Tuesday, May twenty-seventh, late evening.

He then telephoned the *Los Angeles Free Press* to double-check the facts. *Colleen dismissed, November!* Six months ago and she had never mentioned it.

He sat in the living room, feet bare, holding a warm can of Coors. A peanut butter and jelly sandwich curled on a plate. A dill pickle had lost its juice, the skin a green leather.

If he mentioned this to Barbara, she would worry herself sick. She would insist on going to L.A. even if it would serve no purpose.

The bad check—Gypsum, Colorado.

Colleen may have changed her mind, gone elsewhere to seek employment. She might have gone to friends. Might have—

He heard the door slam. *Barbara.* He could tell by her footsteps, she was angry.

"I'd like to know what's wrong with you, Gary?"

"What do you think is wrong?"

"I found Cora in tears. She said she'd never seen such an outburst."

"Maybe I ought to vent steam now and then, Barbara. How damned dumb can Cora be? Three leads and she refers them to the FBI! Does everybody think I publish a paper for my personal amusement?"

"Cora works for me, Gary. Rocky Mountain Rentals pays her salary. She answers the *Sentinel* telephone because it's there. In any case, she's not a newspaper reporter."

"Ah, so that's what we've come to. What's yours is yours, what's mine is mine. Who pays the utility bills? Who sweeps the floor?"

"Don't be ridiculous. My God, what are you eating?"

"I didn't eat it."

She examined the food. "Are you pregnant?"

"If I were," he said, "somebody else would surely report it before I could."

She moved the tray aside, sat on a hassock beside his feet.

"I lost the hardware account," Gary said. "George Nolan pitched a fit at the Staghorn Café. Wanted to poll the businessmen about my responsibility to the community."

"You'll survive that. He's been threatening to quit for a long time. He thinks handbills are better."

"Provincial bastards."

"Does that include me, too?"

"Half the damned businessmen are worried the publicity is bad for them. The others are anticipating reporters with expense accounts."

"Controversy breeds this, Gary."

"Did you know the networks carried the story last night?"

"I saw it."

"You saw it? Why didn't you tell me?"

"Gary—damn—what is this? There's the TV, turn it on now and then."

"The networks came to town and didn't come by the *Sentinel*."

"Why should they?"

"Professional courtesy, if nothing else."

He turned away from her bemused gaze, stared at the bookcases. *Daniel Talbert's* novels, autographed.

Reading his thoughts, Barbara said, "Dan is looking for you. He has an address and telephone number you wanted. Borden's former wife."

"Now that he doesn't need it."

She pulled away. "You're like a petulant child. Dan Talbert is what you always aspired to be. He's bending over backward to be friendly. Despite your rudeness! I see what's eating you."

"You do, do you."

"You haven't had to hustle for so long you've forgotten

how. And you *know* it. Dan Talbert comes to town making it look easy. You've forgotten it is not easy."

"The FBI bared a breast for him."

"He had to cultivate that. You know it takes years to develop contacts and build confidence in your sources."

"Sucking on the federal mammary."

"Yes, of course he is. That's what sources are all about."

"I'm a failure."

"You're an idiot. And shorter than anyone except Cora; don't forget that."

"Balding. Bowlegged. Bent knees. Bad back—"

"But cute. Hang on to cute."

She came into his lap, searching his face. She pushed back a few inches. "At this distance, you're a blur."

"I think you see me as I was, anyway. Not as I am."

"Gary, what can I say? Yes, I see you as you were. On the other hand, I like what I see today. Honey, I'm worn out with this. Not only are you feeling sorry for yourself, you're trying to blame somebody else for your misery. If you are unhappy, do something about it. Don't whimper, *do* something."

He nodded glumly and she kissed his forehead. "You're fighting yourself," she said. "Unless you're unhappy with me—are you?"

"No."

"I wouldn't do to you what you do to yourself. Peanut butter and pickle and beer. Would it make you feel better to know that sixty percent of the Gatlin Pass respondents think your last two issues of the *Sentinel* were more what a paper should be?"

"Where did you get that?"

"Five people called. Three thought it was better."

She took his tray and went into the kitchen. When she returned, Gary asked, casually, "Wonder how Colleen is doing?"

"Doing fine, last I heard." Barbara dialed the office, dismissed Cora for the day. When she hung up, she turned to Gary, smiling. "We are booking faster than ever before. This is going to be a great season."

The telephone. She took a reservation. Gary watched her, depressed about the paper, about Nolan and that goddamned hardware account, worrying about Colleen.

No sooner did Barbara hang up than the phone rang again. He heard her say, "You may speak to him on condition you realize he's normally sweet. Not today, but usually."

She cupped the receiver in a hand. "It's Dan Talbert."

Gary took the phone and Talbert's smooth baritone rumbled in his ear. "How would you like to take a trip, Colter?"

"Where?"

"Montreal."

"Wang?"

"Caught him stealing food in a grocery store. In a scuffle, he pulled a pistol and wounded the guard. There's not much chance we'll get to see him, but we can be there for press releases."

He glanced at Barbara. "It'll take time to get ready. I have to cash a check, pack my bags. Damn, the banks are closed."

"I bought two tickets for a flight that leaves Denver in three hours," Talbert said. "We can run on my credit cards until we get back. We'll split the bills. If I can pick you up in ten minutes, we can make it."

"I'll be ready."

He hung up and turned. Barbara was in the doorway.

"They caught Wang," Gary said. "Talbert bought two tickets for a flight to Montreal. He asked if I want to go."

"Go," she said. "Yes, please go!"

CHAPTER SIXTEEN

P eople who once took a Greyhound bus now flew instead. In the smoking section near the tail of the aircraft, Talbert sat by the aisle, giving Gary the window. The jet settled into a steady drone, the obligatory messages from pilot and stewardess completed, seat belts off, drinks being served.

"Are you married, Talbert?" Gary made conversation.

"Once wed, always so. Even if divorced."

"Children?"

"Boy in junior high, daughter younger."

The moon stepped from cloud to cloud below, racing with their flight. When the drinks arrived, Talbert mixed his bourbon with water.

"My lifestyle is tough on homebodies," he said. "I'm gone most of the year doing research. Then the intensity of writing a book, not to mention rewrites and publicity tours—my wife couldn't accept it. I've noticed you have a similar problem with Barbara."

Surprised, Gary nodded. "Does it show?"

"To nobody else, maybe. It does to me."

Across the aisle a baby fretted. A stewardess asked if they needed anything.

"Why did you ask me to come along?" Gary questioned.

"Oh, I dug up your series on the underworld," Talbert said. "I see you are capable of world-class writing. It deserved the Pulitzer. Maybe I'm curious. Why did you drop out?"

"Going to Gatlin Pass? Because Barbara wasn't happy with my work anymore."

"I was under the impression she was very happy with your work, but you brought it home."

"Is there any other way?"

Talbert swiggled his drink. "No," he said softly, "there is no other way."

"You're trying to tell me you invited me because you're curious?" Gary asked, skeptically.

"As you might suppose, I also have an ulterior motive. Besides being kindred spirits as writers, I see you can get information that isn't available to me. Your interview with Borden Wilson's parents as an example—they refused to see me."

Talbert raised his glass, signaling another order.

The stewardess brought it, pausing. "I've read all your books, Mr. Talbert. I love them."

"Bless your heart."

"My favorite was *Blood and Money*."

"Thank you."

When she withdrew, Gary said, "I thought Tommy Thompson wrote *Blood and Money*."

"He did. I say thanks to anything. I've been congratulated on writing everything but TV commercials and the Bible. I always say 'Bless your heart' and 'thank you.' "

Talbert sipped his drink, watching the rear end of the stewardess as she retrieved pillows from overhead.

"You and Clint Ferguson seem close," Talbert said.

"He's my brother-in-law, as you know."

"Hard man to talk to. I ask questions and he nods or grunts and that's it. He doesn't volunteer a thing."

"He's that way with me, too."

"You're part of the local community," Talbert said. "You know these people to the marrow of their bones. Before I can write about them, I need the essence of the characters involved."

"You're hoping I can provide that?"

"If you will, you can. I offered to share my notes—consider

this journey an extension of that. I would like to be your friend, if you'll allow it."

Talbert burped, cheeks puffed a second. "Have you decided what creates a man like Borden Wilson?"

"I'm going on the assumption insanity isn't a factor," Gary said, cautiously. "I believe Borden was sane, that Wang will be found sane. Do you agree?"

"Yes."

"I once interviewed a Nazi accused of exterminating several thousand men, women, and children," Gary related. "He was living in Chicago at the time and they were trying to deport him for trial. He finally jumped bail and ran away to Argentina. Died in bed, ultimately. The point is, he talked to me quite candidly."

"I think I mentioned something about Nazis by way of proving these killers are sane."

"Yes, you did. My own experience makes me agree. The man I interviewed had no remorse for the atrocities he'd committed. When I asked how he could have done such things, he said he'd thought a lot about it, trying to figure it out for himself."

"That sounds like regrets."

"But it wasn't," Gary said. "He claimed the Nazis created madmen without benefit of insanity. He said they'd conditioned him to do what he did. As a result, he didn't blame himself. He blamed the Nazi state."

"What did he say?"

"It could've been anybody slaughtering the Jews, he said. Anybody could be conditioned to be cruel. He grew up in a genteel home; his mother was a pianist who loved the beauty of nature; his father was a Calvinist by inclination, but as a family they were as close as any Teutonic home of the twenties and thirties. He insisted he'd been brought up in a God-fearing, good house."

Another drink.

"He said something that has haunted me ever since," Gary continued. "He said Americans are conditioning their children the same way the Nazis did."

"Not quite."

"He said Americans give their children war toys at the earliest impressionable age. He said we surround them with movies that glorify violence and exalt the act of killing other humans. He reminded me that Hitler put out propaganda saying it was right to eliminate the undesirable elements in society."

"We don't do that, Colter."

"Abortion was something the Nazis condoned."

"Free choice is what we condone, not abortion."

Gary remembered the soft-spoken old man, recounting the genocide of which he'd been a part. "He insisted that we are numbing our children to human values. The popular music with lyrics that describe masturbation, oral sex at gunpoint, the trend to glorify bondage and rape."

"Yes, well, we know such things are wrong, don't we?"

"We adults do," Gary said. "But if my son wants to see an X-rated film, he can get it. Sex magazines are sold in any drugstore that sells periodicals. Pornography depicts the use of women, or children, or other men in a way that dehumanizes them."

"Human values are learned in the home," Talbert said.

"That's true. You asked why we moved to Gatlin Pass and that's why—we still have a sense of home in Gatlin Pass."

They changed planes in Chicago, the forty-minute layover spent in a bar at O'Hare. Talbert had drunk himself sober.

"There's always been pornography and always will be," Talbert argued. "So why legislate against it?"

"So the viewer knows that society does not condone it," Gary said. "When a child sneaks to see a dirty film, he knows he had to sneak. That in itself tells the child the family would not accept it. When the child knows violence and abuse are unacceptable, he is not conditioned to accept it."

They departed for Dorval Airport in Montreal shortly after one A.M.

"You ever step out on Barbara?" Talbert questioned, bluntly.

"No. I would like to say it's maturity, but I've begun to think it's a diminishing hormonal flow."

"I suspect many an old man's air of maturity is nothing more than diminished hormonal flow." Talbert laughed.

Later, when they arrived at the hotel, Talbert used his credit card to get a cash advance. He gave Gary four hundred dollars. Then, wearily, they retired to separate rooms. As Gary was lying down, the telephone rang.

"Mr. Colter, this is Roger Beecham of the FBI. Are you in the room alone?"

"Yes."

"Could you come see me, Mr. Colter?"

"Now? It's three o'clock in the morning! How did you know I was here?"

"Something unexpected has arisen, Mr. Colter. We would like your opinion."

"I'm unshaven . . . I need a shower—"

"I'll have a car pick you up in front of the hotel in fifteen minutes, if you will come now."

"All right."

"I would appreciate it if you would discuss this with no one. Not Talbert, not anyone."

"All right."

Gary hung up. He felt disoriented. Wished he hadn't tried to match Talbert's drinking.

Hurriedly, he washed his face, changed into a fresh shirt and socks. When he stepped into the hallway, he eased his door shut.

Downstairs, at the entrance, an unmarked police car was waiting.

Roger Beecham talked as they walked rapidly, their foot-steps echoing down a tiled corridor. "We're running into difficulties," he said. "The Canadian authorities have Wang on illegal entry, unlawful weapon charges, and wounding a security guard at a grocery market. He's also accused of stealing."

"What is that compared to murder?" Gary said.

"The difficulty," Beecham said, turning left, "is the matter of extradition. Wang is not a U.S. citizen. If he is deported at all, it might be to Hong Kong. Also, there's no U.S.-Canadian extradition law covering capital crimes. If he had stolen a car we would have a better chance of getting him back."

They made another turn, the walls reverberating with the tap of their shoes.

"Did you tell Talbert where you were going?"

"No. We'd retired for the night."

The agent halted at a steel door, peered through a thick glass window. He knocked, showed his badge, and the door was opened.

The room was small, uncomfortably warm. A video camera was set up to record the proceedings in an adjoining cubicle. Wang sat at a long table, hands in his lap, head hung. He wore blue jeans and a faded blue shirt, sleeves rolled to the elbows revealing tattoos on his forearms. He was smaller than Gary expected, thin and wiry, chest concave. His hair was closely cropped, military style, his head disproportionately large for a neck so frail.

"Ready, Mr. Beecham?"

"Yes. Proceed." Then, to Gary, "We've been questioning him for twenty hours, wearing him down."

Through a mirrored glass, Gary saw an officer enter the room with Wang. His voice came through a speaker, the video camera capturing every move. Wang looked exhausted.

"Now then, Wang," the officer spoke with a slight French accent, "let us begin again. Would you care for a cigarette?"

Wang shook his head, eyes darkly circled, deep brown.

"How did you meet Borden Wilson?"

Wang took a breath, exhaled with a sigh. "He advertised for mercenaries. I forget the magazine."

"You answered the advertisement?"

"Yes."

"When did he first suggest taking prisoners?"

"He said only a particular kind of man could kill like he did in Nam."

"Go on."

"He said you had to do it without hesitation. A woman— could I kill a woman with a knife, he asked."

"Could you?"

"I said I could if I had to."

"Then he said—"

"He said, but I didn't have to. He said I could go back to San Francisco and have no blood on my hands."

The officer drew on his cigarette, listening.

"One thing led to another," Wang said softly.

"Tell me."

"He said I didn't have combat experience. I had to prove myself before anybody would hire me. He said we could make money while I trained."

"Trained to do what?"

"Kill someone."

"How would you make the money?"

"With videotapes. Borden said he'd been doing it a long time already. Who would know? Who would talk? He said we could get a hundred thousand dollars for each tape."

"Was that true?"

"I don't know."

"You never saw such amounts of money?"

"Little now and then. No hundred thousand."

The officer blew smoke away from the mirrored wall. "Wilson did the killing, you say?"

"Always."

"The Americans say otherwise."

"They're lying."

"They say they have the films." The officer pronounced it *fillums*.

"It's a lie."

"You are on camera, they say. Cutting a woman's throat. It will be difficult to deny that."

His head dropped, chin to chest, hands limp in his lap.

"But never mind," the officer said. "Tell me how the people were captured."

"We tracked them. Caught them on the trails, usually. Sometimes we'd track one and let it go."

"Why do that?"

"Up close they didn't look good. Or there were other people too nearby. Just for practice, maybe. Whatever."

"But the ones you captured—tell about them."

Gary felt perspiration gather in his hands. He wiped them against his trousers, watching the young man inhale deeply as if in need of oxygen.

"We'd try to trick them into going to the cabin," Wang said. "It was too far to carry somebody if they were fighting. Borden said it took finesse. He was good at it."

"And once they were there?"

"Get them in the cellar where the cameras were."

"Then?"

"Borden made me act out a scene. Like making a movie."

"Describe one."

"In a castle." Wang sucked air. "*A Virgin in Distress* was the title of one. Borden chained them to a wall, or the bed." He shifted uneasily.

"You're doing fine, Wang. Go on."

"They had to resist—beg—before Borden accepted it. Sometimes they fought. Or curled up and cried. He said to watch their eyes. They had to be scared to turn him on."

"The victim had to be frightened?"

"The woman."

"Your task was to frighten them?"

"Yeah. Sometimes it took a few days. See, that's why I was on camera. I was afraid Borden would kill me. He never let me out of his sight for a long time. He said I was as guilty as he was. He used trick photography, the way he edited the video. I know it looked like I killed some of them, but I never did. I swear it."

"After the killing, what did you do with the bodies?"

"You mean, Borden. He got rid of the bodies. He buried them."

"Where?"

"Anyplace the ground wasn't frozen or shale."

"What did you do with the personal effects of these people? Rings, wallets, purses, the things they wore?"

"You keep saying *me*. I didn't do that shit. Borden did it! He buried everything. Except the money, if there was some. Borden wouldn't keep anything. Earrings, bracelets—he buried all of it."

"What did he do with the tapes that were made?"

"He'd spend days editing them. Moving a piece here and there, it took hours and hours—"

"He did that, too."

"I never did it, not once."

"Having finished the editing, then what?"

"He would send me somewhere to mail them. I don't know anything but the box number and city."

"Tell me."

Wang gave a Los Angeles address.

"All this time you were a prisoner," the officer scoffed.

"I was."

"Yet you went to mail the tapes."

"Alone. I know that. I should've run. I was afraid! He knew where to find me. He said the Mafia would find me. There was no place in the world I could go that they couldn't find me. He said we were being watched all the time by this other guy who was doing the same thing."

"Oh, yes, you mentioned another man—"

"I don't know his name."

"But Wilson claimed he was a former accomplice."

"He taught Borden how to do it, Borden said."

"This other man was out in the mountains capturing people?"

"Yes."

"But you never met him?"

"Not face to face."

"Didn't know his name. Maybe Borden lied to you."

"No. Borden was scared of him like I was scared of Borden."

"But, you said earlier, you once saw him."

"Once. At a distance."

"When was that?"

"Borden and me tracked a girl and boy. Last December. It was heavy snow. They went to a place called Hidden Valley with skis. But they didn't ski. They took pictures of animals. They made it on a blanket in the snow. The boy was taking pictures of her. We were ready to move when this other guy came up behind Borden and warned him not to."

"Where were you?"

"About sixty meters away, maybe more. I was watching Borden for a signal. He wore a white ski mask. The other guy was combat marked, but no mask. He was there. I saw him. I know he was there."

"Very well. Go on."

"He told Borden the boy was the son of a newspaperman in Gatlin Pass. He said if we took him, they would tear the mountains apart looking."

Gary felt his heart pounding. Sweat trickled under his arms.

"I got the signal to withdraw, and I did. When we met at the truck, Borden said, 'That was him. Did you see him? The sonofabitch was on me and I didn't know it until he whispered in my ear. That's who watches us. He's a god-damned ghost. The most cold-blooded man you ever met. What he does makes us look like altar boys.' "

Gary sagged against a wall and Beecham grabbed his arm.

"Tell me about the procedure you followed in mailing the videotapes."

"You keep asking the same things over and over."

"Would you like a cup of coffee?"

"I'm tired. I'm tired of this."

Beecham led Gary into the hallway. They walked slowly, Gary's stomach cramping, his mouth so dry his lips stuck to his teeth.

"How much of that is true, Colter?"

"I don't know."

"Your boy met Charlotte Minoretti. That much is true."
Another killer.
Gary fought off nausea.
Colleen.
No, not possible! It was inconceivable!
"Very troubling," Beecham said. "If there's another killer
out there—we don't want this to get out, Mr. Colter. No-
body knows it but the men in those rooms, Wang, and the
other killer himself, if he exists."
"Jesus, please let it be a lie."
"We must assume otherwise."
"I want to call my wife."
The agent's grip tightened on Gary's arm, almost support-
ive. "Colter, you must not tell anyone of this. If there's
another killer, we must find him before he knows he is a
suspect. You know the people in that region. Will you help
us?"
The thought of Marc, the girl, within seconds of capture
and certain, dreadful—
"Mr. Colter, will you help us?"
"Yes. Of course. How?"
"We're looking for a loner, aren't we?"
Colleen. Missing.
"We can assume he operates like Wilson and Wang," the
agent said. "He is remote, but has electricity to power the
cameras."
Colleen in Colorado, in trouble. Was that true? And if so,
did he dare tell this man? Gary imagined himself in the
kidnapper's place: California girl, traveling alone. But sup-
pose he discovered he had a local girl, with all the heat that
would generate? Wouldn't he kill her immediately, and
flee?
"Colter? Colter! Are you all right?"
"Yes."
"You look ill."
"No sleep. Look. I'll help any way I can, Beecham. I
agree, tell nobody. I'll make inquiries. I'll start right away."
"Good."

"If there is a second killer and if he suspects he's wanted, he'll escape. So don't foul me on this, Beecham. I want your word that you will not give a hint to anybody about the possibility of another killer."

"That's a promise."

Gary's abdomen ached, gastric juices rose to sear his throat. He felt breathless, his hands cold and shaking.

He was taken back to the hotel where he went upstairs and got his unpacked bag, leaving.

"Tell Mr. Talbert I returned home," Gary instructed the hotel desk clerk. "He knows where to reach me."

Had to think clearly.

Tell no one, or Colleen would be in immediate danger.

The irrational tug of sheer panic clouded his mind.

Think like the killer.

Think like Borden Wilson.

Think, and pray—but he must do it alone.

If the FBI knew about Colleen, they would cease telling Gary the bad news, withholding any information that might distress him.

Hold on, Colleen. *Please, God, let it be a lie.* There was no such man!

Hold on, baby—Daddy's coming.

CHAPTER SEVENTEEN

C olleen felt she had never known another person as well as she now knew Joyce. Trapped in perpetual darkness, forced to perform sexual acts, enduring the unendurable, they talked.

The prostitute was a curious blend of abject fatalist and incurable optimist. *Going to die,* she seemed to accept; bad luck had always been her shadow and, somehow, she deserved it. To Joyce, abuse was as common as rain—God's retribution for evil deeds done.

After describing a particularly brutal beating she'd suffered at the hands of her pimp, a man named Posey, Joyce concluded, with a mirthless chuckle, "I asked for it."

Posey was only the latest in a long line of cruel men. Joyce mentioned her first sex act with a stepbrother. Then came other relatives, men who had lived with her mother. She was born in south Georgia in a "shotgun" house. "Look through the front door and see out the back door," Joyce related.

Sitting in the cold dark, listening, Colleen conjured images of deprivation, endless "one-pot meals." Joyce had attended school only to the sixth grade. Her first new dress, "never worn by nobody but me," came in her late teens.

Colleen could imagine a "knobby-kneed" adolescent with shoes that never fit, worn without stockings. No other sibling was so fair in complexion—all the others were "dark" and Joyce endured racial prejudice within her own home.

"Mama never said which white man," Joyce confessed.

"But I suspicioned it was the man who owned our house. He come to collect the rent every Friday and we had to go out in the yard while they 'discussed' it."

The tales were not told morbidly. Rather, Joyce divulged bits and pieces of her past with an earthy humor and, always, fatalism.

She recited the names of her brothers and sisters in a musical litany that betrayed rural southern roots: "Maylene, Betty Sue, Bobby, Billy, Billy Too we called him because he was called for my mama's third man; Lou Ann, Bo, and Wasserman Positive Illegitimate—Mama said the hospital named him—my oldest sister, Jo-Belle, and me. That makes nine."

Wasserman Positive—a joke? It could have been. Joyce laughed and laughed, saying again, "Wasserman Positive Illegitimate Jones!"

To elicit intimacies, Colleen had to give some. Yet she was afraid of this volatile girl, so quick to anger, so easy to yield when Richmond gave her anything she wanted. Colleen knew she must not admit to Joyce she was from here. Her tales of family events were carefully selected, deliberately revealed, meticulously edited to avoid a place or year.

Joyce was exactly what Richmond Bell wanted. She was his prisoner physically and psychologically. With a sadistic cruelty, he manipulated her with cigarettes, beer, and food. From him all good flowed. *Cooperate or suffer.*

Colleen remembered articles she'd read about hostage situations. Joyce had succumbed to a variation of the so-called "Stockholm Syndrome" in which captives begin to identify with their captors. Joyce reviled Richmond to his face, cursing him, attacking his manhood, but if she achieved some small thing, she would later boast to Colleen, "You just got to know how to work him, honey. He's like any man—and if there's anything I do know, it's men!"

Joyce existed for the next meal. She bartered crudely for tiny advantages—batteries for her lamp, magazines of her choice, blankets, liquor, or tobacco.

Don't fall for it. Colleen had decided she must stand apart from the two of them. Use Richmond rather than be maneuvered like Joyce. Stay calm. Do the unexpected.

"What does he ask about you?" she'd questioned Joyce a day or two after capture.

"He don't give a damn about us, honey."

It was true. Except as it served his purpose. Never for "curiosity."

"Joyce, it's important that we tell him about ourselves."

"He doesn't care."

"No, he doesn't. But we have to talk to him—talk about ourselves, about our hopes and dreams."

"I hope he gets close enough to grab him, that's what I hope."

But there was no escape. Even if they caught him, injured or killed him. Richmond was right—they would perish here.

Delay. Make his job difficult without seeming to. But, how?

"Tell me what you wanted to be when you grew up," Colleen suggested.

"Rich bitch!" Joyce crowed. "Wanted me one of those cars with a TV in the back seat. I had me a john once with a car like that. Rolls-Royce Silver-something. Cost him one hundred and twenty-five thousand dollars! Leather seats that didn't stick to your bare ass. Music in the doors. A tinted glass window between us and the driver. And when you wanted a drink! Right there in a little bar. First time I ever tasted rye. I didn't like it, though."

"When you were a little girl," Colleen insisted, "what did you dream about? I mean before you ever heard of a Rolls-Royce. What did you dream?"

"About food, mostly. You remember those road signs with a Snickers candy bar—stretched out with nuts and chocolate? I dreamed about that, once."

Defeated, Colleen lapsed into silence. Minutes later, Joyce said softly, "I wanted to be a singer."

"You did?"

"Feel-good music. I wanted to sing songs like that."

"Can you sing one?"

She heard Joyce giggle, a childlike sound that suggested one hand over her mouth, shyly.

"Hey, how about it, Joyce? Let's sing a song."

"What do you know to sing?"

"How about 'Old MacDonald Had a Farm'?"

" 'Old MacDonald'! I don't know that one."

Colleen sang it like Daddy used to. With each verse she mimicked the sounds of the animal: cluck-cluck chickens, quack-quack ducks, hee-haw mule, arf-arf dog, meow kitty.

Joyce filled their cell with peals of laughter. When Colleen finished, a grand finale of sounds of creatures, Joyce clapped her hands. "That was good, girl!"

"Now you sing one."

And so she did. With a clarity and tenor that stunned Colleen, a hand-clapping hymn from some distant Sunday-school class.

When Is-rael was in E-gypt's land,
Let my people go!
Op-pressed so hard they could not stand,
Let my people go!
Go down, Moses, way down in E-gypt's land—
Tell old Pha-raoh,
Let my people go!

Astonished, Colleen listened to notes so pure, so vibrant, it was thrilling.

Joyce swung from one tempo to the next, a verbal segue, her voice a tremulous bell filling the room with

Amazing Grace, how sweet the sound,
That saved a wretch like me!
I once was lost but now am found,
Was blind but now I see.

Colleen wept softly. Such beauty in this place, this horrible dungeon. Joyce's voice was incredibly alive, exhilarating to hear.

"That was beautiful," Colleen whispered.

"You think so, really?"

"Absolutely—beautiful!"

She heard Joyce sigh. "I wanted to sing," she said softly. "Feel-good songs, that's what I wanted to sing."

Richmond adjusted the lights and studied Colleen's image on a TV monitor. He went to the door and unfastened Joyce's chain, feeding it through an iron eye beside her pallet, giving her enough length to cross over and be with Colleen.

The lights blinding, Colleen said, "I've been thinking, Richmond. You know what's wrong?"

He studied the monitor, rearranged a light.

"You start out with two naked women," Colleen said. "Visually, we have no place to go."

"What do you mean?"

"I mean," she said, "there's no mystique. The way you're directing this, there's no mystery. If you want eroticism, you have to hold something back and build into it."

"I know what I'm doing."

Colleen smiled at him through the camera—he was looking at the monitor.

"You said you wanted quality, I'm trying to help you achieve that."

He removed his glasses, wiping them with a corner of a bandana. "Okay," he said, evenly, "I'm listening."

Colleen sat forward, as if animated. "If we started out with some clothing," she said, "that creates allure. Then, as Joyce seduces me, she removes the clothes one item at a time."

"You're in a prison cell!"

"Even the clothes could be sexy," Colleen insisted. "Ragged shorts or skirt, a tattered blouse. You'd get a hint of thigh, a peek of breast—it would be more enticing."

He put on his glasses again, peered at a wall. "We'd have to start over to do that."

"Start over!" Joyce wailed. "Like hell!"

"Not necessarily," Colleen reasoned. "You could take the footage you have and use it after the disrobing. Don't you see? That way the excitement ascends. But this—going straight to two naked bodies, then sex—it just isn't doing it."

"You do your job and I'll do mine," Richmond instructed.

"Suit yourself." Colleen settled back. "I thought you had pride in this. I guess that was just talk."

He lit a cigarette, bared his teeth inhaling.

"Gimme a smoke, man," Joyce demanded.

Absently, he did so.

"What you're saying is, take the existing work and use it in the middle," Richmond clarified.

"Exactly." Colleen sat forward again. "It wouldn't take any more time, actually. It would certainly be better than what we have so far."

He spit tobacco dryly, puffed again.

"You keep telling me to relax and be natural," Colleen continued. "It has to feel right, you know. We have to build into the mood. But, bam! Here we are, two girls in a cell, supposed to learn to love one another. Women appreciate the chase—men, too, whether they know it or not."

"Ain't that the gospel," Joyce said.

"You have no dialogue," Colleen persisted. "All we have is visual communication with the viewer. Yes, we *do* have to be natural, but we also need to pull the viewer in emotionally."

"Not a bad idea, actually."

"A good idea!" Colleen was on her knees now, earnest and excited.

"I'd have to get clothes, but that's no problem."

"Ragged," Colleen said, "but with eye appeal. You understand? Scanty but sexy. Like the clothes a Hollywood director would put on two women shipwrecked on an island. They can be faded, but color compatible."

He was sitting on his high stool now.

"Okay, okay"—Colleen had pulled to the end of her tether as if caught up in the moment—"Joyce makes her overture, I reject her; Joyce comes back with a morsel of food—"

"We did that already."

"I know that! But with the disrobing we could virtually shoot the same actions again and now they carry emotional weight. Don't you see?"

"Yeah, I do."

"This could be good—I mean, really good," Colleen enthused. "But subtle things make a master director, Richmond. Attention to details. It's more than kissy-licky, as Joyce calls it."

He chuckled. So did Joyce.

"Another thing, another tiny point," Colleen said. "When I'm lying there, when I reach up and stroke Joyce with one hand, it should be more than a stroke of the hand."

"I've been telling you that."

"I know you have. And I agree. I've been thinking about it. First it should be hesitant, then firm, then one finger touching her, then as if I were ready to claw her with my passion."

"That's what I've been talking about!"

"I know." Colleen hung her head in mock shame. "But I didn't *feel* that, before. Now I think I can feel it, Richmond."

He stepped on his cigarette. "Think you got all this, Joyce?"

"Shit's shit, man; I got it by the truckload."

He turned off the brighter lights, put the video camera on the table.

"I'll be glad to help you prepare the clothes," Colleen volunteered. "Joyce and I could do that, couldn't we, Joyce?"

"Do what?"

"Create the costumes."

"Costumes? Piss on costumes. I vote for some outdoor shots!"

Colleen hugged her, laughing. "We can do it, though."

Richmond turned off the TV monitor.

"Gimme another smoke," Joyce demanded.

"No smoking when I'm not here." He halted at the door,

turned to gaze at Colleen. "I like the way you thought this through," he said. "There'll be a bonus for you."

"And Joyce," Colleen amended. "She's going to help with the costumes."

"Back on your side, Joyce." Richmond tugged on the chain, shortening her reach.

"There are a couple of other points, too," Colleen said, "but we can discuss them later."

She saw him falter, recover. "What other points?"

"Oh, little things. They can wait."

"What?" he said, sharply.

Colleen affected a sigh, then a smile. "The camera angles."

"What's wrong with the camera angles?"

"It's static, Richmond. Stationary. We're back to subtle things."

"What!"

"In a well-produced scene, even a one-shot, movement develops conflict. When the president of the United States is sitting at his desk in the Oval Office, on TV, he just sits there, but the camera is *always* moving. Very subtle, but it is moving. It pulls in tighter and tighter, then breaks away to a different angle."

"I don't have a crew here, Colleen."

"You could shoot at higher and lower levels. You could pan—that means turn the camera across a scene—"

"I know what it means."

"You could lean slowly aside while shooting. You could start up high and slowly kneel as you shoot. There are things *you* could do to bring more drama to a scene."

"Joyce." Richmond snapped, "Get on your pallet."

"Hey, I'm going. Jesus."

"The lighting ought to vary a bit," Colleen said.

"Lighting is a fixed thing," Richmond said, brusquely. "You can't capture images in low light without a blur in movement."

"But on a close shot, full face, you don't need intense light in the whole area—light the face and subdue the other lights. But that wasn't what I meant. I meant you could use shadows to enlarge the scene."

"What the hell are you talking about?"

"Bars."

"What bars?"

"It's a prison cell." Colleen gestured. "With the stripes of bars across our bodies, with the curve of our bodies as we move, that could be quite dramatic and very sensual."

"I don't have a staff to build sets and work the goddamned cameras, Colleen. I want quality, but as Joyce is so fond of saying, this is *not* Metro-Goldwyn-Mayer."

"How much time does it take to build a frame with bars? Put a light behind it and the shadows fall across us. It'd make a great effect and it's nothing to do!"

He yanked the door closed, his step quicker than usual, ascending.

"Girl, what *are* you doing?" Joyce murmured.

Colleen pulled a blanket to her, mouth dry. Shivering, she let go of her emotions slightly.

"Costumes and lights?" Joyce questioned. "What you doing?"

"Trying to draw it out, Joyce. Keep him working. It's our only chance."

"Chance for what? More weeks in this hole?"

"It's the only alternative we have."

"He's so pee-ohed we'll be eating stew every meal."

"He wants to do it right. That's his only weakness. If we're smart, we'll help him, but stall."

The lights went out and they were plunged into viscid darkness.

"I used to sew," Joyce said. "Made my little sister's clothes. I'd take old-fashioned things from the Salvation Army and make them stylish."

Colleen worked for saliva to moisten her tongue.

"I made a whole entire evening dress one time," Joyce reminisced. "That was for Betty Sue when she graduated from elementary school. Pink and red. It had those stiff underskirt things—"

"Crinolines."

"Yeah, crinolines. She said she felt like a southern lady in that dress. More like Aunt Jemima go-to-town clothes. I did it with four other dresses—a piece here, a piece there."

"Joyce, we have to seem to help him. We have to delay without seeming to do it. Don't forget how important it is."

"The bastard."

"Yes," Colleen said. "The bastard."

Richmond placed his picnic basket on the worktable and served their plates, his back to them. When he turned to face Joyce, he grinned. "Surprise," he said.

"Spaghetti?"

"I hope you enjoy it. There's plenty of sauce."

Joyce ate eagerly, tearing bread from a half loaf he'd baked.

"Plenty of parmesan cheese, girls," he said pleasantly.

Delicious. Colleen dipped the yeasty bread into sauce, chewing slowly.

As was his ritual, he sat on a stool beside the table, smoking while they ate.

"Too bad we aren't making a musical," Colleen said. "Joyce has a great voice, Richmond."

"Um."

"We were singing songs from our childhood, weren't we, Joyce?"

"I don't know the songs you know, though."

"But, oh, how she sings what she does know," Colleen said. "Joyce comes from a family of nine children. Did you sing together as a family, Joyce?"

"In church."

"Not at home?"

"Sometimes."

"We always sang at home," Colleen recalled. "Especially on holidays. Mom played the piano, Daddy doing um-pah sounds like a tuba because he couldn't carry a tune."

"Didn't have no piano," Joyce said. "We made music with our hands and mouths."

"I think you're great!" Colleen said.

"You not so bad yourself." Joyce laughed. "I like that old MacDonald. Tweets and squawks and oinks."

Richmond listened passively.

"Making music with your mouth," Joyce said. "Like you did with MacDonald and those animals."

Colleen snapped her fingers, slapped a knee, chewing and grinning at Joyce. Joyce tapped her plate with a spoon, swallowed, picking up rhythm.

"Going to lay me down, baby! By your side!"

"You girls want more spaghetti?"

"Gimme more sauce," Joyce said. She returned to her lyrics, improvising, "Going put you down, baby—by my side!"

Colleen shook her head, smiling. "I can't sing harmony to that. We ought to find something we both know."

Joyce ran through a string of titles. Colleen didn't know them.

"How about *Jingle Bells*?" Joyce teased.

"Yeah!"

Instantly, they broke into song. *Dashing through the snow . . .*

Richmond gave Joyce her plate, solemnly. He arched his eyebrows, questioning Colleen. *Want more*? She shook her head, singing along.

. . . one horse open sleigh . . . o'er the fields we go . . .

"Your food is getting cold," Richmond said evenly.

They trailed away, then laughed, and Joyce sucked pasta into her mouth. "Need a fork, not a spoon," she said, irritably.

"You can't appreciate what a voice she has," Colleen spoke to Richmond, "until you hear her sing a cappella and solo."

"A what!" Joyce shrieked.

"By yourself with no music," Colleen said. "Like that song last night—'Amazing Grace.' "

"I'll take your word for it," Richmond said, huskily. "If you're through, pass your plates. If not, please eat."

Without warning, Joyce sang. *Silent night . . . holy night
. . . all is calm . . . all is bright . . .*

For an instant, Richmond seemed startled—her voice—so
rich and her tone perfect. He stared at Joyce, then com-
pressed his lips.

. . . Round yon virgin, mother and child . . .

Colleen watched him watching Joyce. Unblinking eyes
fixed on his captive, motionless, listening.

. . . Holy infant, so tender and mild . . .

The incredible resonance of it, the tingling it brought to
Colleen's neck, the way the sounds curled within their con-
fines seemed to accent every pulsing note.

. . . Sleep in heavenly peace . . .

Richmond's shoulders sagged slightly.

. . . Sleep in heavenly peace . . .

In the still that followed, Colleen gave the mood a long
beat to deepen.

"I've never heard a finer version," she said. "It was
exquisitely beautiful."

"Aw." Joyce flapped a hand at Colleen.

"Wasn't it, Richmond?"

He took their plates. "Well," he said, "we aren't doing a
musical, are we?"

As he started to depart, Colleen struck up "O Little
Town of Bethlehem" and Joyce joined in.

Unnerved him.

Colleen sang louder. Joyce switched, suddenly, changing
to "Silver Bells" . . . then to another, even happier upbeat
song.

The lights went out.

Still they sang.

CHAPTER EIGHTEEN

With daylight, while in Chicago waiting for his next flight, Gary telephoned Clint at home and woke him. "Tell me about Tom Albright." He heard Clint yawn into the telephone.

"Family been here forever."

"Before the park became federal territory?"

"Before the territory became a state."

"How does he make a living?"

"Raises chicken for eggs. Cattle for beef and milk. Kids for hire. Where are you?"

"Chicago."

"Thought you went to Canada."

"I did. Clint, I'm thinking about writing a series on mountain men. Thought I'd run out and talk to Albright."

"He's a mountain man, all right."

"Tell me how to get to his place."

"Long distance?" Clint's yawn was protracted, ending in a groan. "Okay. Two ways."

"The shortest," Gary instructed.

"Take a helicopter—"

"By road, please."

Clint chuckled, yawned again, chuckled some more. "Eight miles up Thompson Canyon, first wooden bridge on the northwest dirt road. Know where it is?"

"I think so." Gary held the phone between his ear and shoulder, taking notes.

"Deer Mountain on your left, lake to the right."

Outside the telephone booth, he saw passengers preparing to board his flight.

"Barn; year-round stream; clothesline fifty yards long."

"Clothesline?"

"Eleven kids. Wash-wash-wash." Clint yawned again. "What time is it?"

"Nearly five-thirty."

"God. Bye."

"Clint! One more thing. Don't tell Barbara anything about Colleen."

He listened to the hum of long-distance lines. Then, "Okay."

"I'll be home this morning, but I'm going straight to Albright about my article."

"What about Wang?"

"Case closed," Gary lied. "Nothing left but mopping up."

He disconnected and ran for his plane.

During the flight to Denver, Gary composed a story aimed at one man—*if* he existed. The headline designed to put him at ease: WANG CAPTURED, CASE CLOSED. By playing down the story, he hoped the killer would be lulled into a sense of false security. They needed time to find him. Time would keep Colleen safe from harm.

He decided to print a picture of the elk, a nature story, dominating the lower half of page one.

In Denver, he rented an automobile and drove straight to Gatlin Pass. Without stopping, he passed the *Sentinel* office, taking Thompson Canyon road through thick white mist, the air cool and clean.

Gary decided that if he told anyone—Clint, Barbara, anyone!—there would be a greater chance the story would leak out and become rumor. When and if a killer discovered he had a Gatlin Pass girl, that could be the end of Colleen immediately. To find this man, he would begin with Tom Albright.

If Tom had lived here before federal intervention, he held his land for life but could never sell it. There had been a few who tried to fight the government, but none had ever won their cases. The wise ones struck an unspoken bargain, keeping their homesteads but relinquishing title in return for live-and-let-live. The park rangers chose to use men like Tom as volunteers when hikers were lost, skiers stranded, or poachers were marauding on federally protected game preserves.

There.

He pulled into a lane between two bluffs, wending away from Thompson Canyon back into rills and gullies that sheltered the homestead from tourists.

As Clint had described it, the long clothesline was strung with garments. A small boy was moving from the barn, hefting a pail one labored step at a time, putting it down every foot or so.

"Your daddy home?" Gary called.

"To dinner."

Immediately, the front porch filled with children, the boys in overalls, barefoot and curious. They lined the rail, watching him approach.

"Daddy home?" he questioned again.

"To dinner."

"Come in!" Tom Albright yelled. The children parted and Gary walked through an open, unscreened door.

"Them that ain't seated ain't eating," Albright roared. Instantly the seats around the table were occupied. The patriarch lifted a boy from his chair by the collar of his shirt and said, "Take your plate so Mr. Colter can sit down."

As Gary did, a clean plate was put before him, biscuits passed, butter in a dishpan, thick slices of ham, and a monstrous cup of coffee that sizzled in the spout as Mrs. Albright poured from a porcelain pot.

"Eat what you will," Tom said. "There's plenty."

The clatter of utensils signaled the young people returning to their meals.

"Find my shotgun?" Tom asked. He was so short his chest was at table level. The children took after their mother, big bones, taller.

"Afraid not, Tom. They caught Wang in Canada, but

they found Borden Wilson's four-wheeler a while back. The gun was gone."

"Damn 'em"

"Damn 'em!" a boy at the end of the table mimicked.

"Still," Tom said, "I wouldn't wish a man dead for a shotgun."

"Turns out there's more to it than that," Gary explained.

"I heard." Albright looked up as his wife took a chair beside him. "You know my missus?"

Gary started to rise and she commanded, "Sit. Eat. When you put your chin in this trough, it don't pay to stop until you finish. These pigs will steal your last scrap."

One of the girls giggled. A boy pushed his finger into one end of a biscuit, poured in syrup.

"Came all this way to say my gun's lost for good?" Tom questioned.

"Part of my reason," Gary said. "I thought maybe you could help me with something."

"Say your piece."

Gary told about the "articles" he planned to write, about men living in the mountains, the ones who preferred solitude to society, fending for themselves in isolation, close to nature.

"How can I help with that?" Tom pointed at a bowl of gravy and it began a relay toward him, hand to hand.

"If you could tell me who they are, how to find them?"

"Don't know but a few."

"Those few, then."

Tom ladled thick milk gravy over biscuits. "There's old man Murtry."

"Rustler," a boy noted.

"Stealing a chicken ain't rustling," Tom said.

"How old is Mr. Murtry, Tom?"

"Ninety, maybe."

"Ninety-five, maybe," Mrs. Albright suggested.

Through the rear door came the small boy with his bucket, clunking across the floor unnoticed by all but Gary. The bucket was filled with milk, but he didn't spill a drop.

'There's Randall Merriwether, living over near Hagues Peak. He don't like company much.''

One of the boys mentioned a name. Another child provided a second identification.

"Them ain't mountain men," Tom said. "Lots of people like that—men back from Asia come out here to get away from the world. But they get government checks, most of them. Don't hunt except as an excuse, don't fish but for fun, and never raised a thing but cain."

"I'm looking for men who keep to themselves—"

"Like Borden Wilson."

"Uh, yes—like Borden."

"Living alone don't make a mountain man," Albright said. "No real mountain man would've stolen nothing. Might not borrow, even."

"How about Richmond Cathedral Bell?" Mrs. Albright said. "He knows about things in the mountains, fishes for food, and hunts, too."

"Never raised nothing."

"Neither did we until we had to, Tom."

"Truth in that," Tom yielded. "You could call Bell a mountain man come lately."

"Come from mountains to mountains," Mrs. Albright said. "Smokies to here."

"Who is he?" Gary asked.

"Drives a big four-wheeler. Owns a thirty-ought-six bolt-action Smith and Wesson."

"Where does he get his money?"

"Never asked."

The child with the bucket was climbing a footstool, the burden threatening to overwhelm him.

"Where does Bell live, Tom?"

The child was on tiptoes, trying to push the pail onto a counter. Oblivious to the boy, Tom gave directions to Bell's place, eating as he talked.

The bucket was almost there—the boy down on the floor again, reaching up to shove it across the counter. The task done, he turned, grinning, and looked at his mother's back.

Without looking up, she said, "Done good, hon. Come get your dinner."

Tom was describing Bell: "Mustache shaped like the horns of a steer, hanging down, not up. Wears round metal-rim glasses, leather hat."

"I've seen him." Gary nodded. "You say his gun and vehicle are expensive?"

"More'n twenty thousand for that Grand Wagoneer," an older boy remarked.

"Paid plenty for the rifle, too," Tom said. He sighed, head down. "Wish I'd got my gun back. One of a kind."

"God give and God took," Mrs. Albright said.

"Didn't give long enough," Tom replied.

One biscuit lay on a platter. Mrs. Albright offered it to Gary and he declined.

"Help yourself, Roy," she said, and a boy speared it with a fork.

Barbara was on the telephone, laughing, as Gary entered the office. "Come now, Dan, it couldn't have been that bad."

Talbert. Gary sat at his desk, moving objects aimlessly. Cora spoke into another phone, taking reservations.

"She said that to you?" Barbara mused. "You probably deserved it."

To feign nonchalance, Gary clasped his hands behind his head, leaned back, peering out at the street. Eddy and Marc drove by in Clint's Travel-All, caught in traffic. The vehicle was full. Not just kids.

"She said you're a hack," Barbara affirmed, "and you said she's an enumerator. So, who won the argument?"

Daytime phone rates. Talbert had more money than good sense.

The Travel-All stopped at the corner, Eddy flirting with Rachel Winthrop, the college-girl cop.

"Okay, Dan," Barbara said, "thanks for calling. See you when you get here."

Barbara hung up, her gaze unwavering as she studied Gary. "That was Dan."

"I guessed."

"He called to see if everything is all right. He said you left as soon as you got there. He was worried because you fled Canada."

"I didn't flee. I flew. In an orderly withdrawal."

"He wants to know what's going on, Gary. So do I."

"Who called him a hack?" Gary questioned.

"A woman reporting for Associated Press. An argument regarding the purity of their respective professions. I think it started over use of a pay telephone. Gary, what happened up there?"

"Did I hear you say he's coming here?"

"Yes. Gary. Are you going to talk to me?"

"There's nothing to say. The story on Wang dried up. I saw what Talbert wanted and I didn't want to help him."

"What did he want?"

"My insights into local people. Essence of the characters, he called it."

"So you flew to Montreal, caught a flight back. Who drove you home?"

"I rented a car. Incidentally, I want Marc and Eddy to return it to Denver."

"Rented a car?"

"I'll pay for it, Barbara."

"That isn't the issue and you know it. What is happening here?"

"Look." He stood up, irritably. "I have a paper to get out tomorrow. I realized I was chasing rainbows. This isn't a daily, it's a weekly. It isn't state, it's local. Talbert was trying to use me. I came to my senses."

Cora was listening and Barbara thrust a paper at her. "Did you contact an electrician about the problem at the duplexes?"

"Yes. Nothing but a blown fuse."

Barbara confronted Gary again, her voice low. "Dan says you owe him nine hundred dollars."

"Nine hundred! Was that call to bill me?"

"No. In fact, I asked him. He said the round-trip plane ticket was five hundred and he let you have four hundred cash."

"Oh, yeah—all right. Barb, I need to get busy."

Outside, the Travel-All halted and Marc jumped out, entering the *Sentinel* whistling.

"Marcus," Barbara said, sharply, "what are you doing?"

"About what?"

"In that van, with Eddy."

"Oh. What did it look like we were doing, Mom?"

"If I knew that, I wouldn't be asking."

"But it looked wrong, right?" He threw an arm around her, squeezing. It was a ploy that sometimes worked and sometimes didn't. Right now, it didn't.

"Marc, I've had all the nonsense I can stand for one day. What are you boys doing?"

"We started a tour-guide service. Eddy got the idea from showing Mr. Talbert around."

"Tour guide?"

"We take them to Rush Falls, to Hidden Valley. You know, showing them the sights."

"What about insurance?" Barbara asked. "Is Clint liable? Do you have a business license? What if—"

Marc's eyes flashed. "I'm sure there's *something* wrong, Mom. Not the least of which is my earning money without cleaning cottages. Keep on looking. Make it insurmountable."

The doorbell tinkled wildly as he slammed out. Marc glanced both ways, ran between cars to cross the street.

Barbara covered her eyes with a hand. Gary came up behind, put his arms around her. "Being Mama is heavy duty. But we love you for it."

He kissed her neck and Cora giggled with nervous relief.

"I'm going crazy," Barbara said softly. "I have this paranoid sense that nothing is right and I can't figure out why. Those boys are up to something."

"I'll look into it, darling."

She twisted to face him. "And you?" she said. "What are you up to?"

Outside the *Sentinel* office, tourists ambled through a cloud that gave the street a foggy ambience. Street lights and neon signs bathed the vapors with color. Car horns blared as local boys greeted one another in passing. Gary set type, composing the front page. Clint examined a proof sheet, his hat pushed back on his head. "What about Wang?"

"It's there," Gary said.

"Says they caught him."

"That's right."

"Case *closed*?"

"That's what it says, Clint."

Clint stared down at the page. "Same elk."

"Clint, how many mountain men do you know?"

"Those local."

"Randall Merriwether?"

"Know him as well as anybody. Keeps to himself."

"You know Tom Albright, of course."

"Gave you directions, remember?"

"Anybody else?"

"There's—no, he died."

"Tom mentioned men who came back from Asia."

"Well, yes. A lot of them."

"Can you name some?"

"Not mountain men."

"They're here, they're loners. They want the solitude," Gary said, carefully. "But they seem to need a bit of civilization, too."

"Like what?"

"Indoor toilets, some of them. Electricity."

Clint chewed a cigar, grunted. "Water runs, commodes flush—tourists."

Eddy and Marc entered, laughing. When the door closed, the boys stood there grinning.

"Did you return the rental car, Marc?"

"Yes, Dad."

"I guess I owe you money for gas, Eddy." Gary pulled out ten dollars.

"Don't sweat it, Mr. C."

"You followed Marc down and back—"

"On us," Eddy said.

The generosity caught Gary by surprise. "Well, thanks, fellows."

"Hey!" Marc looked at the elk. "You really like this shot, don't you, Dad?"

"New tourists every week," Gary said. "Thanks again, boys."

He watched them cross the street to the Staghorn Café. For a moment they seemed to be debating. Then, with purpose, they walked to the Trout House and entered.

"Clint, what are those boys doing with your Travel-All?"

"Hauling tourists."

"Do you worry about liability?"

"They're good drivers. Don't go far."

"Clint picked up their earlier conversation. "You mean like Borden Wilson? Paper says 'Case Closed.' Is that true or not?"

"If it's in the newspaper," Gary replied, "it must be true."

Clint gazed out at the foggy street, ghostly figures passing. "Seems that's what you want folks to think," he said. "Some will. Some won't."

After Clint left, Gary stood alone, despondent. He pushed the start button and watched the press begin a run.

Case closed.

Pray God, one man believed it.

CHAPTER NINETEEN

S itting in the Trout House, Eddy extended his long legs beneath the table, an arm hung over the back of his chair. He rolled a toothpick in his mouth, gazing at Marc.

"I said we'd do good and we have," Eddy said. "I've been right so far, haven't I?"

Marc had allowed Eddy to coerce him into something against his better judgment. They'd printed business cards at the *Sentinel* office: "*A-C* (Anderson-Colter) *SITE-SEE TOURS*."

"So okay," Eddy persisted. "We need more binoculars. It's a capital expenditure that is cost-to-income smart."

They'd started with Marc's jeep, taking tourists up the steep trail to an overlook for a view of Borden Wilson's cabin. Eddy had a spiel. He wore a tie. " . . . mountains formed by glaciers, but mostly by the upward pressure of tectonic plates deep in the earth . . ."

Breathing hard, unaccustomed to the altitude, the tourists came with eyes bright, filled with the adventure of it.

" . . . the crime so terrible, secrecy so important, Borden Wilson needed an inaccessible hideout. He required electricity to power his video equipment."

The toursts loved it. Eddy would give each customer a set of binoculars. He would introduce Marc. "One of the first people to go inside, Marc Colter. What did you discover, Marc?"

Roomful of weapons . . . survival kits . . . pornographic magazines . . .

208

As the tours continued, Eddy coached Marc. "Make your voice quiver. Let your eyes be haunted with the memory of it."

. . . a TV and videocassette player . . .

At that point, Eddy would pick up the tale. "The sheriff, Clint Ferguson, was here to ask about a stolen shotgun. With Sheriff Ferguson was his brother-in-law, Marc's father, Gary Colter, publisher of the *Gatlin Pass Sentinel*. Mr. Colter is a Pulitzer-prizewinning journalist who came to Gatlin Pass over ten years ago. Little did they know they were about to uncover one of the most gruesome acts in the annals of crime."

They could see workmen digging up the grounds below.

. . . over fifty pounds of bones uncovered so far . . .

A helicopter sat in an open field on the other side of the river, blades drooping like the wings of a spent dragonfly.

" . . . direct your attention to the two outbuildings . . ."

The drone of equipment came to their ears, the purring of mechanical kittens. Now and then they caught the whisper of the river, a clank of metal, a snatch of voices breaking through the hubbub of activity. All the while, Eddy mesmerized their audience. "A woodshed by appearance, but in fact, the scene of carnage . . ."

On those first tours, Marc had to breathe deeply, the scent of fir and other conifers helping to settle his stomach.

" . . . shocked, alarmed, Sheriff Ferguson kicked in the door, shouting, 'Sonofabitch!' Then . . . the cellar . . ."

With every presentation, Eddy added a line here, deleted one there, responding to his listeners. If they laughed, he expounded and made the addition a part of his package. If they grew restless, he moved along to gory details, holding them with a vibrancy of voice, a theatrical pause, his eyes "haunted" as if by the memory of them.

" . . . shackles embedded in thick walls . . . the smell of blood . . . the thick musty air . . ."

They did. They loved it.

Eddy always waggled his head, overwrought with emotion.

"Terrified . . . trapped . . . in the hands of men so cold-blooded it was impossible to believe . . ."

Eventually, somebody always asked Marc, "You went in the cellar?"

"Yes," he'd lie. It was what they wanted to hear.

"Despicable acts of cruelty," Eddy intoned. "Cameras recording the horror, their screams muted by walls of thick timber."

The moment of truth: "One of the victims," Eddy would say, "was Charlotte Minoretti—Marc's girlfriend."

That electrifying instant was, according to Eddy, "worth the price of the tour."

At that point, Marc was the star. A lump in his throat, abdomen taut, but less so with each telling. "I recognized Charlotte . . ."

Eddy raised the tour price to five dollars. Even then, they couldn't handle the business. They'd borrowed Uncle Clint's Travel-All, doubling their capacity. Eddy dreamed of extending to a second vehicle, training other guides.

"But they can't replace you," Eddy realized. "It's your involvement that gives it punch, Marc. Don't you agree?"

"Dad is going to kill me if he finds out."

"Your dad? Don't be ridiculous. He can appreciate initiative. He's a capitalist! How much did we make today?"

And they were doing it every day. Eddy recruited friends who worked at the largest motels, "bird dogs" who got a dollar per customer. They looked for the bored guest. Or they responded to questions about the crime itself—"There's a tour, you know."

Why had he agreed to do this? Marc stared at Eddy across the table, his friend's lips moving, urging, cajoling, but Marc wasn't listening.

Eddy had helped Marc's conscience. "This is good therapy, Marc. Anybody else would pay a psychiatrist thousands of dollars to get it out of his system. You're talking about it, purging your soul—that's good for you. Making money while you do it, too!"

There was a kind of twisted logic to that. It had become

easier in the telling. The first time, caught off guard by one of Eddy's questions, Marc had almost become ill.

Eddy embellished the facts a bit. "Literal truth is secondary to drama," he said. He spoke of tours in Mexico City, through catacombs where martyrs had been tortured and killed, a pit full of skulls. He mentioned *In Cold Blood*, Truman Capote's novel about a true murder. He talked about movies such as *The Boston Strangler*, about a villain who raped and killed women in New England.

"How are we different from them?" Eddy insisted. "We're in the right place at the right time. This is American ingenuity, Marc. Besides, *look at the money!*"

By day, in an unreal way, it made sense. In the dazzling brightness of noon, with Eddy extolling the virtues of the area, repulsed by the horror of the moment, it had an unreal reality. But at night—

Out of a sound sleep Marc would vault upright, gasping for air, sucking lungsful as if he'd been underwater. His chest ached, heart hammering, blood roaring in his ears. He would be drenched with sweat, but cold. He'd feel lost, as if in a stranger's home, unable to remember which way to the door, which way to the bathroom.

Nagged by guilt, Marc had told Eddy about Charlotte's knapsack hidden in Mom's cabins. It was a mistake.

"Wow!" Eddy reeled. "Wow, Marc! We've got the makings of something great. The photos you took, Charlotte's things—wow! This is the nucleus of a museum."

Why had he agreed? How could he have?

"Make the photos as large as possible to give the illusion of quantity," Eddy directed. "Can you blow them up to twenty-four inches wide?"

"Well, yeah—"

"Even the bad ones could be printed small just to break up the display," Eddy said. "If we could only get a few shots of the torture chamber itself. Do you think we could sneak up to Borden's cabin and get in the cellar?"

"Hell, no!"

"Okay, okay—forget that. You realize what this means? We can get ten bucks a head for sure. They'll eat it up."

And they did. They came into the laundry storage room to look at Charlotte's underwear, the pictures on the walls, Eddy's monologue hypnotizing them with the monstrosity of the crime.

Marc jolted back to the moment, Eddy's fingers snapping before his face. "Hello?" Eddy called. "Anybody in there?"

"I'm here, Eddy."

"I'm talking myself inside out and you're sitting there staring at the bones of that trout," Eddy said. "For the third time, what do you say? We need to make an executive decision—buy more binoculars."

"I say no."

"Haven't you heard me?" Eddy cried. "We're wasting precious time while people pass around the glasses. Six sets of binoculars cost five hundred dollars. If we save fifteen minutes per tour, five tours a day, we can squeeze in a sixth tour at ten bucks a head—"

"No."

Eddy flung himself backward in his chair. He bit his toothpick so hard it broke. With forced calm, Eddy questioned, "Why do you say no?"

"You saw Dad's paper. The headline says 'Case Closed.' After tomorrow, nobody is going to be interested."

"They still read about the holocaust, don't they? People go to religious shrines where some apostle had his skin ripped off a strip at a time. They run ferries to Alcatraz, don't they? Besides, your dad is wrong. The case isn't closed until Wang is electrocuted. Come on, Marc, damn! We'll make back our money in a week."

"I'll think about it."

Eddy tipped twenty percent on the grounds it was easier to tabulate. He sauntered into the street, low clouds making impenetrable fog, sounds muffled by condensation.

"I have to label the newspaper for mailing," Marc said. "You want to take the Travel-All and go on?"

Eddy got in, ran a hand across the dashboard. "Did you dust this thing?"

"Yes, Eddy. We've been riding with the windows open."

"Cleanliness is a subtle indicator of veracity," Eddy counseled. "Like holes in your underwear are indicators of deception. You can lie, lie, lie, building yourself up to a girl. But when you take off your pants, you'd better not have holes in your underwear. She'll see right through you."

He threw back his head, laughing, ending with snorted inhalations. "See right through you," Eddy repeated. "Okay, listen. You want help labeling the papers?"

"No."

"See you tomorrow, then. First tour is ten o'clock. Don't forget."

Gary awoke to Marc's screams, Barbara stumbling out of bed. "Marc," she said, grabbing a robe. "Having a nightmare."

Gary lay there in the dark, listening to the mumble of voices across the hall. Barbara lulling Marc with motherly assurances, soothing the boy back into slumber.

Gary thought of Colleen, of a potential captor.

Tourists wandered off the trails every year, lost for days or weeks, desperate to be found and actively sought by teams of experienced hunters. Some vanished forever.

The man he wanted would have elevated hiding to a profession: a woodsman acquainted with every back road and desolate canyon. If he were like Borden Wilson, such a man would be trained in camouflage, an expert at tracking.

Out there somewhere in thousands of square miles of wilderness. The enormity of the area was stunning. As sparse as the population was, there were hundreds of inhabitants back in the mountains.

Barbara returned, dropped her robe at the foot of the bed and crawled in beside him. She snuggled nearer, shivered slightly, her breath warm and moist between his shoulders.

"Is Marc all right?" Gary asked.

"I think so. He's having a lot of bad dreams, though. This horrible situation."

She pulled him closer, sighed. "You had nightmares in Chicago," Barbara said softly. "Marc's having them now. Do you remember how Colleen was, after we went to see Hitchcock's film, *The Birds*?"

Colleen was only three years old and they'd mistakenly assumed she was too young to grasp the terror a flock of birds would bring. Colleen had hated birds until her school days. She drew no joy from anything avian.

"I've never had a bad dream," Barbara said. "Not that I can recall anyway. It must be vivid, if Marc and Colleen are any example."

"Never one bad dream?" Gary marveled.

"Not a one."

"How about good dreams?"

"Oh, sure!" She tugged on his chest and giggled. "Some *very* good dreams."

"Barbara? Why didn't we go to Colleen's wedding?"

"They got married too quickly, I guess. There wasn't time for invitations. Justice of the peace thing."

"I guess so."

She breathed evenly for so long Gary thought her asleep. Then, "We didn't have your parents or mine at our wedding, either."

"They lived so far away."

"That wasn't the reason, though. We decided to get married on a Monday and we were sleeping in the same bed a week later. Remember that funny little guy who managed the motel out on Lakeshore Drive? He said we were his first newlyweds and gave us a discount on the room."

"Plus a free TV."

"And a bed that vibrated for a quarter."

They both laughed.

"Mom didn't know until we'd been married a year," Barbara said. "You were nervous for fear she wouldn't approve. Fat chance! I was expecting Colleen by then."

A long silence passed between them, broken when Barbara said, "We still haven't met Timothy."

"I know."

"Talked on the phone." Barbara yawned long and hard. "Doing to us what we did to our parents. Mom told me once, family patterns repeat themselves. I guess she was right."

"I always felt so close to Colleen," Gary said.

"And you are."

"My baby," Gary said, huskily.

"She was that. Doted on her daddy."

How had he become so busy? So absorbed with his work and the business of the newspaper?

He realized how little he knew of Colleen. His perceptions were based on her childhood. How accurate would his assessment be now?

He ached to discuss it with Barbara. It was a burden greater than one person should bear.

But like an infidelity revealed, the act would not be a kindness. Barbara would be destroyed with anguish.

There was still no proof Colleen was anywhere near here. No proof a second killer even existed! Wang would tell any lie to ingratiate himself with his jailers.

Colleen. Grown apart from them these past years. Away at college, then married, now in trouble and keeping it to herself. Gary wished he could hold her as when she was a child, curled in his lap, her head against his chest, wrapped in parental security. He would stroke her hair, tell her how beautiful she was and how much he loved her.

Were they close, really? Or had he wished it so, assumed it to be?

Was he close to Marc? Suffering bad dreams, assailed by subconscious devils—it was Barbara who went in, patted Marc's bottom, whispering him back to sleep.

When Gary assembled a memory of Colleen, it was always of the child. Only she was not a child, was she? Her lithe body had blossomed, her figure supple and full. She had Barbara's eyes—sea-green eyes that could twinkle mischievously, go dark with impending ire. Eyes that were portals to Colleen's soul—sometimes flashing, more often soft, compassionate, forgiving, and gentle.

She didn't deserve unhappiness.

He had a shocking, involuntary image of Charlotte Minoretti on video—mortally wounded, throat slashed—

"God!" Gary yelled and Barbara grabbed him in her sleep.

"It's all right, Gary. Gary? Honey, it's all right."

"I'm sorry, Barbara."

"Shhh, hush." She was still asleep. "It's all right," she whispered.

She stroked his arm, his torso and leg. "Shhh-hh," she soothed. "Go to sleep. Shhhh."

From Marc's room came a low mutter. *Dreaming again.*

Gary willed his muscles to ease, commanded tendons to yield, breathing evenly, deeply, determined to dispel his worries.

The telephone rang and Barbara reacted, automatically. "Gary, honey—phone."

He rolled over, grappled for the receiver. *Three A.M.*

"Gary," the voice said. "Clint. You awake?"

"I am now." He spoke aside to Barbara, "It's all right, baby. Go to sleep."

"Bad news," Clint advised.

His chest locked instantly, so constricted Gary couldn't speak.

"Colleen," Clint said. "They found her car."

CHAPTER TWENTY

B efore dawn, Richmond was awake, anticipating breakfast at the Staghorn Café. With any luck, the video
would be completed tonight. He'd carefully planned the
final, critical scene. Tomorrow it would be ended.

But then, the generator failed. As he served the girls their
morning meal, the light flickered, faded, going from yellow
to brown before surging bright again.

Without constant power, the video would distort.

Cursing, he'd disassembled the regulator, looking for burnt
wires, any indication that something was sticking. He changed
the oil, tightened the fan belt, pulled the starter cord. Again,
the current ebbed.

He resolved to replace every part that might be suspect,
driving to town in traffic so slow it was maddening. Tourists
clogged the roadway, gathering for the opening of the Trail
Ridge Drive day after tomorrow.

At the hardware store, the owner, George Nolan was
harried by customers. "It'll be two weeks," he said. "I'll
have to order repair kits from Chicago."

Two weeks.

Frustration exacerbated distress, muscles tightened, ten-
dons drawn, pain ascending. Richmond went to the Staghorn
Café where he had to wait for his favorite booth in the rear.
When he got it, he took a Percodan with a swallow of water.

Voices bubbled around him, chairs scraped the floor.
Dishes clattered as busboys cleared tables for waiting customers. Every seat was occupied.

217

"What'll it be?" a waitress demanded.

"Coffee."

"Mister, it's lunch hour. Want to sit at the counter?"

"And the special," he said.

She whirled, going to the kitchen.

He cleaned his spectacles with a paper napkin. He couldn't allow days to slip by like this. Every hour the job remained unfinished was an hour in peril. For two weeks they had been sifting soil at Borden's place, using infrared devices to locate hot spots created by decomposition.

Instinct impelled him to hurry.

Two weeks.

He considered buying a new generator, but then he faced the task of hauling it up to his cabin. He couldn't hire help this time, not with the girls there.

Colleen was a cunning bitch. Trying to stall. He'd delayed already to accommodate her. He saw through her tactics but relented because she was right. Costumes *had* added mystique, whetting the prurient appetite as Joyce disrobed her fellow prisoner. This morning Colleen had requested a particular shade of rouge for makeup. *Sure.* Buy women's cosmetics—*fat chance.*

One more day and he'd have been finished.

He was always good with preventive maintenance. But mechanical things seemed to fail just when needed the most. The best-tended weapon had gremlins in battle.

The waitress delivered coffee, slopping it into the saucer.

Richmond added sugar, stirring, staring out at the crowded street. A tow truck passed, followed by a Sheriff's Patrol car.

Then it struck him. The towed vehicle, a dark green Volvo—*Colleen's car.*

He watched them put the car in a fenced compound at the Sheriff's Patrol office. Sheriff Ferguson and the newspaperman, Colter, were looking at it.

Why would they bring it here? Nearly fifty miles over the closed Trail Ridge Drive—why hadn't they taken it to Granby on the western side of the national park?

He saw a locksmith kneel to work on the trunk.

What was Colter's interest, anyway?

Colleen knew him. Richmond remembered her address book. Okay. So they found the abandoned car, ran a routine check on the California tag—Colleen Lichtenfelter—and Colter learned about it somehow.

A nameless, formless warning took shape at the base of Richmond's brain—a primitive alarm he'd never dared to ignore.

The cup quivered in his hands, his chest aching as he watched them catalogue Colleen's belongings.

"We're out of the special," the waitress said. "They went to buy more pork chops. Want something else, or what?"

"I'll wait."

She splashed coffee into his cup, went to the next table.

He watched, eyes squinted, his glasses fogging as steam rose from the cup he held to his lips.

Yes. He'd wait.

Clint slammed the trunk lid, slammed it again and it shut. "Talk to me, Gary," he said.

The clutter in the Volvo suggested a quick move—a scrapbook, framed photographs, a wastebasket filled with cosmetics as if scooped hurriedly from a vanity. Clothes on hangers laid over it all. But no suitcase.

"Talk to me, Gary," Clint said again.

"I can't, Clint." They walked toward the *Sentinel* office passing unhurried tourists strolling the sidewalks.

"See the uniform," Clint said, gruffly. "See the badge and weapon? I'm a cop. Talk to me."

"I can't, goddamn it, Clint, not a word of this to Barbara, understand? Not a word to anybody!"

"She'll know the car."

"No. I didn't. She won't."

"What's going on, Gary?"

"You'll have to ask the FBI."

"FBI?" Clint grabbed Gary's arm and they halted. "Colleen in trouble? Besides the bad check?"

"Talk to the FBI, Clint. But nobody else."

"Missing," Clint said softly. "Keep it quiet. But, why—unless—"

Gary pulled free, walking into the *Sentinel* office. Dan Talbert was sitting at Barbara's desk. Eddy and Marc were there, and Cora.

"Three calls from people who think they recognized a victim," Cora announced. She extended the names and phone numbers, but Gary waved them away. "Tell them to call the FBI," he said.

"But, I thought you said—"

"I did," he snapped. "Now I'm saying call the FBI!"

"Gary," Barbara said sharply, "what's wrong with you?"

"Got something going, don't you?" Talbert grinned. "I knew it. Flew out of Montreal in the dead of night—come on, Colter, what's happening?"

"Marc," Gary commanded, "I need you to take newspapers to the motels."

"Eddy and I have a tour in half an hour, Dad."

"Take the papers first."

Talbert lifted a copy of the *Sentinel*, eyebrows arched, "Case Closed? Tell me, Colter—is this investigative reporting?"

Gary gathered an armload of newspapers, going for the door. "If anybody needs me," he said, "I'll be at the Staghorn delivering these."

Clint stepped aside, gray eyes expressionless. Behind him, Gary heard Talbert laugh. "Anybody get the feeling we've been dismissed?"

Gary filled vending machines on the street. As he did so, he saw Clint return to the Sheriff's Patrol office. Talbert ambled across the street, pausing to chat with people, then went into the Staghorn Café.

Sick at heart, Gary headed that way. He didn't dare deviate from his usual routine.

As he entered the crowded café, the local businessmen were taking a seat for afternoon coffee. In the rear, wearing a leather hat, a cup poised as if to drink, Gary recognized Richmond Bell.

Richmond sat in his booth, against a wall facing the room. He saw the writer Talbert enter, then turn to peer back at Colter, across the street servicing his paper racks. Talbert took a seat with the locals at a central round table. Colter arrived, put his latest edition beside the cash register, and several businessmen went to get a copy.

"Bring me a paper," Richmond told the waitress. She did so and he spread it on the table. The front page seemed back to normal: an article about marauding bears around campsites last season; a story concerning the Deer Creek elk habitat improvement project.

Two columns, page one: "WANG CAPTURED." Subheading: "Case Closed."

Colter joined the other businessmen. Daniel Talbert held their attention, talking about a spate of murders for video in California—*babies and children*.

Late customers kept the waitresses busy. Richmond didn't mind—he was in no hurry. He looked at the newspaper as if reading. *Wang refuses to cooperate*.

Was it over? The culprits dead or in jail—was it over? Nothing in the story suggested otherwise.

With peripheral vision he caught Colter looking his way.

"The chops are here," the waitress said. "Still want the special?"

"Yes."

The swinging double doors thumped, shaking his seat.

"Guess you'll be leaving town now?" somebody asked Talbert.

"Looks that way."

"You ain't going to make us famous?"

"There're better things than infamy," McHenry stated. "Best let this mess fade away and forget it."

"Not likely," George Nolan rejoined. "Not with those boys running folks out to view the remains."

"What does that mean, Nolan?" Colter asked.

"If you don't know, I'm not saying."

"Now, now, boys," McHenry soothed.

"Maybe we'd make a good short story, or a TV movie," somebody prodded Talbert.

"Some stories just don't jell, boys." Talbert raised a hand, summoning a waitress. "How can I write a book about a murderer who is dead on page one?"

"Write about Wang."

"The force behind this crime wouldn't be Wang. He went along for the thrill or the money or whatever, but he was not the mastermind. Borden Wilson is the real story. We know he's dead, so that ends the book before it begins."

"Sure thought we'd be famous for a while there," the owner of the Rocky Mountain Lodge said.

"No way to change your mind?" somebody asked Talbert.

"Oh, sure." Talbert slapped Colter on the back, shook him playfully. "If you can dig up another killer, I'll be right back."

Richmond listened to the laughter, chairs rasping as men started to rise and go back to work.

McHenry was shuffling his newspaper, putting it together again. George Nolan rose, hoisted his britches, letting them settle on angular hipbones, waiting his turn at the cash register. Talbert was shaking Colter's shoulder, joking about another killer, the men laughing.

Colter didn't laugh.

He seemed to jolt, as if Talbert had touched a nerve.

He turned and shot a glance at Richmond.

Their eyes met.

He knew.

Richmond sipped coffee, hands so steady he felt like a gambler rolling for his last dollar, the dice dancing on felt— and before they settle he knows in his bones he is a loser.

"I'd like to take you and Barbara to the Trout House for a farewell dinner," Talbert was offering.

But Colter wasn't listening. His head down, seemingly preoccupied, he was connected to Richmond by some invisible thread, an imaginary umbilical between their brains, each feeding on the other.

He wasn't positive, not yet, but Colter's inadvertent response was as telling as any of his newspaper headlines. It was in his eyes, looking to see if Richmond heard or reacted. It was in his stance, shoulders slightly rounded, avoiding Richmond as if to refute what he'd already revealed.

Oh, yes, he knew there was another one out there.

But, as surely as Richmond drank coffee, hiding a faint smile behind his cup, Colter didn't know who.

Outside the Staghorn Café, Gary turned toward the end of the block to a pedestrian crossing. Talbert stayed beside him.

"I know you're holding out on me," Talbert said. "But I have decided whatever it is it isn't important enough to bear a grudge."

Gary could still feel the tingle of electricity that had passed between Richmond Bell and him a moment ago. The man's eyes, behind round spectacles, staring as if not seeing. But he saw, all right. As if Gary had been naked in a room of cloaked souls, Richmond Bell saw.

"I kept asking myself," Talbert said as he followed across the street, "why would you have bolted from Montreal without talking to me? You interviewed Wang, didn't you, Colter?"

"No."

"Saw him, anyway."

"Talbert, it's of no consequence."

"That bastard, Beecham—he was working us against one another. I knew it!"

They reached the *Sentinel* office door. Across the street, Bell was unlocking his Wagoneer. *Didn't miss a thing.*

"He wanted to divide us and he accomplished it. Am I right, Colter?"

"The story is dead, and we seem to agree."

"You fell for it, Gary, m'man." Talbert grinned. "When a government type pulls you aside for a briefing, look out!

They're always trading something for something even when you can't spot it. Beecham wanted you to head for home. He knew I couldn't be at Sessions of the People Court and cover the prison transfer at the same time."

Eddy and Marc drove by in the Travel-All filled with passengers.

"I have to go, Talbert."

"No hard feelings, Colter." Talbert shook his hand. "We'll get together for dinner at the Trout House tonight, what do you say?"

"Yes. Fine."

"I'll set it up with your lovely wife."

Gary hurried to his car. Bell was driving away west. The Travel-All followed the Trail Ridge Drive.

Colter's kid and the Anderson boy running folks out to view the remains.

Gary circled the block, now following. He saw the Wagoneer leave the main road, going north. The Travel-All continued toward the national park.

Turning toward Barbara's cabins!

Gary kept the distance between them.

At the lane going up to Fawn Run, he waited a minute or two, then turned as the Travel-All had turned.

It was parked outside the storage rooms and laundry area used by tenants during their stay.

Empty.

Gary parked beside the larger vehicle, got out and looked around. *Nobody.* What were those boys—he saw a side door ajar.

He entered behind half a dozen people clustered around a table. The room was lighted, photographs on the walls.

Pictures of Borden's cabin.

"Young Marc Colter had found true love at last." Eddy's voice carried well. "His final mementos are spread before you: a shred of cloth, a worn knapsack—"

Eddy saw Gary and halted, mouth agape.

"What is this?" Gary demanded.

Marc raised downcast eyes and paled.

"What a surprise!" Eddy struggled to recover. "We have the father of this young man in our midst!"

Gary stepped through, looked at the table. Panties, sweater, toothpaste, and a razor.

"Marcus—"

"Dad—"

"Why don't you two step outside in this moment of grief," Eddy suggested. "We can see how overcome you are."

Marc burst into tears.

With thirty dollars in quarters, Richmond sat in his Wagoneer waiting for a young man to vacate the telephone booth. He had used this phone before. Set back from the paved road, in cool shade, he could see the Beaver Meadows entrance to the Rocky Mountain National Park. To the east, he had a half-mile view of cars crawling toward the Trail Ridge Drive.

When he and Borden had negotiated their deal with a distributor, they did it face to face. They had offered their first video for assessment, haggled for price, and settled on a staggered payment. "Fifty thousand for this one," the distributor had agreed, "and fifty thousand as an advance for the next one."

They had left Los Angeles with cash and a series of postal addresses already established to separate them from the underworld. Payment was mailed when a coded message had been delivered, going first to one postal address only to be forwarded to another. The second address had instructions to forward again, then again, until the package of cash arrived wherever they wanted it.

Richmond never gambled with his security. He changed box numbers and set up new forwarding instructions with every video delivered.

"Sorry to keep you waiting," the young man apologized, leaving the telephone, passing the Wagoneer.

Until now, he'd always delivered. After breaking with Borden, he negotiated a separate deal for himself, a new code, and over the telephone it was consummated. Whereas Borden had been careless, he never was.

He dialed a Los Angeles number, fed quarters into a slot until the operator was satisfied.

"This is Zed-Four-Two calling." Richmond altered his voice to a throaty growl. "Let me speak with Mr. Video."

"Say again?"

He repeated the code, "Zed-Four-Two."

"Mr. Video is not available," the male voice replied. "Can he call you back?"

Trying to locate him.

"Get him," Richmond growled.

The seconds ticked away. Flies from a nearby picnic table walked the outside of the glass booth, sampling candy smears left by the hands of a child. Exhaust fumes made the air blue, heat mounting.

"Zed?"

"Yes, Mr. Video."

"Everything all right?"

"No."

The man's voice assumed a sorrowful note. "I'm sorry to hear that, Zed. What's the problem?"

"I can't fulfill our agreement. I'm sending back your last payment."

"What payment is that?"

"You know what payment. I'll mail it in the same form I received it. I'll do it tomorrow."

"Don't do that, Zed."

"I can't finish the project," Richmond said. "You want your money, don't you?"

"I want the product. The money could be embarrassing. Incriminating."

"I'm not an amateur, Mr. Video. I'm not a thief, either. I have your money and you have no product. I'm sending back the money."

"Now, Zed"—the voice hardened slightly—"you must realize we could not accept money from an unknown source. If money were what we were after, we would have kept it. I'm

distressed to hear you have a problem, but it is your problem. If you want to withdraw from our arrangement, you
may do so after delivery of the next shipment. Until then,
you owe us the product. Not money—the product. Is that
clear?"

"Hey, man, don't muscle me. You're barking up a culvert
pipe with that approach. I could've skipped and that would
be that. I'm being honorable. I'm sending back the money
because I can't deliver."

He heard a prolonged sigh. "What is your problem, Zed?"

"Heat. Believe me, if you want to do what's safe for both
of us, you'll forget the project and let me return your
money. My welfare and yours are like one—follow me?"

"As you say, Zed, don't muscle me."

"It will be in the mail tomorrow."

A moment passed, then Video asked, "How is the weather
in Gatlin Pass?"

Richmond felt his palms go moist.

"You see, Zed," Video said amicably, "we can't make
such large investments unless we know who we're dealing
with."

He heard a riffle of papers on the far end of the line.
"Your mother," Mr. Video commented, "is she doing well
with her quail?"

"Then you know what's happened to Borden, you bastard."

"Oh, indeed. But, Zed, you aren't so foolish as your
friend. You have taken proper precautions, have you not?
We've admired your technique, your product is first rate.
We can appreciate the checks and balances you've established. It was designed to protect you but it also protects us,
doesn't it? To bypass the precautions would be a serious
breach. It would jeopardize us as well as you. This is something you can understand, isn't it?"

"I can't finish, goddamn you!"

"You must. You must, Zed."

His leg was quaking, knee banging the side of the booth.
Richmond squeezed hard, stroking toward the knee.

"You must, Zed," Mr. Video intoned. "This has been an

equitable situation. We've always done as we said we would. You've always done what you promised. It must be obvious we could have abrogated the arrangement at will."

"You're bluffing. Borden—the bastard—he didn't know everything and neither do you."

"Zed, we know."

"Yeah? Prove it."

Another sigh, as if suffering a recalcitrant child. "Very well," Mr. Video said. "Wait exactly ten minutes and call your mother."

Mama.

"This will be our final conversation," Mr. Video said.

He hung up, drenched with sweat and threw open the door of the booth for air. Flies buzzed his face. Gnats swarmed. *Mama.*

He went to the Wagoneer, checked the quartz clock in the dashboard. *Ten minutes.* Bluffing. Had to be!

A car pulled in and a man got out.

"I'm waiting for a call, pal!" Richmond yelled.

"Won't take a second."

"Hey, you—stay away from the goddamned phone!"

The man hesitated, debated, withdrew.

Eight minutes.

He could pretend it was his birthday call, a couple of days early. "Glad you had me, Mama!"

He would ask no questions, wait for her to take the lead—Mama was very perceptive, almost extrasensory in her perception of trouble.

Seven minutes.

He swabbed his forehead with the sleeve of his shirt, rolled the cuffs to his elbows. He had to defend the telephone again—the lady drove away without complaint.

Six minutes.

Gnats darted for the wax in his ears, the corners of his eyes. He hurt. God, he hurt. He rounded the Wagoneer, pawed through the glove compartment in search of aspirin. He chewed four, sucking for saliva enough to swallow them.

Four minutes.

Of all the people in his life, Mama was the one person he wanted to please. If he were in court, she would be there. As evidence mounted, she would face the world, standing by her son as a mother should, suffering as a good mother would.

Three minutes. The gnats were smothering. He stared into the haze of noxious fumes along the road.

Borden must have told them. He must have blown the whole security apparatus at some time. Dumb—God, dumb!

Men would murder for the sums they received. Their only safety was anonymity.

Two minutes.

"Whoa!" he yelled at a girl approaching the telephone. "Hey, whoa, sugar—I'm expecting a long-distance call."

"I gotta call my mother."

Richmond grabbed the receiver. "So do I, sugar. There's a phone at the lodge down the road."

He dialed Mama's number.

Busy. Jesus—busy!

The girl stood there, waiting. Richmond turned, hip searing, teeth grinding audibly. "Go away, girl."

"I gotta call my mother."

"Go to the lodge and call her." Richmond scooped several quarters into a hand, gave them to her. "Have an ice cream cone."

Slowly, she walked away, looking back as she did so.

He dialed again. West Virginia. *Chimney Rock.* He could imagine ivy growing up the fieldstone facing of the house, stones his father mortared when he moved there from Virginia. When it rained, drops of water crawled to the tip of each leaf, dripped to the next leaf, the whole wall shimmering as it transported raindrops groundward. He could remember the smell of the house, cool and clean, always uniquely home.

An operator asked for the price of three minutes. Each quarter brought a blip, Mama waiting for him to speak.

"Hiya, Mama! A little early—thanks for having me—"

"Where are you, Richmond?"

"I'm in Gatlin Pass, Mama."

"What kind of trouble this time, Richmond?"

"No trouble, Mama."

"Don't lie to me."

"I'm not lying."

"Just coincidence, I suppose."

"What, Mama?"

"A man called a minute ago. A man asking for *you*."

CHAPTER TWENTY-ONE

"C lint," Gary said, "I wanted you and Barbara here to know what these boys have been doing."

"Not my business," Clint said.

"It's your Travel-All, isn't it?"

Clint sat beside Barbara, her eyes fearful. Marc was still sniffling.

"These two lads started quite a business," Gary said sternly. "They've been rounding up visitors to take them on a tour. They've been telling us about Hidden Valley and Rush Falls. What they neglected to mention was the real destination."

Eddy jiggled his legs nervously, gazing past Gary at the Travel-All parked outside the *Sentinel* window.

"I followed them," Gary said. "To the cabins at Fawn Run, Barbara."

"Our cabins?"

"Where," Gary said, "they have appropriated the storage room as a display case. There are enlarged photographs on the walls—Borden Wilson's cabin, interior and exterior shots. They also have a knapsack and the clothing of Charlotte Minoretti spread for public view. Her toiletries, underwear—"

Barbara closed her eyes.

"Now, Mr. C.," Eddy attempted, "you're making things sound worse than they are."

"In addition," Gary continued, "Eddy has a glib little speech about Marc's lost love and his last mementos."

231

"Whoever heard of a tour without a spiel?" Eddy argued.

"I have never seen a more tasteless and disgusting disregard for a tragedy," Gary said.

"Now, wait a minute." Eddy stood up. "Hold on, Mr. Colter. Okay, so maybe we rubbed you the wrong way—"

"Hush, Eddy," Clint commanded.

Eddy sat again, muscles in his jaws corded, legs jiggling.

"They have been taking people out to a crest overlooking Borden's cabin, handing out binoculars—"

"Do I get a rebuttal?" Eddy demanded. "Even a murderer gets his moment in the courtroom."

"Eddy, shut up," Clint growled.

"I found out," Gary said, "when George Nolan made a snide comment about Marc taking people to show them the remains—"

"Dad, Mom, I'm sorry."

"Why should you be?" Eddy snapped. "Tourist attractions all over the world show the skulls of martyrs, and places where criminals were hung in a tree. We're not doing anything they wouldn't do."

"This crime isn't a century old, however," Barbara said sharply. "You had to know this was something we would not approve, Marcus."

"Yes, ma'am."

"What's so different between us and Clint?" Eddy cried. "If it weren't for criminals he'd be out of a job."

Clint extended a hand. "Keys," he said.

Eddy put them in the huge palm, twisting away, "Aw, damn."

"Eddy," Gary said, "the way you tell your parents about this is up to you."

"Why would I tell them anything? Unless you insist."

"I insist," Barbara said.

"Okay." Eddy slapped his legs, stood up. "I'll say, 'Hey, Dad, we were knocking down a bundle with the tourists and we've lost our wheels. Mr. Colter is offended. Of course, he prints stories about the murders. He goes to interview the parents of the murderer—that sells papers. He's in the business of selling papers.' It was all right for Marc to sell photographs to the wire services, showing the same damned things we show in that storage room. But, okay, because you folks are embarrassed by it, we're supposed to consider this shameful. The logic escapes me."

"Shut up, Eddy," Marc said.

"Marc," Eddy seethed, "stand up and fight! Why are you crying?"

"I cry at movies!" Marc wailed. "I cry at parades! I cry when we lose a ball game and when we win one."

"I, on the other hand, laugh," Eddy said. "But that doesn't make it funny. It also doesn't make it wrong or sad. Mr. Colter, I appeal to your intellect—"

"Eddy," Barbara warned, "this isn't working."

"Clint," Eddy reasoned, "I'll split fifty-fifty with you. We're cleaning up, I tell you."

"No."

"Aw, darn!" Eddy slapped his thighs, turned around. "Okay. I'll put on a sad face and see if I can get anybody else to share my disgrace. I'm sure somebody else will agree with you."

"Eddy, will you shut up?" Marc yelled.

"Boy, what a fizzle to end with," Eddy lamented. "All right, listen. Suppose we get rid of the girl's clothes?"

"No, Eddy."

Eddy used one finger to scratch his eyebrow, lips pursed. "I guess that's it," he said softly. "The end of the entrepreneur. End-of-preneur."

"That's all I have to say," Gary concluded. "You boys may go, so far as I'm concerned."

Together, the boys went outside, stood without speaking, then walked listlessly toward the Staghorn Café.

After a long silence, Clint said, "Remember the time we sold Granddaddy's ducks?"

Barbara laughed, painfully.

"Plucked off every feather," Clint recalled. "Sold them as fresh, ready to cook when slaughtered."

"This isn't funny, Clint," Gary said.

"Will be. Few years. I was getting an early start, that's all."

"You plucked live ducks?" Gary asked Barbara.

"It seemed so sensible at age nine."

"Everybody liked the idea," Clint said, standing, "except Granddaddy and the ASPCA."

Gary dialed the telephone, looking toward the True Value hardware store as he did so.

"True Value!"

"George, this is Gary Colter with the *Sentinel*."

"What can I do for you?"

"You know a man named Bell—wears wire-rim glasses, leather hat, drives a blue Jeep Wagoneer?"

"I know Richmond."

"What can you tell me about him?"

"Good customer. Pays cash for what he buys."

"Beyond that."

"Beyond that," Nolan said, "I don't know anything."

"I saw his Wagoneer parked outside your place earlier. Could you tell me what he wanted?"

There was a long pause. "Suppose you say why you're asking."

"I want to get to know him."

"You don't need me for that."

"Nolan, damn it, what did he buy?"

"Nothing. Wanted repair kits for an electric generator. I special-ordered it out of Chicago."

Generator. "Anything else?"

"Left a deposit."

"Thank you." Gary hung up, dialed again.

His next call was to McHenry's drugstore. Same routine.

"Buys aspirin by the thousand," McHenry reported. "Goes to the military PX for stronger analgesics."

"Such as what?"

"Wouldn't know, except that he once brought me a prescription for Percodan, said he couldn't get to a PX."

"What is Percodan?"

"Painkiller for a man who knows real pain. His pelvic area was smashed in Vietnam."

Gary hung up. He realized Barbara was listening. "Man I met," he explained.

"Something wrong with him?" Barbara asked.

"Typical mountain man. I'm planning a series on mountain men."

The telephone rang and Gary answered at his desk.

"He's short tempered," McHenry rasped. "On a bad day he can be volatile. Most people leave him be."

"Thanks, McHenry."

He hung up, staring at nothing.

"Gary," Barbara said, "mind telling me what's going on?"

"Nothing," he said. He smiled. "Nothing," he insisted.

Richmond spread parts of the generator before him on today's copy of the *Sentinel*. He was sweating profusely despite a cool breeze rising out of the valley.

He had tried to be honorable. Tried to return their money. Instead, he'd further complicated his situation. Now he had to fear the law, that meddling sonofabitch Colter, and a possible hit man lurking out there somewhere to be certain he finished the contract.

No amount of aspirin or Percodan seemed to relieve his pain. *All in the mind.* He knew that. He believed in mental conditioning, the exercise of state-of-mind to create well-being. Going into a dangerous situation, thinking positive eliminated negative results. He was convinced that successful gamblers had perfected such attitudes. They were sure they would win. And they did. For lack of a better term, they called it "luck."

Luck was no whimsy. It had to be created, nurtured, and the attitude of the winner was crucial to winning.

He was losing that. Letting his confidence slip away like grains in an hourglass signaling the end of an era. It didn't have to happen. He could—he *must* reverse the sense of impending doom. By sheer will he could achieve it.

His fingers shook as he cleaned parts of the generator in gasoline.

They had called Mama, that much was proven. No telling how long they'd known about him, who he was, where he was. His only reassurance was that they hadn't come for him before.

Of course, *before* he hadn't threatened to quit.

He held the tiny pieces at arm's length, further proof of failing sight. He blinked stinging perspiration from his eyes. If he could take apart a strange automatic rifle and reassemble it blindfolded, he could certainly do this in the bright light of day. How many booby traps had he disarmed in the dark of a thatched hut where a wily enemy had tried to second-guess his next moves?

There. The minute screw fell into place, threads meshed.

All a matter of attitude.

When he thought of his call to Mama, he altered the conversation unconsciously.

"Who is the man calling here, Richmond?"

"A bill collector, maybe."

"He didn't ask for money. Are you without money?"

"I'm all right, Mama."

Remembering, he edited it to:

"Do you need money, Richmond?"

"I'm all right, Mama."

He knew he altered reality, casting Mama in a light and mood that was not true—but why not? If he chose to think of her with ample breasts, double chin quivering with laughter, must he also remember she was mocking him?

For several years he'd been going to Gatlin Pass, having breakfast at the Staghorn Café. Why had Colter noticed him *this* day?

Why did they bring Colleen's car to Gatlin Pass?

Thinking like a loser. Letting pessimism prevail. Letting dire thoughts permeate his mind. Losers had the smell of penury. They carried themselves as if burdened. Successful men could tell at a glance if a man were born to lose.

He wished Mama were here. To cook for him, to rub his

back and legs with warm oil. To hold his head to her breast and sing him lullabies. He yearned for her cornbread and a pot of black-eyed peas simmering around a ham hock.

"Your father was a real man, Richmond," Mama often said. She would sit in her rocking chair, Father's tinted photograph clasped to her bosom, rocking, singing a lullaby.

"He died for you, Richmond—you must never forget that. He told you not to swim at the mill pond, didn't he?"

"Yes, Mama."

"He told you and told you."

"Yes, Mama."

"But you went swimming anyway."

"Oh, Mama, yes—"

"Your father couldn't swim, but he tried to, didn't he?"

He could remember the creak of rockers on pegged floorboards, a crackle of flames in the fireplace, a blanket of snow trapping the widow and her surviving son.

He always wished Mama would rock him that way.

When she served his meals, the food came with a sigh of remembrance. "This was your father's favorite dish."

She incubated quail because Father had done so, seeding his fields with bird, renting the land to hunters.

He remembered those mornings, the dogs sniffing, hunters with guns at the ready. Between the pines a misty haze gave shelter to the frozen bobwhites, the covey fixed as if turned to stone, the pointer with a foot raised, tail out, nose quivering inches from the quarry.

For an instant, only an instant, the weight of silence was suffocating, the pastoral scene so tranquil it brought an ache to his chest, knowing what came next.

The concussion buffeted him, the thunderous roar of gunfire, the sudden whirring of wings, the flutter of feathers, the bounding dogs, the yells of triumph.

He couldn't eat quail. Not because of an occasional shot found in a small baked breast, but because he could feel the ghost of the bird, its tiny back ramrod straight, motionless, inches from the nose of the hunting dog, seconds away from slaughter.

He'd hunted. Mama insisted on it. Somebody had to guide the men to the best fields. It was their livelihood. It was what Father would have done, had he been able to swim.

It was the least Richmond could do.

After all, Father had died for him. Mama's life of suffering was the result. They had to eat.

He had to hunt.

It was still daylight when Richmond delivered supper to the girls. He was in no mood for nonsense and Joyce began with a threat.

"Better be something good to eat this time, gimp," she railed. "Else I ain't working."

"The generator is down," Richmond said. "No work tonight."

"Richmond, we're cold," Colleen complained. "We need more blankets."

He forked a steak on a plate and extended it to Joyce.

"Now that," she said, "is more like it! I like it rare."

"It's rare." Richmond popped the top of a can of beer and gave it to her.

"May I have a beer?" Colleen asked. He gave her one.

"We have to wait on repairs before we can conclude our production," Richmond said. "The delay is unavoidable."

"Did you buy the cosmetics?" Colleen questioned.

"No cosmetics."

"We need them, Richmond."

"No cosmetics," he said, too sharply. He gave Colleen her plate. Both women had steak knives and forks. He watched them warily.

"You mama raised a good cook," Joyce said. "When you got a mind to be."

"I talked to my mama today," Richmond offered.

The unexpected admission brought disbelieving stares.

"She lives in Chimney Rock, West Virginia. You know where that is?"

"I was born in Georgia," Joyce said.

"Mama raises quail."

"Quail? What she do with quail? You know what a quail is, Colleen?"

"Yes."

"Little bitty bird," Joyce said.

"Their eggs are about this size." Richmond showed the end of his thumb. "People make necklaces with them. They poke holes in both ends and blow out the yolk and albumin. They lacquer the shells to give them strength and make jewelry."

Incredulously, they listened.

"Tiny little empty shells," Richmond said.

"Is that what your mama does?" Joyce asked. "Make necklaces?"

"No, she hatches quail. We would raise them to a certain point and release them in the fields. Now, with me gone, Mama sells the quail to other people who do the same thing."

"Why they do that?" Joyce scoffed.

"Hunters."

"Raise them—to hunt?"

"To hunt, yes. Raise them to hunt. But they have a good life for a short while. All they can eat and drink. No parasites, no predators. They get clean water with antibiotics to keep them healthy."

He opened another beer, offered it. Joyce took the can, drank gustily.

"When I was a child—" Richmond paused to burp. "I thought it was cruel. Biddies so sure life was perfect. Then one day people shooting at them."

He saw goosebumps erupt on Colleen's shoulders, prickling the flesh as they ran down her arms. *Interesting.* Impossible to film.

"One day I told Mama I thought we were cruel."

"Bet she whomped you," Joyce said.

"No, never did that. I can't remember a single spanking. My father didn't believe in it, Mama said. When I needed a spanking, she'd say to thank him when I didn't get it."

"Where was he?"

"Drowned. I was a small boy."

"So what your mama say about them quails?"

"She said, farmers pampered pigs. They raised cattle with tenderness. They took care of chickens."

He gazed away, remembering.

"She told me people once did the same thing with people. A tribe of people called Aztecs."

"Yeah!" Joyce brightened. "Wynona's people came from Aztecs."

"The Aztecs selected the most perfect man in their nation," Richmond continued. "He was the strongest and most handsome. Virile. For a whole year anything he wanted was his. He was a celebrity. He had the best foods, the most beautiful girls. The Aztecs treated him like a god."

He downed his beer, opened another one. Joyce wiggled her fingers and he gave her one.

"At the end of the year," Richmond said, "the Aztecs went to a particular place to worship the sun god. There were feasts, music, dancing—it was a celebration like Easter, Christmas, and New Year's rolled into one."

"Wynona told me about Aztecs," Joyce interjected.

"It was a complex and fabulous culture," Richmond said. Another burp. "Then, that fine young man was taken to the top of a high pyramid. They put him on his back and cut out his heart."

Aghast, Joyce shrank.

"Been me," she said, "I'd live like a queen eleven months, run like hell forever."

"It was an honor!" Richmond countered. "Of course he didn't run. The whole point was his death, don't you see? Like the quail—living to be hunted and killed. The young man had to be sacrificed."

"You're going to kill us, aren't you?" Colleen said.

"No, no, you misunderstand." Richmond chuckled deliberately. "I told you about my mama and the Aztecs to make the opposite point. You haven't been treated like royalty, have you?"

"Sure shit not," Joyce griped.

"We've reversed the procedure, see?"

"Bad times bring good?" Colleen suggested skeptically.

He closed his eyes in a double wink, nodding.

Joyce contemplated her abdomen. "Know what I hate most, gimpy?"

"What?"

"Taking a pee with you sitting there."

"I could step outside."

"Wish you would."

He climbed the steps, pushed open the slanted door overhead. The evening air felt cool. *Blankets*. He crossed the yard leisurely. Painkillers and beer had worked their wonders. He felt better.

One thing Mama taught him: tranquility was essential to health. Frightened quail didn't feed. A sudden scare could make a cow go dry. Worry etched the face as well as the brain.

Tranquil.

He had to keep the girls tranquil until the generator was functional. Pacify them, reassure them, promise them anything—but above all, give them hope. Without it, the final scene would show two worn players unlike the same girls in the first.

He removed blankets from a chest he'd built against a wall. They smelled of cedar chips.

At the Staghorn Café he had reached a critical decision. Colter alone, in the crowd of men, harbored any suspicion— born of what, Richmond could not guess. Born of nothing, maybe. Intuition, possibly. A sixth sense that was certainly a requirement in the news trade. No fact, no reason. A niggling doubt was all it took—that was what Colter had.

In Nam Richmond always studied a sentry as long as possible before striking. Did the man pivot on his right foot, or left? Did he hold a cigarette with one hand, or the other? Making his rounds as sentry, there was always one place where a guard halted to rest a moment, before straightening his back to continue pacing. *That* was not the place to strike. At his resting place, the guard was especially wary, not for an assassin, but for an officer who might catch him loitering.

The psychology of the victim, the human element.

Colter had a bad back. Less so than Richmond, but the newspaperman carried his weight carefully. He sat with his back against a chair, spine straight. He lifted a coffee cup with his right hand, passed salt to a diner with his left— *ambidextrous.*

Always alert. Even if he seemed engrossed with one man speaking, Colter saw people who bought his newspaper. When patrons entered or departed, Colter never failed to notice who.

Never kill without reason. Never without reasonable assurance the objective was worth the risk. And, if it had to be done at all, it must happen in a way that would not connect to Borden Wilson.

If Colter were found shot in his office, who would think of Borden lying dead in his own grave? Wang was in a Canadian prison.

A thief, prowler, a burglar interrupted.

It would seem to be one of those murders that happen every twenty-eight minutes in America. Motive unclear. Suspects: *none.*

He returned to the cellar unhurriedly. A half-moon darted behind clouds rushing west on high winds unfelt down here. Shadows moved across the valley like huge dust motes creeping beneath a bed before the whisk of a broom.

Better yet—if Colter were caught out somewhere alone, the body found where it fell—a hunter's mishap, a hitchhiker from parts afar . . .

"Hey!" Joyce yelled when she heard him. "Bring more beer!"

He placed the blankets at the top of the steps. Lights from their battery-powered lamps cast a yellow rectangle against the wall of the boulder above them.

He got two six-packs from the hillside cooler. As frigid as if iced. City-dwellers would never have believed it possible, using only the altitude, a seep of moisture, and the natural underground temperature as refrigeration.

He heard the *whoo* of an owl, a distant murmur of trees, a lone cricket playing for his fellows now stilled by the chill.

Blankets and beer in hand, he went down the steps one at a time.

Joyce was leaning against a wall, her arms clasped around her knees for warmth. Colleen was curled in a fetal position, sleeping. Richmond covered her with a blanket.

"The kid can't hold her beer," Joyce said. "She ain't no pro, like you and me."

He popped two cans, sat down to join her.

"You mean to waste us," Joyce stated.

For a long time they drank, gazing at one another knowingly. Finally, Joyce blew air into her cheeks. "No way to talk you out of it, is there?"

"Out of what?"

"You know what."

Richmond lit two cigarettes, extending one to her. Joyce inhaled with mouth wide open. "God, that is good," she whispered.

Richmond massaged his tired eyes with thumb and index finger.

"Nothing I could say, nothing I could do," Joyce commented. "My ass is past anyway I cut it. I'm right, ain't I?"

"Don't fret, Joyce."

She snickered mirthlessly. "Don't fret," she murmured. "Jesus, he is cool—don't fret."

"Do you believe in fate?" Richmond inquired.

"Who is she?"

"Fate is the shadow that hovers over all. Fate steals fortunes and casts woe among men of good will. Fate—"

"Fate." Joyce snapped her fingers. "Met that bitch in Vegas once. Yeah, I know Fate. Mean bitch."

"Can be."

"Mister, I never knew otherwise. I've been working the hard side so long I don't think soft is, anymore. If the pimps don't get it, the johns do. If johns don't get it, the cops do. Somebody always gets it except me."

"I know that song, verse and chorus."

"Do you really?" Joyce jeered. "See who wears the chains, don't you?"

Richmond smoked, drinking beer, long lapses between them. Periodically, Joyce mumbled about some injustice from the past, her eyes bleary, tongue thick.

Colleen turned on her back, throwing off the blanket. Richmond spread it again. Her arm fell away, fingers curled.

"Is it going to hurt?" Joyce rasped.

"What?"

"Sonofabitch. You know what."

"No."

She clamped her teeth, staring at Colleen. "First time near true," she said.

Richmond dozed, jerked upright. But Joyce hadn't noticed, her head wobbling as malt softened the muscles of her neck.

"Fate," she muttered. "Mean bitch. Always has been."

CHAPTER TWENTY-TWO

"**O**ne big happy family." Talbert smiled. "You boys have all the cola you want."

Gary watched him pour wine, pass a glass to Barbara, another to Clint.

"I'm down to one customer again," Eddy said to Marc. "Mr. Talbert."

Daniel Talbert laughed. "Went out to see Tom Albright this afternoon," he said to Gary. "Interesting mountain man."

"Why Albright?"

"It was his stolen shotgun that unraveled this whole thing, wasn't it? Besides, he said he talked to you, too."

Damn.

"He sent me to see a fellow named Randall Merriwether," Talbert continued. "Did you interview him?"

One of the mountain men Albright had named. Gary tasted the wine.

"Merriwether near Hagues Peak?" Clint asked.

"That's the man. Lives alone, likes it."

"Reputation is," Clint said, "he isn't friendly."

"No, he wasn't," Talbert confirmed. "Told me to get off his land and cradled a shotgun in his arms while he did it."

Clint chuckled softly.

"I was there," Eddy said. "Merriwether is definitely antisocial."

"What made you go see them?" Gary questioned. "You've said there's no book in all this."

"For the same reason you did, I suspect." Talbert's eyes twinkled cheerfully. "You began with the thesis: solitary, isolated, the psychological profile of Borden Wilson—right?"

Damn—damn!

Talbert laughed heartily. "I knew it," he said. "You get an investigative reporter started and he's like a pup with a rag—can't let go until he shakes it to pieces."

"Four dollars an hour is a long way from what we were making," Eddy confided in Marc. "But we're using Mr. Talbert's rental car and I just point the way to the sites."

"Like what?" Marc asked.

"Fellow that drives the blue Wagoneer—his place."

"Bell?" Gary asked. "Why Bell?"

"Same reason as the other fellow, Colter," Talbert mused. "Please don't insult my intelligence."

"Sat on the side of a mountain six hours with binoculars," Eddy said. "Watching."

"Watching what?" Gary demanded.

"Watching Bell try to fix a generator. Boring."

"Now, Eddy." Talbert was enjoying this. "Don't give away all my trade secrets. Mr. Colter has chosen to take an adversary position with me and I am not obligated to share what I learn."

"He took the same position with me," Eddy noted soberly.

"Folks might not appreciate you spying on them," Clint suggested.

"I won't continue to do so," Talbert said. "It was just a game I was playing with Colter. Following in his footsteps, so to speak. More wine, Sheriff?"

Clint accepted another glass.

"No, for me it's over," Talbert said. "This dinner is my farewell to you all. As of tomorrow night, I'm leaving for Atascadero, California, to pursue a similar story a friend told me about."

"It must cost a fortune to go this far with a book idea and drop it," Barbara said.

"Your husband knows as well as I," Talbert replied. "We

dig a ton of research material to gather a couple of ounces we can use. Right, Colter?"

"Yes."

A man of about thirty stopped at Talbert's side, bending to speak, but clearly heard by all. "Mr. Talbert?"

"Yes?"

"I've read everything you've written, Mr. Talbert."

"Bless your heart."

"My friend at the table over there," the young man said, pointing to an older man, watching, unsmiling. "He's very shy. He's one of your biggest fans, too. He's from Los Angeles originally, but we both live in Las Vegas now. It's our first trip to the mountains."

Talbert's eyes moved from the man afar to points in the room, here, there. "We're having dinner," he said, almost harshly.

"If you could spare a minute. It won't take long to get an autograph. He wants to shake your hand."

"Perhaps later."

Gary saw color rise in the man's face. He bent near, murmured in Talbert's ear.

Talbert turned to look at the man again; still unsmiling, still watching.

"So that's who he is," Talbert said softly. He returned attention to his guests. "I've been corresponding with that man for years, since my first book, but we've never met. I really will have to excuse myself."

"Certainly!" Barbara said. "How nice."

Talbert followed the younger man back to the far table. Gary saw the stranger nod at a chair. *Didn't look cordial.*

"How many times did you go to Bell's cabin, Eddy?" Gary asked.

"Couple times."

"I don't think Mr. Bell is a man to play with," Gary spoke as he watched Talbert and his companions.

"Love that Wagoneer," Eddy said. "It's loaded. Air conditioning, citizens band *and* shortwave radios. You've seen it, haven't you, Marc?"

"It's a beauty, all right."

"I want you boys to stay away from Bell," Gary mandated.

"Mr. Colter," Eddy said, coldly, "I gave up a business that would've paid for college, my first deluxe automobile, and a glorious experience with several as yet unidentified beautiful women. But taking Mr. Talbert around for four bucks an hour is not immoral or illegal."

"Talbert will be gone tomorrow night, Eddy. You'll still be living here with Richmond Bell."

"It doesn't matter," Eddy said. "He didn't see us anyway. Mr. Talbert insisted on it and I made sure of it."

Talbert was doodling on a piece of paper. He pushed it across the table. He shook hands with the older man, nodded to the younger, returning.

"I am sorry to have done that." He laughed, but insincerely. "A person is never what you anticipate from having read his writing. I can only hope he is not as disappointed as I am."

"Probably serves you right," Barbara said. "How many readers expect you to be other than what you are?"

Talbert leaned across the table, speaking to all, voice lowered, "He writes such intellectual letters! Talks about philosophy, the psychology of characters—I assumed he held at least a doctorate."

He shot a glance at the two men, now leaving. "He's a used-car salesman!"

"Looks like one," Clint said.

"Anybody who wears suits and dress shoes is definitely not from here," Marc added.

"Now, then." Talbert lifted his glass, mood restored. "Here's to times past and days to come. I hope we all meet again."

Gary watched the departing men. The younger man paid their bill with cash. At the table, a busboy was gathering their dishes. Food partially eaten.

" . . . this thing in Atascadero is growing interesting . . ."

Clint too was watching the men as they took toothpicks from a holder by the cash register. They had hats hanging beside the entrance, put them on before going outside, each with a toothpick in his mouth.

Gary excused himself and walked toward the bathroom. Talbert's back was to him. He slipped outside. The men were driving away. Too far to see a tag number, but the plates were Nevada.

Clint joined him.

"Had a bad feel to them," Gary said.

Clint nodded. "Bad guys must read, too."

They returned to the table. The trout was growing cold.

". . . look for things like their purchases," Talbert was saying to Barbara. "For example, did Borden Wilson buy unusual items? If we had suspected him, if we'd known about his bulk buys of videotape, that would have been a tip-off."

"But first you have to suspect someone," Gary said, picking up the conversation.

"That's true." Talbert chewed food, pensively. "I suppose you've already checked on people like Merriwether and Bell?"

"No reason to."

"Things like batteries and lamps?"

His appetite ruined, Gary put food in a stomach taut with tension. Talbert had uncovered something—regarding Bell or Merriwether? Whatever it was, Talbert was playing with him. The point of the dinner was probably just that. Onto something, he wanted Gary to know and suffer.

"We'd make quite a team." Talbert put a hand on Gary's shoulder. "If we could trust one another."

Gary and Barbara sat on the deck outside their bedroom. The night air was cold, dry, the heavens black with dazzling jabs of celestial light, stars vivid.

"We don't sit out here much anymore," Barbara commented. "Oh, look—falling star. Did you see it?"

"Yes."

She snuggled next to him on the chaise-longue. "We

bought this house because of the deck and we've stopped using it. Why is that?"

"Too busy."

She sighed, her cheek to his chest. "The years are getting away, aren't they?"

He stroked her hair. From an open window they could hear Marc's radio, the thump of percussions and bass fiddles. Marc's laughter overrode the sound.

"A girl," Barbara said, as if Gary had asked. "He gets popular right before Rooftop Rodeo every year."

"He's popular all the time, Barbara."

"Another star, Gary. See it?" The tail faded away like luminous dust.

When they first came here to live, the far mountainside was a dark hulk every night. But now, a decade later, lights winked where roads had been cut, houses erected. The houses resembled decorations on a permanent Christmas tree, strung across the mountain like tiny shining beads.

"What're you thinking about, Gary?"

"Talbert."

"Don't let him get to you," she said.

"I went to see Tom Albright; he went. I got the names of Merriwether and Bell; he got them. We're stumbling over one another, damn it."

"Tomorrow he's leaving."

"I doubt it. I think he's onto something. He's taunting me."

She sat up. "Gary, are you serious about writing a book?"

"No."

"Then what does it matter? You aren't competing with one another. You're letting silly jealousy eat at you and it's ridiculous! If you were really planning to write a book, I'd be pulling with you every inch of the way. I would hate him for second-guessing your moves. But you aren't writing a book. As it is, neither is he."

"So he says. But if not, why is he still poking around?"

They listened to a scramble of sounds as Marc changed

radio stations. The music mellowed. They heard him say, "I listen to waltzes, too—just not all the time."

"That boy is a snow machine," Barbara grumped.

"I think the FBI is feeding Talbert tips," Gary said. "That makes me angry."

"Forget Talbert. You're out here with a scantily clad sexy woman and you're wasting the moment."

He pulled her to him, stroking her back.

"I wouldn't be surprised if Talbert had the FBI set me up," Gary said. "I go off on a tangent while Talbert gets an exclusive on Wang in Canada."

"My poor baby," Barbara teased. "Doesn't want to be a big city newspaperman, but doesn't want anyone else to be."

"Those two men who came in the Trout House tonight—"

"What two men?"

"The guys who wanted Talbert's autograph."

"Gary." She laughed softly. "Would you really enjoy having people interrupt your meal for a signature?"

"I think they work for Talbert. Here to help him chase his story."

"Dressed the way they were," Barbara predicted, "they won't build much rapport with local folks."

"That whole routine about an autograph—something off center about that."

"Are we going to discuss Dan all night?"

He stroked again, but she pulled away.

"Enough," she said mildly.

"What is it?"

"You're bruising me with your affectionate mauling of flesh. Either I'm over the hill, or you are. Want some hot chocolate?"

"I'm sorry—"

"Don't touch me, brute! I'll give you several minutes to purge your brain of piqued and petty thoughts. I'm going to serve hot chocolate. If you are not romantically inclined by then, you can sleep out here in the cold."

She shut the sliding doors behind her. He heard Marc's radio go off.

"Dad?"

"Yes, Marc."

"Want some advice?"

"What?"

"Think romantic thoughts and forget Mr. Talbert. I've slept on the deck. It gets awfully cold."

"Are you eavesdropping?"

"Would a snow machine do that?"

Marc shouted downstairs. "Make enough for three, Mom!"

Gary poured coffee for himself, served a cup to Eddy. The boy took four donuts from a sack and spread them on Gary's desk. "You said a business proposition?" Eddy grumbled.

"That's what it is, Eddy."

"Decided to rent the storage room at Fawn Run?"

"No."

Eddy ate a donut and took a swallow of coffee, his eyes bleary as his biological clock ticked toward full awareness. "What then?" he questioned.

"I want to hire you to take me where you took Mr. Talbert."

Eddy snorted, choked, drank coffee.

"Every place you took him, take me," Gary said. "I also want to know what he said as well as you remember."

"I love it."

"I also want your word that all of this stays between you and me, Eddy."

"I get four dollars an hour, Mr. C."

"I'll pay that."

"For tour guide," Eddy said. "For silence I get a small stipend as a bonus."

He watched the little bastard wolf a donut, reach for more. Gary forced a smile. "How about an extra dollar an hour?"

"How about double four dollars?"

Creep. Gary bargained lightly. "Make it two dollars and we have a deal. After all, long after Talbert is gone, I'll still be here."

"Coercion," Eddy surmised, agreeably. "Two-fifty."

"Six-fifty an hour total. All right."

Eddy looked at his watch. "Starting now, seven o'clock."

"Then let's go."

"Dressed like that?" Eddy asked. "You'll ruin your slacks and without long sleeves you'll be covered with ticks. You should also wear boots, Mr. C."

"I'll do the best I can, Eddy. Let's go."

As Gary locked the *Sentinel* door, Eddy planned their itinerary. "First we went to see Mr. Albright."

"We can skip that."

"Then we went to see Mr. Merriwether. That's hazardous duty, I warn you."

"We can skip that, too."

"That only leaves the man with the blue Wagoneer."

Gary started the car, backed from his parking place, early traffic beginning to move. "Which way, Eddy?"

"Out Trail Ridge Drive. You got binoculars?"

"In the rear seat."

"This was the time of day Mr. Talbert wanted to go, too. Something about the sun being behind us."

They turned off on lumber trails, followed poorly defined fire lanes, weaving back into the mountains.

"Should've brought a four-wheel drive," Eddy muttered. The soft suspension of Gary's sedan caused the undercarriage to scrape rocks as the wheels fell into ruts.

"I thought Bell lived off the main road farther north," Gary complained.

"He does, but we have to approach on the blind side of a mountain. I told you to wear boots."

"What was Talbert after, Eddy?"

"Wanted to see without being seen, he said. Turn right on the next ranger road."

"What kinds of questions did he ask Merriwether and Albright?"

"He wanted to know if you talked to them."

"Is that all?"

"Seemed to be. Mr. Albright told him you were looking for mountain men to interview. Watch the gully, Mr. C. If we get stuck we'll need help to get out. I wish we'd brought some of that coffee—"

"Talbert talked to Albright and Merriwether, but not Bell," Gary said. "Why not Bell?"

"Hold it, Mr. C. Stop a minute."

Gary sat at the wheel, motor idling. Eddy walked out front, staring at the ground. When he returned, the boy sat with the car door open, jiggling a leg, pondering.

"What is it?" Gary asked.

"Somebody's up there. The tracks are fresh, the ground still moist."

"Talbert?"

"Who else would it be?" Eddy questioned. "If we keep going another mile, we're bound to come up on him."

"Is there any other way to approach the same place?"

"Hard climb. You should've worn boots."

"Is this the only way in?"

"By road. You can't leave the car, Mr. C. If Mr. Talbert comes out before we do, he'll know you're here somewhere."

Gary drove in reverse, bramble squealing against metal, tires clawing shale. At the junction with a second fire cut, he drove north a quarter of a mile and then off the road into a shelter of huge spruce trees.

"He said the same thing you did about Mr. Bell," Eddy spoke as Gary retrieved binoculars from the back seat.

"What was that, Eddy?"

"Mr. Talbert said Mr. Bell was nobody to mess with."

Gary was drenched with perspiration. Breathing was difficult, every move an exertion at this altitude.

"Sure you want to do this, Mr. Colter? That mountainside is straight up."

"I'm sure. Let's go. Be sure Talbert doesn't catch us following him."

They scaled an incline so steep they had to pull them-

selves upward using underbrush and exposed roots for hand-
holds. Gary's arms were bleeding from scratches, face stinging
as they reached the peak. Gary sank to his knees, gasping.

He wiped sweat from his eyes with a forefinger. The view
was magnificent. To the north, slightly higher, a cabin was
built hard against massive boulders, on a narrow ledge.

"That's Mr. Bell's place," Eddy said. "He parks his
Wagoneer in a gulch west of the cabin."

From here the cabin was a mile and a half north, perched
like an eagle's nest, with a clear view of the entire valley,
including this precipice. A thousand yards west of here, on
an adjacent peak, two men.

Eddy took the binoculars, adjusted them. "That isn't Mr.
Talbert," he said softly.

Gary retrieved the binoculars, wiped the lenses with his
shirttail. He focused on the two men.

"Those guys were at the Trout House last night," Gary
murmured.

"Probably getting directions from Mr. Talbert. They aren't
dressed like city slickers now," Eddy observed.

Hiking boots. Camouflage clothing. Each had powerful
binoculars set on tripods for stability, aimed at Bell's cabin.

"Mr. C.—" Eddy hissed. He pointed to Bell's place.

Gary's glasses brought the man nearer, but not close
enough to identify. It was his halting gait that branded him.

"Bad back," Gary said, "and he built where he has to
climb several hundred yards to reach his cabin?"

"That's what Mr. Talbert said. He's built a water reservoir behind the house. Can you see it?"

"I think so."

Bell carried a basket, crossing a barren ledge to a shed.
He lifted a root cellar door.

Gary turned, facing the two strangers, watching them as
they spied on Bell. He saw them speak to one another, sit
back from their binoculars.

Cellar.

"Let's get out of here, Eddy. And don't let them see us."

But Eddy was unmoving, staring across the void between this pinnacle and Bell's lodging.

"Eddy, let's go."

"Boy, am I dense," Eddy whispered. "Right under my nose and I didn't see it."

"Eddy, hurry."

"He's doing what Borden Wilson did, isn't he?"

"We don't know that."

"No way to reach that cabin except from the backside and that would take experienced climbers."

Gary saw the two men pour coffee from a thermos, unwrapping sandwiches.

"Then he *was* tracking Marc," Eddy said. "Marc was as close to death as he'll ever be!"

"What are you talking about?"

Eddy was pale. "Marc has a picture of Charlotte in the snow—she's naked. He didn't want you to see it because she's naked. But when he blew it up, we found two men hiding in the trees, watching. Bell was one of them, sure as we sit here."

"The other one?"

"Wore a ski mask."

"Eddy, let's go."

They scrambled down the mountain recklessly, clothes rending, flesh torn by rocks, pebbles skipping ahead toward the valley.

"You must not discuss this with anyone, Eddy."

"I won't."

"Absolutely nobody—not Clint, not Marc, and most especially, not Talbert. Is that understood?"

"Yes, Mr. C."

His heart slamming, the lack of oxygen bringing anginal pain to his chest, Gary insisted they should trot, walking fast for relief, man and boy gulping air, mouths wide, lips blue.

"Can I trust you with this, Eddy? It's a matter of life and death—can I trust you to keep quiet?"

"I swear it."

They reached the car, slammed the doors and locked them. Gary turned the starter and it whined, fruitlessly.

"Don't flood it, Mr. Colter."

"Sit a minute," Gary cautioned himself. "Let it rest a minute."

Their breathing clouded the windshield, Eddy staring straight ahead. "What are you going to do, Mr. Colter?"

"Call the FBI, Eddy."

"Why not Sheriff Ferguson?"

"The FBI has suspected another killer, Eddy. They have better resources for handling this."

Eddy's eyes reflected awe. "All this time you knew," he marveled. "You are some cool dude, Mr. Colter."

The car started. Gary pulled onto the ranger road, turned for home.

"Some cool dude," Eddy remarked.

But Talbert knew, too.

CHAPTER TWENTY-THREE

M arc stepped through the door of the *Sentinel*, bell ringing as he entered. "Boy, it's hot out there."

Eddy was standing by Gary's desk, moving objects as if his hands were in control of themselves.

"Eddy, will you leave things alone?" Gary snapped.

Eddy sat down, crossed one long leg over the other and his foot began to jiggle.

"Where's Mom?" Marc asked.

"Beats me." Eddy's eyes were bright, watching Gary on the telephone.

"I don't think it can wait until Monday, Beecham."

"Isn't that the FBI guy?" Marc asked Eddy.

"Wouldn't know."

Sensing exclusion, Marc went to the work board, checking for units that had to be cleaned. He saw an envelope addressed to him. Slitting it open, he whooped.

"One hundred eight dollars for photos!"

He might as well have been alone.

"I'm not free to discuss it over the telephone, Beecham," Gary said. "However, I will drive to Denver. Meet you at your office."

"What's going on, Eddy?"

"Beats me."

"You're lying. What is it?"

Eddy shrugged so hard his ears touched shoulders. Eyes alight, he watched Gary.

"Two o'clock," Gary concluded. "I have the address and I'll be punctual."

When he hung up, there were sweaty imprints on the receiver. He looked at Marc as if seeing him for the first time. "Do you have cabins to clean?"

"One."

"Better get on it."

"Want to help, Eddy?"

"No, no; I may have something to do."

"Not with me, you don't," Gary said.

Eddy looked at his wristwatch. "Five and a half hours at six-fifty—"

"You can get a check tomorrow, Eddy. Marcus, *do* you have work to do?"

"Yes, Dad, I said so."

"Then be about it."

Marc held up his check, "The wire service paid me over a hundred dollars for pictures."

"Good for you. Do your work."

Gary dialed a number, rocking his desk chair. "Barbara, I have to go to Denver."

"Tell her I'm going to clean the Rush Falls condo, Dad."

"I may be gone all afternoon," Gary said. "Later, even."

Once more, Marc questioned Eddy, "Will you tell me what's going on?"

"Hey, man, I'm just an unemployed tour guide. I came in to get out of the heat. Ask Mr. C."

His father's expression squelched the thought. Marc took the condo keys from a hook, wrote a note *To Whom It May Concern* . . .

Phone in place again, Gary stared at Eddy so intently the boy said, "Trust me, trust me."

Gary nodded. "I'm gone, boys. Lock up when you leave."

Eddy watched Gary get into his car. Their eyes met and Eddy waved, cheerily. He went to the window, watching the car go east toward flatlands.

"I thought he'd make me go with him," Eddy yelped. "I just knew he would."

"What're you talking about?"

"But he didn't!" Eddy clapped his hands, rubbed them briskly. "My friend, I have a proposition—"

"First, tell me what's going on."

"What's the longest telephoto lens you own?" Eddy asked.

"Four hundred—why?"

"Shooting at a hundred yards, could you identify the subject if you shot a picture with that?"

"Probably."

"Good, good." Eddy jiggled across the room. "Now then, if you're shooting in diminishing light, what film would you select?"

"Kodak Tri-X, 400 ASA."

"Oh, yeah, that's good. Okay. Trust me, Marc. Don't ask questions, just do what I say."

"Not unless you tell me what—"

"Hey!" Eddy yelled. "Hey, listen to me! You got how much from the wire services?"

Marc repeated the figure.

"That"—Eddy grinned—"is nothing. That is a speck on the canvas of future potential. Now, for a fifty-fifty split, I am going to maybe make *two* Pulitzer winners in your family. I will act as agent for the enterprise. You will provide expertise, camera, as much film as we can backpack—"

"Eddy, I've had it with trouble."

Eddy placed both palms against Marc's chest, patting. "I swear," he said, fervently, "this will make you famous. I swear, also, it is not immoral, not illegal—"

"But Dad won't like it," Marc predicted.

"Do what I say," Eddy squealed. "Do it without question. You will never regret it. We'll make a fortune!"

"Eddy—"

Eddy seized him, hands trembling. "Trust me," he whispered. "Trust me."

"Tell me."

"I can't. I swore I wouldn't and I can't. But if you come with me—do what I say—oh, Marc, *please*!"

"What about the condo?"

"Forget the condo! We have a long hard climb and we have to do it before dark. Come on!"

Marc erased the message he'd written, hung the condo key. He hesitated, Eddy waiting at the door, impatiently.

Marc wrote: "Gone with Eddy to shoot pix . . ."

"Got plenty of film?"

"Nine rolls." They got in the Jeep and Marc asked, "Where to?"

"My house for binoculars. Forget the sandwiches, we'll stop and buy hamburgers."

Marc started the motor. "Then where?"

"Someplace you've never been. I'll guide, you drive."

Barbara drove up as they were leaving. Marc read her lips: "Condo?"

"Don't stop," Eddy commanded.

"Are you kidding? I have to come back sooner or later."

Eddy stuck his head out the side, shouting, "We'll take care of everything, Mrs. C.—be gone late—" He pulled in again, speaking from the side of his mouth, "Gun it, Marc. We're going to meet our destiny."

"Mr. Colter, this is Mr. Arthur, my supervisor." Roger Beecham made introductions.

Gary shook hands with an older man.

"And this is Special Agent Wohlman," Beecham said. They sat down.

"You indicated this couldn't wait," Beecham noted.

The elder of the agents looked at his watch, tugged a sleeve to cover the instrument. He studied Gary with steel-blue eyes devoid of expression.

"In Montreal," Gary addressed Beecham, "you said there was the possibility of another killer."

Mr. Arthur, the supervisor, urged, "Tell us what's on your mind, Mr. Colter."

"First of all," Gary demanded, "I need the truth, Beecham—and I mean *truth*! Have you been feeding tips to Daniel Talbert?"

Beecham looked to his superior, who interjected, "Why do you ask?"

"I'd like to know if I'm being used by Beecham and Talbert."

"The answer is no," Beecham said.

"Did you tell Talbert anything Wang said?"

"I did not."

"Did he see Wang?"

"No."

"Do you know about a case in Atascadero, California?" Gary asked.

"Yes."

"Well," Gary said, "Talbert said he's going to follow it up. He said a friend told him about it. That wouldn't be you, would it?"

Beecham placed the tips of his fingers together, rocking in his chair.

"Mr. Colter," Mr. Arthur said as he sat forward, "it's Saturday. These men have families. May we know the purpose of our meeting?"

"On the assumption there might be another killer," Gary said, "I went to see a fellow named Albright, a mountain man who has lived here all his life. I asked him about other such men."

"Toward what end?"

"Looking for isolated individuals with a lifestyle similar to Borden Wilson's."

"What did you intend to do with these isolated men?"

"I intended to report them to Beecham."

"And this," the supervisor said, indicating the room, "is your report?"

"You understand, I could be wrong."

"I do understand," Mr. Arthur said emphatically.

"There's a man named Richmond Cathedral Bell—" Beecham started dialing a telephone.

"He's a Vietnam veteran," Gary said. "He seems to be on disability—"

"Bell," Beecham spoke into the phone. "Richmond Cathedral."

"What makes this man interesting to you?" Mr. Arthur inquired.

"He lives alone, his cabin is inaccessible. He built it where most men would never build."

"Explain that."

"Two precious commodities are water and power," Gary said. "Most men build in valleys to get water. Most men choose a site with electrical power, like Borden Wilson's place. Bell had to haul every nail and shingle up a steep slope—several hundred yards—and he's lame."

"Wanted the view," Wohlman said.

"Wanted the view absolutely," Gary declared. "To build where he did means hard labor hauling food, fuel for a generator—"

"He has a generator?"

"Ordered parts for it, according to the hardware store."

"Go on."

"Water is all the more precious when there's no way to get it except packing it up a mountainside," Gary said. "Bell has a cistern, apparently, probably getting water from seepage. That makes every drop golden."

"You've been to his place?"

"I went out to spy with binoculars."

"Please continue," Mr. Arthur insisted.

"Bell has a root cellar just like Borden Wilson had."

Mr. Arthur drew his chair nearer, leaning forward to lend a sense of intimacy. Gary knew the pose. He had used it many times.

"You came here with a theory, Mr. Colter," the supervisor said. "I've taken the liberty of looking into your background. You don't seem to be a man given to wild flings of imagination."

Intimacy, plus praise . . .

"I'd like you to be candid, Mr. Colter. Withhold nothing. Tell me what you're thinking."

. . . plus valued knowledge.

"I think you ought to question Bell."

"Um-hm." Mr. Arthur nodded, smiling. "Um-hm."

"Would you care for coffee, Mr. Colter?" Wohlman asked.

"No."

Beecham placed a tape recorder on his credenza.

"Writers intrigue me," Mr. Arthur mused. "You are chasing a phantom; Talbert, too—"

"The same phantom," Gary said, acidly.

"A sixth sense is a talent," Mr. Arthur noted. "Great investigators all have it. I knew a homicide detective in New York. It was eerie the way he came up with clues. Out of thin air, it seemed."

Beecham wound tape through the machine. He wore earphones, listening. "We're ready, Mr. Arthur," he advised.

Mr. Arthur reached over, patted Gary's knee in a grandfatherly gesture. "I want you to hear this, Mr. Colter. It's from a wiretap in Los Angeles, California. An unsavory fellow who deals in pornography, primarily. Acts as distributor here and abroad. He goes by the name 'Mr. Video.' Wang provided us with the address. It's where he sent videotapes he and Wilson made."

Beecham flipped a switch, adjusted a knob.

"What you'll hear," Mr. Arthur said, pleasantly, "is the voice of evil."

Richmond spit on his spectacles, wiped them dry, held them up to the sky to look for lint. Thunderheads roiled in billowing columns toward a dazzling blue firmament. He sat in the shade, the noonday sun was scorching, the air utterly still, silence bringing a ring to his ears.

Not even a gnat in flight. The birds were torpid and mute, mammals taking refuge in sheltered retreats. Days of uncomfortable heat were rare in the mountains, the evenings usually cool like last night.

He was sitting in the lee of a boulder that formed part of the ceiling and wall of the cellar below. Even that massive stone was warm to the touch as he leaned back, lighting a cigarette.

Tastes like gasoline. He smoked it nevertheless.

He was restless. Irritated. He'd been working with gasoline motors for most of his life and let one simple fact slip by. He'd checked the wiring, relays, regulator, disassembling everything to clean and adjust the parts. Finally, when all else failed, he took apart the motor itself.

Water.

Warm by day, cool at night, he ran the motor for brief periods and condensation had occurred. He should've guessed that. Should've guessed it first! But he hadn't. Time had been wasted trying to replace parts that were already functional. Precious days lost as he suspected the worst from this mechanical contraption—and it was only water.

He'd discovered rusty scabs of oxidation within the cylinders and only then had he gone to the tank where he'd stored gasoline. Drawing it off into containers, he'd found mercurial globules of water in the bottom of his reservoir.

The good news was, he should be able to shoot the last scene tonight.

The lapse in activity had actually been beneficial. He'd had time to reconsider the final scene, mentally calculating camera angles to depict the ultimate shock with artistic results.

He would transfer Joyce's chain to a wall near Colleen. They were tethered by their ankles and the new position would make it possible for the women to wrestle for supremacy, locked in mortal combat.

Getting them prepared psychologically was imperative. He had to be certain the conclusion was performed slowly, and with realism. In the blur of a fight the camera's location must be perfect, the shot itself designed to show that last fatal act.

He stubbed out his cigarette, shredded paper, scattered tobacco. This heat made him lazy. He wished he could sit here until evening, but he needed the light to finish his task.

The girls were bathing, washing their hair—it took time to

dry and brush. He'd devoted several hours to cleaning the cellar, putting the scene in order for the next performance.

He had decided to change the title. *Virgin War* to *Virgin Whore*. Illogical and contradictory, an arcanum. It had commercial appeal.

Knowing this would be the last video, he was almost rueful. It had taken months to hollow out the cellar, following the line of least resistance, tunneling under the boulder to carve out the room below. He'd had to engineer a natural flow of air, defeat the persistent seep of ground water, wire for lights and set up the video equipment. Over the entrance he had constructed the facade of a woodshed. He'd done a good job. A shame to abandon it.

With the final scene about to be consummated, he'd convinced himself the title had to be shot again. He'd set up the title board tomorrow morning. It would only take a few minutes to put it on tape. As for the last editing, that would be in some remote motel next week after all the evidence here had been destroyed. Like a master craftsman who continues to polish a piece of furniture he's designed and built, he was glad to be done, while wishing he were not.

He also wished he had not telephoned Mr. Video. He had seriously considered another call to reassure his distributor. But the truth was, he did need to get away from here. Go to the Orient, stay in nice hotels, eat exotic foods, and sate himself until he wearied of it. Maybe in a few years he would want to produce more videos. But for now, he needed a rest.

He was more exhausted than he'd realized. Emotionally drained by tension and frustration. Borden had turned the world awry. What Richmond felt sitting here was reminiscent of the lulls following a mission in combat—too weary to move, but impatient to be active. It was time for R&R. Enjoy the fruits of his labors.

Spend some money on his health. He'd heard of an osteopath in Baltimore—there had to be others in Japan, equally proficient.

Daydreaming.

It was not like him. He'd seldom indulged in fantasy, even as a child. Dreamed dreams with a reasonable expectation of achieving them. Such bemusement fell in a category with window-shopping. If one had money to buy, it was productive. If destitute, gazing at the unattainable was depressing.

Now, of course, he had the financial resources to do almost anything he wished. Five hundred thousand dollars was buried around this mountainside, wrapped in plastic garbage bags, sealed in glass to prevent the rot of currency. He was, by the standards of most men, wealthy.

Except for the possible return of nightmares, he was going to be all right. If the specters came again—well, he'd deal with that when and if.

For now he had the world on a leash. Gary Colter could thank his God another week would not pass before the generator was working properly. If Colter meddled anymore, he would die.

Daydreaming!

He hoisted himself to a standing position. He sucked fluid through a hose, building siphon flow. Vinegar-white petrol flowed into a bucket. *Running out of containers.* In the pail, drops of water settled, glimmering beneath the gas, heady fumes rising as the fuel evaporated.

Somewhere distantly, an alien snap rode breathless air. Richmond pinched the hose, lifted his head to listen.

So quiet.

He stepped into a shaded nook, turned to peer across the valley at peaks afar. Quadrant by quadrant, he studied squares of terrain.

Nothing moved. No glint of reflected light.

But a nervous tingle fluttered in his abdomen. He ambled toward the cabin as if preoccupied. Inside, he got his .357 magnum, tucked it in his waistband, and covered it with his shirt. He had an inviolate rule: never take a weapon into the cellar. If the girls got it, that would be the end of him. The end of them, for that matter. Chained and helpless, they would run out of water, food, chamber pots filled. But in the passion of a moment such things wouldn't occur to Joyce; she would shoot first, lament later.

He stood back from the windows, shutters lifted, using binoculars to scan the valley and distant peaks.

Nothing.

But he kept the pistol with him, nevertheless.

CHAPTER TWENTY-FOUR

Hyperactive and impatient, Eddy insisted they go on. "You said there'd be climbing," Marc argued. "That means I have to get my boots, Eddy. We'll need jackets and gear and—"

"All right, all right!"

While Marc gathered nylon lines, packed light blankets and climbing equipment, Eddy filled one thermos with cold cola, another with hot coffee. They stopped at a fast-food restaurant, bought a sack of hamburgers and French-fried potatoes.

"Wasted an hour at least," Eddy grumbled.

Using four-wheel drive, Marc eased his jeep over obstacles, traveling four miles up a canyon along a riverbed gone dry. Hundreds of years of flash floods had piled debris at every curve, sweeping away dirt to leave a jumbled mass of boulders. From there, they hiked another hour.

"This is it." Eddy collapsed beside his backpack, breathless.

Marc gazed up a sheer cliff on one side, a tangle of vines, tree roots, and flaking shale on the other side. "This is what, Eddy?"

"Thank God for my brilliant mind." Eddy sprawled on his back, arms extended. "My body won't make it."

"Eddy, this is *what*? Where are we?"

Eddy sat up, pawed through his knapsack for the thermos of cola. "This is the back side of a mountain," he said. "On the other side, halfway down, is a cabin which is our objective. As I have said, I cannot break my oath of silence."

"How would you like me to break your neck?"

"Under the threat of attack, I can say this: you and I will be witness to a spectacle of such proportions—"

"What is it, Eddy?"

Eddy swigged cola, extended the cup to Marc. "The fellow with the blue Grand Wagoneer, wears a leather hat, limps."

"Richmond Bell?"

"At this very moment the legal establishment is marshaling helicopters, marksmen—"

"What is going on—and you'd better level with me or I'm leaving."

"Bell is a killer, like Borden Wilson."

"How do you know that?"

"Your father paid me to bring him out to see what Mr. Talbert saw. Mr. Talbert has two guys watching the other side of the mountain facing the cabin. Bell has a generator for electricity and a cellar. Mr. C. has gone to consult the FBI. Believe me, Bell's a killer."

"What are we supposed to do about it?"

"Take pictures."

"I should've known better than to come. I've been in enough trouble because of you."

Eddy peered up the cliff. "That's going to be tough."

"Tough? It's impossible!"

"Your tendency to pessimism is unattractive, Marc."

"We need more gear, more rope—"

"We've made harder climbs."

"That damn mountain is a thousand feet straight up!"

"I figured two thousand."

"Well, I'm not going."

"Yes, you are," Eddy said. "If we shoot a series of the capture—maybe a gigantic shoot-out—you will be rich and famous. Remember the photographers, the great ones, guys who put themselves in danger to get prizewinning shots? In battle, fires, riots—pictures that immortalized their names."

"It'll be dark by the time we reach the other side, Eddy."

"Then we will wait for dawn."

"Suppose police come in the dark?"

"We lose."

"You know they're coming?"

"Your father is at the FBI office in Denver. If I'm right, they're coming."

Reading Marc's doubt, Eddy said, "Remember the *Life* magazine photo of men assaulting Normandy Beach in World War II? Coming through spikes of tank barriers, stumbling under the weight of battle gear—one man fell, slain. Well, Marc, the photographer got there *first*—looked back."

"All night up there." Marc resisted. "We'll freeze. The insects will be awful."

"If it's cold, insects won't be there. If there are insects, we'll be warm."

Eddy drew an imaginary map on a piece of shale. "There's a huge boulder by which Bell built the cellar. Probably tunneled under it. The cabin is built on a ledge. I sat across the valley looking at the place for six hours with Mr. Talbert—I know every inch, Marc. We can beat Mr. Talbert *and* your dad."

Seeing his point needed more weight, Eddy lowered his voice. "Remember that fantastic shot of a race car in midair tumbling toward the photographer poised at trackside?"

"The car killed him."

"We can do it, Marc," Eddy soothed. "We'd be fools not to. Want a hamburger?"

"We'd better eat here," Marc said begrudgingly. "We won't have another chance until we reach the peak. You said two thousand feet?"

"More or less. If you don't want onions, may I have them?"

"I want the onions, Eddy. I don't have a date."

Eddy muffled a laugh. "One other thing," he said softly. "You know how sound travels up here. We have to be quiet."

Marc remembered a photograph Dad always admired—the German dirigible *Hindenburg* docking after its first ocean crossing, bursting with flames, collapsing as the photographer stood his ground, shooting, shooting, shooting.

Sam Shere. Dad knew his name. "That took courage, luck, and know-how," Dad had commented.

Robert Capa's shot of a Spanish soldier at the instant of impact from an enemy bullet—it made Capa world famous.

"You'd better be right, Eddy," Marc muttered. "Dad is going to skin me alive."

"If I'm wrong, he's wrong," Eddy said, confidently. "He knew about Bell all along. Man, he is some cool dude."

Dad would be furious—and proud.

"This is Zed-Four-Two calling." The voice was a throaty growl. "Let me speak with Mr. Video."

Gary and the three FBI agents listened intently.

". . . not available . . ."

"Get him," the caller commanded.

Mr. Arthur, the senior agent, spoke to Gary, "Listen closely."

"Zed . . . everything all right?"

"No."

Mr. Video sounded sad. "I'm sorry to hear that, Zed. What's the problem?"

"I can't fulfill our agreement. I'm sending back your last payment."

Mr. Arthur stopped the machine. "Do you recognize the voice, Colter? Could it be Bell?"

"I've never talked to him."

"The implication is," Mr. Arthur said, "Mr. Video prepaid for services rendered. Is that what it sounds like to you, Mr. Colter?"

"If he's about to send back money—yes."

"Um-hm." Mr. Arthur nodded. "Um-hm. This makes the conversation incriminating, Mr. Colter. It means, if Video paid in advance he was *commissioning* murder. How do we prove that?"

The tape recorder started again.

"What payment is that?" Mr. Video asked.

"You know what payment. I'll mail it in the same form I received it—"

Mr. Arthur interjected, "Probably cash."

On the tape, Mr. Video insisted, "I want the product. The money could be embarrassing. Incriminating."

"There!" Mr. Arthur said. "Mr. Video knows a return of cash would be proof he had commissioned the murders."

". . . not a thief . . . have your money and you have no product . . . sending back the money . . ."

The voice of Mr. Video sharpened, insisting the caller must produce.

". . . withdraw from our arrangement . . . *after* delivery of the next shipment . . . you owe us the product."

Mr. Arthur turned off the recorder, stroked his platinum hair over one ear. "The implication is—a video is unfinished, but in progress. A murder about to happen."

A chill swept Gary's body.

The reels turned again, the caller angrily insisting he could not deliver.

A long whispery sigh and Mr. Video inquired, "What is your problem, Zed?"

"Heat . . . let me return your money."

Mr. Arthur held up a finger to ensure attention.

"How is the weather in Gatlin Pass?"

The chill swept him again and Gary shivered.

"You see, Zed, we can't make such large investments unless we know who we're dealing with . . . your mother, is she doing well with her quail?"

"Then you know what's happened to Borden, you bastard!"

"Oh, indeed. But, Zed, you aren't so foolish as your friend . . ."

"I can't finish, goddamn you!"

"You must. You must, Zed."

"You're bluffing," the caller challenged. "Borden—the bastard—he didn't know everything and neither do you."

". . . we know . . ."

"Prove it!"

". . . wait exactly ten minutes and call your mother . . ."

Mr. Arthur shut off the machine. "Out of hundreds of incoming calls, this is the one that will hang them. If we can prove the prepayment of money, not only will we bag the killer, we'd bag the banker."

Quaking violently, Gary gasped, feeling faint.

"Colter, are you all right?"

"My daughter—"

"What about your daughter?"

"Colleen—God—he's got Colleen."

"What makes you think that?"

Gary fought nausea, struggling to explain—the landlady in Los Angeles, Timothy Lichtenfelter, the bad check, Colleen's car.

"He's got her," Gary croaked.

"Colter, that's so improbable—"

"He's got her!"

Wohlman brought Gary a glass of water. For a long moment they said nothing.

"Assume he does," Arthur said. "As improbable as it is, assume he does. They mentioned Gatlin Pass and Borden Wilson. The killer is there. He is facing delivery of 'the product,' which means he hasn't finished."

"What kind of animals are these?" Gary cried. "One man—he's insane! But a group of men? What kind of men are these?"

"Pornography is the third-largest form of income for the underworld," Arthur said. "There are fifty companies producing in the United States alone. The law has been emasculated by the courts on grounds of free speech. Local authorities can seize material only if it involves children, infants, animals, or obvious social taboos such as incest. It is difficult to convict. We have no law to stop people from owning a film in which a murder takes place, so long as the film is shown in the privacy of a home and not for the purpose of selling tickets. Even if caught, even if convicted, the defendant usually gets a fine and probation. Weigh the penalty against potential income and you can see why any deviate with a camera might be tempted into business."

Arthur returned to the tape recorder, held an earphone, listening as the tape ran forward at high speed.

"Immediately following the call you heard, this conversation took place."

He adjusted the tape. Mr. Video's voice again. "This is Video."

"Yessir?"

"Regarding Zed-Four-Two: call his mother and squeeze."

"Will do."

A dial tone.

"That call went to a number in Las Vegas which we subsequently identified as a known underworld connection," Arthur said. "That particular phone isn't sanctioned for interception, so we have no idea whether they called the 'mother' mentioned by Mr. Video. We can assume that Zed-Four-Two thought himself secure. The call to his mother was designed to prove how vulnerable he is, bringing pressure to bear."

"There you have it, Colter," Beecham said. "If it's Bell, he must be apprehended immediately. But if it is *not* Bell, we must locate the right man."

"Bell lives on a mountain," Gary quavered. "He has a clear view of the valley and lesser peaks. He'll see you coming."

"Could we land a helicopter on the site?" Arthur asked.

"I viewed it from a distance. I can't be positive, but on a mountainside wind shear is common."

Mr. Arthur pondered a moment. He spoke as if distracted, "We'll need experienced mountain climbers, Wohlman."

"There's one man who might get up there without being seen," Gary said. "His name is Tom Albright. He's climbed every peak in the area at one time or another."

"Get him," Arthur commanded. "Better contact the marshals at Rocky Mountain National Park for assistance. They'll have topography maps. We'll need a base of operations—"

"The Sheriff's Patrol office in Gatlin Pass," Beecham said. "Deputy Clint Ferguson is related to Colter by marriage."

Mr. Arthur seemed to grow older as Gary watched. "Let's

keep this as tightly organized as possible, gentlemen. Colter, if Bell is not the right man, we'll have spooked the real killer. You understand that?"

"Yes." The nausea surged and Gary swallowed repeatedly.

"If Bell is the man," Arthur said, "if he has a hostage, we don't want him killing anyone in a panic. When may we expect reports on Bell, Wohlman?"

"Washington is working on it now."

Arthur pulled his chair directly in front of Gary, their knees almost touching. He patted Gary's leg in a comforting, grandfatherly way. "Let's talk about your girl, Mr. Colter. I want to know as much as possible. What kind of girl is she—what's her name?"

"Colleen," Gary said hoarsely. "Colleen Lichtenfelter . . ."

Avoiding the flank of the mountain meant climbing almost straight up. Marc led the way, using pitons sparingly, driving the metal spikes into rock, fitting them with a carabiner, a spring-loaded clip which held his rope. Below, heavily laden with his pack, taking up some of the pitons for future use, Eddy followed.

Marc paused, wheezing. To the east he could see the Jeep where they had left it. To the west the canyon twisted away in sheer walls. If they fell, nobody would find them. Only fools would camp in a draw so obviously scarred by flash floods from the past.

He clipped his rope to the next piton, inched to one side, feeling for holds with his fingertips and toes. Shale tore loose, plummeted past Eddy as he sheltered his head.

Not properly equipped.

Marc struggled over an outcrop, pulling himself up with diminishing strength. His muscles ached, his lungs burned. They faced a final sharp pitch before the summit, but the worst was over. He secured himself, hoisting Eddy up when the rope slackened. He heard Eddy swear softly, a clatter of debris falling away.

The sun was touching the most westerly peak now. Soon it would be dusk—unsafe to proceed.

"Gimme a minute," Eddy called sotto voce. "Damned pack strap is cutting me."

Feet scotched, Marc wrapped the rope around himself, then secured it to a piton in case Eddy slipped. More than fifteen hundred feet up, the view was breathtaking, the evening sun painting snowcaps red and orange, the hues of a distant spur glowing like a fixed streak of golden lightning.

A shrill trilling rose in his ears and he twisted to see a male broad-tailed hummingbird hovering a few feet away. The rose-red throat was a laughing gash set in iridescent green. "What're you doing up here?" Marc asked softly, and the bird darted away with a whirr.

"Okay," Eddy called, "pull me up."

He winched, held, pulled, secured the line, hauling Eddy to the brink of the overhang. Eddy's face was streaming sweat, complexion ruddy, freckles submerged in a ruby glow.

Together, spent, they leaned back while Eddy caught his breath. "Want some cola?"

"We don't have time, Eddy. We're losing our light."

Eddy wiped his eyes with the sleeves of both arms, looked up behind them. "Five hundred feet, maybe; what'ya think?"

"About that."

They gave themselves a few more minutes, then Marc took the lead again. *Easier going.* The frost line was here. Snow trapped in winter had melted away, loosening rocks. But the pitch was better, letting Marc scramble across fifty yards of incline before he paused to sink another piton.

The peak—gray serrated stone teeth denuded of all but lichen. Marc collapsed, waiting for Eddy.

Strength sapped by lack of oxygen, they rested. Finally, Eddy turned on his stomach, took his binoculars, and scanned a far side of the valley. "There they are," he said. "The two men Mr. Talbert staked out to watch Bell."

Marc took the binoculars. Following Eddy's clues, he located the peak. He could barely see them.

"Have to be careful two ways," Eddy counseled. "Bell below; them afar."

"What can they do to us?"

"Take pictures," Eddy guessed. "Tell Mr. Talbert we're here. They might tip off Bell without meaning to."

They felt their way down the southerly slope, reaching the tree line, the descent more secure than that of the north side. Periodically, Eddy paused to spy on the two men who spied on Richmond Bell below.

The sun blinked like a flickering candle, flowing away.

"We have about thirty minutes before dark, Eddy."

"Hey!" Eddy whispered. "Look at this."

A wire stretched between two scrub firs. Eddy followed it without touching the strand. "Look at this," he whispered. "An alarm."

Trip wire. If they had struck it, a cannister would have dumped pebbles down the slope, clattering a warning of their approach.

"Now I know he's up to something," Eddy vowed. "Watch for more of these."

Long shadows spread into a dusky pool in the valley below. The last direct light disappeared, the change in illumination altering perception, making footing more critical.

"Another trip wire, Eddy."

"Yeah. Be careful."

Eddy kicked a stone, then scrambled through scrub brush to stop its fall.

"There." Eddy pointed.

Roof of the cabin. Barely visible beyond a last boulder.

"Circle east," Eddy said. "There's a place where we should be able to see everything."

"We'll be exposed.

"In the dark?"

Marc felt for each step. It was getting colder. Eddy took the point, recklessly it seemed, but without a sound he slipped along a face of boulders, wending his way to the desired destination.

"This is it," Eddy murmured. "Over that ledge is the cabin." His teeth were white in a grin. "We got him now!"

Their packs eased to the ground and, using a twisted fir for leverage, they climbed a boulder, flat on their stomachs.

With a jolt, Marc realized they were right on top of the site. In the cabin a lantern bathed open windows and doorway with yellowed light. They could see a shed built under the lip of a massive boulder, a slanted cellar door seemingly a portal into stone.

"How's this for pictures?" Eddy gloated.

"Too dark."

"But we're here." Eddy beamed. "Best seat in the house!"

They heard the clang of a metal pan, surprisingly loud.

"Be very quiet," Eddy said needlessly.

Eddy used his binoculars, focusing on the cabin. "Cooking," he reported. "Eats late, doesn't he? I see the generator, the water reservoir. Nice place."

Shivering, Marc slipped down to their packs. He found the thermos of hot coffee, poured a cup. The aroma was so strong he worried that Richmond Bell would smell it. He unwrapped a cold package of limp fried potatoes, and began eating them. Eddy slid down and joined him.

"I wish I had 1000 ASA film," Marc whispered. "I could shoot in this light, but the pictures would be very grainy."

"Don't worry about it." Eddy shared the fries. "Maybe nothing will happen before daylight."

"If it does," Marc advised, "I don't have a flash."

They wrapped themselves in the blankets Marc had thought to bring. By the time they finished the coffee, the first stars were glowing overhead.

He heard Eddy sigh. "This is the most exciting night of my life," Eddy said. He pulled close to Marc's ear. "Thanks for coming."

Marc nodded.

Dad would be furious. Mom would die if she knew they were here—and now, overnight.

"Don't worry." Eddy squeezed Marc's arm. "Everything will work out in the end. You'll see."

Furious, worried.

Beyond the boulder came the sound of a cough, Bell clearing his throat. A faint lilt made Marc sit up, trying to identify it.

Bell. Humming as he prepared his supper.

CHAPTER TWENTY-FIVE

C lint's office had become a command center, the Sheriff's Patrol building a focal point for various agencies. The atmosphere of tension and anticipation gave a festive air to the gathering of marshals, park rangers, the sheriff and his deputies, state patrolmen, and the FBI agents helping direct plans.

Eleven o'clock. Gary threw a styrofoam cup into a wastebasket overflowing with cups. Rachel Winthrop, the student cop, was brewing coffee in an urn borrowed from the Staghorn Café.

"I need climbers who can pick a tick off a hound at four hundred yards," Tom Albright said. "I can name three who are here—we've hunted together."

Agent Wohlman presented a teletyped message to his superior and Mr. Arthur donned glasses to read it.

Maps of roadways, park trails, and fire lanes were spread on a counter in the reception area. Topography maps were being examined by Tom Albright and his choice of climbers. The wavy lines which depicted contours of terrain looked like the purl of a pond being pelted by rain.

"Bell's cabin is here." Albright touched a point with a pencil. "Even that is a hard climb. Never did understand why he built there."

"We have a piece of moon tonight," somebody reported. "Weather forecast is for clear skies, temperature in the low fifties, Fahrenheit."

"Good night for game," a climber joked.

"This game can shoot back," Albright warned. "And he *can* shoot. I saw him drop a buck at one thousand yards. Incidentally, it was almost dark. He has an infrared scope for that rifle."

Sobered, the men reexamined topography maps.

"Bell was severely wounded in Vietnam," Mr. Arthur said, condensing what he'd read. "A booby trap blew up under him. Took his genitalia."

"Jesus."

"Repeated surgery," Arthur continued. "Plastic ball for a hip joint. Highly decorated for bravery, career soldier who lost his profession."

"So what makes us think he's dangerous?" the sheriff from Fort Collins questioned.

Mr. Arthur lifted silvery eyebrows, biting his lower lip for a pensive moment. "Underwent two years of psychiatric observation," he said. "He was bitter about the American public's response to what he and others had been through. Suffers swings of mood, extreme depression, and recurring nightmares. A tendency to paranoia, according to the doctors at Walter Reed Hospital."

"Antisocial," Roger Beecham concluded.

"What's it mean?" Clint queried.

"It means," the sheriff noted, "Bell is about like any of us would be if we'd experienced what he has."

"Then, what the hell are we doing?" One of the climbers slapped at the maps irritably.

Mr. Arthur ignored him. "Next of kin is his mother. She lives in Chimney Rock, West Virginia. We have an agent going there now."

"What are we supposed to do?" a marshal asked. "Get in position and wait—arrest him—what?"

"If Bell is the man we think," Mr. Arthur said, "we must assume there is a hostage."

"You are *assuming* with Bell," the sheriff said, sharply. "Get these men wandering around in the dark and somebody's apt to be hurt."

"Radio ain't worth using back in there," a climber commented to Albright. "How we going to get instructions?"

Gary accepted another cup of coffee from Rachel. Outside, uniformed and waiting, men laughed as they talked.

". . . set up a radio relay about here . . ."

Clint was on the telephone in his office. He beckoned Gary with a wiggle of a finger. "It's Barbara," he said, "and she's hot."

"Barb, honey, I'm sorry I didn't call earlier."

"Gary, have you seen Marcus?"

"Not since noon."

"That boy," she exhaled into the receiver. "He and Eddy have gone off together. They ought to be spanked, their size notwithstanding. What's going on down there? I saw the cars."

"Barbara, can you come here?"

He could feel apprehension in her silence.

"Like you said," Gary reasoned, "Marc and Eddy are probably together. Did you call Eddy's parents?"

"They haven't heard from them. When I came home I found some of Marc's climbing gear strewn around the garage. Gary, has something happened?"

Icy dread forbade a response.

"Marc left a note on the work board," Barbara worried. "He said he was going with Eddy to take pictures."

Damn that Eddy. Damn him!

"Did he say where?"

"No." Her tone faltered. "Marc was scheduled to clean the condo at Rush Falls. I went up there after it got dark. There are dirty dishes in the sink. Towels to be laundered. I have it booked for tomorrow morning, Gary."

"Barbara, I want you to come to Clint's office."

"I have to clean the condo—"

"Barbara, baby, come here."

He heard her sob. "The boys. There's been an accident."

"No, the boys are all right so far as I know. Do you want me to come get you?"

"Get me?. No—Gary, what is it?"

A moment passed. "You don't suppose they're stranded somewhere?" Barbara questioned. "It isn't like Marc to be irresponsible, despite what I say when I'm angry."

Holding the phone, Gary went to the office door and called Rachel. "Have you seen Marc and Eddy?"

"Not today."

Gary closed the door, muting crowd noises. Alone in Clint's office he fought anger and fear. *Gone to take pictures with Eddy.*

He'd debated dragging the little twerp to Denver. But Eddy swore—*swore!* Gary's chest constricted, heart quickening. Tom Albright was making final preparations to scale that mountain under the cover of darkness. The potential for disaster was alarming. A jittery marksman, a moving shadow, an unanswered challenge, shots fired—

"Barbara, I'm sending Rachel Winthrop to get you. Stay there."

"Like hell. I'm on my way."

"Barbara—" She'd hung up.

Gary dialed the number of the motel where Talbert was staying. "May I speak with Daniel Talbert?"

"Mr. Talbert has checked out."

"Checked out?" Gary cupped his forehead with a hand. *Checked out?*

"This is Gary Colter with the *Sentinel*—"

"Oh, hi, Mr. Colter. Marc and I are in the same grade."

"Have you—have you seen Marc this evening?"

"No, I haven't."

"Did Mr. Talbert say where he was going?"

"I overheard him talking to the manager," the young girl confided. "He's catching a plane out of Denver in the morning. Going to California, he said."

"He wouldn't spend the night in an airport."

"No, sir—wait a minute—Mr. Colter, we booked his reservations for tonight in Denver at the Executive Inn."

He hung up, head buzzing. *If Talbert was gone . . .*

He'd planned to ask Talbert to consult with his men who

were watching Richmond Bell's cabin. If Marc and Eddy were up there, perhaps Talbert's men had seen them.

Why leave with men on lookout?

Gary sank into Clint's chair. Maybe Talbert lied. Maybe out there now, with his men—doing what?

Mr. Arthur let himself into Clint's office, closed the door, and leaned against it. He held a sheaf of papers. "Our agent talked to Bell's mother in West Virginia."

"Mr. Arthur, there's a good chance my son and a friend of his have gone out to take photographs of Bell's cabin. They're both climbers—"

The agent's gaze ranged afar without leaving Gary's face. "That's unfortunate," he said. "Bell is our man, I'm afraid."

"What makes you sure?"

"Remember the conversation between Mr. Video and Zed-Four-Two? Mr. Video said, 'Your mother, is she doing well with her quail?' "

"Yes?"

Mr. Arthur flicked the sheaf of papers. "Bell's mother raises quail."

Richmond pulled the starter rope and the motor roared to life. From the opened cellar door a shaft of light pierced the night. A steady 110 volts—*good*! He regulated the flow of electricity, monitoring the generator for a few minutes, watching for any surge that could make a video recording distort.

He heard Joyce screaming, her words unintelligible at this distance, with the motor running so near his ear.

He'd prepared tuna salad sandwiches, made with pickles, onions, and celery. From a can he'd divided a cocktail mix of fruits in sweet syrup.

He took the picnic basket, crossing the yard to the open cellar door. Descending the stairs, he shut the door behind him and, by force of habit, bolted it from inside.

"About time," Joyce shouted. "Treat us like dogs! Better be plenty food too, fool."

"Will we work today?" Colleen asked.

"We'll finish tonight," Richmond said. With his back to

them, he put his pistol on the worktable, placed the basket so they couldn't see the weapon.

"What is this?" Joyce screeched. "Sandwiches? Fishy sandwiches?"

"Don't you like tuna?"

"Do we be cats? Hell, no, I don't like tuna."

"Well," Richmond said mildly, "that's what we have."

"And *this*?" Joyce peered into the bowl of mixed fruits.

"I like it," Colleen said, spooning juice.

"How about another steak, you sonofabitch?" Joyce demanded. "How about a baked potato and sour cream?"

"And a linen tablecloth?" Richmond teased.

"Damn right."

Richmond set up his tripod, placed the video camera and secured it.

Her food shoved aside, Joyce glowered at Richmond as he adjusted overhead lights, examined the scene for hot spots or shadows.

Richmond spoke to Joyce casually, "Eat your dinner. You'll need your strength."

"For what?"

Richmond peered at her through the camera, the image showing on a TV monitor mounted over the video table.

"How about a beer, you bastard?" Joyce said.

"No beer tonight."

"No beer, no work."

"No beer," Richmond said. He checked the camera, lowered it slightly. On the TV monitor, Joyce was making a vulgar sign with one finger.

"Are you going to eat your fruit?" Colleen asked.

"Haven't decided."

Colleen held the bowl close, spooning pears, peaches, grapes, and cherries to her lips.

"What will you buy with your money, Joyce?" Richmond questioned.

"A gun to shoot a gimpy bastard."

Electrical flow constant. The color was good. Richmond

sat down, lit a cigarette. Let them eat—let the generator run to be certain it was in good repair.

"Tonight's it," Colleen predicted, her voice low.

"This is it." Richmond extended a cigarette and Joyce took it, inhaled eagerly.

"What do you want us to do?" Colleen asked.

"In due time," Richmond said. "Enjoy your meal." He saw a flicker of doubt in her green eyes as Colleen tried to assess his mood. Joyce took another puff, drew it deep into her lungs.

"You can have this fruit," Joyce told Colleen. "I'm eating nicotine."

Colleen drank the last juice from one bowl, began on the next. "Richmond," she said, "I have several ideas for the ending."

"The ending is fixed."

"I've been thinking about our last session," Colleen said. "I think we could do it better."

"No more delays, Colleen."

"Wish this was pot," Joyce murmured. "Getting a buzz off Liggett and Myers ain't the same."

Richmond stroked his mustache with a finger, first one way, then the other.

"My suggestions wouldn't take long, Richmond," Colleen said. "We could shoot it over this time and—"

"No more delays, Colleen."

Joyce trickled smoke from her lips, surveying Richmond with contempt and suspicion. "Gimme another smoke," she said.

He tossed her one and she lit it from the embers of the first cigarette.

"Girls, I have good news for one of you," Richmond said.

"Bet it ain't no telegram."

"Joyce is a woman of perception." Richmond stabbed his cigarette against the earthen floor. "She has seen me well all along."

He stripped the butt, sprinkled tobacco on the floor.

"The final scene must be shot in a particular way," he said. "It must be exciting, real, breathtaking."

Joyce smoked sullenly, eyes darting from Richmond to Colleen, back again.

"Remember our story," Richmond reminded. "Two captive women sharing the same cell, attracted to one another, first advances rebuffed. Finally, the consummate act—"

"Cecil Beeee Dee-Mill," Joyce scoffed.

"Every love story has a tragic conclusion," Richmond said. "Ours is no exception."

He heard Colleen swallow.

"The captives have a dispute," Richmond said.

"Dispute," Joyce mimed.

"Each confronts the other." Richmond unlocked Joyce's chain, giving her length to move toward Colleen.

"A fight takes place," he continued. "This is the critical part, girls. Listen closely."

"Gimme a goddamn smoke."

He hesitated, lit another cigarette, gave it to Joyce. "In movies the last scene is the one toward which everything builds," Richmond directed. "If it is executed properly, the project is a success. If not—well, if not, we all lose."

He sat on his stool again, awaiting questions. Both women watched him.

"One of you walks out of here with all the money," Richmond said softly.

Joyce drew her lips tight against her teeth, sucking smoke into her throat.

"One of us?" Colleen queried.

"One of you."

"What—what about the other one?"

"I take no favorite in this," Richmond assured them. "The victor is the victor. I will not influence the outcome once we begin."

"What about the other one?" Colleen persisted.

"But, if the last scene is unsatisfactory, the penalty is— neither of you get out of here."

Colleen's chin tucked downward in motions like clicks of a gear.

"Splatter film," Joyce said. "He makes splatter films."

Mouth wide, Colleen scrambled backward, swaying on all fours, watching Richmond. He withdrew two stainless steel knives from the picnic basket. The blades curved upward, catching light in a flash as he turned the bone handles appreciatively.

"When one of you has achieved dominance," Richmond said, "you're to halt before the final thrust. That's imperative. Do not follow through until I've adjusted the camera, until I'm sure we have the proper angle."

Like a cornered animal, swaying from side to side, Colleen followed every move with eyes gone wild.

"Is everything clear, girls?"

"Ain't going to do it," Joyce said amiably.

"Yes, you will." Richmond put his pistol on the front edge of the worktable.

"Shoot me, then, you miserable piece of—"

He grabbed the gun and thrust it at her so violently Joyce hurtled away without being touched.

"Makes no difference to me," Richmond said, quietly. "If I have to get two girls and begin again, I will. No more crap from you, Joyce. If you want all the money, do what I say. If Colleen wins, she gets the money and goes free."

"You liar!" Joyce screamed. "You gone kill us both."

Colleen moaned, rocking like a metronome.

"The winner gets all the money and goes free," Richmond said, emphatically. He put the pistol on the table again, sat down.

"If we cut one another up, do what he say do," Joyce said to Colleen, "then he kill the other. He got to, don't you see that?"

Colleen's moan rose to a low wail.

"We won't do it," Joyce argued. "He can't do nothing. Nothing!"

"I'll kill you both," Richmond warned softly.

*　　*　　*

The roar of an engine brought Marc upright. Beside him, Eddy dozed, snoring sibilantly. The fir growing from a crevice in stone stirred as a breeze swept up the mountainside out of the valley. The night was cold, yet he was perspiring. Marc looked at the luminous dial of his watch. *After midnight.* He clambered up the boulder. The initial roar of the engine had subsided to a steady drone. Out of the opened cellar door a shaft of illumination gave an eerie glow to the entire ledge. Bell was at the generator. The cabin was dark.

At first, Marc thought his ears were playing tricks on his mind. But, no—*a woman—screaming obscenities.*

The wind lifted in a gust, the bough of the fir sweeping the back of his head. Bell moved with a lurching gait toward the cellar door. His body cast a grotesque shadow up the boulder over the cellar as he heaved into light. One step at a time, he descended, closing the door behind him.

Except for the purr of the distant motor, silence.

The fir soughed, shushed; the breeze lulled. A platinum arc was rising, a dull quarter-moon set in a pincushion sky of glittering stars.

Somebody was in there—a woman.

Marc slid down to Eddy. "Eddy, did you hear that?"

"What?" Eddy said aloud. Marc clapped a hand over Eddy's mouth. "*Shh-hh!* Are you awake?"

Eddy pushed Marc's hand away. "I am now."

"Bell has a woman in the cellar."

Shivering, Eddy rubbed his face with both hands. "You're sure?"

"I heard her! Cursing Bell."

Below them, in the dark valley, tips of trees bent under a stroke of wind, leaves reflecting the dim light of stars and the waning moon.

"What can we do?" Marc questioned.

"Take pictures," Eddy said, with finality. "That's what we came to do."

"But he's holding somebody in there."

"Ours is not to interfere, but—"

Marc cursed aloud. "If he's a killer like Borden Wilson, we can't just stay here and do nothing!"

"Well, what do you suggest?" Eddy said. "If he's a killer like Borden Wilson, he also has guns."

"I'm going down there."

"Like hell you are." Eddy grabbed his arm in a vise grip. "You're here to take pictures. I'll go down there."

"What if he finds you?"

"Take pictures."

"What if he shoots you?"

"Then you damn well better take pictures—or I'll *kill* you."

Eddy secured their nylon climbing rope to the fir and they went to the top of the boulder. The generator motor was a thrum under which they could hear yelling as if from a distance.

Eddy slid down to the ledge. So dark he was barely visible. Marc watched Eddy's shadowy figure run in a gangly crouch under the overhanging boulder. He stopped at the cellar door, bent low, listening.

No gun. Not even a knife! Marc wasn't sure he would use a weapon if he had one.

Appalled, he watched Eddy bypass the cellar door, running toward the cabin. *Fool!* If Bell emerged, Eddy would be trapped. Marc used the binoculars to follow Eddy's passage. He disappeared into shadows at the rear of the cabin, then appeared at the front. Eddy strolled the brink of the ledge, looking down at the valley. The shouting intensified.

Eddy mounted the cabin steps and Marc lost sight of him. He could hear blood pulsing in his ears, his heart a triphammer slamming ribs. Eddy appeared, jumped off the porch and walked across the open ledge. Maddeningly, he raised both arms and did a disjointed spool doll dance, flinging his limbs for Marc's benefit.

Back to the cellar door—listening, listening. So long he lingered, Marc forced himself not to shout, *Hurry!*

At last, Eddy dragged himself up the boulder, hand over

hand. His face a pale visage in diminished light, his breath smelled of onions.

"He has two women," he reported. "He's talking about killing them."

"Oh, God, Eddy."

Eddy took the binoculars, bracing against the fir, elbows on his knees to create a bodily tripod. He searched the valley with slow sweeps. "If there's anybody down there," he rasped, "I don't see them."

"We've got to get help, Eddy."

"How, you idiot? Go back the way we came? We'll fall and be killed. If we go down this slope, he may hear us, see us—and we'd face a three-hour trot to town anyway. There's nothing we can do but wait."

Marc brought up blankets and they wrapped themselves, teeth chattering. An hour passed, then another, Eddy scanning the valley.

"If they're coming," Eddy reasoned, "it'll be right at daylight. If they're coming, they're down there now, moving into position."

Thirty minutes later, unconvincingly, Eddy said, "Probably a hundred guys out there moving toward us."

Mom would be distraught by now. Dad at a peak of fury and worry. They would have called Uncle Clint, discovered the uncleaned condo—

The muted shrill of a woman's voice caused Eddy to lower the binoculars, listening.

"He said he was going to kill them, Eddy?"

"Sounded like it." The screams ascended.

Then, as if the wind and woman were one, silence.

The yelp of a dog miles away came rippling up canyons in echoes. The generator was a puttering monotone.

"Bell parks his Wagoneer down the farthest slope from here," Eddy said. "Think we could hot-wire it?"

"Hell, no, Eddy. I couldn't do it if I had all day and good light."

"Me either. I flunked auto theft in high school mechanics."

A bloodcurdling scream ripped the night. Rigid, Marc sat absolutely still, holding his breath involuntarily.

The eyes.

He swallowed and his tongue glued to the roof of his mouth.

Charlotte's eyes. The desperation, her throat sliced. *Groping.*

"Eddy," he said, "we have to do something."

Eddy's face was a white mask. "Well, yeah, I guess we do. I don't see anybody down there."

The scream held . . . held . . .

Eddy threw off his blanket. "You better take pictures, Marc. First light, by God, you better."

The shriek in the cellar fell to soft peeps, like covered birds.

"I don't want you so excited you forget the pictures, Marc. Don't let anything distract you."

"Goddamn, Eddy!"

"Remember the great ones," Eddy instructed. "Remember to stay calm and shoot the damned pictures. I mean it."

"What're you going to do?"

"I don't know." Eddy stood up, examined the ledge, the cellar to their right, the huge boulder over it. "How long until daybreak, Marc?"

"An hour. Ninety minutes, maybe."

Eddy shook his hands, wrists limp, shifting from foot to foot like a sprinter preparing for a burst of energy. "I've got to stall him until daylight," Eddy said, "and I'm so scared I may pee."

"There must be some way—burn the cabin—somebody will see it."

"Yes and he'll know we're here," Eddy wheezed. "But in any event, take pictures with first light. Understand?"

"Yes."

"Swear it."

"I swear, Eddy. Please be careful."

Eddy tried to grin and it was a sick grimace. "I wouldn't go," he quavered, "but he's going to kill them if I don't."

CHAPTER TWENTY-SIX

I t was Barbara's nature to take bad news calmly. Over the years, Gary had seen her accept family tragedies with a stoic demeanor that lasted for days.

"Timothy left Colleen?"

"It appears that way," Gary said.

"Why didn't she tell us?"

"I don't know."

Numbed, exhausted, they sat in Clint's office, Gary bringing Barbara up to the moment—the bad check, Colleen's car. Pale, face drawn, she listened grimly.

"A killer," Barbara said. "Like Borden Wilson."

"We think so."

"Do—do Marc and Eddy know Colleen is up there?"

"Honey, *we* don't know it for a fact. But no, they don't."

In the outer reception area, Cora was delivering sandwiches and coffee to the few men remaining. Rachel Winthrop was asleep on a wooden bench.

"Why do you suppose Colleen didn't confide in us?" Barbara anguished. "Why didn't she call for money?"

"I don't know."

Everything that could be done was done. Tom Albright and his best climbers were scaling the north wall of Bell's mountain by the dim beam of miner's lamps, with electrical tape reducing the lights to a sliver.

They had found Marc's jeep. The boys were positively up there. "Nobody shoots unless he draws first fire," the marksmen had been told. And yet, there was always the possibility of error.

"The horror," Barbara whispered. "Unbelievable horror—"

Gary put his arm around her, kissed her forehead. He returned to sit in Clint's chair, fingertips to his temples, elbows on the desk. He had tried repeatedly to call Daniel Talbert. Midnight. One A.M., then two o'clock. No answer. Finally, he left word with the night desk at the Executive Inn. *Important—return call immediately.*

Talbert's men were on watch, they were aware of what was happening from their peak south of Richmond Bell's cabin. But the niggling inconsistency was—why had Talbert sent them there only to leave himself?

Up to something. *What?*

"Gary, do you want coffee or a sandwich?" Cora stood in the office doorway.

"No."

"Barbara, honey?"

"No, Cora. Thank you."

Cora put a beefy arm around the sitting woman's shoulders, consoling her. "Everything is going to be all right," she said, lamely.

Barbara nodded, eyes red, dark circles adding years to her age.

"Clint called in a moment ago," Cora related. "He said he'll give us a report when he knows anything."

Gary dialed Denver again, asking the operator for Daniel Talbert.

"I'm sorry," the hotel receptionist responded, "Mr. Talbert cannot be disturbed."

"He's there?"

"Yes, sir."

"This is Gary Colter. Did you give him my message? It's urgent."

"I gave him your message, Mr. Colter."

"Wake him up!"

"Mr. Colter, I can't do that."

"It's an emergency—wake him up!"

An excruciating wait, the girl speaking to someone aside. "Mr. Colter, his instructions were quite explicit."

"You wake him, hear me? Do it now—"

A different voice came on the line, a man. "May I help you?"

"I have an emergency call for Daniel Talbert," Gary said. "It *is* an emergency."

"Mr. Colter, your message was delivered to Mr. Talbert. If he wished to answer your call, he would have done so."

"Listen, damn you—this is an emergency. You want the police to call for me?"

"If the police telephone, I will wake him."

Gary slammed the receiver, quaking with anger.

"Why are you doing that?" Barbara questioned.

"Why is he in Denver and not here?" Gary rejoined.

"Who cares?"

Gary pressed his temples, fighting the rising thud of a headache. "He's up here chasing this story—two men staked out to watch Bell—he knew as much as I did. Yet he left. Won't return my call. Now why is he doing that, Barbara?"

"Gary," she said, wearily, "who *cares*?"

"His men could tell us if they've seen Marc and Eddy. Tell us where they are on that mountain."

Barbara turned aside, her gesture close to disgust. She watched Cora serving coffee, talking to a park ranger at the admissions desk.

Gary walked out, down the hall to the radio room. "Can you raise Clint Ferguson for me?"

The dispatcher announced Clint's code and a moment later Clint's baritone replied.

"Clint," Gary spoke into the microphone, "directly south of Bell's cabin there are two lower peaks. The most westerly peak has the advantage of viewing Bell's place."

"Right."

"Daniel Talbert has two men on stakeout there," Gary said. "Can you send someone to ask them if they've seen Marc and Eddy?"

"Our men are up there, Gary."

Gone?

Gary relinquished the microphone to the dispatcher, who signed off transmission. The radio crackled, messages between units in the field.

Something wrong.

Absently, Gary poured coffee.

"Tom Albright is nearing the crest of Bell's mountain," the dispatcher reported.

Gary sorted facts, redistributing theories along the line of *What if . . .*

What if Daniel Talbert didn't know what was happening here? What if the two men were not working for him at all? *What if—*

Gary touched the dispatcher's shoulder. "How many radio frequencies are you using?"

"One for the park rangers and federal marshals, one of our own, plus the walkie-talkies and state patrol. Four."

"Can you reach Beecham of the FBI?"

The dispatcher flicked a switch, calling.

Beecham's voice, "Yes, Colter."

"Beecham, is anybody going up the mountain besides Tom Albright?"

"Yes."

"Two men on the south slope?"

"We see them. Colter, what is it, please?"

"Whose men are they?" Gary asked.

"Sheriff's, probably."

"Stand by, Beecham." Gary spoke to the dispatcher. "Get the sheriff."

He posed the same questions. "I see them. Two men."

"Are they your men, Sheriff?"

"Negative."

Gary stared at the wall.

"Could be state patrol," the dispatcher said. "But they're supposed to be on roadblocks, not assault."

"Get Beecham again."

"Colter, what is it?" Beecham snapped.

"You do see two men ascending the southern slopes?"

"Yes."

"Is it daylight?"

"No. We're using night scopes."

"Are they armed?"

"Yes, Colter."

"Beecham," he said, "those are hit men. Repeat, hit men."

Pause . . . pause . . .

"Affirmative, Colter. Out."

Frantically, Marc searched the valley for sign of movement. *Nothing!* In the predawn darkness, Eddy scaled the boulder over the cellar, stones skittering off the edge to rain down on the ledge below.

The wind had died. Utter stillness magnified the drone of the generator. The sound reverberated away to return in overlapping echoes from other peaks.

Eddy staggered out of undergrowth over the boulder, edging toward the drop-off carrying a stone larger than the breadth of his own body. Blind to the ledge immediately below him, he put down the rounded missile, fell flat on his stomach, and with legs splayed, inched forward to assess the intended trajectory.

Once more, Marc scanned the valley. *Where were they? Was Eddy wrong? Maybe nobody was coming. Nobody knew!*

Eddy slithered away from the overhanging cliff, back to his rock. He moved it left, shoved.

Damn! The stone rolled to within a few feet of the sharply inclined drop, and halted. Eddy went into the trees again.

Please, God. Send help.

The screams had ceased. The closed cellar door covered a potential atrocity. Marc held his breath, lying on his belly, watching the boulder over the cellar, waiting for Eddy to reappear. *There.* With an even larger stone! Rolling it one turn at a time toward the boulder.

The stars seemed pale, the first light of day so soft the scene was all the more brooding. The thump of the turning stone marked Eddy's progress, the boy's exertion making him grunt with each flip of the rock.

Eddy sat down, using his feet to push the stone, bracing himself with both hands, pushing, pushing.

It fell.

The blow was so muted, Marc heard Eddy swear fervently. Missed the cellar door by inches. Eddy strained for the first rock, using his toe, pushing, pushing.

Wham!

The cellar door was the head of a drum, the falling rock smashing it dead center. Eddy scrambled, slipping, clawing his way upward again.

The puttering engine rumbled.

Marc slid beneath the bough of his sheltering fir, waiting.

The cellar door opened, partially blocked by the rock, and then with a heave, Richmond Bell threw it aside.

A pistol.

Marc saw Eddy pull into foliage directly over Bell's head.

The shaft of light from the cellar was less intense. The graying sky cloaked minor stars as the unseen sun crept toward the eastern lip of the world.

Bell limped into full sight now, looking here, there, examining the two stones, going out to look back and up at the boulder over the cellar.

A woman's cry came to Marc's ears in a sustained moan.

Marc set the camera at the widest aperture, shutter speed of one second. Placing the camera flat against the boulder, it clattered, metal against rock, until he held it firm. *Click.*

The trip of the shutter was an alien sound, masked only by the motor of the generator. Bell seemed to be studying the boulder overhead. Gun in hand, he walked to the rim of the ledge, gazing down the slope, into the valley.

Click.

There was almost no chance he had a photo, but any impression was better than none. *Click.*

Bell patrolled the ledge, staring into the darkness beneath his domain. *Click.*

A shriek rose from the cellar door, the words unintelligible, but the cry so filled with agony it was like an electrical shock.

Bell was looking this way, walking in his halting gait—this way. Marc pressed himself to the cold stone surface, the bough making a needled lace pattern between his eyes and Bell's image.

"Bastard!" the woman shrilled. "Bastard!"

He was not more than thirty feet distant, looking down the slope again. Marc felt as if his heart were throwing him upward with every beat. He put his cheek to the boulder, holding his breath.

A moment later, Bell's shuffling feet passed beneath Marc, going back toward the cellar. Marc brought up his head, shaking, and forced himself to exhale carefully.

The cellar door shut.

Marc hurled away shivers like a dog rising from water. He saw Eddy peek out. Marc waved, "All clear."

Wham!

Gunshot. *Was he killing them?*

A minute later, Eddy was beside Marc again, breathing hard. "Lot of good that did," he said, in a normal voice. "I think he shot one."

Wham! Another shot.

"Take pictures," Eddy gasped. He dropped down to the ledge, ran past the closed cellar door toward the cabin. He disappeared inside. Marc heard the clink of metal, something fell.

A moment later, Eddy's head appeared over the crest of the cabin roof. He waved at Marc, then pretended to hold a camera, with a finger to shutter release, miming, "Pictures."

The highest peaks began to shine with the first reflected light. A teasing breeze murmured, died.

An agonizing scream rose again. Marc closed his eyes and shuddered.

"Marc! I went in looking for a gun," Eddy said. "Think I should look again?"

"No, Eddy."

"I'm going to knock out the generator," Eddy advised. "When I do, he'll be looking for us."

Marc waved.

"Pictures!" Eddy reminded. He slid out of view down the far side of the cabin roof. Marc reset his aperture, adjusted the shutter speed. Enough light now, maybe, to get a reasonable print.

Eddy reached the rear of the cabin, stood over the generator a few seconds as if uncertain how to do what he wanted. Marc saw him reach down and snatch something loose.

Into the ebbing echoes of the last putter came a quiet so heavy it was palpable. Eddy sprinted away behind the cabin again, back to the roof.

Somewhere below, a noise.

Bell threw open the cellar door, cursing. His gun in hand, he vaulted toward his generator, took one look at it and ducked into a crouch. With his back to the cliff wall, he held his pistol at the ready.

Click. The shadows defeated the film. Marc shot anyway. *Click.*

Another noise from below and Marc continued to shoot, advancing the film, tripping the shutter as Bell ran in the back door of his cabin. When he came out the front, he was armed with a shotgun.

Click.

Bell moved across the yard, shotgun held at his waist, finger on the trigger. The pistol was in his belt again.

"Okay, you sonofabitch," Bell said, evenly, "you might as well come out."

Marc saw Eddy flatten himself on the roof, going below the crown so Bell couldn't see him from the center of the ledge.

"One last chance," Bell said.

His voice seemed to unleash panic in the cellar, shrieking pleas. "Help! Help, somebody! Help!"

At the cellar door, Bell yelled, "Shut up, goddamn you!"

He backed toward the rim of the ledge, turning full circle,

warily. He looked up at the boulder where Eddy had dropped the stones. He looked toward Marc, their line of sight meeting for an agonizing instant before Bell looked away, searching.

He turned and peered into the valley.

Then, Marc saw what Bell could not see—a man hidden below, scarcely fifty yards to Bell's left.

Another man! Moving while Bell's back was turned, now behind a rock, motionless.

Click. Click.

Bell wheeled, staring this way.

Remember the great ones. *Click!*

Bell advanced, shotgun bore looming like a tunnel, pointing at Marc. Behind him, Eddy hit the ground, running to another hiding place nearer Bell, nearer the cellar.

"Who's up there?" Bell demanded.

At the far edge of the ledge, a figure darted behind the cabin. Below Bell, the second and nearer man advanced upward.

"Come on down," Bell commanded.

Marc couldn't have hugged the boulder more closely if he'd been liquid. Bell's breathing was a throaty rasp.

"Come down or I fire," Bell warned.

A low warbling whistle—Eddy. Idiot! Bell spun about, pointing the shotgun. He limped toward Eddy, the shrill from the cellar a steady mix of oaths and supplications.

As Bell approached Eddy, Marc whistled. Bell twisted, halted, shotgun leveled.

Come on, come on! Marc mentally urged the man below, now climbing steadily toward them.

He advanced film, shooting images. He set a new bracket for aperture and speed of shutter.

Click. Click.

The man behind the cabin made a hand signal to his advancing companion and the climbing man hurried.

Marc whistled again, softly. *Click.*

The tumble of dislodged stones beyond the rim of the

ledge warned Bell and he did a one-leg hop-step toward the unsuspecting climber below.

"Bell!" the man at the cabin yelled.

He wheeled and each held his weapon on the other.

Grinning, Eddy emerged from hiding, a few steps from the cellar door.

The climber stepped into sight.

Click.

"Drop it, Bell!" he shouted.

Click.

Somewhere above, a man shouted, "Police! Hold it! Police!"

For an instant nothing moved. As if a living portrait, everyone stood transfixed.

The man at the cabin whirled, fired.

Bell spun to face the man behind him and both shotguns erupted.

Eddy reeled, grabbed for air, and hurtled into the dark chasm of the open cellar door.

Mechanically, Marc took pictures capturing it all.

Both strangers fell under a fusillade from above the boulder over the cellar. Bell threw himself to the ground, screaming obscenities.

Echo . . . echo . . . echo . . . like thunder going away.

A blue haze hung over it all.

Marc heard the gentle whump of helicopter blades, the low wail of sirens.

Tom Albright stepped into the clearing, a miniature of a man.

Click. Click.

He walked from one body to the other.

Click.

Other men disarmed Richmond Bell.

Click. Click.

"Bell," Albright said, pleasantly, "we saved your life."

CHAPTER TWENTY-SEVEN

T he radio dispatcher stepped out of the communications room into the hall. "They want Doc Johnson to meet them here," he called. "Send for him."

Eddy's parents began to weep, Barbara and Cora trying to console them when both needed solace themselves.

"The boys?" Gary demanded of the dispatcher. "Did they find a girl?"

"No word yet, Mr. Colter."

The crackle of the radio quickened, reports between men in the field. Out of a burst of static came a monotone, ". . . Dead and injured . . . medical helicopter waiting for one to be brought down now . . ."

"Oh, dear Lord," Barbara cried, she and Gary holding one another.

Rachel Winthrop stood beside Cora, behind the dispatcher, both women quivering.

"The boys," Gary insisted. "Ask about the boys. Ask if they found a girl."

The radioman raised Clint, making inquiries.

"I'm not up there," Clint said. "Sheriff and I have Bell. Bringing him in. Try the marshals, park frequency."

The dispatcher switched frequencies, asking.

The wait was interminable. Distantly, a shrill of sirens came in pulsating waves. Barbara held Gary with cold hands, both of them trembling.

"Is Colter there?" Beecham's voice on the radio. Gary's

heart plunged. He heard the dispatcher as if through a long tunnel. "He's listening, sir."

"Colter, your boy was not hurt."

Thank you, God. Colleen?

"Your daughter is here—alive. We'll bring them in as soon as we can."

Barbara slumped in Gary's arms and he eased her onto a chair.

Beecham's voice again, "Can you send for the Anderson boy's parents, Colter?"

"They're here, Beecham."

"He's in a helicopter going to Denver," Beecham said. "There's a trauma team waiting."

Mrs. Anderson wailed, Barbara and Cora rushing to comfort her.

"How bad, Beecham?"

"I didn't see him."

"Find someone who did, damn it!"

The reception room was becoming crowded, the ululating warble of sirens screaming up mountain walls, wave upon wave of noise rousting the town as cars rushed into Gatlin Pass.

"Colter?"

"Yes, Beecham?"

"Albright says the boy was shot, but he was conscious when the helicopter left here."

"Rachel, can you drive Mr. and Mrs. Anderson to Denver?"

"Yes, Mr. Colter."

"Be careful—don't get carried away."

"Yes, Mr. Colter."

Clint and the sheriff burst through as Eddy's parents turned to leave. Richmond Bell was manacled, hands behind his back, teeth bared, feet dragging. When Clint wrenched him forward, Bell cursed lustily, lips drawn.

Mr. Anderson moved to intercept and Gary blocked his way. "Go to Denver, Mr. Anderson. Go see about Eddy. Let us know."

". . . Two men dead . . ." The radio brought the information.

Clint and the sheriff returned, their faces ashen. "Put a suicide watch on the bastard," Clint commanded a subordinate. He dropped Bell's shoelaces, belt, shirt, and trousers on the admissions desk. "Catalogue these."

Someone poured coffee and the sheriff took a cup. Clint said to Gary, "Eddy was hit."

"How bad?"

"Don't know. Marc is okay. Colleen was there. Shock, bruises, couple of cuts—but she'll be all right." Clint raised his voice suddenly. "Anybody who has no business here, get out!"

He spoke to Gary again. "There was another woman, too. Bell was making one of those goddamned films. That scum—he's yelling because of his hip. Nobody shot him."

"The dead men?"

"If you hadn't called in saying they were hit men," the sheriff interrupted, "it would've been worse. We warned Tom Albright, otherwise some of our men might be dead, too."

"Bell, for sure," Clint said.

Mr. Arthur and FBI agent Wohlman arrived, clothes torn and muddied, a stubble of beard giving their faces a shade of weariness that accentuated their eyes. They supervised the delivery of videotapes and equipment, other officers bringing more.

"Copy everything," Arthur directed. "Impound the originals." He turned to Gary. "Beecham is bringing your daughter. She'll be okay."

The radio dispatcher called to the sheriff. "They want to know about putting a cordon around the cabin and grounds."

"I'm going back out there," he replied. "Tell them to stand by."

Outside, the crowd noises lulled and as Gary glanced up a young black woman wrapped in a blanket was being helped from the rear of a squad car.

"Damnedest thing you ever saw," a deputy remarked. "He was forcing them to kill one another."

Doc Johnson joined the officer and woman, helping her enter.

"Wanted us to cut one another," she cried. "Kept shooting at my head. Said he'd kill me if I didn't. I had to do it—I had to!"

Doc took her in a room, prepared a syringe. Arthur was quietly questioning the woman.

"The boys saved her life," Agent Wohlman related. "They pulled the plug on the generator. Hadn't been for that, the girls would be dead."

Marc appeared as if from ether. Pale and expressionless, he stood before Barbara and Gary, his camera around his neck, photo supply bag slung across his chest.

"Marc, of all the idiotic things I ever heard about!" Gary lunged for the boy and grabbed him in a hug.

"I'm okay, Dad." Over Gary's shoulder, Marc said, "I'm all right, Mom. Dad—Colleen was there."

"I know. I know."

Barbara burst into tears, Marc pulling her to him.

"Eddy got shot, Mom. He was pretty bloody."

"Are you hurt?"

"I'm fine, Mom. I was lucky. Two cops got killed."

"They weren't police, Marc."

He nodded without questioning it. "When the shooting started, Eddy was in the middle of it. Know what he said when I got to him? He said, 'Take my picture.' "

"He made us do it!" The black woman's voice came through a closed door. "We didn't want to. He made us do it!"

When Mr. Arthur emerged, Gary pulled him aside. "I want you to get some information on Talbert for me."

"Later, Colter."

"Now," Gary said, firmly. "Start now."

"Where is Colleen?" Barbara cried.

"She's coming, Mrs. Colter. She's with Mr. Beecham. She's going to be all right."

A deputy came in from the jail section. "Bell is asking for a painkiller. Is Doc Johnson still here?"

The woman under interrogation was weeping, her tears broken by bursts of obscenities, pleas for understanding, alternately crying and shouting.

Mr. Arthur examined a list Gary had made. Grimly, he nodded. "Almost no chance we can prove any of this," he said to Gary. "The hit men are dead. Complicity is not easy to show."

"Talbert was feeding information to Video," Gary said. "That's why he was the first reporter here after Borden Wilson killed himself. That's how Talbert knew about Richmond Bell. Eddy Anderson took him out to spy on Bell the first week Talbert came to town. Video was using Talbert as a conduit, keeping up with the progress of the investigation. When I began to move on Bell, Talbert must've told Video. Then the hit men were sent."

"But we can't prove it, Colter."

"That's how Talbert knew about the case in Atascadero, California. He's a step ahead of the police all the way."

"All conjecture, Colter."

"Make inquiries," Gary insisted. "Get on the phone and start the ball rolling. Have an agent pick up Talbert at the Executive Inn before he leaves Denver."

"He'd have to come voluntarily."

"*Ask* him, goddamn it! He'll come."

Arthur massaged his eyes, tiredly. "Wohlman, take a look at these notes."

Wohlman read what Gary had written. "We'll never prove a connection between Video and Talbert."

"He'll hire a hotshot lawyer in Houston and get a million dollars worth of publicity out of it," Mr. Arthur declared. "His next book will be a best-seller."

"I saw him talking to the two hit men in the Trout House," Gary said. "The next day I saw them on the same peak where Eddy Anderson took Talbert to spy on Richmond Bell."

"We went there, too. That isn't proof. That means the

peak was the best vantage for watching the cabin, that's all."

"Are you going to let Talbert get away with this?" Gary demanded, angrily.

"Nobody is letting him do anything, Colter. He's an investigative reporter. He pumps us for information, he pumps the underworld. He gives us tips, and no doubt, he gives the underworld tips, too. But that doesn't make him guilty of conspiracy to murder."

"Damn it," Gary shouted. "Get on the phone and make these calls. Get that information and bring Talbert here. It's worth a try, isn't it?"

Arthur's head wiggled a bit, his cheeks sunken, eyes dulled by exhaustion. "This is the weekend. I don't know how much we can do but, okay, Wohlman—let's give it a try."

An ambulance passed by, lights revolving, siren off. Another came a few minutes later, going toward the flatlands and the mortuaries. Across the street, the Staghorn Café was open for business and some of the crowd was moving that way.

"Where is Colleen?" Barbara questioned Arthur. "I want to know and I want to know now."

Arthur went to the communications room. "Raise Beecham. Where's the other girl?"

The reply: "Coming in now."

Barbara ran to the unmarked car and snatched open the door. She crawled inside with Colleen, both crying.

"She was cut," Beecham explained. "Just superficial, but we had to do some first aid. It took time to get her loose. The bastard had them chained, but the black girl's chain could be pulled through a stanchion. Sorry it took so long."

"Daddy?" Colleen threw herself into his arms and Gary held her, sobbing. "I wouldn't take the knife, Daddy. I tried to fool him, making him think I'd become catatonic. Then when he came to put it in my hand, I grabbed him. Joyce and I nearly had him. I—I tried to kill him, Daddy."

Gary holding one arm, Barbara the other, they took

Colleen inside. When Colleen saw Joyce she pulled away and embraced the black woman.

"My ears ringing yet!" Joyce shrieked, laughing. "That sonofabitch shot at me twice and I don't hear nothing."

Joyce drew back, peeled aside Colleen's blanket. "I tried to cut shallow so scars wouldn't show."

Then they were hugging again.

"All on the videotape," Clint murmured in Gary's ear. "Want to see it?"

"No."

"Splinters flying—shooting at them. Colleen did all right."

Mr. Arthur came out of a rest room, drying his face and hands. He'd found a razor somewhere, nicked himself shaving.

"These girls need to go to a hospital?" Beecham asked Doc Johnson.

"Not unless they want to."

Wohlman spoke to Arthur, "Talbert is on his way. We'll have to bluff him. Maybe you can use these reports on Bell. Any more hot water for shaving?"

Cora and Barbara took Colleen and Joyce out a rear door. *Going home,* they told Gary.

Daniel Talbert arrived to a greeting less warm than his last. His passage through the reception area was under scrutiny of all. Nobody was smiling.

"What is this?" Talbert demanded of Beecham.

"Sit down, Talbert," Mr. Arthur said. "Mr. Colter has an interesting theory he wants to share with you."

Talbert caught Marc's eye through the office door and smiled. Marc turned away. Gary saw perspiration at the hairline of Talbert's forehead, the writer nervously squeezing his hands. He sat down, crossed his legs, and lifted his eyebrows. "The theory?"

"I wondered how you seemed to read my mind," Gary began. "One step in front, no more than a single step behind me."

"We're talking about?"

"Richmond Bell."

"This commotion—" Talbert indicated the outer room. "This relates to Bell?"

"I saw you talking to the two hit men in the Trout House, Talbert."

"Hit men?" Talbert laughed softly.

"You directed them to Bell's cabin and the peak from which you spied on Bell."

"Is this a joke?"

"You said a friend told you about Atascadero, California," Gary continued. "Tell us the name of your friend."

"You know I can't reveal confidential sources, Colter."

"I think his name is Mr. Video."

Talbert blinked once, then his smile resumed. "Don't think I know the gentleman. Quaint name, though."

"He sends you to the hot spots, doesn't he?" Gary persisted. "You set up shop with the local newspaper, feed the story to wire services, but your real purpose is to keep Video informed."

"Video—now who do you say he is?"

"He finances people like Borden Wilson and Richmond Bell," Mr. Arthur said. "He is facing murder one. It appears you face a conspiracy charge at the least."

"This is absurd." Talbert laughed.

Mr. Arthur turned pages of a teletype report. "I have a rather lengthy statement from your publishers, Mr. Talbert. Your royalty payments, your book titles, the number of copies in the warehouses."

"Maybe you should be my agent."

"Mr. Colter suggested we speak to them about your book sales. We have those figures, too."

Talbert pinched the septum of his nose, bemused.

"Every new book goes straight to the top," Gary said. "Before publication date, you get some juicy film deals and a lot of publicity. You're on your way to a hit even before a book is distributed."

"I've been fortunate."

Outside, Marc was listening. Everyone was.

Mr. Arthur turned pages of the report. "We're looking into the financing of your films, Mr. Talbert. Thus far, it seems, Mr. Video and his ancillary businesses have backed every movie project."

"The reputed connection of the underworld to the film industry has long been a rumor," Talbert said huskily.

"I think we have a case, Talbert," Arthur stated. "I'm advising you to seek legal assistance."

"Oh, I will," Talbert said nonchalantly. "But I'll beat this in court and end up a winner. Bank on it."

"You may," Gary said, standing. "You have the money and the contacts to get the best. But you're through, Talbert. Even if you come out acquitted, you're through. I'm going to write the book we talked about. The one that addresses the question, 'What makes such men and the evil they do?' With a good attorney you may win in court. But public opinion will finish you. The one thing crooks can't stand is publicity. I'll see that you get plenty of it."

Gary paused at the door and turned. "Would you like to tell me what creates men like Borden Wilson and Bell?"

"You tell *me*, Colter."

"Money," Gary replied. "They may kill for the pleasure of it, for the excitement. But Video financed it for the profits he'd make. He employed you to protect him with inside information."

"That's a lie."

"And you did it for book sales and hit movies," Gary said. "Money."

"Hey, man," Talbert snapped, "be sure you ask the public to examine themselves. The real question is, What makes people buy the damned things?"

"Yes," Gary said. "That worries me most of all."

He took Marc's arm. "Let's go home, son."

From upstairs came the peals of laughter, like girls at a slumber party. It made Gary think of Colleen's school days. *A hundred years ago.* He sat on a high stool in the kitchen, watching Barbara prepare mashed potatoes and gravy, a pot roast, hot biscuits. It was what the girls had requested.

"Clint wants to know if Joyce can stay here a day or two," he reported. "They'll want to ask questions, he said. Colleen, too."

Marc entered, hair damp from a shower. "They used all the hot water." He lifted a lid, asking, "What's for dinner?"

"Pot roast. Get away from the stove, snoop."

More laughter; singing.

"They don't act traumatized," Marc said. "They're sitting on Colleen's bed painting their toenails."

"But they are traumatized," Gary noted.

"I think Joyce is a hooker, Dad. Keeps talking about johns and Las Vegas."

"She's our guest," Barbara said, curtly. "For the moment, she's Colleen's best friend."

"Yeah. That's what Colleen told me. Mom? May I have a biscuit?"

"What's taking so long?" Gary questioned.

"Repeated baths and feminine considerations," Barbara said. "Marc, don't drop crumbs on the floor."

"I wish somebody would call with news about Eddy," Marc said. Then, realizing his parents were looking at him worriedly, he choked down a bite and smiled. "Biscuit's good, Mom."

The girls came downstairs and Joyce halted, looking at the table. "Real plates," she said. "That's nice."

Heads bowed, Gary gave fervent thanks, everybody holding hands. With "Amen," they looked up and Colleen was crying. Immediately, Joyce blinked away tears.

"I never thought I'd be here again, Daddy."

"But you are."

"I thought I'd never see any of you."

Barbara moved toward Colleen and suddenly Marc sobbed.

"Why are *you* crying?" Colleen laughed.

"I cry at parades, I cry at movies—"

Abruptly, they all laughed. Gary served the roast.

"Joyce is a terrific singer."

"Aw, I don't know . . ."

"We sang Christmas songs."

"Old MacDonald is what I liked!"

Then, unexpectedly, more tears as Joyce spoke of a girl named "Wynona."

"Dumb little Chicano, sweet as stewed berries."

Then, laughter as Colleen and Joyce related tales they'd told one another in the black of the unlighted cellar.

"Will you be going home, Joyce?" Barbara asked.

"Home?" Joyce seemed surprised. "Me back to Georgia . . ." She pushed food with her fork, head down. "No ma'am, I won't be going home. They wouldn't know what to do with me."

"You're welcome here as long as you like."

"Thank you."

Silence.

"You think 'home' and this is what you know," Joyce said softly. "I never had anything like this. I wouldn't know which way to eat if Colleen hadn't told me. Don't pick up the knife and fork at the same time, she said."

Colleen put a hand on Joyce's wrist, squeezed gently.

"Then this can be home for both of you," Barbara attempted.

"I appreciate it, Mrs. Colter. But soon as things get settled, I'll go back to Vegas. I have friends there and all."

It was not an easy meal. To Gary, Colleen seemed older, her maturity deeper. Married, separated . . . the recent days . . .

As if she'd detected his thoughts, Colleen took Gary's hand and held it.

"My little girl," he said.

"And always will be, Daddy."

The telephone rang and Barbara answered.

"You can call him tomorrow at the *Sentinel* office," Barbara said. Then, gently, "Oh. Yes, of course, I'll accept the call."

"It's Eddy," she said to the room at large. Back to the phone again. "Yes, Eddy, hello! How are you?"

Barbara cupped the receiver, smiling, "He's all right."

Gary saw her expression alter and Barbara said, "He wants to know if the *Sentinel* would like to bid on the pictures!"

Gary faced Marc and the boy shrugged helplessly.

"Dad—he's my agent."